D0914576

WHERE DO WE GO FROM HERE?

Science Fiction by Isaac Asimov

PEBBLE IN THE SKY
I, ROBOT
THE STARS, LIKE DUST ...
FOUNDATION
FOUNDATION AND EMPIRE
THE CURRENTS OF SPACE
*DAVID STARR: SPACE RANGER
SECOND FOUNDATION
*LUCKY STARR AND THE PIRATES OF THE ASTEROIDS
THE CAVES OF STEEL
THE MARTIAN WAY AND OTHER STORIES
*LUCKY STARR AND THE OCEANS OF VENUS
THE END OF ETERNITY
*LUCKY STARR AND THE BIG SUN OF MERCURY
THE NAKED SUN
*LUCKY STARR AND THE MOONS OF JUPITER
EARTH IS ROOM ENOUGH
*LUCKY STARR AND THE RINGS OF SATURN
NINE TOMORROWS
THE REST OF THE ROBOTS
FANTASTIC VOYAGE
THROUGH A GLASS, CLEARLY
ASIMOV'S MYSTERIES
NIGHTFALL AND OTHER STORIES

Science Fiction Anthologies edited by Isaac Asimov

THE HUGO WINNERS
**FIFTY SHORT SCIENCE FICTION TALES
TOMORROW'S CHILDREN

*under the pseudonym of Paul French
**in collaboration with Groff Conklin

WHERE DO WE GO FROM HERE?

edited by

Isaac Asimov

London

MICHAEL JOSEPH

First published in Great Britain by MICHAEL JOSEPH LTD.
52 Bedford Square, London, W.C.1
1973

ISBN 0 7181 1134 6

Set and printed in Great Britain by
Northumberland Press Limited, Gateshead
in Pilgrim ten on twelve point on paper supplied by
P. F. Bingham Ltd., and bound by
James Burn at Esher, Surrey

Dedication

To Judy-Lynn Benjamin

who is full of surprises,

birthday and otherwise.

Grateful acknowledgement is made to the following for permission to reprint the articles included in this book:

'Pâté de Fois Gras' by Isaac Asimov, first published in *Astounding Science Fiction*, September 1956. Copyright © 1956 by Street & Smith Publications, Inc. Reprinted by permission of the author;

'The Holes Around Mars' by Jerome Bixby, first published in *Galaxy Magazine*, January 1954. Copyright © 1970 by Jerome Bixby. Reprinted by permission of the author;

'Surface Tension' by James Blish, first published in *Galaxy Magazine*, August 1952. Copyright © 1957 by James Blish. Reprinted by permission of the author and Robert P. Mills, Ltd.;

'The Deep Range' by Arthur C. Clarke, first published in *Stars Science Fiction* no. 3, edited by Fredrik Pohl. Copyright © 1954 by Ballantine Books, Inc. Reprinted by permission of the author and the author's agents, Scott Meredith Literary Agency, Inc.;

'Dust Rag' by Hal Clement, first published in *Astounding Science Fiction*, September 1956. Copyright © 1956 by Street & Smith Publications, Inc. 'Proof' by Hal Clement, first published in *Astounding Science Fiction*, June 1942. Copyright 1942 by Street & Smith Publications, Inc. Copyright © 1970 by Harry C. Stubbs. Reprinted by arrangement with the author.

'The Day Is Done' by Lester del Ray, first published in *Astounding Science Fiction*, May 1939. Copyright 1939 by Street & Smith Publications, Inc. Reprinted by permission of the author and his agents, Scott Meredith Literary Agency Inc.;

'A Subway Named Mobius' by A. J. Deutsch, first published in *Astounding Science Fiction*, December 1950. Copyright 1950 by Street & Smith Publications, Inc.;

'Heavy Planet' by Milton A. Rothman, first published under the name of Lee Gregor, in *Astounding Science Fiction*, August 1939. Copyright 1939 by Street & Smith Publications, Inc. Reprinted by permission of the author;

'The Cave of Night' by James E. Gunn, first published in *Galaxy Magazine*, February 1955. Copyright 1954 by Galaxy Publishing Corporation. Reprinted by permission of the author and his agents, Scott Meredith Literary Agency, Inc.;

'—And He Built a Crooked House—' by Robert A. Heinlein, first published in *Astounding Science Fiction*, February 1941. Copyright 1940 by Street & Smith Publications, Inc. Reprinted by permission of the author's agents Lurton Blassingame;

'Omnilingual' by H. Beam Piper, first published in *Astounding Science Fiction*, February 1957. Copyright © 1957 by Street & Smith Publications, Inc. Reprinted by permission of the estate of the late H. Beam Piper;

'Country Doctor' by William Morrison from *Stars Science Fiction* no. 1, edited by Fredrik Pohl. Copyright 1953 by Ballantine Books, Inc. Reprinted by permission of the author;

'Neutron Star' by Larry Niven, first published in *Worlds of IF*, October 1966. Copyright © 1966 by Galaxy Publishing Corporation. Published in *Neutron Star* by Larry Niven. Reprinted by permission of the author and Ballantine Books, Inc.;

'Night' by Don A. Stuart, first published in *Astounding Stories*, October 1935. Copyright © 1935 by Street & Smith Publications, Inc. Copyright © renewed 1963 by the Condé Nast Publications, Inc. Reprinted by permission of the author and his agents, Scott Meredith Literary Agency, Inc.;

'The Big Bounce' by Walter S. Tevis, first published in *Galaxy Magazine*, February 1958. Copyright © 1958 by Galaxy Publishing Corporation;

'A Martian Odyssey' by Stanley G. Weinbaum, first published in *Wonder Stories*, July 1934. Copyright 1934 by Continental Publications, Inc.; Copyright renewed 1962 by Margaret Weinbaum Kay. Published by arrangement with Forrest J. Ackerman representing the author's estate.

Contents

Introduction

I have long maintained that science fiction has potential as an inspiring and useful teaching device. For this anthology, therefore, I have selected seventeen stories which, I think, can inspire curiosity and can lead the student into lines of questioning of his own that may interest and excite him, and may even help determine the future direction of his career.

This is not to say that the stories are all scientifically accurate though some, of course, are indeed accurate by the standards of their times. After all, a science fiction story cannot be (except by inspired guessing) more accurate than the scientific knowledge of the time makes possible. A story written in 1925 can only by accident deal accurately with Pluto, the ninth planet; and the situation is similar in stories about the atomic bomb written in 1935; artificial satellites written in 1945; quasars written in 1955, and so on.

In many science fiction stories, a scientific principle is deliberately bent for the sake of making a particular plot possible. This can be done skilfully by an author knowledgeable in science or clumsily by another who is less well versed in the matter. In either case, even in the latter, the story can be useful. A law of nature ignored or distorted can rouse more interest, sometimes, than a law of nature explained. Are the events in the story possible? If not, why not? And in tracking that down, the student may sometimes learn more about science than from any number of correct classroom demonstrations.

This anthology is prepared, then, on several different levels.

In the first place, the seventeen stories included are all good ones, all clever and exciting in their own right. Anyone who wishes can read them for themselves alone, need make no conscious effort to learn from them, and may totally ignore my own comments after each story.

For those who would probe a little deeper, I have placed after each story a few hundred words of commentary in which I talk about the scientific points made in the story, pointing out their validity or, sometimes, explaining their errors.

Finally, after each comment, I have appended a series of suggestions and questions designed to direct the reader's curiosity in possibly fruitful directions. These are not simple, nor are they intended to be simple; sometimes indeed I ask questions that have no known answers. Nevertheless, I give no hints and there are no answers in the back of the book. I have, however, in an appendix at the end of the book, listed two items for each story that might interest anyone who found himself gripped by the science involved. The further reading may not give the answers to the questions I posed but they will answer other questions which I did not ask and they will very likely lure the reader onward.

Even this appendix, rough and non-specific though it is, I present reluctantly. I want the reader completely on his own. I don't want to give answers but to stimulate thought; I don't want to point out solutions but to rouse the kind of curiosity that may begin a self-directed drive.

There is, after all, no requirement that any reader follow up all or even any of the lines of inquiry I suggest, but a few might, out of a desire nurtured by the stories in this anthology, or even by just one particular story.

If that happens, then for each reader that finds even one thread of suggestion exciting and proceeds to lose himself in the search for knowledge, I win immensely more than I would have won by merely providing an interesting anthology.

And the involved readers win immensely more as well.

1. A Martian Odyssey

Stanley G. Weinbaum

Jarvis stretched himself as luxuriously as he could in the cramped general quarters of the *Ares*.

'Air you can breathe!' he exulted. 'It feels as thick as soup after the thin stuff out there!' He nodded at the Martian landscape stretching flat and desolate in the light of the nearer moon, beyond the glass of the port.

The other three stared at him sympathetically—Putz, the engineer, Leroy, the biologist, and Harrison the astronomer and captain of the expedition. Dick Jarvis, of course, was chemist of the famous crew, the *Ares* expedition, first human beings to set foot on the mysterious neighbour of the earth, the planet Mars. This, of course, was in the old days, less than twenty years after the mad American Doheny perfected the atomic blast at the cost of his life, and only a decade after the equally mad Cardoza rode on it to the moon. They were true pioneers, these four of the *Ares*. Except for a half-dozen moon expeditions and the ill-fated de Lancey flight aimed at the seductive orb of Venus, they were the first men to feel other gravity than earth's, and certainly the first successful crew to leave the earth-moon system. And they deserved that success when one considers the difficulties and discomforts—the months spent in acclimatization chambers back on earth, learning to breathe air as tenuous as that of Mars, the challenging of the void in the tiny rocket driven by the cranky reaction motors of the twenty-first century, and mostly the facing of an absolutely unknown world.

Jarvis stretched again and fingered the raw and peeling tip of his frost-bitten nose. He sighed again contentedly.

'Well,' exploded Harrison abruptly, 'are we going to hear what happened? You set out all shipshape in an auxiliary rocket, we don't get a peep for ten days, and finally Putz here picks you out of a lunatic ant-heap with a freak ostrich as your pal! Spill it, man!'

'"Speel"?' queried Leroy perplexedly. 'Speel what?'

'He means *"spiel"*,' explained Putz soberly. 'It iss to tell.'

Jarvis met Harrison's amused glance without the shadow of a smile. 'That's right, Karl,' he said in grave agreement with Putz. *'Ich spiel es!'* He grunted comfortably and began.

'According to orders,' he said, 'I watched Karl here take off towards the North, and then I got into my flying sweat-box and headed South. You'll remember, Cap—we had orders not to land, but just scout about for points of interest. I set the two cameras clicking and buzzed along, riding pretty high—about two thousand feet—for a couple of reasons. First, it gave the cameras a greater field, and second, the under-jets travel so far in this half-vacuum they call air here that they stir up dust if you move low.'

'We know all that from Putz,' grunted Harrison. 'I wish you'd saved the films, though. They'd have paid the cost of this junket; remember how the public mobbed the first moon pictures?'

'The films are safe,' retorted Jarvis. 'Well,' he resumed, 'as I said, I buzzed along at a pretty good clip; just as we figured, the wings haven't much lift in this air at less than a hundred miles per hour, and even then I had to use the under-jets.

'So, with the speed and the altitude and the blurring caused by the under-jets, the seeing wasn't any too good. I could see enough, though, to distinguish that what I sailed over was just more of this grey plain that we'd been examining the whole week since our landing—same blobby growths and same eternal carpet of crawling little plant-animals, or biopods, as Leroy calls them. So I sailed along, calling back my position every hour as instructed, and not knowing whether you heard me.'

'I did?' snapped Harrison.

'A hundred and fifty miles south,' continued Jarvis imperturbably, 'the surface changed to a sort of low plateau, nothing but desert and orange-tinted sand. I figured that we were right in our guess, then, and this grey plain we dropped on was really the Mare Cimmerium which would make my orange desert the region called Xanthus. If I were right, I ought to hit another grey plain, the Mare Chronium in another couple of hundred miles, and then another orange desert, Thyle I or II. And so I did.'

'Putz verified our position a week and a half ago!' grumbled the Captain. 'Let's get to the point.'

'Coming!' remarked Jarvis. 'Twenty miles into Thyle—believe it or not—I crossed a canal!'

'Putz photographed a hundred! Let's hear something new!'

'And did he also see a city?'

'Twenty of 'em, if you call those heaps of mud cities!'

'Well,' observed Jarvis, 'from here on I'll be telling a few things Putz didn't see!' He rubbed his tingling nose, and continued. 'I knew that I had sixteen hours of daylight at this season, so eight hours—eight hundred miles—from here, I decided to turn back. I was still over Thyle, whether I or II I'm not sure, not more than twenty-five miles into it. And right there, Putz's pet motor quit!'

'Qvit? How?' Putz was solicitous.

'The atomic blast got weak. I started losing altitude right away, and suddenly there I was with a thump right in the middle of Thyle! Smashed my nose on the window, too!' He rubbed the injured member ruefully.

'Did you maybe try vashing der combustion chamber mit acid sulphuric?' inquired Putz. 'Sometimes der lead giffs a secondary radiation—'

'Naw!' said Jarvis disgustedly. 'I wouldn't try that, of course—not more than ten times! Besides, the bump flattened the landing gear and busted off the under-jets. Suppose I got the thing working—what then? Ten miles with the blast coming right out of the bottom and I'd have melted the floor from under me!' He rubbed his nose again. 'Lucky for me a pound only weighs seven ounces here, or I'd have been mashed flat!'

'I could have fixed!' ejaculated the engineer. 'I bet it vas not serious.'

'Probably not,' agreed Jarvis sarcastically. 'Only it wouldn't fly. Nothing serious, but I had my choice of waiting to be picked up or trying to walk back—eight hundred miles, and perhaps twenty days before we had to leave! Forty miles a day! Well,' he concluded, 'I chose to walk. Just as much chance of being picked up, and it kept me busy.'

'We'd have found you,' said Harrison.

'No doubt. Anyway, I rigged up a harness from some seat straps, and put the water tank on my back, took a cartridge belt and revolver, and some iron rations, and started out.'

'Water tank!' exclaimed the little biologist, Leroy. 'She weigh one-quarter ton!'

'Wasn't full. Weighed about two hundred and fifty pounds earth-weight, which is eighty-five here. Then, besides, my own personal two hundred and ten pounds is only seventy on Mars, so, tank and all, I grossed a hundred and fifty-five, or fifty-five pounds less than my everyday earth-weight. I figured on that when I undertook the forty-mile daily stroll. Oh—of course I took a thermo-skin sleeping bag for these wintry Martian nights.'

'Off I went, bouncing along pretty quickly. Eight hours of daylight meant twenty miles or more. It got tiresome, of course—plugging along over a soft sand desert with nothing to see, not even Leroy's crawling biopods. But an hour or so brought me to the canal—just a dry ditch about four hundred feet wide, and straight as a railroad on its own company map.

'There'd been water in it sometime, though. The ditch was covered with what looked like a nice green lawn. Only, as I approached, the lawn moved out of my way!'

'Eh?' said Leroy.

'Yeah; it was a relative of your biopods. I caught one—a little grass-like blade about as long as my finger, with two thin, stemmy legs.'

'He is where?' Leroy was eager.

'He is let go! I had to move, so I ploughed along with the walking grass opening in front and closing behind. And then I was out on the orange desert of Thyle again.

'I plugged doggedly along, cussing the sand that made going so tiresome, and, incidentally, cussing that cranky motor of yours, Karl. It was just before twilight that I reached the edge of Thyle, and looked down over the grey Mare Chronium. And I knew there was seventy-five miles of *that* to be walked over, and then a couple of hundred miles of that Xanthus desert, and about as much more Mare Cimmerium. Was I pleased? I started cussing you fellows for not picking me up!'

'We were trying, you sap!' said Harrison.

'That didn't help. Well, I figured I might as well use what was left of daylight in getting down the cliff that bounded Thyle. I found an easy place, and down I went. Mare Chronium was just the same sort of place as this—crazy leafless plants and a bunch of crawlers; I gave it a glance and hauled out my sleeping bag. Up to that time, you know, I hadn't seen anything worth worrying about on this half-dead world—nothing dangerous, that is.'

'Did you?' queried Harrison.

'*Did* I! You'll hear about it when I come to it. Well, I was just about to turn in when suddenly I heard the wildest sort of shenanigans!'

'Vot iss shenanigans!' inquired Putz.

'He say, *"Je ne sais quoi",*' explained Leroy. 'It is to say, "I don't know what".'

'That's right,' agreed Jarvis. 'I didn't know what, so I sneaked over to find out. There was a racket like a flock of crows eating a bunch of canaries—whistles, cackles, caws, trills, and what have you. I rounded a clump of stumps, and there was Tweel!'

'Tweel?' said Harrison, and 'Tveel?' said Leroy and Putz.

'That freak ostrich,' explained the narrator. 'At least, Tweel is as near as I can pronounce it without sputtering. He called it something like "Trrrweerrlll".'

'What was he doing?' asked the Captain.

'He was being eaten! And squealing, of course, as any one would.'

'Eaten! By what?'

'I found out later. All I could see then was a bunch of black ropy arms tangled around what looked like, as Putz described it to you, an ostrich. I wasn't going to interfere, naturally; if both creatures were dangerous, I'd have one less to worry about.

'But the bird-like thing was putting up a good battle, dealing vicious blows with an eighteen-inch beak, between screeches. And besides, I caught a glimpse or two of what was on the end of those arms!' Jarvis shuddered. 'But the clincher was when I noticed a little black bag or case hung about the neck of the bird-like thing! It was intelligent! That or tame, I assumed. Anyway, it clinched my decision. I pulled out my automatic and fired into what I could see of its antagonist.

'There was a flurry of tentacles and a spurt of black corruption, and then the thing, with a disgusting sucking noise, pulled itself and its arms into a hole in the ground. The other let out a series of clacks, staggered around on legs about as thick as golf sticks, and turned suddenly to face me. I held my weapon ready, and the two of us stared at each other.

'The Martian wasn't a bird, really. It wasn't even bird-like, except just at first glance. It had a beak all right, and a few feathery appendages, but the beak wasn't really a beak. It was somewhat flexible; I could see the tip bend slowly from side to side; it was almost like a cross between a beak and a trunk. It had four-toed feet, and four-fingered things—hands, you'd have to call them, and a little roundish body, and a long neck ending in a tiny head—and that beak. It stood an inch or so taller than I, and—well, Putz saw it!'

The engineer nodded. 'Yah! I saw!'

CHAPTER II
Tweel of Mars

Jarvis continued. 'So—we stared at each other. Finally the creature went into a series of clackings and twitterings and held out its hands towards me, empty. I took that as a gesture of friendship.'

'Perhaps,' suggested Harrison, 'it looked at that nose of yours and thought you were its brother!'

'Huh! You can be funny without talking! Anyway, I put up my gun and said, "Aw, don't mention it," or something of the sort, and the thing came over and we were pals.

'By that time, the sun was pretty low and I knew that I'd better build a fire or get into my thermo-skin. I decided on the fire. I picked a spot at the base of the Thyle cliff, where the rock could reflect a little heat on my back. I started breaking off chunks of this desiccated Martian vegetation, and my companion caught the idea and brought in an armful. I reached for a match, but the Martian fished into his pouch and brought out something that looked like a glowing coal; one touch of it, and the fire was blazing—and you all know what a job we have starting a fire in this atmosphere!

'And that bag of his!' continued the narrator. 'That was a manufactured article, my friends; press an end and she popped open—press the middle, and she sealed so perfectly you couldn't see the line. Better than zippers.

'Well, we stared at the fire a while and I decided to attempt some sort of communication with the Martian. I pointed at myself and said "Dick"; he caught the drift immediately, stretched a bony claw at me and repeated "Tick". Then I pointed at him, and he gave that whistle I called Tweel; I can't imitate his accent. Things were going smoothly; to emphasize the names, I repeated "Dick", and then, pointing at him, "Tweel".

'There we stuck! He gave some clacks that sounded negative, and said something like "P-p-p-proot". And that was just the beginning; I was always "Tick", but as for him—part of the time he was "Tweel", and part of the time he was "P-p-p-proot", and part of the time he was sixteen other noises!

'We just couldn't connect! I tried "rock", and I tried "star", and "tree", and "fire", and Lord knows what else, and try as I would, I couldn't get a single word! Nothing was the same for two successive minutes, and if that's a language, I'm an alchemist! Finally I gave it up and called him Tweel, and that seemed to do.

'But Tweel hung on to some of my words. He remembered a couple of them, which I suppose is a great achievement if you're used to a language you have to make up as you go along. But I couldn't get the hang of his talk; either I missed some subtle point or we just didn't *think* alike—and I rather believe the latter view.

'I've other reasons for believing that. After a while I gave up the language business, and tried mathematics. I scratched two plus two equals four on the ground, and demonstrated it with pebbles. Again Tweel caught the idea, and informed me that three plus three equals six. Once more we seemed to be getting somewhere.

'So, knowing that Tweel had at least a grammar school education, I drew a circle for the sun, pointing first at it, and then at the last glow of the sun. Then I sketched in Mercury, and Venus, and Mother Earth, and Mars, and finally, pointing to Mars, I swept my hand around in a sort of inclusive gesture to indicate that Mars was our current environment. I was working up to putting over the idea that my home was on the earth.

'Tweel understood my diagram all right. He poked his beak at it, and with a great deal of trilling and clucking, he added Deimos and Phobos to Mars, and then sketched in the earth's moon!

'Do you see what that proves? It proves that Tweel's race uses telescopes—that they're civilized!'

'Does not!' snapped Harrison. 'The moon is visible from here as a fifth magnitude star. They could see its revolution with the naked eye.'

'The moon, yes!' said Jarvis. 'You've missed my point. Mercury isn't visible! And Tweel knew of Mercury because he placed the moon at the *third* planet, not the second. If he didn't know Mercury, he'd put the earth second, and Mars third, instead of fourth? See?'

'Humph!' said Harrison.

'Anyway,' proceeded Jarvis, 'I went on with my lesson. Things were going smoothly, and it looked as if I could put the idea over. I pointed at the earth on my diagram, and then at myself, and then, to clinch it, I pointed to myself and then to the earth itself shining green almost at the zenith.

'Tweel set up such an excited clacking that I was certain he understood. He jumped up and down, and suddenly he pointed at himself and then at the sky, and then at himself and at the sky again. He pointed at his middle and then at Arcturus, at his head and then at Spica, at his feet and then at half a dozen stars, while I just gaped at him. Then, all of a sudden, he gave a tremendous leap. Man, what a hop! He shot straight up into the starlight, seventy-five feet if an inch! I saw him silhouetted against the sky, saw him turn and come down at me head first, and land smack on his beak like a javelin! Then he stuck square in the centre of my sun-circle in the sand—a bull's-eye!'

'Nuts!' observed the Captain. 'Plain nuts!'

'That's what I thought, too! I just stared at him open-mouthed while he pulled his head out of the sand and stood up. Then I figured he'd missed my point, and I went through the whole blamed rigmarole again, and it ended the same way, with Tweel on his nose in the middle of my picture!'

'Maybe it's a religious rite,' suggested Harrison.

'Maybe,' said Jarvis dubiously. 'Well, there we were. We could exchange ideas up to a certain point, and then—blooey! Something in us was different, unrelated; I don't doubt that Tweel thought me just as screwy as I thought him. Our minds simply looked at the world from different viewpoints, and perhaps his viewpoint is as true as ours. But—we couldn't get together, that's all. Yet, in spite of all difficulties, I *liked* Tweel, and I have a queer certainty that he liked me.'

'Nuts!' repeated the Captain. 'Just daffy!'

'Yeah? Wait and see. A couple of times I've thought that perhaps we—' He paused, and then resumed his narrative. 'Anyway, I finally gave it up, and got into my thermo-skin to sleep. The fire hadn't kept me any too warm, but that damn sleeping bag did. Got stuffy five minutes after I closed myself in. I opened it a little and bingo! Some eighty-below-zero air hit my nose, and that's when I got this pleasant little frostbite to add to the bump I acquired during the crash of my rocket.

'I don't know what Tweel made of my sleeping. He sat around, but when I woke up, he was gone. I'd just crawled out of my bag, though, when I heard some twittering, and there he came, sailing down from that three-storey Thyle cliff to alight on his beak beside me. I pointed to myself and towards the north, and he pointed at himself and towards the south, but when I loaded up and started away, he came along.

'Man, how he travelled!—a hundred and fifty feet at a jump, sailing through the air stretched out like a spear, and landing on his beak. He seemed surprised at my plodding, but after a few moments he fell in beside me, only every few minutes he'd go into one of his leaps, and stick his nose into the sand a block ahead of me. Then he'd come shooting back at me; it kept me nervous at first to see that beak of his coming at me like a spear, but he always ended in the sand at my side.

'So the two of us plugged along across the Mare Chronium. Same sort of place as this—same crazy plants and same little green biopods growing in the sand, or crawling out of your way. We talked—not that we understood each other, you know, but just for company. I sang songs, and I suspect Tweel did too; at least, some of his trillings and twitterings had a subtle sort of rhythm.

'Then, for variety, Tweel would display his smattering of English words. He'd point to an outcropping and say "rock", and point to a pebble and say it again; or he'd touch my arm and say "Tick", and then repeat it. He seemed terrifically amused that the same word meant the same thing twice in succession, or that the same word could apply to two different objects. It set me wondering if perhaps his language wasn't like the primitive speech of earth people—you know, Captain, like the Negritoes, for instance, who haven't any generic words. No word for food or water or man—words for good food and bad food, or rain water and sea water, or strong man and weak man—but no names for general classes. They're too primitive to understand that rain water and sea water are just different aspects of the same thing. But that wasn't the case with Tweel; it was just that we were somehow mysteriously different—our minds were alien to each other. And yet—we *liked* each other!'

'Looney, that's all,' remarked Harrison. 'That's why you two were so fond of each other.'

'Well, I like *you*!' countered Jarvis wickedly. 'Anyway,' he resumed, 'don't get the idea that there was anything screwy about Tweel. In fact, I'm not so sure but that he couldn't teach our highly praised human intelligence a trick or two. Oh, he wasn't an intellectual superman, I guess; but don't overlook the point that he managed to understand a little of my mental workings, and I never even got a glimmering of his.'

'Because he didn't have any!' suggested the Captain, while Putz and Leroy blinked attentively.

'You can judge of that when I'm through,' said Jarvis. 'Well, we plugged along across the Mare Chronium all that day, and all the next. Mare Chronium—Sea of Time! Say, I was willing to agree with Schiaparelli's name by the end of that march! Just that grey, endless plain of weird plants, and never a sign of any other life. It was so monotonous that I was even glad to see the desert of Xanthus towards the evening of the second day.

'I was fair worn out, but Tweel seemed as fresh as ever, for all I never saw him drink or eat. I think he could have crossed the Mare Chronium in a couple of hours with those block-long nosedives of his, but he stuck along with me. I offered him some water once or twice; he took the cup from me and sucked the liquid into his beak, and then carefully squirted it all back into the cup and gravely returned it.

'Just as we sighted Xanthus, or the cliffs that bounded it, one of those nasty sand clouds blew along, not as bad as the one we had here, but mean to travel against. I pulled the transparent flap of my thermo-skin bag across my face and managed pretty well, and I noticed that Tweel used some feathery appendages growing like a moustache at the base of his beak to cover his nostrils, and some similar fuzz to shield his eyes.'

'He is desert creature!' ejaculated the little biologist, Leroy.

'Huh? Why?'

'He drink no water—he is adapt' for sand storm—'

'Proves nothing! There's not enough water to waste anywhere on this desiccated pill called Mars. We'd call all of it desert on earth, you know.' He paused. 'Anyway, after the sand storm blew over, a little wind kept blowing in our faces, not strong enough to stir the sand. But suddenly things came drifting along from the Xanthus cliffs—small, transparent spheres, for all the world like glass tennis balls! But light—they were almost light enough to float even in this thin air—empty, too; at least, I cracked open a couple and nothing came out but a bad smell. I asked Tweel about them, but all he said was "No, no, no", which I took to mean that he knew nothing about them. So they went bouncing by like tumbleweeds, or like soap bubbles, and we plugged on towards Xanthus. Tweel pointed at one of the crystal balls once and said "rock", but I was too tired to argue with him. Later I discovered what he meant.

'We came to the bottom of the Xanthus cliffs finally, when there wasn't much daylight left. I decided to sleep on the plateau if possible; anything dangerous, I reasoned, would be more likely to prowl through the vegetation of the Mare Chronium than the sand of Xanthus. Not that I'd seen a single sign of menace, except the rope-armed black thing that had trapped Tweel, and apparently that didn't prowl at all, but lured its victims within reach. It couldn't lure me while I slept, especially as Tweel didn't seem to sleep at all, but simply sat patiently around all night.

I wondered how the creature had managed to trap Tweel, but there wasn't any way of asking him. I found that out too, later; it's devilish!

'However, we were ambling around the base of the Xanthus barrier looking for an easy spot to climb. At least, I was. Tweel could have leaped it easily, for the cliffs were lower than Thyle—perhaps sixty feet. I found a place and started up, swearing at the water tank strapped to my back—it didn't bother me except when climbing—and suddenly I heard a sound that I thought I recognized!

'You know how deceptive sounds are in this thin air. A shot sounds like the pop of a cork. But this sound was the drone of a rocket, and sure enough, there went our second auxiliary about ten miles to westward, between me and the sunset!'

'Vas me!' said Putz. 'I hung for you.'

'Yeah; I knew that, but what good did it do me? I hung on to the cliff and yelled and waved with one hand. Tweel saw it too, and set up a trilling and twittering, leaping to the top of the barrier and then high into the air. And while I watched, the machine droned on into the shadows to the south.

'I scrambled to the top of the cliff. Tweel was still pointing and trilling excitedly, shooting up towards the sky and coming down head-on to stick upside down on his beak in the sand. I pointed towards the south and at myself, and he said, "Yes—Yes—Yes"; but somehow I gathered that he thought the flying thing was a relative of mine, probably a parent. Perhaps I did his intellect an injustice; I think now that I did.

'I was bitterly disappointed by the failure to attract attention. I pulled out my thermo-skin bag and crawled into it, as the night chill was already apparent. Tweel stuck his beak into the sand and drew up his legs and arms and looked for all the world like one of those leafless shrubs out there. I think he stayed that way all night.'

'Protective mimicry!' ejaculated Leroy. 'See? He is desert creature!'

CHAPTER III
The Pyramid Being

'In the morning,' resumed Jarvis, 'we started off again. We hadn't gone a hundred yards into Xanthus when I saw something queer! This is one thing Putz didn't photograph, I'll wager!

'There was a line of little pyramids—tiny ones, not more than six inches high, stretching across Xanthus as far as I could see! Little buildings made of pygmy bricks, they were, hollow inside and truncated, or at least broken at the top and empty. I pointed at them and said "What?" to Tweel, but he gave some negative twitters to indicate, I suppose, that he didn't know. So off we went, following the row of pyramids because they ran north, and I was going north.

'Man, we trailed that line for hours! After a while, I noticed another queer thing: they were getting larger. Same number of bricks in each one, but the bricks were larger.

'By noon they were shoulder high. I looked into a couple—all just the same, broken at the top and empty. I examined a brick or two as well; they were silica, and old as creation itself!'

'How you know?' asked Leroy.

'They were weathered—edges rounded. Silica doesn't weather easily even on earth, and in this climate—!'

'How old you think?'

'Fifty thousand—a hundred thousand years. How can I tell? The little ones we saw in the morning were older—perhaps ten times as old. Crumbling. How old would that make *them?* Half a million years? Who knows?' Jarvis paused a moment. 'Well,' he resumed, 'we followed the line. Tweel pointed at them and said "rock" once or twice, but he'd done that many times before. Besides, he was more or less right about these.

'I tried questioning him. I pointed at a pyramid and asked "People?" and indicated the two of us. He set up a negative sort of clucking and said, "No, no, no. No one-one-two. No two-two-four," meanwhile rubbing his stomach. I just stared at him and he went through the business again. "No one-one-two. No two-two-four." I just gaped at him.'

'That proves it!' exclaimed Harrison. 'Nuts!'

'You think so?' queried Jarvis sardonically. 'Well, I figured it out different! "No one-one-two!" You don't get it, of course, do you?'

'Nope—nor do you!'

'I think I do! Tweel was using the few English words he knew to put over a very complex idea. What, let me ask, does mathematics make you think of?'

'Why—of astronomy. Or—or logic!'

'That's it! "No one-one-two!" Tweel was telling me that the builders of the pyramids weren't people!—or that they weren't intelligent, that they weren't reasoning creatures! Get it?'

'Huh! I'll be damned!'

'You probably will.'

'Why,' put in Leroy, 'he rub his belly?'

'Why? Because, my dear biologist, that's where his brains were! Not in his tiny head—in his middle!'

'C'est impossible!'

'Not on Mars, it isn't! This flora and fauna aren't earthly; your biopods prove that!' Jarvis grinned and took up his narrative. 'Anyway, we plugged along across Xanthus and in about the middle of the afternoon, something else queer happened. The pyramids ended.'

'Ended!'

'Yeah; the queer part was that the last one—and now they were ten-footers—was capped! See? Whatever built it was still inside; we'd trailed 'em from their half-million-year-old origin to the present.

'Tweel and I both noticed it about the same time. I yanked out my automatic (I had a clip of Boland explosive bullets in it) and Tweel, quick as a sleight-of-hand trick, snapped a queer little glass revolver out of his bag. It was much like our weapons, except that the grip was larger to accommodate his four-taloned hand. And we held our weapons ready while we sneaked up along the lines of empty pyramids.

'Tweel saw the movement first. The top tiers of bricks were heaving, shaking, and suddenly slid down the sides with a thin crash. And then—something—something was coming out!

'A long, silver-grey arm appeared, dragging after it an armoured body. Armoured, I mean, with scales, silver-grey and dull-shining. The arm heaved the body out of the hole; the beast crashed to the sand.

'It was a nondescript creature—body like a big grey cask, arm and a sort of mouth-hole at one end; stiff, pointed tail at the other—and that's all. No other limbs, no eyes, ears, nose—nothing! The thing dragged itself a few yards, inserted its pointed tail in the sand, pushed itself upright, and just sat.

'Tweel and I watched it for ten minutes before it moved. Then, with a creaking and rustling like—oh, like crumpling stiff paper—its arm moved to the mouth-hole and out came a brick! The arm placed the brick carefully on the ground, and the thing was still again.

'Another ten minutes—another brick. Just one of Nature's bricklayers. I was about ready to slip away and move on when Tweel pointed at the thing and said "rock"! I went "huh?" and he said it again. Then, to the accompaniment of some of his trilling, he said, "No—no—," and gave two or three whistling breaths.

'Well, I got his meaning, for a wonder! I said, "No breath?" and demonstrated the word. Tweel was ecstatic; he said, "Yes, yes, yes! No, no, no breet!" Then he gave a leap and sailed out to land on his nose about one pace from the monster!

'I was startled, you can imagine! The arm was going up for a brick, and I expected to see Tweel caught and mangled, but—nothing happened! Tweel pounded on the creature, and the arm took the brick and placed it neatly beside the first. Tweel rapped on its body again, and said "rock", and I got up nerve enough to take a look myself.

'Tweel was right again. The creature *was* rock, and it didn't breathe!'

'How you know?' snapped Leroy, his black eyes blazing interest.

'Because I'm a chemist. The beast was made of silica! There must have been pure silicon in the sand, and it lived on that. Get it? We, and Tweel, and those plants out there, and even the biopods are *carbon* life; this thing lived by a different set of chemical reactions. It was silicon life!'

'La vie silicieuse!' shouted Leroy. 'I have suspect, and now it is proof! I must go see! *Il faut que je—*'

'All right! All right!' said Jarvis. 'You can go see. Anyhow, there the thing was, alive and not alive, moving every ten minutes, and then only to remove a brick. Those bricks were its waste matter. See, Frenchy? We're carbon, and our waste is carbon dioxide, and this thing is silicon, and *its* waste is silicon dioxide—silica. But silica is a solid, hence the bricks. And it built itself in, and when it was covered, it moved over to a fresh place to start over. No wonder it creaked! A living creature half a million years old!'

'How you know how old?' Leroy was frantic.

'We trailed its pyramids from the beginning, didn't we? If this weren't the original pyramid builder, the series would have ended somewhere before we found him, wouldn't it?—ended and started over with the small ones. That's simple enough, isn't it?

'But he reproduces, or tries to. Before the third brick came out, there was a little rustle and out popped a whole stream of those little crystal balls. They're his spores, or eggs, or seeds—call 'em what you want. They went bouncing by across Xanthus just as they'd bounced by us back in the Mare Chronium. I've a hunch how they work, too—this is for your information, Leroy. I think the crystal shell of silica is no more than a protective covering, like an eggshell, and that the active principle is the smell inside. It's some sort of gas that attacks silicon, and if the shell is broken near a supply of that element, some reaction starts that ultimately develops into a beast like that one.'

'You should try!' exclaimed the little Frenchmen. 'We must break one to see!'

'Yeah? Well, I did. I smashed a couple against the sand. Would you like to come back in about ten thousand years to see if I planted some pyramid monsters? You'd most likely be able to tell by that time!' Jarvis paused and drew a deep breath. 'Lord! That queer creature! Do you picture it? Blind, deaf, nerveless, brainless—just a mechanism, and yet—immortal! Bound to go on making bricks, building pyramids, as long as silicon and oxygen exist, and even afterwards it'll just stop. It won't be dead. If the accidents of a million years bring it its food again, there it'll be, ready to run again, while brains and civilizations are part of the past. A queer beast—yet I met a stranger one!'

'If you did, it must have been in your dreams!' growled Harrison.

'You're right!' said Jarvis soberly. 'In a way, you're right. The dream-beast! That's the best name for it—and it's the most fiendish, terrifying creation one could imagine! More dangerous than a lion, more insidious than a snake!'

'Tell me!' begged Leroy. 'I must go see!'

'Not *this* devil!' He paused again. 'Well,' he resumed, 'Tweel and I left the pyramid creature and ploughed along through Xanthus. I was tired and a little disheartened by Putz's failure to pick me up, and Tweel's trilling got on my nerves, as did his flying nosedives. So I just strode along without a word, hour after hour across that monotonous desert.

'Towards mid-afternoon we came in sight of a low dark line on the horizon. I knew what it was. It was a canal; I'd crossed it in the rocket and it meant that we were just one-third of the way across Xanthus. Pleasant thought, wasn't it? And still, I was keeping up to schedule.

'We approached the canal slowly; I remembered that this one was bordered by a wide fringe of vegetation and that mud-heap city was on it.'

CHAPTER IV
The Dream-Beast

'I was tired, as I said. I kept thinking of a good hot meal, and then from that I jumped to reflections of how nice and home-like even Borneo would seem after this crazy planet, and from that, to thoughts of little old New York, and then to thinking about a girl I know there—Fancy Long. Know her?'

''Vision entertainer,' said Harrison. 'I've tuned her in. Nice blonde—dances and sings on the *Yerba Mate* hour.'

'That's her,' said Jarvis ungrammatically. 'I know her pretty well—just friends, get me?—though she came down to see us off in the *Ares*. Well, I was thinking about her, feeling pretty lonesome, and all the time we were approaching that line of rubbery plants.

'And then—I said, "What 'n hell!" and stared. And there she was—Fancy Long, standing plain as day under one of those crack-brained trees, and smiling and waving just the way I remembered her when we left!'

'Now you're nuts, too!' observed the Captain.

'Boy, I almost agreed with you! I stared and pinched myself and closed my eyes and then stared again—and every time, there was Fancy Long smiling and waving! Tweel saw something, too; he was trilling and clucking away, but I scarcely heard him. I was bounding towards her over the sand, too amazed even to ask myself questions.

'I wasn't twenty feet from her when Tweel caught me with one of his flying leaps. He grabbed my arm, yelling, "No—no—no!" in his squeaky voice. I tried to shake him off—he was as light as if he were built of bamboo—but he dug his claws in and yelled. And finally some sort of sanity returned to me and I stopped less than ten feet from her. There she stood, looking as solid as Putz's head!'

'Vot?' said the engineer.

'She smiled and waved, and waved and smiled, and I stood there dumb as Leroy, while Tweel squeaked and chattered. I *knew* it couldn't be real, yet—there she was!

'Finally I said, "Fancy! Fancy Long!" She just kept on smiling and waving, but looking as real as if I hadn't left her thirty-seven millions miles away.

'Tweel had his glass pistol out, pointing it at her. I grabbed his arm, but he tried to push me away. He pointed at her and said, "No breet! No breet!" and I understood that he meant that the Fancy Long thing wasn't alive. Man, my head was whirling!

'Still, it gave me the jitters to see him pointing his weapon at her. I don't know why I stood there watching him take careful aim, but I did. Then he squeezed the handle of his weapon; there was a little puff of steam, and Fancy Long was gone! And in her place was one of those writhing, black, rope-armed horrors like the one I'd saved Tweel from!

'The dream-beast! I stood there dizzy, watching it die while Tweel trilled and whistled. Finally he touched my arm, pointed at the twisting thing, and said, "You one-one-two, he one-one-two." After he'd repeated it eight or ten times, I got it. Do any of you?'

'Oui!' shrilled Leroy. *'Moi—je le comprends!* He mean you think of something, the beast he know, and you see it! *Un chien*—a hungry dog, he would see the big bone with meat! Or smell it—not?'

'Right!' said Jarvis. 'The dream-beast uses its victim's longings and desires to trap its prey. The bird at nesting season would see its mate, the fox, prowling for its own prey, would see a helpless rabbit!'

'How he do?' queried Leroy.

'How do I know? How does a snake back on earth charm a bird into its very jaws? And aren't there deep-sea fish that lure their victims into their mouths? Lord!' Jarvis shuddered. 'Do you see how insidious the monster is? We're warned now—but henceforth we can't trust even our eyes. You might see me—I might see one of you—and back of it may be nothing but another of those black horrors!'

'How'd your friend know?' asked the Captain abruptly.

'Tweel? I wonder! Perhaps he was thinking of something that couldn't possibly have interested me, and when I started to run, he realized that I saw something different and was warned. Or perhaps the dream-beast can only project a single vision, and Tweel saw what I saw—or nothing. I couldn't ask him. But it's just another proof that his intelligence is equal to ours or greater.'

'He's daffy, I tell you!' said Harrison. 'What makes you think his intellect ranks with the human?'

'Plenty of things! First, the pyramid-beast. He hadn't seen one before; he said as much. Yet he recognized it as a dead-alive automaton of silicon.'

'He could have heard of it,' objected Harrison. 'He lives around here, you know.'

'Well, how about the language? I couldn't pick up a single idea of his and he learned six or seven words of mine. And do you realize what complex ideas he put over with no more than those six or seven words? The pyramid-monster—the dream-beast! In a single phrase he told me that one was a harmless automaton and the other a deadly hypnotist. What about that?'

'Huh!' said the Captain.

'*Huh* if you wish! Could you have done it knowing only six words of English? Could you go even further, as Tweel did, and tell me that another creature was of a sort of intelligence so different from ours that understanding was impossible—even more impossible than that between Tweel and me?'

'Eh? What was that?'

'Later. The point I'm making is that Tweel and his race are worthy of our friendship. Somewhere on Mars—and you'll find I'm right—is a civilization and culture equal to ours, and maybe more than equal. And communication is possible between them and us; Tweel proves that. It may take years of patient trial, for their minds are alien, but less alien than the next minds we encountered—if they *are* minds.'

'The next ones? What next ones?'

'The people of the mud-heap cities along the canals.' Jarvis frowned, then resumed his narrative. 'I thought the dream-beast and the silicon-monster were the strangest beings conceivable, but I was wrong. These creatures are still more alien, less understandable than either and far less comprehensible than Tweel, with whom friendship is possible, and even, by patience and concentration, the exchange of ideas.

'Well,' he continued, 'we left the dream-beast dying, dragging itself back into its hole, and we moved towards the canal. There was a carpet of that queer walking-grass scampering out of our way, and when we reached the bank, there was a yellow trickle of water flowing. The mound city I'd noticed from the rocket was a mile or so to the right and I was curious enough to want to take a look at it.

'It had seemed deserted from my previous glimpse of it, and if any creatures were lurking in it—well, Tweel and I were both armed. And by the way, that crystal weapon of Tweel's was an interesting device; I took a look at it after the dream-beast episode. It fired a little glass splinter, poisoned, I suppose, and I guess it held at least a hundred of 'em to a load. The propellant was steam—just plain steam!'

'Shteam!' echoed Putz. 'From vot come shteam?'

'From water, of course! You could see the water through the transparent handle, and about a gill of another liquid, thick and yellowish. When Tweel squeezed the handle—there was no trigger—a drop of water and a drop of the yellow stuff squirted into the firing chamber, and the water vapourized—pop! —like that. It's not so difficult; I think we could develop the same principle. Concentrated sulphuric acid will heat water almost to boiling, and so will quicklime, and there's potassium and sodium—

'Of course, his weapon hadn't the range of mine, but it wasn't so bad in this thin air, and it *did* hold as many shots as a cowboy's gun in a Western movie. It was effective, too, at least against Martian life; I tried it out, aiming at one of the crazy plants, and darned if the plant didn't wither up and fall apart! That's why I think the glass splinters were poisoned.

'Anyway, we trudged along towards the mud-heap city and I began to wonder whether the city builders dug the canals. I pointed to the city and then at the canal, and Tweel said "No—no—no!" and gestured towards the south. I took it to mean that some other race had created the canal system, perhaps Tweel's people. I don't know; maybe there's still another intelligent race on the planet, or a dozen others. Mars is a queer little world.'

CHAPTER V
The Barrel-People

'A hundred yards from the city we crossed a sort of road—just a hard-packed mud trail, and then, all of a sudden, along came one of the mound builders!

'Man, talk about fantastic beings! It looked rather like a barrel trotting along on four legs with four other arms or tentacles. It had no head, just body and members and a row of eyes completely around it. The top end of the barrel-body was a diaphragm stretched as tight as a drum head, and that was all. It was pushing a little coppery cart and tore right past us like the proverbial bat out of Hell. It didn't even notice us, although I thought the eyes on my side shifted a little as it passed.

'A moment later another came along, pushing another empty cart. Same thing—it just scooted past us. Well, I wasn't going to be ignored by a bunch of barrels playing train, so when the third one approached, I planted myself in the way—ready to jump, of course, if the thing didn't stop.

'But it did. It stopped and set up a sort of drumming from the diaphragm on top. And I held out both hands and said mildly, "We are friends!" And what do you suppose the thing did?'

'Said, "Pleased to meet you," I'll bet!' suggested Harrison.

'I couldn't have been more surprised if it had! It drummed on its diaphragm, and then suddenly boomed out, "We are v-r-r-riends!" and gave its pushcart a vicious poke at me! I jumped aside, and away it went while I stared dumbly after it.

'A minute later another one came hurrying along. This one didn't pause, but simply drummed out, "We are v-r-r-riends!" and scurried by. How did it learn the phrase? Were all of the creatures in some sort of communication with each other? Were they all parts of some central organism? I don't know, though I think Tweel does.

'Anyway, the creatures went sailing past us, every one greeting us with the same statement. It got to be funny; I never thought to find so many friends on this God-forsaken ball! Finally I made a puzzled gesture to Tweel; I guess he understood, for he said, "One-one-two—yes!—two-two-four—no!" Get it?'

'Sure,' said Harrison. 'It's a Martian nursery rhyme.'

'Yeah! Well, I was getting used to Tweel's symbolism, and I figured it out this way. 'One-one-two—yes!" The creatures were intelligent. "Two-two-four—no!" Their intelligence was not of our order, but something different and beyond the logic of two and two is four. Maybe I missed his meaning. Perhaps he meant that their minds were of low degree, able to figure out the simple things—"One-one-two—yes!"—but not more difficult things—"Two-two-four—no!" But I think from what we saw later that he meant the other.

'After a few moments, the creatures came rushing back—first one, then another. Their pushcarts were full of stones, sand, chunks of rubbery plants, and such rubbish as that. They droned out their friendly greeting, which didn't really sound so friendly, and dashed on. The third one I assumed to be my first acquaintance and I decided to have another chat with him. I stepped into his path again and waited.

'Up he came, booming out his "We are v-r-r-riends" and stopped. I looked at him; four or five of his eyes looked at me. He tried his password again and gave a shove of his cart, but I stood firm. And then the—the dashed creature reached out one of his arms, and two finger-like nippers tweaked my nose!'

'Haw!' roared Harrison. 'Maybe the things have a sense of beauty!'

'Laugh!' grumbled Jarvis. 'I'd already had a nasty bump and a mean frostbite on that nose. Anyway, I yelled "Ouch!" and jumped aside and the creature dashed away; but from then on, their greeting was "We are v-r-r-riends! Ouch!" Queer beasts!

'Tweel and I followed the road squarely up to the nearest mound. The creatures were coming and going, paying us not the slightest attention, fetching their loads of rubbish. The road simply dived into an opening, and slanted down like an old mine, and in and out darted the barrel-people, greeting us with their eternal phrase.

'I looked in; there was a light somewhere below, and I was curious to see it. It didn't look like a flame or torch, you understand, but more like a civilized light, and I thought that I might get some clue as to the creatures' development. So in I went and Tweel tagged along, not without a few trills and twitters, however.

'The light was curious; it sputtered and flared like an old arc light, but came from a single black rod set in the wall of the corridor. It was electric, beyond doubt. The creatures were fairly civilized, apparently.

'Then I saw another light shining on something that glittered and I went on to look at that, but it was only a heap of shiny sand. I turned towards the entrance to leave, and the Devil take me if it wasn't gone!

'I suppose the corridor had curved, or I'd stepped into a side passage. Anyway, I walked back in the direction I thought we'd come, and all I saw was more dim-lit corridor. The place was a labyrinth! There was nothing but twisting passages running every way, lit by occasional lights, and now and then a creature running by, sometimes with a pushcart, sometimes without.

'Well, I wasn't much worried at first. Tweel and I had only come a few steps from the entrance. But every move we made after that seemed to get us in deeper. Finally I tried following one of the creatures with an empty cart, thinking that he'd be going out for his rubbish, but he ran around aimlessly, into one passage and out another. When he started dashing around a pillar like one of these Japanese waltzing mice, I gave up, dumped my water tank on the floor, and sat down.

'Tweel was as lost as I. I pointed up and he said "No—no—no!" in a sort of helpless trill. And we couldn't get any help from the natives; they paid us no attention at all, except to assure us they were friends—ouch!

'Lord! I don't know how many hours or days we wandered around there! I slept twice from sheer exhaustion; Tweel never seemed to need sleep. We tried following only the upward corridors, but they'd run uphill a ways and then curve downwards. The temperature in that damned ant-hill was constant; you couldn't tell night from day and after my first sleep I didn't know whether I'd slept one hour or thirteen, so I couldn't tell from my watch whether it was midnight or noon.

'We saw plenty of strange things. There were machines running in some of the corridors, but they didn't seem to be doing anything—just wheels turning. And several times I saw two barrel-beasts with a little one growing between them, joined to both.'

'Parthenogenesis!' exulted Leroy. 'Parthenogenesis by budding—like *les tulipes!*'

'If you say so, Frenchy,' agreed Jarvis. 'The things never noticed us at all, except, as I say, to greet us with "We are v-r-r-riends! Ouch!" They seemed to have no home-life of any sort, but just scurried around with their pushcarts, bringing in rubbish. And finally I discovered what they did with it.

'We'd had a little luck with a corridor, one that slanted upwards for a great distance. I was feeling that we ought to be close to the surface when suddenly the passage debouched into a domed chamber, the only one we'd seen. And man!—I felt like dancing when I saw what looked like daylight through a crevice in the roof.

'There was a—a sort of machine in the chamber, just an enormous wheel that turned slowly, and one of the creatures was in the act of dumping his rubbish below it. The wheel ground it with a crunch—sand, stones, plants, all into powder that sifted away somewhere. While we watched, others filed in, repeating the process, and that seemed to be all. No rhyme nor reason to the whole thing—but that's characteristic of this crazy planet. And there was another fact that's almost too bizarre to believe.

'One of the creatures, having dumped his load, pushed his cart aside with a crash and calmly shoved himself under the wheel! I watched him crushed, too stupefied to make a sound, and a moment later, another followed him! They were perfectly methodical about it, too; one of the cartless creatures took the abandoned pushcart.

'Tweel didn't seem surprised; I pointed out the next suicide to him, and he just gave the most human-like shrug imaginable, as much as to say, "What can I do about it?" He must have known more or less about these creatures.

'Then I saw something else. There was something beyond the wheel, something shining on a sort of low pedestal. I walked over; there was a little crystal about the size of an egg, fluorescing to beat Tophet. The light from it stung my hands and face, almost like a static discharge, and then I noticed another funny thing. Remember that wart I had on my left thumb? Look!' Jarvis extended his hand. 'It dried up and fell off—just like that! And my abused nose—say, the pain went out of it like magic! The thing had the property of hard X rays or gamma radiations, only more so; it destroyed diseased tissue and left healthy tissue unharmed!

'I was thinking what a present *that'd* be to take back to Mother Earth when a lot of racket interrupted. We dashed back to the other side of the wheel in time to see one of the push-carts ground up. Some suicide had been careless, it seems.

'Then suddenly the creatures were booming and drumming all around us and their noise was decidedly menacing. A crowd of them advanced towards us; we backed out of what I thought was the passage we'd entered by, and they came rumbling after us, some pushing carts and some not. Crazy brutes! There was a whole chorus of "We are v-r-r-riends! Ouch!" I didn't like the "ouch"; it was rather suggestive.

'Tweel had his glass gun out and I dumped my water tank for greater freedom and got mine. We backed up the corridor with the barrel-beasts following—about twenty of them. Queer thing—the ones coming in with loaded carts moved past us inches away without a sign.

'Tweel must have noticed that. Suddenly, he snatched out that glowing coal cigar-lighter of his and touched a cartload of plant limbs. Puff! The whole load was burning—and the crazy beast pushing it went right along without a change of pace! It created some disturbance among our "V-r-r-riends", however—and then I noticed the smoke eddying and swirling past us, and sure enough, there was the entrance.

'I grabbed Tweel and out we dashed and after us our twenty pursuers. The daylight felt like Heaven, though I saw at first glance that the sun was all but set, and that was bad, since I couldn't live outside my thermo-bag in a Martian night—at least, without a fire.

'And things got worse in a hurry. They cornered us in an angle between two mounds, and there we stood. I hadn't fired nor had Tweel; there wasn't any use in irritating the brutes. They stopped a little distance away and began their booming about friendship and ouches.

'Then things got still worse! A barrel-brute came out with a pushcart and they all grabbed into it and came out with handfuls of foot-long copper darts—sharp-looking ones—and all of a sudden one sailed past my ear—zing! And it was shoot or die then.

'We were doing pretty well for a while. We picked off the ones next to the pushcart and managed to keep the darts at a minimum, but suddenly there was a thunderous booming of "v-r-r-riends" and "ouches", and a whole army of 'em came out of their hole.

'Man! We were through and I knew it! Then I realized that Tweel wasn't. He could have leaped the mound behind us as easily as not. He was staying for me!

'Say, I could have cried if there'd been time! I'd liked Tweel from the first, but whether I'd have the gratitude to do what he was doing—suppose I *had* saved him from the first dream-beast—he'd done as much for me, hadn't he? I grabbed his arm, and said "Tweel", and pointed up, and he understood. He said, "No—no—no, Tick!" and popped away with his glass pistol.

'What could I do? I'd be a goner anyway when the sun set, but I couldn't explain that to him. I said, "Thanks, Tweel. You're a man!" and felt that I wasn't paying him any compliment at all. A man! There are mighty few men who'd do that.

'So I went "bang" with my gun and Tweel went "puff" with his, and the barrels were throwing darts and getting ready to rush us, and booming about being friends. I had given up hope. Then suddenly an angel dropped right down from Heaven in the shape of Putz, with his under-jets blasting the barrels into very small pieces!

'Wow! I let out a yell and dashed for the rocket; Putz opened the door and I went, laughing and crying and shouting! It was a moment or so before I remembered Tweel; I looked around in time to see him rising in one of his nosedives over the mound and away.

'I had a devil of a job arguing Putz into following! By the time we got the rocket aloft, darkness was down; you know how it comes here—like turning off a light. We sailed out over the desert and put down once or twice. I yelled "Tweel!" and yelled it a hundred times, I guess. We couldn't find him; he could travel like the wind and all I got—or else I imagined it—was a faint trilling twittering drifting out of the south. He'd gone, and damn it! I wish—I wish he hadn't!'

The four men of the *Ares* were silent—even the sardonic Harrison. At last little Leroy broke the stillness.

'I should like to see,' he murmured.

'Yeah,' said Harrison. 'And the wart cure. Too bad you missed that; it might be the cancer cure they've been hunting for a century and a half.'

'Oh, that!' muttered Jarvis gloomily. 'That's what started the fight!' He drew a glistening object from his pocket.

'Here it is.'

A MARTIAN ODYSSEY

The story was written in 1934. It was one of the first stories to deal with extraterrestrial beings realistically; that is, to suppose that they might really be alien.

Earlier stories set on Mars had used the name of the planet and a few salient facts, such as its possession of two moons, but no more. Except for that, the setting might just as well have been some fairy-tale extension of Earth. What's more, intelligent Martians were pictured as essentially Earthmen, differing only in superficial detail. In fact, Martian princesses were often human enough to be objects of romantic longing for Earthmen-heroes.

A Martian Odyssey changed all that. It was the first published science fiction story of Stanley G. Weinbaum who, at one bound, became the most popular author in the field. It was not just the realism of his alien other-world creatures, but it was also his light and easy style, a far cry from the creakiness of the writings of most of the s.f. authors of the early thirties. For two years, he retained his popularity and then, as suddenly as he came, he vanished, for in 1936, at the age of thirty-six, he died of cancer.

Weinbaum was careful, in this story, to keep his description of Mars realistic, but he could do so only in terms of the time in which it was written. At that time it was known that the Martian atmosphere was thinner than ours, but not exactly how much thinner. Nor was its composition known. Obviously, Weinbaum assumed it would be thick enough and have oxygen enough for a human being to be able to breathe without an extraneous air supply, although he was realistic enough to suppose men would have to be acclimated to the thin air. The Martian air, as pictured by Weinbaum, could also support quite complicated animal life and could support fires as well.

This, alas, has proved to be much too optimistic. Later information, including the data sent back by Mars-probes (thirty years after the story was written) make Weinbaum's picture of the planet impossible.

The expedition to Mars took place, according to Weinbaum, in the twenty-first century. This may turn out to be correct, but he had it take place ten years after the first landing on the Moon and less than twenty years after the invention of the 'atomic blast'.

The atomic bomb was first exploded in 1945 (probably at least half a century sooner than Weinbaum expected) which would have made the first Mars landing come before 1965. Then, too, Weinbaum says, 'Remember how the public mobbed the first Moon pictures?' Clearly, he is thinking of moving pictures, and never envisaged the live television coverage of the Moon landings.

A particularly fascinating part of Weinbaum's picture of Martian life is that of the 'pyramid being'. Silicon is similar to carbon in many of its chemical properties and in its electronic structure, so that one might imagine complicated molecules built out of long chains and rings of silicon atoms instead of carbon atoms. Unfortunately, silicon atoms are sufficiently larger than carbon atoms to make the chemical bonds between the former much weaker than between the latter. Even short chains of silicon atoms are quite unstable.

Furthermore, Weinbaum makes the implication that the pyramid being lived on elementary silicon, oxidizing it for energy and producing silicon dioxide (also called silica, or quartz). This, too, is most unlikely, for silicon never appears in elementary form in the Earth's crust and is almost certain not to do so in the Martian crust, either.

Despite the scientific shortcomings in the story, it has held up over the decades. In 1969, the membership of the Science Fiction Writers of America selected the best science fiction short stories of all time and *A Martian Odyssey* finished in second place.

Questions and Suggestions

1. The attempts of Dick Jarvis to communicate with Tweel remind one of modern suggestions at communication with

possible intelligences from other planetary systems. How would you use radio signals to communicate with an alien intelligence which does not know your language or anything about you? How would you describe your own appearance?

2. Look up the current information about the Martian surface and atmosphere and decide how the story would have to be changed to meet it. What characteristics of the surface does Weinbaum mention that aren't there; what does he leave out that *are* there?

3. Is Weinbaum correct in suggesting that Mercury is not visible to the naked eye from Mars? How bright would Mercury seem and how far from the Sun would it appear to be at most? How would Earth appear as seen from Mars? How about our Moon?

4. Look up the chemistry of silicon and determine whether it might conceivably form the basis of life in some form a little more complicated than pure chains of silicon atoms? Are there any other non-carbon chemistries that might form a basis for life by building up sufficiently complicated molecules?

2. Night

Don A. Stuart

Condon was staring through the glasses with a face tense and drawn, all his attention utterly concentrated on that one almost invisible speck infinitely far up in the blue sky, and saying over and over again in the most horribly absent-minded way, 'My Lord—my Lord—'

Suddenly he shivered and looked down at me, sheer agony in his face. 'He's never coming down. Don, he's never coming down—'

I knew it, too—knew it as solidly as I knew the knowledge was impossible. But I smiled and said: 'Oh, I wouldn't say that. If anything, I'd fear his coming down. What goes up comes down.'

Major Condon trembled all over. His mouth worked horribly for a moment before he could speak. 'Talbot—I'm scared—I'm horribly scared. You know—you're his assistant—you know he's trying to defy gravity. Men aren't meant to—it's wrong—wrong—'

His eyes were glued on those binoculars again, with the same terrible tensity, and now he was saying over and over in that absent-minded way, 'wrong—wrong—wrong—'

Simultaneously he stiffened, and stopped. The dozen or so other men standing on that lonely little emergency field stiffened; then the major crumpled to the ground. I've never before seen a man faint, let alone an army officer with a D.S. medal. I didn't stop to help him, because I knew something had happened. I grabbed the glasses.

Far, far up in the sky was that little orange speck—far, where there is almost no air, and he had been forced to wear a stratosphere suit with a little alcohol heater. The broad, orange wings were overlaid now with a faint-glowing, pearl-grey light. And it was falling. Slowly, at first, circling aimlessly downward. Then it dipped, rose, and somehow went into a tail spin.

It was horrible. I know I must have breathed, but it didn't seem so. It took minutes for it to fall those miles, despite the speed. Eventually it whipped out of that tail spin—through sheer speed, whipped out and into a power dive. It was a ghastly, flying coffin, hurtling at more than half a thousand miles an hour when it reached the Earth, some fifteen miles away.

The ground trembled, and the air shook with the crash of it. We were in the cars and roaring across the ground long before it hit. I was in Bob's car, with Jeff, his laboratory technician—Bob's little roadster he'd never need again. The engine picked up quickly, and we were going seventy before we left the field, jumped a shallow ditch and hit the road—the deserted, concrete road that led off towards where he must be. The engine roared as Jeff clamped down on the accelerator. Dimly, I heard the major's big car coming along behind us.

Jeff drove like a maniac, but I didn't notice. I knew the thing had done ninety-five but I think we must have done more. The wind whipped tears in my eyes so I couldn't be sure whether I saw mounting smoke and flame or not. With Diesel fuel there shouldn't be—but that plane had been doing things it shouldn't. It had been trying out Carter's anti-gravity coil.

We shot up the flat, straight road across wide, level country, the wind moaning a requiem about the car. Far ahead I saw the side road that must lead off towards where Bob should be, and lurched to the braking of the car, the whine and sing of violently shrieking tyres, then to the skidding corner. It was a sand road; we slithered down it and for all the lightness and power, we slowed to sixty-five, clinging to the seat as the soft sand gripped and clung.

Violently Jeff twisted into a branching cow path, and somehow the springs took it. We braked to a stop a quarter of a mile from the plane.

It was in a fenced field of pasture and wood lot. We leaped the fence, and raced towards it; Jeff got there first, just as the major's car shrieked to a stop behind ours.

The major was cold and pale when he reached us. 'Dead,' he stated.

And I was very much colder and probably several times as pale. 'I don't know!' I moaned. 'He isn't there!'

'Not there!' The major almost screamed it. 'He must be—he has to be. He had no parachute—wouldn't take one. They say he didn't jump—'

I pointed to the plane, and wiped a little cold sweat from my forehead. I felt clammy all over, and my spine prickled. The solid steel of the huge Diesel engine was driven through the stump of a tree, down into the ground perhaps eight or nine feet, and the dirt and rock had splashed under that blow like wet mud.

The wings were on the other side of the field, flattened, twisted straws of dural alloy. The fuselage of the ship was a perfect silhouette—a longitudinal projection that had flattened in on itself, each separate section stopping only as it hit the ground.

The great torus coil with its strangely twined wrappings of hair-fine bismuth wire was intact! And bent over it, twisted, utterly wrecked by the impact, was the main-wing stringer—the great dural-alloy beam that supported most of the ship's weight in the air. It was battered, crushed on those hair-fine, fragile bismuth wires—and not one of them was twisted or displaced or so much as skinned. The back frame of the ponderous Diesel engine—the heavy supercharger was the anvil of that combination—was cracked and splintered. And not one wire of the hellish bismuth coil was strained or skinned or displaced.

And the red pulp that should have been there—the red pulp that had been a man—wasn't. It simply wasn't there at all. He hadn't left the plane. In the clear, cloudless air, we could see that. He was gone.

We examined it, of course. A farmer came, and another, and looked, and talked. Then several farmers came in old, dilapidated cars with their wives and families, and watched.

We set the owner of the property on watch and went away—went back to the city for workmen and a truck with a derrick. Dusk was falling. It would be morning before we could do anything, so we went away.

Five of us—the major of the army air force, Jeff Rodney, the two Douglass Co. men whose names I never remembered and I—sat in my—our—room. Bob's and Jeff's and mine. We'd been sitting there for hours trying to talk, trying to think, trying to remember every little detail, and trying to forget every ghastly detail. We couldn't remember the detail that explained it, nor forget the details that rode and harried us.

And the telephone rang. I started. Then slowly got up and answered. A strange voice, flat and rather unpleasant, said: 'Mr. Talbot?'

'Yes.'

It was Sam Gantry, the farmer we'd left on watch. 'There's a man here.'

'Yes? What does he want?'

'I dunno. I dunno where he came from. He's either dead or out cold. Gotta funny kind of an aviator suit on, with a glass face on it. He looks all blue, so I guess he's dead.'

'Lord! Bob! Did you take that helmet off?' I roared.

'No, sir, no—no, sir. We just left him the way he was.'

'His tanks have run out. Listen. Take a hammer, a wrench, anything, and break that glass faceplate! Quick! We'll be there.'

Jeff was moving. The major was, too, and the others. I made a grab for the half-empty bottle of Scotch, started out, and ducked back into the closet. With the oxygen bottle under my arm I jumped into the crowded little roadster just as Jeff started it moving. He turned on the horn, and left it that way.

We dodged, twisted, jumped and stopped with jerks in traffic, then leaped into smooth, roaring speed out towards the farmer's field. The turns were familiar now; we scarcely slowed for them, slewing around them. This time Jeff charged through the wire fence. A headlight popped; there was a shrill scream of wire, the wicked *zing* of wire scratching across the hood and mud guards, and we were bouncing across the field.

There were two lanterns on the ground; three men carried others; more men squatted down beside a still figure garbed in a fantastic, bulging, airproof stratosphere suit. They looked at us, open-mouthed as we skidded to a halt, moving aside as the major leaped out and dashed over with the Scotch. I followed close behind with the oxygen bottle.

Bob's faceplate was shattered, his face blue, his lips blue and flecked with froth. A long gash across his cheek from the shattered glass bled slowly. The major lifted his head without a word, and glass tinkled inside the helmet as he tried to force a little whisky down his throat.

'Wait!' I called. 'Major, give him artificial respiration, and this will bring him round quicker—better.' The major nodded, and rose, rubbing his arm with a peculiar expression.

'That's cold!' he said, as he flipped Bob over, and straddled his back. I held the oxygen bottle under Bob's nose as the major swung back in his arc, and let the raw, cold oxygen gas flow into his nostrils.

In ten seconds Bob coughed, gurgled, coughed violently, and took a deep shuddering breath. His face turned pink almost instantly under that lungful of oxygen, and I noticed with some surprise that he seemed to exhale almost nothing, his body absorbing the oxygen rapidly.

He coughed again; then: 'I could breathe a heck of a sight better if you'd get off my back,' he said. The major jumped up, and Bob turned over and sat up. He waved me aside, and spat. 'I'm—all right,' he said softly.

'Lord, man, what happened?' demanded the major.

Bob sat silent for a minute. His eyes had the strangest look —a hungry look—as he gazed about him. He looked at the trees beyond and at the silent, watching men in the light of the lanterns; then up, up to where a myriad stars gleamed and danced and flickered in the clear night sky.

'I'm back,' he said softly. Then suddenly he shivered, and looked horribly afraid. 'But—I'll have to be—then—too.'

He looked at the major for a minute, and smiled faintly. And at the two Douglass Co. men. 'Your plane was all right. I started up on the wings, as arranged, went way up, till I thought surely I was at a safe height, where the air wasn't too dense and the field surely wouldn't reach to Earth—Lord!—reach to Earth! I didn't guess how far that field extended. It touched Earth—twice.

'I was at forty-five thousand when I decided it was safe, and cut the engine. It died, and the stillness shocked me. It was so quiet. So quiet.

'I turned on the coil circuit, and the dynamotor began to hum as the tubes warmed up. And then—the field hit me. It paralysed me in an instant. I never had a chance to break the circuit, though I knew instantly something was wrong—terribly wrong. But the very first thing it did was to paralyse me, and I had to sit there and watch the instruments climb to positions and meanings they were never meant for.

'I realised I alone was being affected by that coil—I alone, sitting directly over it. I stared at the meters and they began to fade, began to seem transparent, unreal. And as they faded into blankness I saw clear sky beyond them; then for a hundredth of a second, like some effect of persistence of vision, I thought I saw the plane falling, twisting down at incredible speed, and the light faded as the Sun seemed to rocket suddenly across the sky and vanish.

'I don't know how long I was in that paralysed condition, where there was only blankness—neither dark nor light nor time nor any form—but I breathed many times. Finally, form crawled and writhed into the blankness, and seemed to solidify beneath me as, abruptly, the blankness gave way to a dull red light. I was falling.

'I thought instantly of the forty-five thousand feet that lay between me and the solid Earth, and stiffened automatically in terror. And in the same instant I landed in a deep blanket of white snow, stained by the red light that lighted the world.

'Cold. Cold—it tore into me like the fang of a savage animal. What cold! The cold of ultimate death. It ripped through that thick, insulated suit and slashed at me viciously, as though there were no insulation there. I shivered so violently I could scarcely turn up the alcohol valves. You know I carried alcohol tanks and catalyst grids for heating, because the only electric fields I wanted were those of the apparatus. Even used a Diesel instead of gas engine.

'I thank the Lord for that then. I realised that whatever had happened I was in a spot indescribably cold and desolate. And in the same instant, realised that the sky was black. Blacker than the blackest night, and yet before me the snow field stretched to infinity, tainted by the blood-red light, and my shadow crawled in darker red at my feet.

'I turned around. As far as the eye could see in three directions the land swept off in very low, very slightly rolling hills, almost plains—red plains of snow dyed with the dripping light of sunset. I thought.

'In the fourth direction, a wall—a wall that put the Great Wall of China to shame—loomed up half a mile—a blood-red wall that had the lustre of metal. It stretched across the horizon, and looked a scant hundred yards away, for the air was utterly clear. I turned up my alcohol burners a bit more and felt a little better.

'Something jerked my head around like a giant hand—a sudden thought. I stared at the Sun and gulped. It was four times—six times—the size of the Sun I knew. And it wasn't setting. It was forty-five degrees from the horizon. It was red. Blood-red. And there wasn't the slightest bit of radiant heat reaching my face from it. That Sun was cold.

'I'd just automatically assumed I was still on Earth, whatever else might have happened, but now I knew I couldn't be. It must be another planet of another sun—a frozen planet—for that snow was frozen air. I knew it absolutely. A frozen planet of a dead sun.

'And then I changed even that. I looked up at the black sky above me, and in all the vast black bowl of the heavens, not three-score stars were visible. Dim, red stars, with one single sun that stood out for its brilliance—a yellowish-red sun perhaps a tenth as bright as our Sun, but a monster here. It was another —a dead—space. For if that snow was frozen air, the only atmosphere must have been neon and helium. There wasn't any hazy air to stop the light of the stars, and that dim, red sun didn't obscure them with its light. The stars were gone.

'In that glimpse, my mind began working by itself; I was scared.

'Scared? I was so scared I was afraid I was going to be sick. Because right then I knew I was never coming back. When I felt that cold, I'd wondered when my oxygen bottles would give out, if I'd get back before they did. Now it was not a worry. It was simply the limiting factor on an already-determined thing, the setting on the time bomb. I had just so much more time before I died right there.

'My mind was working out things, working them out all by itself, and giving answers I didn't want, didn't want to know about. For some reason it persisted in considering this was Earth, and the conviction became more and more fixed. It was right. That was Earth. And it was old Sol. Old—old Sol. It was the time axis that coil distorted—not gravity at all. My mind worked that out with a logic as cold as that planet.

'If it was time it had distorted, and this was Earth, then it had distorted time beyond imagining to an extent as meaningless to our minds as the distance a hundred million light years is. It was simply vast—incalculable. The Sun was dead. The Earth was dead. And Earth was already, in our time, two billions of years old, and in all that geological time, the Sun had not changed measurably. Then how long was it since my time? The Sun was dead. The very stars were dead. It must have been, I thought even then, billions on billions of years. And I grossly underestimated it.

'The world was old—old—old. The very rocks and ground radiated a crushing aura of incredible age. It was old, older than—but what is there? Older than the hills? Hills? Gosh, they'd been born and died and been born and worn away again, a million, a score of million times! Old as the stars? No, that wouldn't do. The stars were dead—then.

'I looked again at the metal wall, and set out for it, and the aura of age washed up at me, and dragged at me, and tried to stop this motion when all motion should have ceased. And the thin, unutterably cold wind whined in dead protest at me, and pulled at me with the ghost hands of the million million million that had been born and lived and died in the countless ages before I was born.

'I wondered as I went. I didn't think clearly; for the dead aura of the dead planet pulled at me. Age. The stars were dying, dead. They were huddled there in space, like decrepit old men, huddling for warmth. The galaxy was shrunk. So tiny, it wasn't a thousand light years across, the stars were separated by miles where there had been light years. The magnificent, proudly sprawling universe I had known, that flung itself across a million million light years, that flung radiant energy through space by the millions of millions of tons was—gone.

'It was dying—a dying miser that hoarded its last broken dregs of energy in a tiny cramped space. It was broken and shattered. A thousand billion years before the cosmical constant had been dropped from that broken universe. The cosmical constant that flung giant galaxies whirling apart with ever greater speed had no place here. It had hurled the universe in broken fragments, till each spattered bit felt the chill of loneliness, and wrapped space about itself, to become a universe in itself while the flaming galaxies vanished.

'That had happened so long ago that the writing it had left in the fabric of space itself had worn away. Only the gravity constant remained, the hoarding constant, that drew things together, and slowly the galaxy collapsed, shrunken and old, a withered mummy.

'The very atoms were dead. The light was cold; even the

red light made things look older, colder. There was no youth in the universe. I didn't belong, and the faint protesting rustle of the infinitely cold wind about me moved the snow in muted, futile protest, resenting my intrusion from a time when things were young. It whinnied at me feebly, and chilled the youth of me.

'I plodded on and on, and always the metal wall retreated, like one of those desert mirages. I was too stupefied by the age of the thing to wonder; I just walked on.

I was getting nearer, though. The wall was real; it was fixed. As I drew slowly nearer, the polished sheen of the wall died and the last dregs of hope died. I'd thought there might be someone still living behind that wall. Beings who could build such a thing might be able to live even here. But I couldn't stop then; I just went on. The wall was broken and cracked. It wasn't a wall I'd seen; it was a series of broken walls, knitted by distance to a smooth front.

'There was no weather to age them, only the faintest stirring of faint, dead winds—winds of neon and helium, inert and uncorroding—as dead and inert as the universe. The city had been dead a score of billions of years. That city was dead for a time ten times longer than the age of our planet tody. But nothing destroyed it. Earth was dead—too dead to suffer the racking pains of life. The air was dead, too dead to scrape away metal.

'But the universe itself was dead. There was no cosmic radiation then to finally level the walls by atomic disintegration. There had been a wall—a single metal wall. Something—perhaps a last wandering meteor—had chanced on it in a time incalculably remote, and broken it. I entered through the great gap. Snow covered the city—soft, white snow. The great red sun stood still just where it was. Earth's restless rotation had long since been stilled—long, long since.

'There were dead gardens above, and I wandered up to them. That was really what convinced me it was a human city, on Earth. There were frozen, huddled heaps that might once have been men. Little fellows with fear forever frozen on their faces huddled helplessly over something that must once have been a heating device. Dead perhaps, since the last storm old Earth had known, tens of billions of years before.

'I went down. There were vastnesses in that city. It was huge. It stretched forever, it seemed, on and on, in its deadness. Machines, machines everywhere. And the machines were dead, too. I went down, down where I thought a bit of light and heat might linger. I didn't know then how long death had been there; those corpses looked so fresh, preserved by the eternal cold.

'It grew dark down below, and only through rents and breaks did that bloody light seep in. Down and down, till I was below the level of the dead surface. The white snow persisted, and then I came to the cause of that final, sudden death. I could understand then. More and more I had puzzled, for those machines I'd seen I knew were far and beyond anything we ever conceived—machines of perfection, self-repairing, and self-energizing, self-perpetuating. They could make duplicates of themselves, and duplicate other, needed machines; they were intended to be eternal, everlasting.

'But the designers couldn't cope with some things that were beyond even their majestic imaginations—the imaginations that conceived these cities that had lived beyond—a million times beyond—what they had dreamed. They must have conceived some vague future. But not a future when the Earth died, and the Sun died, and even the universe itself died.

'Cold had killed them. They had heating arrangements, devices intended to maintain forever the normal temperature despite the wildest variations of the weather. But in every electrical machine, resistances, balance resistances, and induction coils, balance condensers, and other inductances. And cold, stark, spatial cold, through ages, threw them off. Despite the heaters, cold crept in colder—cold that made their resistance balances and their induction coils superconductors! That destroyed the city. Superconduction—like the elimination of friction, on which all things must rest. It is a drag and a thing engineers fight forever. Resistance and friction must finally be the rest and the base of all things, the force that holds the great red bolts firm and the brakes that stop the machines when needed.

'Electrical resistance died in the cold and the wonderful machines stopped for the replacement of defective parts. And when they were replaced, they, too, were defective. For what months must that constant stop—replacement—start—stop—replacement have gone on before, at last defeated forever, those vast machines must bow in surrender to the inevitable? Cold had defeated them by defeating and removing the greatest obstacle of the engineers that built them—resistance.

'They must have struggled forever—as we would say—through a hundred billion years against encroaching harshness of nature, forever replacing worn, defective parts. At last, defeated forever, the great power plants, fed by dying atoms, had been forced into eternal idleness and cold. Cold conquered them at last.

'They didn't blow up. Nowhere did I see a wrecked machine; always they had stopped automatically when the defective resistance made it impossible to continue. The stored energy that was meant to re-start those machines after repairs had been made had long since leaked out. Never again could they move, I knew.

'I wondered how long they had been, how long they had gone on and on, long after the human need of them had vanished. For that vast city contained only a very few humans at the end. What untold ages of lonely functioning perfection had stretched behind those at-last-defeated mechanisms?

'I wandered out, to see perhaps more, before the necessary end came to me, too. Through the city of death. Everywhere little self-contained machines, cleaning machines that had kept that perfect city orderly and neat stood helpless and crushed by eternity and cold. They must have continued functioning for years after the great central power stations failed, for each contained its own store of energy, needing only occasional recharge from the central stations.

'I could see where breaks had occurred in the city, and, clustered about those breaks were motionless repair machines, their mechanisms in positions of work, the débris cleared away and carefully stacked on motionless trucks. The new beams and plates were partly attached, partly fixed and left, as the last dregs of their energy was fruitlessly expended in the last, dying attempts of that great body to repair itself. The death wounds lay unmended.

'I started back up. Up to the top of the city. It was a long climb, an infinite, weary climb, up half a mile of winding ramps, past deserted, dead homes; past, here and there, shops and restaurants; past motionless little automative passenger cars.

'Up and up, to the crowning gardens that lay stiff and brittle and frozen. The breaking of the roof must have caused a sudden chill, for their leaves lay green in sheaths of white, frozen air. Brittle grass, green and perfect to the touch. Flowers, blooming in wonderful perfection showed still; they didn't seem dead, but it didn't seem they could be otherwise under the blanket of cold.

'Did you ever sit up with a corpse?' Bob looked up at us—through us. 'I had to once, in my little home town where they always did that. I sat with a few neighbours while the man died before my eyes. I knew he must die when I came there. He died—and I sat there all night while the neighbours filed out, one by one, and the quiet settled. The quiet of the dead.

'I had to again. I was sitting with a corpse then. The corpse of a dead world in a dead universe, and the quiet didn't have to settle there; it had settled a billion years ago, and only my coming had stirred those feeble, protesting ghosts of eon-dead hopes of that planet to softly whining protest—protest the wind tried to sob to me, the dead wind of the dead gases. I'll never be able to call them inert gases again. I know. I know they are dead gases, the dead gases of dead worlds.

'And above, through the cracked crystal of the roof, the

dying suns looked down on the dead city. I couldn't stay there. I went down. Down under layer after layer of buildings, buildings of gleaming metal that reflected the dim, blood light of the Sun outside in carmine stains. I went down and down, down to the machines again. But even there hopelessness seemed more intense. Again I saw that agonizing struggle of the eternally faithful machines trying to repair themselves once more to serve the masters who were dead a million million years. I could see it again in the frozen, exhausted postures of the repair machines, stilled forever in their hopeless endeavours, the last poor dregs of energy spilled in fruitless conflict with time.

'It mattered little. Time himself was dying now, dying with the city and the planet and the universe he had killed.

'But those machines had tried so hard to serve again—and failed. Now they could never try again. Even they—the deathless machines—were dead.

'I went out again, away from those machines, out into the illimitable corridors, on the edge of the city. I could not penetrate far before the darkness became as absolute as the cold. I passed the shops where goods, untouched by time in this cold, still beckoned those strange humans, but humans for all that; beckoned the masters of the machines that were no more. I vaguely entered one to see what manner of things they used in that time.

'I nearly screamed at the motion of the thing in there, heard dimly through my suit the strangely softened sounds it made in the thin air. I watched it stagger twice—and topple. I cannot guess what manner of storage cells they had—save that they were marvellous beyond imagination. That stored energy that somehow I had released by entering was some last dreg that had remained through a time as old as our planet now. Its voice was stilled forever. But it drove me out—on.

'It had died while I watched. But somehow it made me more curious. I wondered again, less oppressed by utter death. Still, some untapped energy remained in this place, stored unimaginably. I looked more keenly, watched more closely.

And when I saw a screen in one office, I wondered. It was a screen. I could see readily it was television of some type. Exploratively, I touched a stud. Sound! A humming, soft sound!

'To my mind leaped a picture of a system of these. There must be—interconnected—a vast central office somewhere with vaster accumulator cells, so huge, so tremendous in their power once, that even the little microfraction that remained was great. A storage system untouchable to the repair machines—the helpless, hopeless power machines.

'In an instant I was alive again with hope. There was a strange series of studs and dials, unknown devices. I pulled back on the stud I had pressed, and stood trembling, wondering. Was there hope?

'Then the thought died. What hope? The city was dead. Not merely that. It had been dead, dead for untold time. Then the whole planet was dead. With whom might I connect? There were none on the whole planet, so what mattered it that there was a communication system.

'I looked at the thing more blankly. Had there been—how could I interpret its multitudinous devices? There was a thing on one side that made me think of a telephone dial for some reason. A pointer over a metal sheet engraved with nine symbols in a circle under the arrow of the pointer. Now the pointer was over what was either the first or the last of these.

'Clumsily, in these gloves, I fingered one of the little symbol buttons inlaid in the metal. There was an unexpected click, a light glowed on the screen, a lighted image! It was a simple projection—but what a projection! A three-dimensional sphere floated, turning slowly before my eyes, turning majestically. And I nearly fell as understanding flooded me abruptly. The pointer was a selector! The studs beneath the pointer I understood! Nine of them. One after the other I pressed, and nine spheres—each different—swam before me.

'And right there I stopped and did some hard thinking. Nine

spheres. Nine planets. Earth was shown first—a strange planet to me, but one I knew from the relative size and the position of the pointer must be Earth—then, in order, the other eight.

'Now—might there be life? Yes. In those nine worlds there might be, somewhere.

'Where? Mercury—nearest the Sun? No, the Sun was too dead, too cold, even for warmth there. And Mercury was too small. I knew, even as I thought, that I'd have one good chance because whatever means they had for communication wouldn't work without tremendous power. If those incredible storage cells had the power for even one shot, they had no more. Somehow I guessed that this apparatus might incorporate no resistance whatever. Here would be only very high frequency alternating current, and only condensers and inductances would be used in it. Supercooling didn't bother them any. It improved them. Not like the immense direct-current power machinery.

'But where to try? Jupiter? That was big. And then I saw what the solution must be. Cold had ruined these machines, thrown them off by making them too-perfect conductors. Because they weren't designed to defend themselves against spatial cold. But the machines—if there were any—on Pluto for instance, must originally have been designed for just such conditions! There it had always been cold. There it always would be cold.

'I looked at that thing with an intensity that should have driven my bare eyesight to Pluto. It was a hope. My only hope. But—how to signal Pluto? They could not understand! If there were any 'they'.

'So I had to guess—and hope. Somehow, I knew, there must be some means of calling the intelligent attendant, that the user might get aid. There was a bank of little studs—twelve of them—with twelve symbols, each different, in the centre of the panel, grouped in four rows of three. I guessed. Duodecimal system.

'Talk of the problems of interplanetary communication! Was there ever such a one? The problem of an anachronism in the city of the dead on a dead planet, seeking life somewhere, somehow.

'There were two studs, off by themselves, separate from the twelve—one green, one red. Again I guessed. Each of these had a complex series of symbols on it, so I turned the pointer on the right to Pluto, wavered, and turned it to Neptune. Pluto was farther. Neptune had been cold enough; the machines would still be working there, and it would be, perhaps, less of a strain on the dregs of energy that might remain.

'I depressed the green symbol hoping I had guessed truly, that red still meant danger, trouble and wrongness to men when that was built—that it meant release and cancellation for a wrongly pressed key. That left green to be an operative call signal.

'Nothing happened. The green key alone was not enough. I looked again, pressed the green key and that stud I had first pressed.

'The thing hummed again. But it was deeper note now, an entirely different sound, and there was a frenzied clicking inside. Then the green stud ticked back at me. The Neptune key under the pointer glowed softly; the screen began to shimmer with a greyish light. And, abruptly, the humming groaned as though at a terrific overload; the screen turned dull; the little signal light under Neptune's key grew dim. The signal was being sent—hurled out.

'Minute after minute I stood there, staring. The screen grew very slowly, very gently duller, duller. The energy was fading. The last stored driblet was being hurled away—away into space. "Oh," I groaned, "it's hopeless—hopeless to—"

'I'd realized the thing would take hours to get to that distant planet, travelling at the speed of light, even if it had been correctly aligned. But the machinery that should have done that through the years probably had long since failed for lack of power.

'But I stood there till the groaning motors ceased altogether, and the screen was as dark as I'd found it, the signal light black. I released the stud then, and backed away, dazed by the utter collapse of an insane hope. Experimentally I pressed the Neptune symbol again. So little power was left now, that only the faintest wash of murky light projected the Neptune image, little energy as that would have consumed.

'I went out. Bitter. Hopeless. Earth's last picture was long, long since painted—and mine had been the hand that spent Earth's last poor resource. To its utter exhaustion, the eternal city had strived to serve the race that created it, and I, from the dawn of time had, at the end of time, drained its last poor atom of life. The thing was a thing done.

"Slowly I went back to the roof and the dying suns. Up the miles of winding ramp that climbed a half mile straight up. I went slowly—only life knows haste—and I was of the dead.

'I found a bench up there—a carved bench of metal in the midst of a riot of colourful, frozen flowers. I sat down, and looked out across the frozen city to the frozen world beyond, and the freezing red Sun.

'I do not know how long I sat there. And then something whispered in my mind.

' "We sought you at the television machine."

'I leaped from the bench and stared wildly about me.

'It was floating in the air—a shining dirigible of metal, ruby-red in that light, twenty feet long, perhaps ten in diameter, bright, warm orange light gleaming from its ports. I stared at it in amazement.

' "It—it worked!" I gasped.

' "The beam carried barely enough energy to energize the amplifiers when it reached Neptune, however," replied the creature in the machine.

'I couldn't see him—I knew I wasn't hearing him, but somehow that didn't surprise me.

' "Your oxygen has almost entirely given out, and I believe your mind is suffering from lack of oxygen. I would suggest you enter the lock; there is air in here."

'I don't know how he knew, but the gauges confirmed his statement. The oxygen was pretty nearly gone. I had perhaps another hour's supply if I opened the valves wide—but it was a most uncomfortably near thing, even so.

'I got in. I was beaming, joyous. There was life. This universe was not so dead as I had supposed. Not on Earth, perhaps, but only because they did not choose! They had space ships! Eagerly I climbed in, a strange thrill running through my body as I crossed the threshold of the lock. The door closed behind me with a soft *shush* on its soft gaskets, locked, and a pump whined somewhere for a moment; then the inner door opened. I stepped in—and instantly turned off my alcohol burners. There was heat—heat and light and air!

'In a moment I had the outer lacings loose, and the inner zipper down. Thirty seconds later I stepped out of the suit, and took a deep breath. The air was clean and sweet and warm, invigorating, fresh-smelling, as though it had blown over miles of green, Sun-warmed fields. It smelled alive, and young.

'Then I looked for the man who had come for me. There was none. In the nose of the ship, by the controls, floated a four-foot globe of metal, softly glowing with a warm, golden light. The light pulsed slowly or swiftly with the rhythm of his thoughts, and I knew that this was the one who had spoken to me.

'"You had expected a human?" he thought to me. "There are no more. There have been none for a time I cannot express in your mind. Ah, yes, you have a mathematical means of expression, but no understanding of that time, so it is useless. But the last of humanity was allowed to end before the Sun changed from the original G-O stage—a very, very long time ago."

'I looked at him and wondered. Where was he from? Who—what—what manner of thing? Was it an armour-encased living creature or another of the perfect machines?

'I felt him watching my mind operate, pulsing softly in his golden light. And suddenly I thought to look out of the ports. The dim red suns were wheeling across those ports at an unbelievable rate. Earth was long since gone. As I looked, a dim, incredibly dim, red disc suddenly appeared, expanded—and I looked in awe at Neptune.

'The planet was scarcely visible when we were already within a dozen millions of miles. It was a jewelled world. Cities—the great, perfect cities—still glowed. They glowed in soft, golden light above, and below, the harsher, brighter blue of mercury vapour lighted them.

'He was speaking again. "We are machines—the ultimate development of man's machines. Man was almost gone when we came.

'"With what we have learned in the uncounted dusty mega-years since, we might have been able to save him. We could not then. It was better, wiser, that man end than that he sink down so low as he must, eventually. Evolution is the rise under pressure. Devolution is the gradual sinking that comes when there is no pressure—and there is no end to it. Life vanished from this system—a dusty infinity I cannot sort in my memory—my type memory, truly, for I have complete all the memories of those that went before me that I replace. But my memory cannot stretch back to that time you think of—a time when the constellations—

'"It is useless to try. Those memories are buried under others, and those still buried under the weight of a billion centuries.

'"We enter"—he named a city; I cannot reproduce that name—"now. You must return to Earth though in some seven and a quarter of your days, for the magnetic axis stretches back in collapsing field strains. I will be able to inject you into it, I believe."

'So I entered that city, the living city of machines, that had been when time and the universe were young.

'I did not know then that, when all this universe had dissolved away, when the last sun was black and cold, scattered dust in a fragment of a scattered universe, this planet with its machine cities would go on—a last speck of warm light in a long-dead universe. I did not know then.

'"You still wonder that we let man die out?" asked the

machine. "It was best. In another brief million years he would have lost his high estate. It was best.

' "Now we go on. We cannot end, as he did. It is automatic with us."

'I felt it then, somehow. The blind, purposeless continuance of the machine cities I could understand. They had no intelligence, only functions. These machines—these living, thinking, reasoning investigators—had only one function, too. Their function was slightly different—they were designed to be eternally curious, eternally investigating. And their striving was the more purposeless of the two, for theirs could reach no end. The cities fought eternally only the blind destructiveness of nature, wear, decay, erosion.

'But their struggle had an opponent forever, so long as they existed. The intelligent—no, not quite intelligent, but something else—curious machines were without opponents. They had to be curious. They had to go on investigating. And they had been going on in just this way for such incomprehensible ages that there was no longer anything to be curious about. Whoever, whatever designed them gave them function and forgot purpose. Their only curiosity was the wonder if there might, somewhere, be one more thing to learn.

'That—and the problem they did not want to solve, but must try to solve, because of the blind functioning of their very structure.

'Those eternal cities were limited. The machines saw now that limit, and so the hope of final surcease in it. They worked on the energy of the atom. But the masses of the suns were yet tremendous. They were dead for want of energy. The masses of the planets were still enormous. But they, too, were dead for want of energy.

'The machines there on Neptune gave me food and drink—strange, synthetic foods and drinks. There had been none on all the planet. They, perforce, started a machine, unused in a billion years and more, that I might eat. Perhaps they were glad to do so. It brought the end appreciably nearer, that vast consumption of mine.

'They used so very, very little, for they were so perfectly efficient. The only possible fuel in all the universe is one—hydrogen. From hydrogen, the lightest of elements, the heaviest can be built up, and energy released. They knew how to destroy matter utterly to energy, and could do it.

'But while the energy release of hydrogen compounding to the heavy elements is controllable, the destruction of matter to energy is a self-regenerative process. Started once, it spreads while matter lies within its direct, contiguous reach. It is wild, uncontrollable. It is impossible to utilize the full energy of matter.

'The suns had found that. They had burned their hydrogen until it was a remnant so small the action could not go on.

'On all Earth there was not an atom of hydrogen—nor was there on any planet, save Neptune. And there the store was not great. I used an appreciable fraction while I was there. That is their last hope. They can see the end, now.

'I stayed those few days, and the machines came and went. Always investigating, always curious. But there is in all that universe nothing to investigate save the one problem they do not want to solve—the problem they are sure they cannot solve.

'The machine took me back to Earth, set up something near me that glowed with a peculiar, steady, grey light. It would fix the magnetic axis on me, on my location, within a few hours. He could not stay near when the axis touched again. He went back to Neptune, but a few millions of miles distant, in this shrunken mummy of the solar system.

'I stood alone on the roof of the city, in the frozen garden with its deceptive look of life.

'And I thought of that night I had spent, sitting up with the dead man. I had come and watched him die. And I sat up with him in the quiet. I had wanted someone, anyone to talk to.

'I did then. Overpoweringly it came to me I was sitting

up in the night of the universe, in the night and quiet of the universe, with a dead planet's body, with the dead, ashen hopes of countless, nameless generations of men and women. The universe was dead, and I sat up alone—alone in the dead hush.

'Out beyond, a last flicker of life was dying on the planet Neptune—a last, false flicker of aimless life, but not life. Life was dead. The world was dead.

'I knew there would never be another sound here. For all the little remainder of time. For this was the dark and the night of time and the universe. It was inevitable, the inevitable end that had been simply more distant in my day—in the long, long-gone time when the stars were mighty lighthouses of a mighty space, not the dying, flickering candles at the head of a dead planet.

'It had been inevitable then; the candles must burn out for all their brave show. But now I could see them guttering low, the last, fruitless dregs of energy escaping as the machines below had spent their last dregs of energy in that hopeless, utterly faithful gesture—to attempt the repair of the city already dead.

'The universe had been dead a billion years. It had been. This, I saw, was the last radiation of the heat of life from an already-dead body—the feel of life and warmth, imitation of life by a corpse. Those suns had long and long since ceased to generate energy. They were dead, and their corpses were giving off the last, lingering life heat before they cooled.

'I ran. I think I ran—down away from the flickering, red suns in the sky. Down to the shrouding blackness of the dead city below, where neither light, nor heat, nor life, nor imitation of life bothered me.

'The utter blackness quieted me somewhat. So I turned off my oxygen valves, because I wanted to die sane, even here, and I knew I'd never come back.

'The impossible happened! I came to with that raw oxygen in my face. I don't know how I came—only that here is warmth and life.

'Somewhere, on the far side of that bismuth coil, inevitable still, is the dead planet and the flickering, guttering candles that light the death watch I must keep at the end of time.'

NIGHT

The story contains two notions that are very common in science fiction: anti-gravity and time-travel. Both are quite impossible in the light of our present knowledge of the Universe.

According to Einstein's theory of relativity there is no way of insulating one's self from the effect of a gravitational field, nor is there such a thing as gravitational repulsion.

As for time-travel, that would seriously compromise the law of cause-and-effect, one of the fundamentals on which science is based. Breaking that law would introduce unusual paradoxes. Suppose you travelled back in time and killed your grandfather when he was still a baby. In that case you would never have been born; but if you had never been born, how could you have gone back to kill him?

Science fiction writers have written very ingenious stories to take care of such paradoxes, but orthodox science will have none of it.

Don A. Stuart, whose name is listed here as the author of this story, is, in reality, John W. Campbell, Jr., who has edited the magazine *Astounding Science Fiction* (from which more than half the stories in this book have been taken) ever since 1938.* Campbell had an excellent training in science and we can be sure he is careful about his details. He uses anti-gravity and time-travel just the same, because they give rise to such interesting plots that they must be used even when they are known to be non-scientific. (Faster-than-light travel is another item so useful to science fiction writers that its impossibility is ignored or hastily argued away.)

Stuart pictures a far-distant future, long after the Sun has

* In 1960, the magazine changed its name to *Analog Science Fact-Fiction.*

'died'. His picture of that death is of a cool Sun, barely red-hot. It appears very large in the sky, perhaps because in all the ages the Earth has crept closer to it, or perhaps because it has expanded. He does not specify.

This was reasonable at the time the story was published in 1935. Since then, however, much more has been learned of the evolution of stars. The Sun indeed is supported by the fusion of hydrogen atoms (which Campbell correctly calls the fundamental fuel of the Universe) but when its hydrogen begins to run low, other types of nuclear reactions take place. Far from cooling down, the Sun is expected to heat up with time and eventually expand greatly into a red giant. The Earth is very likely to be scorched, perhaps even vapourized at this time, which, however, will not come for another 8 billion years at least.

At one point, Campbell states that 'Earth was already, in our time, two billions of years old'. This was indeed thought to be so by astronomers in the 1930s, but geologists were sure that Earth was much older, and it turned out that the geologists were right. The Earth has existed in solid form, it is now believed, about 4.7 billion years.

Questions and Suggestions

1. Some scientists wonder if 'anti-particles' might possess anti-gravitational forces and might therefore repel ordinary particles. What are anti-particles? Suppose you had an anti-particle and a particle near each other, could you measure the gravitational force between them and decide whether it was an attraction or a repulsion? How strong is gravitational force anyway, compared to electromagnetic force, for instance?

2. Look up information on stellar evolution and find out what is likely to happen to the Sun after the red giant stage. Some stars pass through a 'supernova' stage in the course of their development? What is a supernova and is the Sun ever likely to become one?

3. Why did astronomers think the Universe was no more than

2 billion years old in the 1930s? Why did geologists, in those days, insist the Earth was more than 2 billion years old? When and why did the astronomers change their minds and how old do they think the Universe may be nowadays? Suppose you had only the astronomical and geological information of the 1930s. Would you have believed the Universe to be young or old and why?

4. Campbell mentions the far-future Earth as having an atmosphere of helium and neon. Why those two gases? Are there any other possibilities. Campbell also mentions 'super-conduction' (more often called 'superconductivity'). Look up superconductivity. What is it? At what temperatures does it exist? What is its relationship to electrical resistance? Do you think the men of the future might have built machinery that would not have been put out of order by superconductivity?

3. The Day Is Done

Lester del Rey

Hwoogh scratched the hair on his stomach and watched the sun climb up over the hill. He beat listlessly on his chest and yelled at it timidly, then grumbled and stopped. In his youth, he had roared and stumped around to help the god up, but now it wasn't worth the effort. Nothing was. He found a fine flake of sweaty salt under his hair, licked it off his fingers, and turned over to sleep again.

But sleep wouldn't come. On the other side of the hill there was a hue and cry, and somebody was beating a drum in a throbbing chant. The old Neanderthaler grunted and held his hands over his ears, but the Sun-Warmer's chant couldn't be silenced. More ideas of the Talkers.

In his day, it had been a lovely world, full of hairy grumbling people; people a man could understand. There had been game on all sides, and the caves about had been filled with the smoke of cooking fires. He had played with the few young that were born—though each year fewer children had come into the tribe—and had grown to young manhood with the pride of achievement. But that was before the Talkers had made this valley one of their hunting grounds.

Old traditions, half told, half understood, spoke of the land in the days of old, when only his people roamed over the broad tundra. They had filled the caves and gone out in packs too large for any animal to withstand. And the animals swarmed into the land, driven south by the Fourth Glaciation. Then the great cold had come again, and times had been hard. Many of his people had died.

But many had lived, and with the coming of the warmer, drier climate again, they had begun to expand before the Talkers arrived. After that—Hwoogh stirred uneasily—for no good reason he could see, the Talkers took more and more of the land, and his people retreated and diminished before them. Hwoogh's father had made it understood that their little band in the valley were all that were left, and that this was the only place on the great flat earth where Talkers seldom came.

Hwoogh had been twenty when he first saw them, great long-legged men, swift of foot and eye, stalking along as if they owned the earth, with their incessant mouth noises. In the summer that year, they pitched their skin-and-wattle tents at the back of the hill, away from the caves, and made magic to their gods. There was magic on their weapons, and the beasts fell their prey. Hwoogh's people had settled back, watching fearfully, hating numbly, finally resorting to begging and stealing. Once a young buck had killed the child of a Talker, and been flayed and sent out to die for it. Thereafter, there had been a truce between Cro-Magnon and Neanderthaler.

Now the last of Hwoogh's people were gone, save only himself, leaving no children. Seven years it had been since Hwoogh's brother had curled up in the cave and sent his breath forth on the long journey to his ancestors. He had always been dispirited and weak of will, but he had been the only friend left to Hwoogh.

The old man tossed about and wished that Keyoda would return. Maybe she would bring food from the Talkers. There was no use hunting now, when the Talkers had already been up and killed all the easy game. Better that a man should sleep all the time, for sleep was the only satisfying thing left in the topsy-turvy world; even the drink the tall Cro-Magnons made from mashed roots left a headache the next day.

He twisted and turned in his bed of leaves at the edge of the cave, grunting surlily. A fly buzzed over his head provocatively, and he lunged at it. Surprise lighted his features as his fingers closed on the insect, and he swallowed it with a momentary flash of pleasure. It wasn't as good as the grub in the forest, but it made a tasty appetizer.

The sleep god had left, and no amount of lying still and snoring would lure him back. Hwoogh gave up and squatted down on his haunches. He had been meaning to make a new head for his crude spear for weeks, and he rummaged around in the cave for materials. But the idea grew farther away the closer he approached work, and he let his eyes roam idly over the little creek below him and the fleecy clouds in the sky. It was a warm spring, and the sun made idleness pleasant.

The sun god was growing stronger again, chasing the old fog and mist away. For years, he had worshipped the sun god as his, and now it seemed to grow strong again only for the Talkers. While the god was weak, Hwoogh's people had been mighty; now that its long sickness was over, the Cro-Magnons spread out over the country like the fleas on his belly.

Hwoogh could not understand it. Perhaps the god was mad at him since gods are utterly unpredictable. He grunted, wishing again for his brother who had understood such things better.

Keyoda crept around the boulder in front of the cave, interrupting his brooding. She brought scraps of food from the tent village and the half-chewed leg of a horse, which Hwoogh seized on and ripped at with his strong teeth. Evidently the Talkers had made a big kill the day before, for they were lavish with their gifts. He grunted at Keyoda, who sat under the cave entrance in the sun, rubbing her back.

Keyoda was as hideous as most of the Talkers were to Hwoogh, with her long dangling legs and short arms, and the ungainly straightness of her carriage. Hwoogh remembered the young girls of his own day with a sigh; they had been beautiful, short and squat, with forward-jutting necks and nice low foreheads. How the flat-faced Cro-Magnon women could get mates had been a puzzle to Hwoogh, but they seemed to succeed.

Keyoda had failed, however, and in her he felt justified in

his judgment. There were times when he felt almost in sympathy with her, and in his own way he was fond of her. As a child, she had been injured, her back made useless for the work of a mate. Kicked around by the others of her tribe, she had gradually drifted away from them, and when she stumbled on Hwoogh, his hospitality had been welcome to her. The Talkers were nomads who followed the herds north in the summer, south in the winter, coming and going with the seasons, but Keyoda stayed with Hwoogh in his cave and did the few desultory tasks that were necessary. Even such a half-man as the Neanderthaler was preferable to the scornful pity of her own people, and Hwoogh was not unkind.

'Hwunkh?' asked Hwoogh. With his stomach partly filled, he felt more kindly towards the world.

'Oh, they come out and let me pick up their scraps—me, who was once a chief's daughter!—same as they always do.' Her voice had been shrewish, but the weariness of failure and age had taken the edge from it. '"Poor, poor Keyoda," thinks they, "let her have what she wants, just so it don't mean nothin' we like." Here.' She handed him a roughly made spear, flaked on both sides of the point, but with only a rudimentary barb, unevenly made. 'One of 'em give me this—it ain't the like of what they'd use, I guess, but it's good as you could make. One of the kids is practising.'

Hwoogh examined it; good, he admitted, very good, and the point was fixed nicely in the shaft. Even the boys, with their long limber thumbs that could twist any which way, made better weapons than he; yet once, he had been famous among his small tribe for the nicety of his flint work.

Making a horse gesture, he got slowly to his feet. The shape of his jaw and the attachment of his tongue, together with a poorly developed left frontal lobe of his brain, made speech rudimentary, and he supplemented his glottals and labials with motions that Keyoda understood well enough. She shrugged and waved him out, gnawing on one of the bones.

Hwoogh wandered about without much spirit, conscious that

he was growing old. And vaguely, he knew that age should not have fallen upon him for many snows; it was not the number of seasons, but something else, something that he could feel but not understand. He struck out for the hunting fields, hoping that he might find some game for himself that would require little effort to kill. The scornful gifts of the Talkers had become bitter in his mouth.

But the sun god climbed up to the top of the blue cave without Hwoogh's stumbling on anything. He swung about to return, and ran into a party of Cro-Magnons returning with the carcass of a reindeer strapped to a pole on their shoulders. They stopped to yell at him.

'No use, Hairy One!' they boasted, their voices light and gay. 'We caught all the game this way. Turn back to your cave and sleep.'

Hwoogh dropped his shoulders and veered away, his spear dragging limply on the ground. One of the party trotted over to him lightly. Sometimes Legoda, the tribal magic man and artist, seemed almost friendly, and this was one of the times.

'It was my kill, Hairy One,' he said tolerantly. 'Last night I drew strong reindeer magic, and the beast fell with my first throw. Come to my tent and I'll save a leg for you. Keyoda taught me a new song that she got from her father, and I would repay her.'

Legs, ribs, bones! Hwoogh was tired of the outer meat. His body demanded the finer food of the entrails and liver. Already his skin was itching with a rash, and he felt that he must have the succulent inner parts to make him well; always, before, that had cured him. He grunted, between appreciation and annoyance, and turned off. Legoda pulled him back.

'Nay, stay, Hairy One. Sometimes you bring good fortune to me, as when I found the bright ochre for my drawing. There is meat enough in the camp for all. Why hunt today?' As Hwoogh still hesitated, he grew more insistent, not from kindness, but more from a wish to have his own way. 'The wolves are running near today, and one is not enough against them. We carve the reindeer at the camp as soon as it comes from the poles. I'll give you first choice of the meat!'

Hwoogh grunted a surly acquiescence and waddled after the party. The dole of the Talkers had become gall to him, but liver was liver—if Legoda kept his bargain. They were chanting a rough marching song, trotting easily under the load of the reindeer, and he lumbered along behind, breathing hard at the pace they set.

As they neared the village of the nomads, its rough skin tents and burning fires threw out a pungent odour that irritated Hwoogh's nostrils. The smell of the long-limbed Cro-Magnons was bad enough without the dirty smell of a camp and the stink of their dung-fed fires. He preferred the accustomed mouldy stench of his own musty cave.

Youths came swarming out at them, yelling with disgust at being left behind on this easy hunt. Catching sight of the Neanderthaler, they set up a howl of glee and charged at him, throwing sticks and rocks and jumping at him with play fury. Hwoogh shivered and crouched over, menacing them with his spear, and giving voice to throaty growls. Legoda laughed.

'In truth, O Hairy Chokanga, your voice should drive them from you. But see, they fear it not. Kuck, you two-legged pests! Out and away! Kuck, I say!' They leaped back at his voice and dropped behind, still yelling. Hwoogh eyed them warily, but so long as it suited the pleasure of Legoda, he was safe from their pranks.

Legoda was in a good mood, laughing and joking, tossing his quips at the women until his young wife came out and silenced it. She sprang at the reindeer with her flint knife, and the other women joined her.

'Heyo,' called Legoda. 'First choice goes to Chokanga, the Hairy One. By my word, it is his.'

'Oh, fool!' There was scorn in her voice and in the look she gave Hwoogh. 'Since when do we feed the beasts of the caves and the fish of the river? Art mad, Legoda. Let him hunt for himself.'

Legoda tweaked her back with the point of his spear, grinning. 'Aye, I knew thou'dst cry at that. But then, we owe his kind some pay—this was his hunting ground when we were but pups, straggling into this far land. What harm to give to an old man?' He swung to Hwoogh and gestured. 'See, Chokanga, my word is good. Take what you want, but see that it is not more than your belly and that of Keyoda can hold this night.'

Hwoogh darted in and came out with the liver and the fine sweet fat from the entrails. With a shrill cry of rage, Legoda's mate sprang for him, but the magic man pushed her back.

'Nay, he did right! Only a fool would choose the haunch when the heart of the meat was at hand. By the gods of my father, and I expected to eat of that myself! O Hairy One, you steal the meat from my mouth, and I like you for it. Go, before Heyo get free.'

Tomorrow, Hwoogh knew, Legoda might set the brats on him for this day's act, but tomorrow was in another cave of the sun. He drew his legs under him and scuttled off to the left and around the hill, while the shrill yells of Heyo and the lazy good humour of Legoda followed. A piece of liver dangled loose, and Hwoogh sucked on it as he went. Keyoda would be pleased, since she usually had to do the begging for both of them.

And a little of Hwoogh's self-respect returned. Hadn't he outsmarted Legoda and escaped with the choicest meat? And had Keyoda ever done as well when she went to the village of the Talkers? Ayeee, they had a thing yet to learn from the cunning brain of old Hwoogh!

Of course the Talkers were crazy; only fools would act as Legoda had done. But that was none of his business. He patted the liver and fat fondly and grinned with a slight return of good humour. Hwoogh was not one to look a gift horse in the mouth.

The fire had shrunk to a red bed of coals when he reached the cave, and Keyoda was curled up on his bed, snoring loudly, her face flushed. Hwoogh smelled her breath, and his suspicions were confirmed. Somehow, she had drunk of the devil brew of the Talkers, and her sleep was dulled with its stupor. He prodded her with his toe, and she sat up bleary-eyed.

'Oh, so you're back. Ayeee, and with liver and fat! But that never came from your spear throw; you been to the village and stole it. Oh, but you'll catch it!' She grabbed at the meat greedily and stirred up the fire, spitting the liver over it.

Hwoogh explained as best he could, and she got the drift of it. 'So? Eh, that Legoda, what a prankster he is, and my own nephew, too.' She tore the liver away, half raw, and they fell to eagerly, while she chuckled and cursed by turns. Hwoogh touched her nose and wrinkled his face up.

'Well, so what if I did?' Liquor had sharpened her tongue. 'That no-good son of the chief come here, after me to be telling him stories. And to make my old tongue free, he brings me the root brew. Ah, what stories I'm telling—and some of 'em true, too!' She gestured towards a crude pot. 'I reckon he steals it, but what's that to us? Help yourself, Hairy One. It ain't ever' day we're getting the brew.'

Hwoogh remembered the headaches of former experiments, but he smelled it curiously and the lure of the magic water caught at him. It was the very essence of youth, the fire that brought life to his legs and memories to his mind. He held it up to his mouth, gasping as the beery liquid ran down his throat. Keyoda caught it before he could finish and drained the last quart.

'Ah, it strengthens my back and puts the blood a-running hot through me again.' She swayed on her feet and sputtered out the fragments of an old skin-scraping song. 'Now, there you go—can't you never learn not to drink it all to once? That way, it don't last as long, and you're out before you get to feeling good.'

Hwoogh staggered as the brew took hold of him, and his knees bent even farther under him. The bed came up in his face, his head was full of bees buzzing merrily, and the cave spun around him. He roared at the cave, while Keyoda laughed.

'Heh! To hear you a-yelling, a body might think you was the only Chokanga left on earth. But you ain't—no, you ain't!'

'Hwunkh?' That struck home. To the best of Hwoogh's knowledge, there were no others of his kind left on earth. He grabbed at her and missed, but she fell and rolled against him, her breath against his face.

'So? Well, it's the truth. The kid up and told me. Legoda found three of 'em, just like you, he says, up the land to the east, three springs ago. You'll have to ask him—I dunno nothing about it.' She rolled over against him, grunting half-formed words, and he tried to think of this new information. But the brew was too strong for his head, and he was soon snoring beside her.

Keyoda was gone to the village when he awoke, and the sun was a spear length high on the horizon. He rummaged around for a piece of the liver, but the flavour was not as good as it had been, and his stomach protested lustily at going to work again. He leaned back until his head got control of itself, then swung down to the creek to quench a thirst devil that had seized on him in the night.

But there was something he should do, something he half remembered from last night. Hadn't Keyoda said something about others of his people? Yes, three of them, and Legoda knew. Hwoogh hesitated, remembering that he had bested Legoda the day before; the young man might resent it today. But he was filled with an overwhelming curiosity, and there was a strange yearning in his heart. Legoda must tell him.

Reluctantly, he went back to the cave and fished around in a hole that was a secret even from Keyoda. He drew out his treasures, fingering them reverently, and selecting the best. There were bright shells and coloured pebbles, a roughly drilled necklace that had belonged to his father, a sign of completed manhood, bits of this and that with which he had intended to make himself ornaments. But the quest for knowledge was stronger than the pride of possession; he dumped them out into his fist and struck out for the village.

Keyoda was talking with the women, whining the stock formula that she had developed, and Hwoogh skirted around the camp, looking for the young artist. Finally he spotted the Talker out behind the camp, making odd motions with two sticks. He drew near cautiously, and Legoda heard him coming.

'Come near, Chokanga, and see my new magic.' The young man's voice was filled with pride, and there was no threat to it. Hwoogh sighed with relief, but sidled up slowly. 'Come nearer, don't fear me. Do you think I'm sorry of the gift I made? Nay, that was my own stupidity. See.'

He held out the sticks and Hwoogh fingered them carefully. One was long and springy, tied end to end with a leather thong, and the other was a little spear with a tuft of feather on the blunt end. He grunted a question.

'A magic spear, Hairy One, that flies from the hand with wings, and kills beyond the reach of other spears.'

Hwoogh snorted. The spear was too tiny to kill more than rodents, and the big stick had not even a point. But he watched as the young man placed the sharp stick to the tied one, and drew back on it. There was a sharp twang, and the little spear sailed out and away, burying its point in the soft bark of a tree more than two spear throws away. Hwoogh was impressed.

'Aye, Chokanga, a new magic that I learned in the south last year. There are many there who use it, and with it they can throw the point farther and better than a full-sized spear. One man may kill as much as three!'

Hwoogh grumbled; already they killed all the good game, and yet they must find new magic to increase their power. He held out his hand curiously, and Legoda gave him the long stick and another spear, showing him how it was held. Again there was a twang, and the leather thong struck at his wrist, but the weapon sailed off erratically, missing the tree by yards. Hwoogh handed it back glumly—such magic was not for his kind. His thumbs made the handling of it even more difficult.

Now, while the magic man was pleased with his superiority, was a good time to show the treasure. Hwoogh spread it out on the bare earth and gestured at Legoda, who looked down thoughtfully.

'Yes,' the Talker conceded. 'Some of it is good, and some would make nice trinkets for the women. What is it you want —more meat, or one of the new weapons? Your belly was filled yesterday; and with my beer, that was stolen, I think, though for that I blame you not. The boy has been punished already. And this weapon is not for you.'

Hwoogh snorted, wriggled and fought for expression, while the young man stared. Little by little, his wants were made known, partly by signs, partly by the questions of the Cro-Magnon. Legoda laughed.

'So, there is a call of the kind in you, Old Man?' He pushed the treasure back to Hwoogh, except one gleaming bauble. 'I would not cheat you, Chokanga, but this I take for the love I bear you, as a sign of our friendship.' His grin was mocking as he stuck the valuable in a flap of his clout.

Hwoogh squatted down on his heels, and Legoda sat on a rock as he began. 'There is but little to tell you, Hairy One. Three years ago I did run on to a family of your kind—a male and his mate, with one child. They ran from us, but we were near their cave, and they had to return. We harmed them not, and sometimes gave them food, letting them accompany us on the chase. But they were thin and scrawny, too lazy to hunt. When we returned next year, they were dead, and so far as I know, you are the last of your kind.'

He scratched his head thoughtfully. 'Your people die too easily, Chokanga; no sooner do we find them and try to help them than they cease hunting and become beggars. And then they lose interest in life, sicken and die. I think your gods must be killed off by our stronger ones.'

Hwoogh grunted a half assent, and Legoda gathered up his bow and arrows, turning back towards camp. But there was a strange look on the Neanderthaler's face that did not escape the young man's eyes. Recognizing the misery in Hwoogh's expression, he laid a hand on the old man's shoulder and spoke more kindly.

'That is why I would see to your well-being, Hairy One. When you are gone, there will be no more, and my children will laugh at me and say I lie when I spin the tale of your race at the feast fire. Each time that I kill, you shall not lack for food.'

He swung down the single street towards the tent of his family, and Hwoogh turned slowly back towards his cave. The assurance of food should have cheered him, but it only added to his gloom. Dully, he realized that Legoda treated him as a small child, or as one whom the sun god had touched with madness.

Hwoogh heard the cries and laughter of children as he rounded the hill, and for a minute he hesitated before going on. But the sense of property was well developed in him, and he leaped forward grimly. They had no business near his cave.

They were of all ages and sizes, shouting and chasing each other about in a crazy disorder. Having been forbidden to come on Hwoogh's side of the hill, and having broken the rule in a bunch, they were making the most of their revolt. Hwoogh's fire was scattered down the side of the hill into the creek, and they were busily sorting through the small store of his skins and weapons.

Hwoogh let out a savage yell and ran forward, his spear held out in jabbing position. Hearing him, they turned and jumped back from the cave entrance, clustering up into a tight group. 'Go on away, Ugly Face,' one yelled. 'Go scare the wolves! Ugly Face, Ugly Face, waaaah!'

He dashed in among them, brandishing his spear, but they darted back on their nimble legs, slipping easily from in front of him. One of the older boys thrust out a leg and caught him, tripping him down on the rocky ground. Another dashed in madly and caught his spear away, hitting him roughly with it. From the time of the first primate, the innate cruelty of thoughtlessness had changed little in children.

Hwoogh let out a whooping bellow, scrambled up clumsily and was in among them. But they slipped nimbly out of his clutching hands. The little girls were dancing around gleefully, chanting: 'Ugly Face ain't got no mother, Ugly Face ain't got no wife, waaaah on Ugly Face!' Frantically he caught at one of the boys, swung him about savagely, and tossed him on the ground, where the youth lay white and silent. Hwoogh felt a momentary glow of elation at his strength. Then somebody threw a rock.

The old Neanderthaler was tied down crudely when he swam back to consciousness, and three of the boys sat on his chest, beating the ground with their heels in time to a victory chant. There was a dull ache in his head, and bruises were swelling on his arms and chest where they had handled him roughly. He growled savagely, heaving up, and tumbled them off, but the cords were too strong for him. As surely as if grown men had done it, he was captured.

For years they had been his enemies, ever since they had found that Hwoogh-baiting was one of the pleasant occupations that might relieve the tedium of camp life. Now that the old feud was about finished, they went at the business of subduing him with method and ingenuity.

While the girls rubbed his face with soft mud from the creek, the boys ransacked the cave and tore at his clothes. The rough bag in which he had put his valuables came away in their hands, and they paused to distribute this new wealth. Hwoogh howled madly.

But a measure of sanity was returning to them, now that the first fury of the fight was over, and Kechaka, the chief's eldest son, stared at Hwoogh doubtfully. 'If the elders hear of this,' he muttered unhappily, 'there will be trouble. They'd not like our bothering Ugly Face.'

Another grinned. 'Why tell them? He isn't a man, anyway, but an animal; see the hair on his body! Toss old Ugly Face in the river, clean up his cave, and hide these treasures. Who's to know?'

There were half-hearted protests, but the thought of the beating waiting for them added weight to the idea. Kechaka nodded finally, and set them to straightening up the mess they had made. With broken branches, they eliminated the marks of their feet, leaving only the trail to the creek.

Hwoogh tossed and pitched in their arms as four of them picked him up; the bindings loosened somewhat, but not enough to free him. With some satisfaction, he noted that the boy he had caught was still retching and moaning, but that was no help to his present position. They waded relentlessly into the water, laid him on it belly down, and gave him a strong push that sent him gliding out through the rushing stream. Foaming and gasping, he fought the current, struggling against his bonds. His lungs ached for air, and the current buffeted him about; blackness was creeping up on his mind.

With a last desperate effort he tore loose the bonds and pushed up madly for the surface, gulping in air greedily. Water was unpleasant to him, but he could swim, and struck out for the bank. The children were disappearing down the trail, and were out of sight as he climbed from the water, bemoaning his lost fire that would have warmed him. He lumbered back to his cave and sank soddenly on the bed.

He, who had been a mighty warrior, bested by a snarling pack of Cro-Magnon brats! He clenched his fists savagely and growled, but there was nothing he could do. Nothing! The futility of his own effort struck down on him like a burning knife. Hwoogh was an old man, and the tears that ran from his eyes were the bitter, aching tears that only age can shed.

Keyoda returned late, cursing when she found the fire gone, but her voice softened as she spied him huddled in his bed, staring dully at the wall of the cave. Her old eyes spotted the few footprints the boys had missed, and she swore with a vigour that was almost youthful before she turned back to Hwoogh.

'Come, Hairy One, get out of that cold, wet fur!' Her hands were gentle on the straps, but Hwoogh shook her aside. 'You'll be sick, lying there on them few leaves, all wet like that. Get off the fur, and I'll go back to the village for fire. Them kids! Wait'll I tell Legoda!'

Seeing there was nothing he would let her do for him, she turned away down the trail. Hwoogh sat up to change his furs, then lay back. What was the use? He grumbled a little when Keyoda returned with fire, but refused the delicacies she had wheedled at the village, and tumbled over into a fitful sleep.

The sun was long up when he awoke to find Legoda and Keyoda fussing over him. There was an unhappy feeling in his head, and he coughed. Legoda patted his back. 'Rest, Hairy One. You have the sickness devil that burns the throat and runs at the nose, but that man can overcome. Ayeee, how the boys were whipped! I, personally, attended to that, and this morning not one is less sore than you. Before they bother you again, the moon will eat up the sun.'

Keyoda pushed a stew of boiled liver and kidneys at him, but he shoved it away. Though the ache in his head had gone down, a dull weight seemed to rest on his stomach, and he could not eat. It felt as though all the boys he had fought were sitting on his chest and choking him.

Legoda drew out a small painted drum and made heavy magic for his recovery, dancing before the old man and shaking the magic gourd that drove out all sickness devils. But this was a stronger devil. Finally the young man stopped and left for the village, while Keyoda perched on a stone to watch over the sick man. Hwoogh's mind was heavy and numb, and his heart was leaden in his breast. She fanned the flies away, covering his eyes with a bit of skin, singing him some song that the mothers lulled their children with.

He slept again, stirring about in a nightmare of Talker mockery, with a fever flushing his face. But when Legoda came back at night, the magic man swore he should be well in three days. 'Let him sleep and feed him. The devil will leave him soon. See, there is scarce a mark where the stone hit.'

Keyoda fed him, as best she could, forcing the food that she begged at the village down his throat. She lugged water from the creek as often as he cried for it, and bathed his head and chest when he slept. But the three days came and went, and still he was not well. The fever was little higher, and the cold little worse, than he had gone through many times before. But he did not throw it off as he should have done.

Legoda came again, bringing his magic and food, but they were of little help. As the day drew to a close, he shook his head and spoke low words to Keyoda. Hwoogh came out of a half stupor and listened dully.

'He tires of life, Keyoda, my father's sister.' The young man shrugged. 'See, he lies there not fighting. When a man will not try to live, he cannot.'

'Ayyeah!' Her voice shrilled dolefully. 'What man will not live if he can? Thou art foolish, Legoda.'

'Nay. His people tire easily of life, O Keyoda. Why, I know not. But it takes little to make them die.' Seeing that Hwoogh had heard, he drew closer to the Neanderthaler. 'O Chokanga, put away your troubles, and take another bite out of life. It can still be good, if you choose. I have taken your gift as a sign of friendship, and I would keep my word. Come to my fire, and hunt no more; I will tend you as I would my father.'

Hwoogh grunted. Follow the camps, eat from Legoda's hunting, be paraded as a freak and a half-man! Legoda was kind, sudden and warm in his sympathy, but the others were scornful. And if Hwoogh should die, who was to mourn him? Keyoda would go back to her people, Legoda would forget him, and not one Chokanga would be there to show them the ritual for burial.

Hwoogh's old friends had come back to him in his dream, visiting him and showing the hunting grounds of his youth. He had heard the grunts and grumblings of the girls of his race, and they were awaiting him. That world was still empty of the Talkers, where a man could do great things and make his own kills, without hearing the laughter of the Cro-Magnons. Hwoogh sighed softly. He was tired, too tired to care what happened.

The sun sank low, and the clouds were painted a harsh red. Keyoda was wailing somewhere, far off, and Legoda beat on his drum and muttered his magic. But life was empty, barren of pride.

The sun dropped from sight, and Hwoogh sighed again, sending his last breath out to join the ghosts of his people.

THE DAY IS DONE

The first Neanderthal skeleton was discovered in 1856. It was the first indication that species of men had once existed that were more 'primitive' than the kind of man now living.

The most noticeable thing about the Neanderthal skeleton was that it had a skull with a receding forehead and a receding chin, and that there were bony ridges over the eye sockets. In these respects, it seemed midway between a gorilla and man and the notion arose that it represented an 'ape-man'.

In 1908, a French scientist, Marcellin Boule, studied a nearly complete Neanderthal skeleton and published a careful description of it. From that description, it would seem that Neanderthal man was short, just a little over five feet high. He was pictured as having such bowlegs that he had to walk on the outside part of his soles, with his knees bent. Combine that with the bony ridges, prominent teeth, receding forehead and chin, and he seemed an ugly creature indeed.

When artists drew sketches of what they thought a Neanderthal man would look like in the flesh, they were influenced by the 'ape-man' notion. They drew him with a messy stubble of hair all over his face and gave him a savage, brutish expression.

Another type of man living towards the end of Neanderthal times was Cro-Magnon man. He was 'true' man, very much like ourselves; six feet in height with a straight forehead, a pronounced chin, and no bony ridges over the eyes. He was always drawn clean-shaven and was given a noble and handsome expression.

Most people supposed that Cro-Magnon man wiped out Neanderthal man quickly whenever they collided, and felt that the much superior Cro-Magnon would easily manage to slaughter the much inferior Neanderthal.

Del Rey, however, suggests something else. He supposes that while many Neanderthal men may have been killed in battle with Cro-Magnon man, the crucial killing factor was the feeling of inferiority. It was this that ruined the poor 'ape-men'. They died through sheer chagrin at being outclassed even by the young adolescents of the superior species.

But was this true? It turned out eventually that the skeleton that Boule had so carefully studied was a victim of severe arthritis which had deformed the spinal column and other bones. Other Neanderthal skeletons have since been discovered which represented healthier specimens and their bones, all except those of the skull, are completely manlike. In other words, Neanderthal man didn't shamble; he walked upright just as easily and gracefully as Cro-Magnon man did.

Then, too, Neanderthal man had a large brain, just as large as that of Cro-Magnon man. To be sure, the Neanderthal brain was differently shaped. It was larger in back and smaller in front. If the front part of the brain is involved in higher-thought processes, then perhaps Neanderthal man wasn't quite as bright as Cro-Magnon, but that is by no means sure. There is certainly no real reason to think Neanderthal man couldn't talk.

In fact, nowadays, anthropologists consider both Cro-Magnon man and Neanderthal man to be the same species—*Homo sapiens*. Why did Neanderthal man die out then? Well, he didn't exactly die out. He developed into 'true' man, and those that remained of the Neanderthal variety may have interbred with the 'true' variety. In short, we are all descended from the Neanderthals in all likelihood.

Questions and Suggestions

1. Look up the details of the discovery of the first Neanderthal skeleton and the controversy that was conducted over it. What made it difficult for some people to accept the Neanderthal skeleton as a primitive kind of man?

2. When the story first appeared in *Astounding Science Fiction* the editor of the magazine (John W. Campbell, Jr.) followed it with a note to the effect that the Tasmanians, the native inhabitants of the island of Tasmania off the southeast coast of Australia, died out because of a feeling of inferiority to the incoming white man, and that the Australian aborigines were dying out for the same reason. Look up the history of

Tasmania and decide for yourself why the Tasmanians died out? Are the Australian aborigines dying out now?

3. What do you think about the whole matter of 'superior' and 'inferior' varieties of man? Do you belong to a group that is superior to other groups? Or inferior? How can you tell? How does one measure such things? Look up methods of IQ testing and decide how accurately they measure intelligence when the man devising the test and the man taking the test are of different cultures.

4. How would you treat someone whom you felt was superior to you? How would you expect to be treated by him? How would you treat someone whom you felt was inferior to you? How would you expect to be treated by him? Suppose you felt someone was inferior to you and he happened to feel you were inferior to him—how ought you to treat each other? What difficulties is the United States experiencing over questions such as these and how might those difficulties be resolved?

4. Heavy Planet

Milton A. Rothman

Ennis was completing his patrol of Sector EM, Division 426 of the Eastern Ocean. The weather had been unusually fine, the liquid-thick air roaring along in a continuous blast that propelled his craft with a rush as if it were flying, and lifting short, choppy waves that rose and fell with startling suddenness. A short savage squall whirled about, pounding down on the ocean like a million hammers, flinging the little boat ahead madly.

Ennis tore at the controls, granite-hard muscles standing out in bas-relief over his short, immensely thick body, skin gleaming scalelike in the slashing spray. The heat from the sun that hung like a huge red lantern on the horizon was a tangible intensity, making an inferno of the gale.

The little craft, that Ennis manoeuvred by sheer brawn, took a leap into the air and seemed to float for many seconds before burying its keel again in the sea. It often floated for long distances, the air was so dense. The boundary between air and water was sometimes scarcely defined at all—one merged into the other imperceptibly. The pressure did strange things.

Like a dust mote sparking in a beam, a tiny speck of light above caught Ennis's eye. A glider, he thought, but he was puzzled. Why so far out here on the ocean? They were nasty things to handle in the violent wind.

The dust mote caught the light again. It was lower, tumbling down with a precipitancy that meant trouble. An upward blast caught it, checked its fall. Then it floated down gently for a space until struck by another howling wind that seemed to distort its very outlines.

Ennis turned the prow of his boat to meet the path of the falling vessel. Curious, he thought; where were its wings? Were they retracted, or broken off? It ballooned closer, and it wasn't a glider. Far larger than any glider ever made, it was of a ridiculous shape that would not stand up for an instant. And with the sharp splash the body made as it struck the water —a splash that fell in almost the same instant it rose—a thought seemed to leap up in his mind. A thought that was more important than anything else on that planet; or was to him, at least. For if it was what he thought it was—and it had to be that—it was what Shadden had been desperately seeking for many years. What a stroke of inconceivable luck, falling from the sky before his very eyes.

The silvery shape rode the ragged waters lightly. Ennis's craft came up with a rush; he skilfully checked its speed and the two came together with a slight jar. The metal of the strange vessel dented as if it were made of rubber. Ennis stared. He put out an arm and felt the curved surface of the strange ship. His finger prodded right through the metal. What manner of people were they who made vessels of such weak materials?

He moored his little boat to the side of the larger one and climbed to an opening. The wall sagged under him. He knew he must be careful; it was frightfully weak. It would not hold together very long; he must work fast if it were to be saved. The atmospheric pressure would have flattened it out long ago, had it not been for the jagged rent above which had allowed the pressure to be equalized.

He reached the opening and lowered himself carefully into the interior of the vessel. The rent was too small; he enlarged it by taking the two edges in his hands and pulling them apart. As he went down he looked askance at the insignificant plates and beams that were like tissue paper on his world. Inside was wreckage. Nothing was left in its original shape. Crushed, mutilated machinery, shattered vacuum tubes, sagging members, all ruined by the gravity and the pressure.

There was a pulpy mess on the floor that he did not examine closely. It was like red jelly, thin and stalky, pulped under a gravity a hundred times stronger and an atmosphere ten thousand times heavier than that it had been made for.

He was in a room with many knobs and dials on the walls, apparently a control room. A table in the centre with a chart on it, the chart of a solar system. It had nine planets; his had but five.

Then he knew he was right. If they came from another system, what he wanted must be there. It could be nothing else.

He found a staircase, descended. Large machinery bulked there. There was no light, but he did not notice that. He could see well enough by infrared, and the amount of energy necessary to sustain his compact gianthood kept him constantly radiating.

Then he went through a door that was of a comfortable massiveness, even for his planet—and there it was. He recognized it at once. It was big, squat, strong. The metal was soft, but it was thick enough even to stand solidly under the enormous pull of this world. He had never seen anything quite like it. It was full of coils, magnets, and devices of shapes unknown to him. But Shadden would know. Shadden, and who knows how many other scientists before him, had tried to make something which would do what this could do, but they had all failed. And without the things this machine could perform, the race of men on Heavyplanet was doomed to stay down on the surface of the planet, chained there immovably by crushing gravity.

It was atomic energy. That he had known as soon as he knew that the body was not a glider. For nothing else but atomic energy and the fierce winds were capable of lifting a body from the surface of Heavyplanet. Chemicals were impotent. There is no such thing as an explosion where the atmosphere pressed inward with more force than an explosion could press outward. Only atomic, of all the theoretically possible sources of energy, could supply the work necessary to lift a vessel away from the planet. Every other source of energy was simply too weak.

Yes, Shadden, all the scientists must see this. And quickly, because the forces of sea and storm would quickly tear the ship to shreds, and, even more vital, because the scientists of Bantin and Marak might obtain the secret if there was delay. And that would mean ruin—the loss of its age-old supremacy—for his nation. Bantin and Marak were war nations; did they obtain the secret they would use it against all the other worlds that abounded in the Universe.

The Universe was big. That was why Ennis was so sure there was atomic energy on this ship. For, even though it might have originated on a planet that was so tiny that *chemical energy*—although that was hard to visualize—would be sufficient to lift it out of the pull of gravity, to travel the distance that stretched between the stars only one thing would suffice.

He went back through the ship, trying to see what had happened.

There were pulps lying behind long tubes that pointed out through clever ports in the outer wall. He recognized them as weapons, worth looking into.

There must have been a battle. He visualized the scene. The forces that came from atomic energy must have warped even space in the vicinity. The ship pierced, the occupants killed, the controls wrecked, the vessel darting off at titanic speed, blindly into nothing. Finally it had come near enough to Heavyplanet to be enmeshed in its huge web of gravity.

Weeaao-o-ow! It was the wailing roar of his alarm siren, which brought him spinning around and dashing for his boat. Beyond, among the waves that leaped and fell so suddenly, he saw a long, low craft making way towards the derelict spaceship. He glimpsed a flash of colour on the rounded, grey superstructure, and knew it for a battleship of Marak. Luck was going strong both ways; first good, now bad. He could easily have eluded the battleship in his own small craft, but he couldn't leave the derelict. Once lost to the enemy he could never regain it, and it was too valuable to lose.

The wind howled and buffeted about his head, and he strained his muscles to keep from being blasted away as he crouched there, half on his own boat and half on the derelict. The sun had set and the evening winds were beginning to blow. The hulk scudded before them, its prow denting from the resistance of the water it pushed aside.

He thought furiously fast. With a quick motion he flipped the switch of the radiophone and called Shadden. He waited with fierce impatience until the voice of Shadden was in his ear. At last he heard it, then: 'Shadden! This is Ennis. Get your glider, Shadden, fly to a45j on my route! Quickly! It's come, Shadden! But I have no time. Come!'

He flipped the switch off, and pounded the valve out of the bottom of his craft, clutching at the side of the derelict. With a rush the ocean came up and flooded his little boat and in an instant it was gone, on its way down to the bottom. That would save him from being detected for a short time.

Back into the darkness of the spaceship. He didn't think he had been noticed climbing through the opening. Where could he hide? Should he hide? He couldn't defeat the entire battleship singlehanded, without weapons. There were no weapons that could be carried anyway. A beam of concentrated actinic light that ate away the eyes and the nervous system had to be powered by the entire output of a battleship's generators. Weapons for striking and cutting had never been developed on a world where flesh was tougher than metal. Ennis was skilled in personal combat, but how could he overcome all that would enter the derelict?

Down again, into the dark chamber where the huge atomic generator towered over his head. This time he looked for something he had missed before. He crawled around it, peering into its recesses. And then, some feet above, he saw the opening, and pulled himself up to it, carefully, not to destroy the precious thing with his mass. The opening was shielded with a heavy, darkly transparent substance through which seeped a dim glow from within. He was satisfied then. Somehow, matter was still being disintegrated in there, and energy could be drawn off if he knew how.

There were leads—wires of all sizes and busbars, and thick, heavy tubes that bent under their own weight. Some must lead in and some must lead out; it was not good to tamper with them. He chose another track. Upstairs again, and to the places where he had seen the weapons.

They were all mounted on heavy, rigid swivels. He carefully detached the tubes from the bases. The first time he tried it he was not quite careful enough, and part of the projector itself was ripped away, but next time he knew what he was doing and it came away nicely. It was a large thing, nearly as thick as his arm and twice as long. Heavy leads trailed from its lower end and a lever projected from behind. He hoped it was in working condition. He dared not try it; all he could do was to trace the leads back and make sure they were intact.

He ran out of time. There came a thud from the side, and then smaller thuds, as the boarding party incautiously leaped over. Once there was a heavy sound, as someone went all the way through the side of the ship.

'Idiots!' Ennis muttered, and moved forward with his weapon towards the stairway. Noises came from overhead, and then a loud crash buckled the plates of the ceiling. Ennis leaped out of the way, but the entire section came down, with two men on it. The floor sagged, but held for the moment. Ennis, caught beneath the downcoming mass, beat his way free. He came up with a girder in his hand, which he bent over the head of one of the Maraks. The man shook himself and struck out for Ennis, who took the blow rolling and countered with a buffet that left a black splotch on a skin that was like armour plate and sent the man through the opposite wall. The other was upon Ennis, who whirled with the quickness of one who manoeuvres habitually under a pressure of ten thousand atmospheres, and shook the Marak from him, leaving him unconscious with a twist in a sensitive spot.

The first opponent returned, and the two grappled, searching for nerve centres to beat upon. Ennis twisted frantically, conscious of the real danger that the frail vessel might break to pieces beneath his feet. The railing of a staircase gave behind the two, and they hurtled down it, crashing through the steps to the floor below. Their weight and momentum carried them through. Ennis released his grip on the Marak, stopped his fall by grasping one of the girders that was part of the ship's framework. The other continued his devastating way down, demolishing the inner shell, and then the outer shell gave way with a grinding crash that ominously became a burbling rush of liquid.

Ennis looked down into the space where the Marak had fallen, hissed with a sudden intake of breath, then dived down himself. He met rising water, gushing in through a rent in the keel. He braced himself against a girder which sagged under his hand and moved onward against the rushing water. It geysered through the hole in a heavy stream that pushed him back and started to fill the bottom level of the ship. Against that terrific pressure he strained forward slowly, beating against the resisting waves, and, with a mighty flounder, was at the opening. Its edges had been folded back upon themselves by the inrushing water, and they gaped inward like a jagged maw. He grasped them in a huge hand and exerted force. They strained for a moment and began to straighten. Irresistibly he pushed and stretched them into their former position, and then took the broken ends in his hands and *squeezed*. The metal grew soft under his grip and began to flow. The edges of the plate welded under that mighty pressure. He moved down the crack and soon it was watertight. He flexed his hands as he rose. They ached; even his strength was beginning to be taxed.

Noises from above; pounding feet. Men were coming down to investigate the commotion. He stood for a moment in thought, then turned to a blank wall, battered his way through it, and shoved the plates and girders back into position. Down to the other end of the craft, and up a staircase there. The corridor above was deserted, and he stole along it, hunting for the place he had left the weapon he had prepared. There was a commotion ahead as the Maraks found the unconscious man.

Two men came pounding up the passageway, giving him barely enough time to slip into a doorway to the side. The room he found himself in was a sleeping chamber. There were two red pulps there, and nothing that could help him, so he stayed in there only long enough to make sure that he would not be seen emerging into the hall. He crept down it again, with as little noise as possible. The racket ahead helped him: it sounded as though they were tearing the ship apart. Again he cursed their idiocy. Couldn't they see how valuable this was?

They were in the control room, ripping apart the machinery with the curiosity of children, wondering at the strange weakness of the paperlike metal, not realizing that, on the world where it was fabricated, it was sufficiently strong for any strain the builders could put upon it.

The strange weapon Ennis had prepared was on the floor of the passage, and just outside the control room. He looked anxiously at the trailing cables. Had they been stepped on and broken? Was the instrument in working condition? He had to get it and be away; no time to experiment to see if it would work.

A noise from behind, and Ennis again slunk into a doorway as a large Marak with a coloured belt around his waist strode jarringly through the corridor into the control room. Sharp orders were barked, and the men ceased their havoc with the machinery of the room. All but a few left and scattered through the ship. Ennis's face twisted into a scowl. This made things more difficult. He couldn't overcome them all singlehanded, and he couldn't use the weapon inside the ship if it was what he thought it was from the size of the cables.

A Marak was standing immediately outside the room in which Ennis lurked. No exit that way. He looked around the room; there were no other doors. A porthole in the outer wall was a tiny disc of transparency. He looked at it, felt it with his hands, and suddenly pushed his hands right through it. As quietly as he could, he worked at the edges of the circle until the hole was large enough for him to squeeze through. The jagged edges did not bother him. They felt soft, like a ragged pat of butter.

The Marak vessel was moored to the other side of the spaceship. On this side the wind howled bleakly, and the sawtooth waves stretched on and on to a horizon that was many miles distant. He cautiously made his way around the glistening rotundity of the derelict, past the prow, straining silently against the vicious backward sweep of the water that tore at every inch of his body. The darker hump of the battleship loomed up as he rounded the curve, and he swam across the tiny space to grasp a row of projections that curved up over the surface of the craft. He climbed up them, muscles that were hard as carborundum straining to hold against all the forces of gravity and wind that fought him down. Near the top of the curve was a rounded, streamlined projection. He felt around its base and found a lever there, which he moved. The metal hump slid back, revealing a rugged swivel mounting with a stubby cylindrical projector atop it.

He swung the mounting around and let loose a short, sudden blast of white fire along the naked deck of the battleship. Deep voices yelled within and men sprang out, to fall back with abrupt screams clogged in their throats as Ennis caught them in the intolerable blast from the projector. Men, shielded by five thousand miles of atmosphere from actinic light, used to receiving only red and infrared, were painfully vulnerable to this frightful concentration of ultraviolet.

Noise and shouts burst from the derelict spaceship alongside, sweeping away eerily in the thundering wind that seemed to pound down upon them with new vigour in that moment. Heads appeared from the openings in the craft.

Ennis suddenly stood up to his full height, bracing himself against the wind, so dense it made him buoyant. With a deep bellow he bridged the space to the derelict. Then as a squad of

Maraks made their difficult, slippery way across the flank of the battleship towards him, and as the band that had boarded the spaceship crowded out on its battered deck to see what the noise was about, he dropped down into a crouch behind his ultraviolet projector, and whirled it around, pulling the firing lever.

That was what he wanted. Make a lot of noise and disturbance, get them all on deck, and then blow them to pieces. The ravening blast spat from the nozzle of the weapon, and the men on the battleship dropped flat on the deck. He found he could not depress the projector enough to reach them. He spun it to point at the spaceship. The incandescence reached out, and then seemed to waver and die. The current was shut off at the switchboard.

Ennis rose from behind the projector, and then hurtled from the flank of the battleship as he was struck by two Maraks leaping on him from behind the hump of the vessel. The three struck the water and sank, Ennis struggling violently. He was on the last lap, and he gave all his strength to the spurt. The water swirled around them in little choppy waves that fell more quickly than the eye could follow. Heavier blows than those from an Earthly trip hammer were scoring Ennis's face and head. He was in a bad position to strike back, and suddenly he became limp and sank below the surface. The pressure of the water around him was enormous, and it increased very rapidly as he went lower and lower. He saw the shadowy bulk of the spaceship above him. His lungs were fighting for air, but he shook off his pretended stupor and swam doggedly through the water beneath the derelict. He went on and on. It seemed as though the distance were endless, following the metal curve. It was so big from beneath, and trying to swim the width without air made it bigger.

Clear, finally, his lungs drew in the saving breaths. No time to rest, though. He must make use of his advantage while it was his; it wouldn't last long. He swam along the side of the ship looking for an opening. There was none within reach from the water, so he made one, digging his stubby fingers into the metal, climbing up until it was safe to tear a rent in the thick outer and inner walls of the ship.

He found himself in one of the machine rooms of the second level. He went out into the corridor and up the stairway which was half-wrecked, and found himself in the main passage near the control room. He darted down it, into the room. There was nobody there, although the noises from above indicated that the Maraks were again descending. There was his weapon on the floor, where he had left it. He was glad that they had not got around to pulling that instrument apart. There would be one thing saved for intelligent examination.

The clatter from the descending crowd turned into a clamour of anger as they discovered him in the passageway. They stopped there for a moment, puzzled. He had been in the ocean, and had somehow magically reappeared within the derelict. It gave him time to pick up the weapon.

Ennis debated rapidly and decided to risk the unknown. How powerful the weapon was he did not know, but with atomic energy it would be powerful. He disliked using it inside the spaceship; he wanted to have enough left to float on the water until Shadden arrived; but they were beginning to advance on him, and he had to start something.

He pulled a lever. The cylinder in his arms jerked back with great force; a bolt of fierce, blinding energy tore out of it and passed with the quickness of light down the length of the corridor.

Unmindful of the heat from the object in his hands, he turned and directed it at the battleship that was plainly outlined through the space that had been once the walls of the derelict. Before the men on the deck could move, he pulled the lever again.

And the winds were silenced for a moment. The natural elements were still in fear at the incredible forces that came from the destruction of atoms. Then with an agonized scream the hurricane struck again, tore through the spot where there had been a battleship.

Far off in the sky Ennis detected motion. It was Shadden, speeding in a glider.

Now would come the work that was important. Shadden would take the big machine apart and see how it ran. That was what history would remember.

HEAVY PLANET

We are used to considering Earth's gravity and air pressure as so normal we are hardly aware of it. In ordinary fiction, it is never mentioned, except of course in connection with falls or storms.

In science fiction, however, such matters as gravity and air pressure are important for they vary from world to world. To be sure, we are not likely to be exposed to gravitational fields more intense or air pressures greater than those we are used to. Excluding the Sun itself, there are only four objects in the Solar system with gravitational fields more powerful than that of the Earth—these are the giant planets, Jupiter, Saturn, Uranus, and Neptune. In the foreseeable future, we are not likely to attempt landings on those planets.

These giant planets also have giant atmospheres—far denser, far deeper, involving far greater pressures at their bottoms than is true of Earth's atmosphere.

The worlds we are likely to reach will all have gravitational fields and air pressures smaller than that to which we are accustomed. The Moon has a gravitational field at its surface only $\frac{1}{6}$ ours, and has no atmosphere at all; Mars's gravity at its surface is $\frac{2}{5}$ ours and its atmospheric pressure is no more than $\frac{1}{100}$ ours.

In science fiction stories, alien worlds outside our Solar system usually are very like Earth, but many stories must deal with the Moon and Mars so that low-gravitational, low-atmospheric worlds are familiar to its readers. Less familiar are pictures of conditions on Jupiter-like planets, as Heavyplanet is. Rothman labours hard to make the strange conditions on its surface come alive for us.

At the time the story was written, Milton A. Rothman was a

bright college student majoring in physics, and he has since become a respected research physicist. Yet even so, he could not move ahead of the times.

The story was published in the August 1939 issue of *Astounding Science Fiction,* at which time uranium fission was on the edge of being discovered. Yet the story did not anticipate it, and it would have been unfair to expect it to. No details are given of the atomic device on board the weak-walled ship from outer space (presumably from Earth). Apparently, the device releases a beam of energy that breaks down atoms that it encounters so that the author can say, 'Everything that had been in the way of the projector was gone, simply disappeared.' On the other hand it might simply mean that the great heat originating from the processes within the device vaporized everything.

And yet we must not underestimate the value of this much, either. Science fiction writers at least assumed that nuclear power could be tapped and put to work. Few scientists of the 1930s dared think so.

Questions and Suggestions

1. What is known concerning the planet Jupiter beneath the upper edge of the atmosphere—which is all we really see? What is the chemical nature of the atmosphere? How deep is it? What is its air pressure at the solid surface? What is the solid surface like? What about the other three giant planets; what are they like?

2. The story states that Heavyplanet is part of a system containing five planets altogether. The Heavyplanet being knows that, so his people had apparently developed astronomy. But suppose we imagine a race of intelligent beings on Jupiter's solid surface—what would they know about astronomy? What could they see of the heavens through Jupiter's atmosphere? What methods could be used to gain astronomical knowledge even in the absence of direct vision?

3. Venus is an unusual planet. Its surface gravity is only $\frac{4}{5}$ that of Earth, but its atmospheric pressure at the surface is perhaps fifty times that of Earth. What do we know of con-

ditions on Venus's surface thanks to discoveries of the 1960s? How will men manage to explore that surface?

4. Disintegrator guns were a staple of science fiction prior to the 1940s. Do you think a disintegrator gun is possible? Some people call lasers disintegrating rays because they can make things disappear in the path of their radiation. Why? How do they work? Do they disintegrate atoms?

5. '—And He Built a Crooked House—'

Robert A. Heinlein

Americans are considered crazy anywhere in the world.

They will usually concede a basis for the accusation but point to California as the focus of the infection. Californians stoutly maintain that their bad reputation is derived solely from the acts of the inhabitants of Los Angeles County. Angelenos will, when pressed, admit the charge but explain hastily, 'It's Hollywood. It's not our fault—we didn't ask for it; Hollywood just grew.'

The people in Hollywood don't care; they glory in it. If you are interested, they will drive you up Laurel Canyon '—where we keep the violent cases'. The Canyonites—the brown-legged women, the trunks-clad men constantly busy building and rebuilding their slap-happy unfinished houses—regard with faint contempt the dull creatures who live down in the flats, and treasure in their hearts the secret knowledge that they, and only they, know how to live.

Lookout Mountain Avenue is the name of a side canyon which twists up from Laurel Canyon. The other Canyonites don't like to have it mentioned; after all, one must draw the line somewhere!

High up on Lookout Mountain at number 8775, across the street from the Hermit—the original Hermit of Hollywood—lived Quintus Teal, graduate architect.

Even the architecture of southern California is different. Hot dogs are sold from a structure built like and designated 'The Pup'. Ice cream cones come from a giant stucco ice cream cone, and neon proclaims 'Get the Chili Bowl Habit!' from the roofs of buildings which are indisputably chili bowls. Gasoline, oil, and free road maps are dispensed beneath the wings of tri-motored transport planes, while the certified rest rooms, inspected hourly for your comfort, are located in the cabin of the plane itself. These things may surprise, or amuse, the tourist, but the local residents, who walk bareheaded in the famous California noonday sun, take them as a matter of course.

Quintus Teal regarded the efforts of his colleagues in architecture as faint-hearted, fumbling, and timid.

'What is a house?' Teal demanded of his friend, Homer Bailey.

'Well—' Bailey admitted cautiously, 'speaking in broad terms, I've always regarded a house as a gadget to keep off the rain.'

'Nuts! You're as bad as the rest of them.'

'I didn't say the definition was complete—'

'Complete! It isn't even in the right direction. From that point of view we might just as well be squatting in caves. But I don't blame you,' Teal went on magnanimously, 'you're no worse than the lugs you find practising architecture. Even the Moderns—all they've done is to abandon the Wedding Cake School in favour of the Service Station School, chucked away the gingerbread and slapped on some chromium, but at heart they are as conservative and traditional as a county courthouse. Neutra! Schindler! What have those bums got? What's Frank Lloyd Wright got that I haven't got?'

'Commissions,' his friend answered succinctly.

'Huh? Wha' d'ju say?' Teal stumbled slightly in his flow of words, did a slight double take, and recovered himself. 'Commissions. Correct. And why? Because I don't think of a house as an upholstered cave; I think of it as a machine for living, a vital process, a live dynamic thing, changing with the mood of the dweller—not a dead, static, oversized coffin. Why should we be held down by the frozen concepts of our ancestors? Any fool with a little smattering of descriptive geometry can design a house in the ordinary way. Is the static geometry of Euclid the only mathematics? Are we to completely disregard the Picard-Vessiot theory? How about modular systems?—to say nothing of the rich suggestions of stereochemistry. Isn't there a place in architecture for transformation, for homomorphology, for actional structures?'

'Blessed if I know,' answered Bailey. 'You might just as well be talking about the fourth dimension for all it means to me.'

'And why not? Why should we limit ourselves to the— Say!' He interrupted himself and stared into distances. 'Homer, I think you've really got something. After all, why not? Think of the infinite richness of articulation and relationship in four dimensions. What a house, what a house—' He stood quite still, his pale bulging eyes blinking thoughtfully.

Bailey reached up and shook his arm. 'Snap out of it. What the hell are you talking about, four dimensions? Time is the fourth dimension; you can't drive nails into *that.*'

Teal shrugged him off. 'Sure. Sure. Time is *a* fourth dimension, but I'm thinking about a fourth spatial dimension, like length, breadth and thickness. For economy of materials and convenience of arrangement you couldn't beat it. To say nothing of the saving of ground space—you could put an eight-room house on the land now occupied by a one-room house. Like a tesseract—'

'What's a tesseract?'

'Didn't you go to school? A tesseract is a hypercube, a square figure with four dimensions to it, like a cube has three, and a square has two. Here, I'll show you.' Teal dashed out into the kitchen of his apartment and returned with a box of toothpicks which he spilled on the table between them, brushing glasses and a nearly empty Holland gin bottle carelessly aside. 'I'll need some plasticine. I had some around here last week.' He burrowed into a drawer of the littered desk which crowded one corner of his dining room and emerged with a lump of oily sculptor's clay. 'Here's some.'

'What are you going to do?'

'I'll show you.' Teal rapidly pinched off small masses of the clay and rolled them into pea-sized balls. He stuck toothpicks into four of these and hooked them together into a square. 'There! That's a square.'

'Obviously.'

'Another one like it, four more toothpicks, and we make a cube.' The toothpicks were now arranged in the framework of a square box, a cube, with the pellets of clay holding the corners together. 'Now we make another cube just like the first one, and the two of them will be two sides of the tesseract.'

Bailey started to help him roll the little balls of clay for the second cube, but became diverted by the sensuous feel of the docile clay and started working and shaping it with his fingers.

'Look,' he said, holding up his effort, a tiny figurine, 'Gypsy Rose Lee.'

'Looks more like Gargantua; she ought to sue you. Now pay attention. You open up one corner of the first cube, interlock the second cube at one corner, and then close the corner. Then take eight more toothpicks and join the bottom of the first cube to the bottom of the second, on a slant, and the top of the first to the top of the second, the same way.' This he did rapidly, while he talked.

'What's that supposed to be?' Bailey demanded suspiciously.

'That's a tesseract, eight cubes forming the sides of a hypercube in four dimensions.'

'It looks more like a cat's cradle to me. You've only got two cubes there anyhow. Where are the other six?'

'Use your imagination, man. Consider the top of the first cube in relation to the top of the second; that's cube number three. Then the two bottom squares, then the front faces of each cube, the back faces, the right hand, the left hand—eight cubes.' He pointed them out.

'Yeah, I see 'em. But they still aren't cubes; they're whatchamucallems—prisms. They are not square, they slant.'

'That's just the way you look at it, in perspective. If you drew a picture of a cube on a piece of paper, the side squares would be slantwise, wouldn't they? That's perspective. When you look at a four-dimensional figure in three dimensions, naturally it looks crooked. But those are all cubes just the same.'

'Maybe they are to you, brother, but they still look crooked to me.'

Teal ignored the objections and went on. 'Now consider this as the framework of an eight-room house; there's one room on the ground floor—that's for service, utilities, and garage. There are six rooms opening off it on the next floor, living room, dining room, bath, bedrooms, and so forth. And up at the top, completely enclosed and with windows on four sides, is your study. There! How do you like it?'

'Seems to me you have the bathtub hanging out of the living room ceiling. Those rooms are interlaced like an octopus.'

'Only in perspective, only in perspective. Here, I'll do it another way so you can see it.' This time Teal made a cube of toothpicks, then made a second of halves of toothpicks, and set it exactly in the centre of the first by attaching the corners of the small cube to the large cube by short lengths of toothpick. 'Now—the big cube is your ground floor, the little cube inside is your study on the top floor. The six cubes joining them are the living rooms. See?'

Bailey studied the figure, then shook his head. 'I still don't see but two cubes, a big one and a little one. Those other six things, they look like pyramids this time instead of prisms, but they still aren't cubes.'

'Certainly, certainly, you are seeing them in different perspective. Can't you see that?'

'Well, maybe. But that room on the inside, there. It's completely surrounded by the thingamujigs. I thought you said it had windows on four sides.'

'It has—it just looks like it was surrounded. That's the grand feature about a tesseract house, complete outside exposure for every room, yet every wall serves two rooms and an eight-room house requires only a one-room foundation. It's revolutionary.'

'That's putting it mildly. You're crazy, bud; you can't build a house like that. That inside room is on the inside, and there she stays.'

Teal looked at his friend in controlled exasperation. 'It's guys like you that keep architecture in its infancy. How many square sides has a cube?'

'Six.'

'How many of them are inside?'

'Why, none of 'em. They're all on the outside.'

'All right. Now listen—a tesseract has eight cubical sides, *all on the outside*. Now watch me. I'm going to open up this tesseract like you can open up a cubical pasteboard box, until it's flat. That way you'll be able to see all eight of the cubes.' Working very rapidly he constructed four cubes, piling one on top of the other in an unsteady tower. He then built out four more cubes from the four exposed faces of the second cube in the pile. The structure swayed a little under the loose coupling of the clay pellets, but it stood, eight cubes in an inverted cross, a double cross, as the four additional cubes stuck out in four directions. 'Do you see it now? It rests on the ground floor room, the next six cubes are the living rooms, and there is your study, up at the top.'

Bailey regarded it with more approval than he had the other figures. 'At least I can understand it. You say that is a tesseract, too?'

'That is a tesseract unfolded in three dimensions. To put it back together you tuck the top cube on to the bottom cube, fold those side cubes in till they meet the top cube and there you are. You do all this folding through a fourth dimension of course; you don't distort any of the cubes, or fold them into each other.'

Bailey studied the wobbly framework further. 'Look here,' he said at last, 'why don't you forget about folding this thing up through a fourth dimension—you can't anyway—and build a house like this?'

'What do you mean, I can't? It's a simple mathematical problem—'

'Take it easy, son. It may be simple in mathematics, but you could never get your plans approved for construction. There isn't any fourth dimension; forget it. But this kind of a house—it might have some advantages.'

Checked, Teal studied the model. 'Hm-m-m— Maybe you got something. We could have the same number of rooms, and we'd save the same amount of ground space. Yes, and we would set that middle cross-shaped floor northeast, southwest, and so forth, so that every room would get sunlight all day long. That central axis lends itself nicely to central heating. We'll put the dining room on the northeast and the kitchen on the southeast, with big view windows in every room. O.K., Homer, I'll do it! Where do you want it built?'

'Wait a minute! Wait a minute! I didn't say you were going to build it for me—'

'Of course I am. Who else? Your wife wants a new house; this is it.'

'But Mrs. Bailey wants a Georgian house—'

'Just an idea she has. Women don't know what they want—'

'Mrs. Bailey does.'

'Just some idea an out-of-date architect has put in her head. She drives a 1941 car, doesn't she? She wears the very latest styles—why should she live in an eighteenth-century house? This house will be even later than a 1941 model; it's years in the future. She'll be the talk of the town.'

'Well—I'll have to talk to her.'

'Nothing of the sort. We'll surprise her with it. Have another drink.'

'Anyhow, we can't do anything about it now. Mrs. Bailey and I are driving up to Bakersfield tomorrow. The company's bringing in a couple of wells tomorrow.'

'Nonsense. That's just the opportunity we want. It will be a surprise for her when you get back. You can just write me a cheque right now, and your worries are over.'

'I oughtn't to do anything like this without consulting her. She won't like it.'

'Say, who wears the pants in your family anyhow?'

The cheque was signed about halfway down the second bottle.

* * *

Things are done fast in southern California. Ordinary houses there are usually built in a month's time. Under Teal's impassioned heckling the tesseract house climbed dizzily skywards in days rather than weeks, and its cross-shaped second storey came jutting out at the four corners of the world. He had some trouble at first with the inspectors over these four projecting rooms but by using strong girders and folding money he had been able to convince them of the soundness of his engineering.

By arrangement, Teal drove up in front of the Bailey residence the morning after their return to town. He improvised on his two-tone horn. Bailey stuck his head out of the front door. 'Why don't you use the bell?'

'Too slow,' answered Teal cheerfully. 'I'm a man of action. Is Mrs. Bailey ready? Ah, there you are, Mrs. Bailey! Welcome home, welcome home. Jump in, we've got a surprise for you!'

'You know Teal, my dear,' Bailey put in uncomfortably.

Mrs. Bailey sniffed. 'I know him. We'll go in our own car, Homer.'

'Certainly, my dear.'

'Good idea,' Teal agreed; ''sgot more power than mine; we'll get there faster. I'll drive, I know the way.' He took the keys from Bailey, slid into the driver's seat, and had the engine started before Mrs. Bailey could rally her forces.

'Never have to worry about my driving,' he assured Mrs. Bailey, turning his head as he did so, while he shot the powerful car down the avenue and swung on to Sunset Boulevard, 'it's a matter of power and control, a dynamic process, just my meat —I've never had a serious accident.'

'You won't have but one,' she said bitingly. 'Will you *please* keep your eyes on the traffic?'

He attempted to explain to her that a traffic situation was a matter, not of eyesight, but intuitive integration of courses, speeds, and probabilities, but Bailey cut him short. 'Where is the house, Quintus?'

'House?' asked Mrs. Bailey suspiciously. 'What's this about a house, Homer? Have you been up to something without telling me?'

Teal cut in with his best diplomatic manner. 'It certainly is a house, Mrs Bailey. And what a house? It's a surprise for you from a devoted husband. Just wait till you see it—'

'I shall,' she agreed grimly. 'What style is it?'

'This house sets a new style. It's later than television, newer than next week. It must be seen to be appreciated. By the way,' he went on rapidly, heading off any retort, 'did you folks feel the earthquake last night?'

'Just a little one,' Teal continued, 'about two a.m. If I hadn't been awake, I wouldn't have noticed it.'

Mrs. Bailey shuddered. 'Oh, this awful country! Do you hear that, Homer? We might have been killed in our beds and never have known it. Why did I ever let you persuade me to leave Iowa?'

'But my dear,' he protested hopelessly, 'you wanted to come out to California; you didn't like Des Moines.'

'We needn't go into that,' she said firmly. 'You are a man; you should anticipate such things. Earthquakes!'

'That's one thing you needn't fear in your new home, Mrs. Bailey,' Teal told her. 'It's absolutely earthquake-proof; every part is in perfect dynamic balance with every other part.'

'Well, I hope so. Where is this house?'

'Just around this bend. There's the sign now.' A large arrow sign, of the sort favoured by real estate promoters, proclaimed in letters that were large and bright even for southern California:

THE HOUSE OF THE FUTURE!!!

COLOSSAL—AMAZING—
REVOLUTIONARY

SEE HOW YOUR GRANDCHILDREN
WILL LIVE!

Q. Teal, Architect

'Of course that will be taken down,' he added hastily, noting her expression, 'as soon as you take possession.' He slued around the corner and brought the car to a squealing halt in front of the House of the Future. *'Voilà!'* He watched their faces for response.

Bailey stared unbelievingly, Mrs. Bailey in open dislike. They saw a simple cubical mass, possessing doors and windows, but no other architectural features, save that it was decorated in intricate mathematical designs. 'Teal,' Bailey asked slowly, 'what have you been up to?'

Teal turned from their faces to the house. Gone was the crazy tower with its jutting second-storey rooms. No trace remained of the seven rooms above ground floor level. Nothing remained but the single room that rested on the foundations. 'Great jumping cats!' he yelled, 'I've been robbed!'

He broke into a run.

But it did him no good. Front or back, the story was the same: the other seven rooms had disappeared, vanished completely. Bailey caught up with him, and took his arm. 'Explain yourself. What is this about being robbed? How come you built anything like this—it is not according to agreement.'

'But I didn't. I built just what we had planned to build, an eight-room house in the form of a developed tesseract. I've been sabotaged; that's what it is! Jealousy! The other architects in town didn't dare let me finish this job; they knew they'd be washed up if I did.'

'When were you last here?'

'Yesterday afternoon.'

'Everything all right then?'

'Yes. The gardeners were just finishing up.'

Bailey glanced around at the faultlessly manicured landscaping. 'I don't see how seven rooms could have been dismantled and carted away from here in a single night without wrecking this garden.'

Teal looked around, too. 'It doesn't look it. I don't understand it.'

Mrs Bailey joined them. 'Well? Well? Am I to be left to amuse myself? We might as well look it over as long as we are here, though I'm warning you, Homer, I'm not going to like it.'

'We might as well,' agreed Teal, and drew a key from his pocket with which he let them in the front door. 'We may pick up some clues.'

The entrance hall was in perfect order, the sliding screens that separated it from the garage space were back, permitting them to see the entire compartment. 'This looks all right,' observed Bailey. 'Let's go up on the roof and try to figure out what happened. Where's the staircase? Have they stolen that, too?'

'Oh, no,' Teal denied, 'look—' He pressed a button below the light switch; a panel in the ceiling fell away and a light, graceful flight of stairs swung noiselessly down. Its strength members were the frosty silver of duralumin, its treads and risers transparent plastic. Teal wriggled like a boy who has successfully performed a card trick, while Mrs. Bailey thawed perceptibly.

It was beautiful.

'Pretty slick,' Bailey admitted. 'Howsomever it doesn't seem to go any place—'

'Oh, that—' Teal followed his gaze. 'The cover lifts up as you approach the top. Open stair wells are anachronisms. Come on.' As predicted, the lid of the staircase got out of their way as they climbed the flight and permitted them to debouch at the top, but not, as they had expected, on the roof of the single room. They found themselves standing in the middle one of the five rooms which constituted the second floor of the original structure.

For the first time on record Teal had nothing to say. Bailey echoed him, chewing on his cigar. Everything was in perfect order. Before them, through open doorway and translucent partition lay the kitchen, a chef's dream of up-to-the-minute domestic engineering monel metal, continuous counter space, concealed lighting, functional arrangement. On the left the formal, yet gracious and hospitable dining room awaited guests, its furniture in parade-ground alignment.

Teal knew before he turned his head that the drawing room

and lounge would be found in equally substantial and impossible existence.

'Well, I must admit this *is* charming,' Mrs. Bailey approved, 'and the kitchen is just *too* quaint for words—though I would never have guessed from the exterior that this house had so much room upstairs. Of course *some* changes will have to be made. That secretary now—if we moved it over *here* and put the settle over *there*—'

'Stow it, Matilda,' Bailey cut in brusquely. 'Wha'd yuh make of it, Teal?'

'Why, Homer Bailey! The very id—'

'Stow it, I said. Well, Teal?'

The architect shuffled his rambling body. 'I'm afraid to say. Let's go on up.'

'How?'

'Like this.' He touched another button; a mate, in deeper colours, to the fairy bridge that had let them up from below offered them access to the next floor. They climbed it, Mrs. Bailey expostulating in the rear, and found themselves in the master bedroom. Its shades were drawn, as had been those on the level below, but the mellow lighting came on automatically. Teal at once activated the switch which controlled still another flight of stairs, and they hurried up into the top floor study.

'Look, Teal,' suggested Bailey when he had caught his breath, 'can we get to the roof above this room? Then we could look around.'

'Sure, it's an observatory platform.' They climbed a fourth flight of stairs, but when the cover at the top lifted to let them reach the level above, they found themselves, not on the roof, but *standing in the ground floor room where they had entered the house.*

Mr. Bailey turned a sickly grey. 'Angels in heaven,' he cried, 'this place is haunted. We're getting out of here.' Grabbing his wife he threw open the front door and plunged out.

Teal was too much preoccupied to bother with their departure. There was an answer to all this, an answer that he did not believe.

But he was forced to break off considering it because of hoarse shouts from somewhere above him. He lowered the staircase and rushed upstairs. Bailey was in the central room over Mrs. Bailey, who had fainted. Teal took in the situation, went to the bar built into the lounge, and poured three fingers of brandy, which he returned with and handed to Bailey. 'Here—this'll fix her up.'

Bailey drank it.

'That was for Mrs. Bailey,' said Teal.

'Don't quibble,' snapped Bailey. 'Get her another.' Teal took the precaution of taking one himself before returning with a dose earmarked for his client's wife. He found her just opening her eyes.

'Here, Mrs. Bailey,' he soothed, 'this will make you feel better.'

'I never touch spirits,' she protested, and gulped it.

'Now tell me what happened,' suggested Teal. 'I thought you two had left.'

'But we did—we walked out the front door and found ourselves up here, in the lounge.'

'The hell you say! Hm-m-m—wait a minute.' Teal went into the lounge. There he found that the big view window at the end of the room was open. He peered cautiously through it. He stared, not out at the California countryside, but into the ground floor room—or a reasonable facsimile thereof. He said nothing, but went back to the stair well which he had left open and looked down it. The ground floor room was still in place. Somehow, it managed to be in two different places at once, on different levels.

He came back into the central room and seated himself opposite Bailey in a deep, low chair, and sighted him past his upthrust bony knees. 'Homer,' he said impressively, 'do you know what has happened?'

'No, I don't—but if I don't find out pretty soon, something is going to happen and pretty drastic, too!'

'Homer, this is a vindication of my theories. This house is a real tesseract.'

'What's he talking about, Homer?'

'Wait, Matilda—now Teal, that's ridiculous. You've pulled some hanky-panky here and I won't have it—scaring Mrs. Bailey half to death, and making me nervous. All I want is to get out of here, with no more of your trapdoors and silly practical jokes.'

'Speak for yourself, Homer,' Mrs. Bailey interrupted, 'I was *not* frightened; I was just took all over queer for a moment. It's my heart; all of my people are delicate and highstrung. Now about this tessy thing—explain yourself, Mr. Teal. Speak up.'

He told her as well as he could in the face of numerous interruptions the theory back of the house. 'Now as I see it, Mrs. Bailey,' he concluded, 'this house, while perfectly stable in three dimensions, was not stable in four dimensions. I had built a house in the shape of an unfolded tesseract; something happened to it, same jar or side thrust, and it collapsed into its normal shape—it folded up.' He snapped his fingers suddenly. 'I've got it! The earthquake!'

'Earthquake?'

'Yes, yes, the little shake we had last night. From a four-dimensional standpoint this house was like a plane balanced on edge. One little push and it fell over, collapsed along its natural joints into a stable four-dimensional figure.'

'I thought you boasted about how safe this house was.'

'It *is* safe—three-dimensionally.'

'I don't call a house safe,' commented Bailey edgily, 'that collapses at the first little tremblor.'

'But look around you, man!' Teal protested. 'Nothing has been disturbed, not a piece of glassware cracked. Rotation through a fourth dimension can't affect a three-dimensional figure any more than you can shake letters off a printed page. If you had been sleeping in here last night, you would never have awakened.'

'That's just what I'm afraid of. Incidentally, has your great genius figured out any way for us to get out of this booby trap?'

'Huh? Oh, yes, you and Mrs. Bailey started to leave and landed back up here, didn't you? But I'm sure there is no real difficulty—we came in, we can go out. I'll try it.' He was up and hurrying downstairs before he had finished talking. He flung open the front door, stepped through, and found himself staring at his companions, down the length of the second floor lounge. 'Well, there does seem to be some slight problem,' he admitted blandly. 'A mere technicality, though—we can always go out a window.' He jerked aside the long drapes that covered the deep French windows set in one side wall of the lounge. He stopped suddenly.

'Hm-m-m,' he said, 'this is interesting—very.'

'What is?' asked Bailey, joining him.

'This.' The window stared directly into the dining room, instead of looking outdoors. Bailey stepped back to the corner where the lounge and the dining room joined the central room at ninety degrees.

'But that can't be,' he protested, 'that window is maybe fifteen, twenty feet from the dining room.'

'Not in a tesseract,' corrected Teal. 'Watch.' He opened the window and stepped through, talking back over his shoulder as he did so.

From the point of view of the Baileys he simply disappeared.

But not from his own viewpoint. It took him some seconds to catch his breath. Then he cautiously disentangled himself from the rosebush to which he had become almost irrevocably wedded, making a mental note the while never again to order landscaping which involved plants with thorns, and looked around him.

He was outside the house. The massive bulk of the ground floor room thrust up beside him. Apparently he had fallen off the roof.

He dashed around the corner of the house, flung open the front door and hurried up the stairs. 'Homer!' he called out, 'Mrs. Bailey! I've found a way out!'

Bailey looked annoyed rather than pleased to see him. 'What happened to you?'

'I fell out. I've been outside the house. You can do it just as easily—just step through those French windows. Mind the rose-bush, though—we may have to build another stairway.'

'How did you get back in?'

'Through the front door.'

'Then we shall leave the same way. Come, my dear.' Bailey set his hat firmly on his head and marched down the stairs, his wife on his arm.

Teal met them in the lounge. 'I could have told you that wouldn't work,' he announced. 'Now here's what we have to do: as I see it, in a four-dimensional figure a three-dimensional man has two choices every time he crosses a line of juncture, like a wall or a threshold. Ordinarily he will make a ninety-degree turn through the fourth dimension, only he doesn't feel it with his three dimensions. Look.' He stepped through the very window that he had fallen out of a moment before. Stepped through and arrived in the dining room, where he stood, still talking.

'I watched where I was going and arrived where I intended to.' He stepped back into the lounge. 'The time before I didn't watch and I moved on through normal space and fell out of the house. It must be a matter of subconscious orientation.'

'I'd hate to depend on subconscious orientation when I step out for the morning paper.'

'You won't have to; it'll become automatic. Now to get out of the house this time— Mrs. Bailey, if you will stand here with your back to the window, and jump backward, I'm pretty sure you will land in the garden.'

Mrs. Bailey's face expressed her opinion of Teal and his ideas. 'Homer Bailey,' she said shrilly, 'are you going to stand there and let him suggest such—'

'But Mrs. Bailey,' Teal attempted to explain, 'we can tie a rope on you and lower you down eas—'

'Forget it, Teal,' Bailey cut him off brusquely. 'We'll have to find a better way than that. Neither Mrs. Bailey nor I are fitted for jumping.'

Teal was temporarily nonplussed; there ensued a short silence. Bailey broke it with, 'Did you hear that, Teal?'

'Hear what?'

'Someone talking off in the distance. D'you s'pose there could be someone else in the house, playing tricks on us, maybe?'

'Oh, not a chance. I've got the only key.'

'But I'm sure of it,' Mrs. Bailey confirmed. 'I've heard them ever since we came in. Voices. Homer, I can't stand much more of this. Do something.'

'Now, now, Mrs. Bailey,' Teal soothed, 'don't get upset. There can't be anyone else in the house, but I'll explore and make sure. Homer, you stay here with Mrs. Bailey and keep an eye on the rooms on this floor.' He passed from the lounge into the ground floor room and from there to the kitchen and on into the bedroom. This led him back to the lounge by a straight-line route, that is to say, by going straight ahead on the entire trip he returned to the place from which he started.

'Nobody around,' he reported. 'I opened all of the doors and windows as I went—all except this one.' He stepped to the window opposite the one through which he had recently fallen and thrust back the drapes.

He saw a man with his back towards him, four rooms away. Teal snatched upon the French window and dived through it, shouting, 'There he goes now! Stop thief!'

The figure evidently heard him; it fled precipitately. Teal pursued, his gangling limbs stirred to unanimous activity, through drawing room, kitchen, dining room, lounge—room after room, yet in spite of Teal's best efforts he could not seem to cut down the four-room lead that the interloper had started with.

He saw the pursued jump awkwardly but actively over the low sill of a French window and in so doing knock off his hat. When he came up to the point where his quarry had lost his headgear, he stopped and picked it up, glad of an excuse to stop and catch his breath. He was back in the lounge.

'I guess he got away from me,' he admitted. 'Anyhow, here's his hat. Maybe we can identify him.'

Bailey took the hat, looked at it, then snorted, and slapped it on Teal's head. It fitted perfectly. Teal looked puzzled, took the hat off, and examined it. On the sweat band were the initials 'Q. T.' It was his own.

Slowly comprehension filtered through Teal's features. He went back to the French window and gazed down the series of rooms through which he had pursued the mysterious stranger. They saw him wave his arms semaphore fashion. 'What are you doing?' asked Bailey.

'Come see.' The two joined him and followed his stare with

their own. Four rooms away they saw the backs of three figures, two male and one female. The taller, thinner of the men was waving his arms in a silly fashion.

Mrs. Bailey screamed and fainted again.

Some minutes later, when Mrs. Bailey had been resuscitated and somewhat composed, Bailey and Teal took stock. 'Teal,' said Bailey, 'I won't waste any time blaming you; recriminations are useless and I'm sure you didn't plan for this to happen, but I suppose you realize we are in a pretty serious predicament. How are we going to get out of here? It looks now as if we would stay until we starve; every room leads into another room.'

'Oh, it's not that bad. I got out once, you know.'

'Yes, but you can't repeat it—you tried.'

'Anyhow we haven't tried all the rooms. There's still the study.'

'Oh, yes, the study. We went through there when we first came in, and didn't stop. Is it your idea that we might get out through its windows?'

'Don't get your hopes up. Mathematically, it ought to look into the four side rooms on this floor. Still we never opened the blinds; maybe we ought to look.'

''Twon't do any harm anyhow. Dear, I think you had best just stay here and rest—'

'Be left alone in this horrible place? I should say not!' Mrs. Bailey was up off the couch where she had been recuperating even as she spoke.

They went upstairs. 'This is the inside room, isn't it, Teal?' Bailey inquired as they passed through the master bedroom and climbed on up towards the study. 'I mean it was the little cube in your diagram that was in the middle of the big cube, and completely surrounded.'

'That's right,' agreed Teal. 'Well, let's have a look. I figure this window ought to give into the kitchen.' He grasped the cords of Venetian blinds and pulled them.

It did not. Waves of vertigo shook them. Involuntarily they fell to the floor and grasped helplessly at the pattern on the rug to keep from falling. 'Close it! Close it!' moaned Bailey.

Mastering in part a primitive atavistic fear, Teal worked his way back to the window and managed to release the screen. The window had looked *down* instead of *out,* down from a terrifying height.

Mrs. Bailey had fainted again.

Teal went back after more brandy while Bailey chafed her wrists. When she had recovered, Teal went cautiously to the window and raised the screen a crack. Bracing his knees, he studied the scene. He turned to Bailey. 'Come look at this, Homer. See if you recognize it.'

'You stay away from there, Homer Bailey!'

'Now, Matilda, I'll be careful.' Bailey joined him and peered out.

'See up there? That's the Chrysler Building, sure as shooting. And there's the East River, and Brooklyn.' They gazed straight down the sheer face of an enormously tall building. More than a thousand feet away a toy city, very much alive, was spread out before them. 'As near as I can figure it out, we are looking down the side of the Empire State Building from a point just above its tower.'

'What is it? A mirage?'

'I don't think so—it's too perfect. I think space is folded over through the fourth dimension here and we are looking past the fold.'

'You mean we aren't really seeing it?'

'No, we're seeing it all right. I don't know what would happen if we climbed out this window, but I for one don't want to try. But what a view! Oh, boy, what a view! Let's try the other windows.'

They approached the next window more cautiously, and it was well that they did, for it was even more disconcerting, more reason-shaking, than the one looking down the gasping height of the skyscraper. It was a simple seascape, open ocean and blue sky—but the ocean was where the sky should have been, and contrariwise. This time they were somewhat braced for it, but they felt seasickness about to overcome them at the sight of waves rolling overhead; they lowered the blind quickly without giving Mrs. Bailey a chance to be disturbed by it.

Teal looked at the third window. 'Game to try it, Homer?'

'Hrrumph—well, we won't be satisfied if we don't. Take it easy.' Teal lifted the blind a few inches. He saw nothing, and raised it a little more—still nothing. Slowly he raised it until the window was fully exposed. They gazed out at—nothing.

Nothing, nothing at all. What colour is nothing? Don't be silly! What shape is it? Shape is an attribute of *something*. It had neither depth nor form. It had not even blackness. It was *nothing*.

Bailey chewed at his cigar. 'Teal, what do you make of that?'

Teal's insouciance was shaken for the first time. 'I don't know, Homer, I don't rightly know—but I think that window ought to be walled up.' He stared at the lowered blind for a moment. 'I think maybe we looked at a place where space *isn't*. We looked around a fourth-dimensional corner and there wasn't anything here.' He rubbed his eyes. 'I've got a headache.'

They waited for a while before tackling the fourth window. Like an unopened letter, it might *not* contain bad news. The doubt left him. Finally the suspense stretched too thin and Bailey pulled the cord himself, in the face of his wife's protests.

It was not so bad. A landscape stretched away from them, right side up, and on such a level that the study appeared to be a ground floor room. But it was distinctly unfriendly.

A hot, hot sun beat down from lemon-coloured sky. The flat ground seemed burned a sterile, bleached brown and incapable of supporting life. Life there was, strange stunted trees that lifted knotted, twisted arms to the sky. Little clumps of spiky leaves grew on the outer extremities of these misshapen growths.

'Heavenly day,' breathed Bailey, 'where is that?'

Teal shook his head, his eyes troubled. 'It beats me.'

'It doesn't look like anything on Earth. It looks more like another planet—Mars, maybe.'

'I wouldn't know. But, do you know, Homer, it might be

worse than that, worse than another planet, I mean.'

'Huh? What's that you say?'

'It might be clear out of our space entirely. I'm not sure that that is our Sun at all. It seems too bright.'

Mrs. Bailey had somewhat timidly joined them and now gazed out at the outré scene. 'Homer,' she said in a subdued voice, 'those hideous trees—they frighten me.'

He patted her hand.

Teal fumbled with the window catch.

'What are you doing?' Bailey demanded.

'I thought if I stuck my head out the window I might be able to look around and tell a bit more.'

'Well—all right,' Bailey grudged, 'but be careful.'

'I will.' He opened the window a crack and sniffed. 'The air is all right, at least.' He threw it open wide.

His attention was diverted before he could carry out his plan. An uneasy tremor, like the first intimation of nausea, shivered the entire building for a long second, and was gone.

'Earthquake!' They all said it at once. Mrs. Bailey flung her arms around her husband's neck.

Teal gulped and recovered himself, saying:

'It's all right, Mrs. Bailey. This house is perfectly safe. You know you can expect settling tremors after a shock like last night.' He had just settled his features into an expression of reassurance when the second shock came. This one was no mild shimmy but the real seasick roll.

In every Californian, native born or grafted, there is a deep-rooted primitive reflex. An earthquake fills him with soul-shaking claustrophobia which impels him blindly to *get outdoors!* Model boy scouts will push aged grandmothers aside to obey it. It is a matter of record that Teal and Bailey landed on top of Mrs. Bailey. Therefore, she must have jumped through the window first. The order of precedence cannot be attributed to chivalry; it must be assumed that she was in readier position to spring.

They pulled themselves together, collected their wits a little, and rubbed sand from their eyes. Their first sensations were relief at feeling the solid sand of the desert land under them. Then Bailey noticed something that brought them to their feet and checked Mrs. Bailey from bursting into the speech that she had ready.

'Where's the house?'

It was gone. There was no sign of it at all. They stood in the centre of flat desolation, the landscape they had seen from the window. But, aside from the tortured, twisted trees there was nothing to be seen but the yellow sky and the luminary overhead, whose furnace-like glare was already almost insufferable.

Bailey looked slowly around, then turned to the architect. 'Well, Teal?' His voice was ominous.

Teal shrugged helplessly. 'I wish I knew. I wish I could even be sure that we were on Earth.'

'Well, we can't stand here. It's sure death if we do. Which direction?'

'Any, I guess. Let's keep a bearing on the Sun.'

They had trudged on for an undetermined distance when Mrs. Bailey demanded a rest. They stopped. Teal said in an aside to Bailey, 'Any ideas?'

'No . . . no, none. Say, do you hear anything?'

Teal listened. 'Maybe—unless it's my imagination.'

'Sounds like an automobile. Say, it *is* an automobile!'

They came to the highway in less than another hundred yards. The automobile, when it arrived, proved to be an elderly, puffing light truck, driven by a rancher. He crunched to a stop at their hail. 'We're stranded. Can you help us out?'

'Sure. Pile in.'

'Where are you headed?'

'Los Angeles.'

'Los Angeles? Say, where is this place?'

'Well, you're right in the middle of the Joshua-Tree National Forest.'

The return was as dispiriting as the Retreat from Moscow.

Mr. and Mrs. Bailey sat up in front with the driver while Teal bumped along in the body of the truck, and tried to protect his head from the Sun. Bailey subsidized the friendly rancher to detour to the tesseract house, not because they wanted to see it again, but in order to pick up their car.

At last the rancher turned the corner that brought them back to where they had started. But the house was no longer there.

There was not even the ground floor room. It had vanished. The Baileys, interested in spite of themselves, poked around the foundations with Teal.

'Got any answers for this one, Teal?' asked Bailey.

'It must be that on that last shock it simply fell through into another section of space. I can see now that I should have anchored it at the foundations.'

'That's not all you should have done.'

'Well, I don't see that there is anything to get downhearted about. The house was insured, and we've learned an amazing lot. There are possibilities, man, possibilities! Why, right now I've got a great new revolutionary idea for a house—'

Teal ducked in time. He was always a man of action.

'—AND HE BUILT A CROOKED HOUSE—'

Robert Heinlein, in this story, spends a good part of the beginning describing a tesseract. He does an excellent job, but words alone would go for nothing without a diagram. And even with a diagram, they go for very little. A three-dimensional structure would be bad enough for, as Heinlein says, this would merely be a distorted projection of the four-dimensional tesseract. A diagram on paper is a two-dimensional distorted projection of the three-dimensional distorted projection of a four-dimensional tesseract (see Figure 1).

The house described in the story as being in the shape of an 'opened-up' tesseract would look like Figure 2. The simpler analogue of an 'opened-up' cube is in Figure 3. If you cut out a shape like Figure 3 in thin cardboard and fold along the creases through the third dimension you can form a cube. Theoretically if you build a three-dimensional structure like Figure 2 and fold the eight cubes through the fourth dimension, you can form a tesseract.

The trouble is you can't actually fold the opened-up tesseract through the fourth dimension, either by means of an earthquake or anything else. A real tesseract in four spatial dimensions cannot exist in our three-dimensional world.

(At the time this story appeared in February 1941, by the way, Heinlein himself lived at 1776 Lookout Mountain Avenue' in Los Angeles, so that he himself is the 'Hermit of Hollywood' and in the first three paragraphs he is making himself the target for his own satire.)

Questions and Suggestions

1. From Figure 1, build the representation of a tesseract in three dimensions, using Tinker Toy materials. Compare it with a representation of a cube drawn in two dimensions. Are the distortions similar? Can you find the eight cubes (six of them distorted) in the tesseract structure?

2. The tesseract can also be called a 'hypercube'. In those terms what would a hypersphere be? You could also have a hypertetrahedron, a hyperellipsoid and so on. Indeed, you could have an entire four-dimensional geometry of 'hyperspace'. What can you find out about this four-dimensional geometry?

3. What do you suppose *n*-dimensional geometry is?

4. Heinlein says 'Time is *a* fourth dimension.' In what way is it a fourth dimension? Do purely three-dimensional objects have real existence in our world? What is an 'instantaneous cube'? How could you detect one? What effect would it have on its surroundings? Can something that can neither be detected nor affect its surroundings be said to exist?

5. If time is a fourth dimension, in what way does it differ from the other three? What are the units of measurement of time as compared with the other three? How does travel through time differ from travel through the other three? If you can

rotate an object through three dimensions, converting length into breadth and so on, could you rotate it through time also, making the length extend into the future, for instance?

6. In Einstein's theory of relativity, 'space-time' is an important concept. What is it?

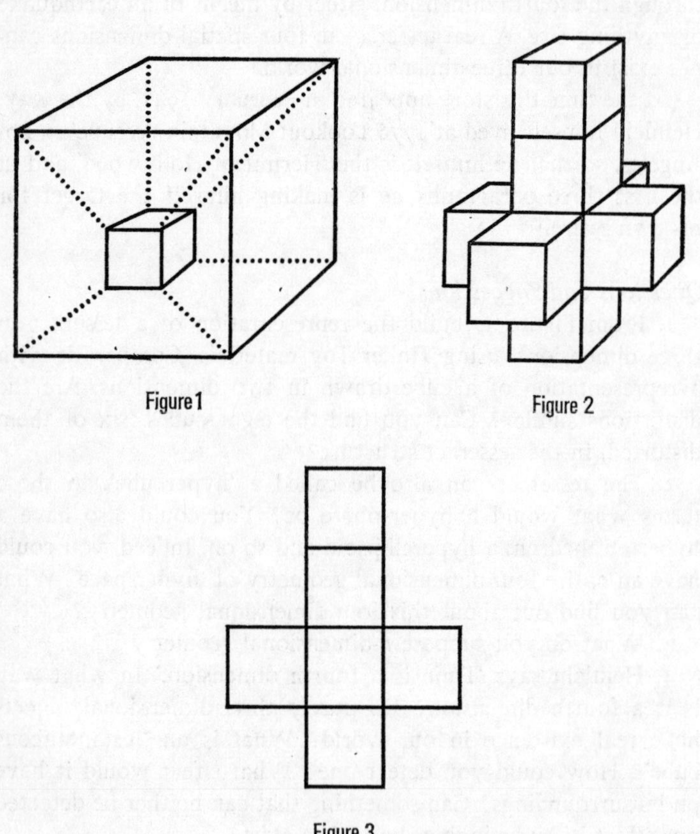

Figure 1

Figure 2

Figure 3

6. Proof

Hal Clement

Kron held his huge freighter motionless, feeling forward for outside contact. The tremendous interplay of magnetic and electrostatic fields just beyond the city's edge was as clearly perceptible to his senses as the city itself—a mile-wide disc ringed with conical field towers, stretching away behind and to each side. The ship was poised between two of the towers; immediately behind it was the field from which Kron had just taken off. The area was covered with cradles of various forms—cup-shaped receptacles which held city craft like Kron's own: long, boat-shaped hollows wherein reposed the cigarlike vessels which plied between the cities; and towering skeleton frameworks which held upright the slender double cones that hurtled across the dark, lifeless regions between stars.

Beyond the landing field was the city proper; the surface of the disc was covered with geometrically shaped buildings—cones, cylinders, prisms, and hemispheres, jumbled together.

Kron could 'see' all this as easily as a human being in an aeroplane can see New York; but no human eyes could have perceived this city, even if a man could have existed anywhere near it. The city, buildings and all, glowed a savage, white heat; and about and beyond it—a part of it, to human eyes—raged the equally dazzling, incandescent gases of the solar photosphere.

The freighter was preparing to launch itself into that fiery ocean; Kron was watching the play of the artificial reaction fields that supported the city, preparatory to plunging through them at a safe moment.

There was considerable risk of being flattened against the edge of the disc if an inauspicious choice was made, but Kron was an experienced flier, and slipped past the barrier with a sudden, hurtling acceleration that would have pulped any body of flesh and bone. The outer fringe of the field flung the globe sharply downward; then it was free, and the city was dwindling above them.

Kron and four others remained at their posts; the rest of the crew of thirty relaxed, their spherical bodies lying passive in the cuplike rests distributed through the ship, bathing in the fierce radiance on which those bodies fed, and which was continually streaming from a three-inch spheroid at the centre of the craft. That an artificial source of energy should be needed in such an environment may seem strange, but to these creatures the outer layers of the sun were far more inhospitable to life than is the stratosphere of Earth to human beings.

They had evolved far down near the solar core, where pressures and temperatures were such that matter existed in the 'collapsed' state characteristic of the entire mass of white dwarf stars. Their bodies were simply constructed: a matrix of close-packed electrons—really an unimaginably dense electrostatic field, possessing quasi-solid properties—surrounded a core of neutrons, compacted to the ultimate degree. Radiation of sufficient energy, falling on the 'skin', was stabilized, altered to the pattern and structure of neutrons; the tiny particles of neutronium which resulted were borne along a circulatory system—of magnetic fields, instead of blood—to the nucleus, where it was stored.

The race had evolved to the point where no material appendages were needed. Projected beams and fields of force were their limbs, powered by the annihilation of some of their own neutron substance. Their strange senses gave them awareness not only of electromagnetic radiation, permitting them to 'see' in a more or less normal fashion, but also of energies still undreamed of by human scientists. Kron, hundreds of miles below the city now, was still dimly aware of its location, though radio waves, light and gamma rays were all hopelessly fogged in the clouds of free electrons. At his goal, far down in the solar interior, 'seeing' conditions would be worse—anything more than a few hundred yards distant would be quite indetectable even to him.

Poised beside Kron, near the centre of the spheroidal sun ship, was another being. Its body was ovid in shape, like that of the Solarian, but longer and narrower, while the ends were tipped with pyramidal structures of neutronium, which projected through the 'skin'. A second, fainter static aura enveloped the creature outside the principal surface; and as the crew relaxed in their cups, a beam of energy from this envelope impinged on Kron's body. It carried a meaning, transmitting a clear thought from one being to the other.

'I still find difficulty in believing my senses,' stated the stranger. 'My own worlds revolve about another which is somewhat similar to this; but such a vast and tenuous atmosphere is most unlike conditions at home. Have you ever been away from Sol?'

'Yes,' replied Kron, 'I was once on the crew of an interstellar projectile. I have never seen your star, however; my acquaintance with it is entirely through hearsay. I am told it consists almost entirely of collapsed matter, like the core of our own; but there is practically no atmosphere. Can this be so? I should think, at the temperature necessary for life, gases would break free of the core and form an envelope.'

'They tend to do so, of course,' returned the other, 'but our surface gravity is immeasurably greater than anything you have here; even your core pull is less, since it is much less dense than our star. Only the fact that our worlds are small, thus causing a rapid diminution of gravity as one leaves them, makes it possible to get a ship away from them at all; atoms, with only their original velocities, remain within a few miles of the surface.

'But you remind me of my purpose on this world—to check certain points of a new theory concerning the possible behaviour of aggregations of normal atoms. That was why I arranged a trip on your flier; I have to make density, pressure, temperature, and a dozen other kinds of measurements at a couple of thousand different levels, in your atmosphere. While I'm doing it, would you mind telling me why you make these regular trips—and why, for that matter, you live so far above your natural level? I should think you would find life easier below, since there would be no need to remain in sealed buildings, or to expend such a terrific amount of power in supporting your cities.'

Kron's answer was slow.

'We make the journeys to obtain neutronium. It is impossible to convert enough power from the immediate neighbourhood of the cities to support them; we must descend periodically for more, even though our converters take so much as to lower the solar temperature considerably for thousands of miles around each city.

'The trips are dangerous—you should have been told that. We carry a crew of thirty, when two would be enough to man this ship, for we must fight, as well as fly. You spoke truly when you said that the lower regions of Sol are our natural home; but for æons we have not dared to make more than fleeting visits, to steal the power which is life to us.

'Your little worlds have been almost completely subjugated by your people, Sirian; they never had life forms sufficiently powerful to threaten your domination. But Sol, whose core alone is far larger than the Sirius B pair, did develop such creatures. Some are vast, stupid, slow-moving or immobile; others are semi-intelligent, and rapid movers; all are more than willing to ingest the ready-compacted neutronium of another living being.'

Kron's tale was interrupted for a moment, as the Sirian sent a ray probing out through the ship's wall, testing the physical state of the inferno beyond. A record was made, and the Solarian resumed.

'We, according to logical theory, were once just such a race

—of small intelligence, seeking the needs of life among a horde of competing organisms. Our greatest enemy was a being much like ourselves in size and power—just slightly superior in both ways. We were somewhat ahead in intelligence, and I suppose we owe them some thanks—without the competition they provided, we should not have been forced to develop our minds to their present level. We learned to co-operate in fighting them, and from that came the discovery that many of us together could handle natural forces that a single individual could not even approach, and survive. The creation of force effects that had no counterpart in nature was the next step; and, with the understanding of them, our science grew.

'The first cities were of neutronium, like those of today, but it was necessary to stabilize the neutrons with fields of energy; at core temperature, as you know, neutronium is a gas. The cities were spherical and much smaller than our present ones. For a long time, we managed to defend them.

'But our enemies evolved, too; not in intelligence, but in power and fecundity. With overspecialization of their physical powers, their mentalities actually degenerated; they became little more than highly organized machines, driven, by an age-old enmity towards our race, to seek us out and destroy us. Their new powers at last enabled them to neutralize, by brute force, the fields which held our cities in shape; and then it was that, from necessity, we fled to the wild, inhospitable upper regions of Sol's atmosphere. Many cities were destroyed by the enemy before a means of supporting them was devised; many more fell victims to forces which we generated, without being able to control, in the effort. The dangers of our present-day trips seem trivial beside those our ancestors braved, in spite of the fact that ships not infrequently fail to return from their flights. Does that answer your question?'

The Sirian's reply was hesitant. 'I guess it does. You of Sol must have developed far more rapidly than we, under that drive; your science, I know, is superior to ours in certain ways, although it was my race which first developed space flight.'

'You had greater opportunities in that line,' returned Kron.

'Two small stars, less than a diameter apart, circling a larger one at a distance incomparably smaller than the usual interstellar interval, provided perfect ground for experimental flights; between your world and mine, even radiation requires some one hundred and thirty rotations to make the journey, and even the nearest other star is almost half as far.

'But enough of this—history is considered by too many to be a dry subject. What brings you on a trip with a power flier? You certainly have not learned anything yet which you could not have been told in the city.'

During the conversation, the Sirian had periodically tested the atmosphere beyond the hull. He spoke, rather absently, as though concentrating on something other than his words.

'I would not be too sure of that, Solarian. My measurements are of greater delicacy than we have ever before achieved. I am looking for a very special effect, to substantiate or disprove an hypothesis which I have recently advanced—much to the detriment of my prestige. If you are interested, I might explain: laugh afterwards if you care to—you will not be the first.

'The theory is simplicity itself. It has occurred to me that matter—ordinary substances like iron and calcium—might actually take on solid form, like neutronium, under the proper conditions. The normal gas, you know, consists of minute particles travelling with considerable speed in all directions. There seems to be no way of telling whether or not these atoms exert appreciable forces on each other; but it seems to me that if they were brought closely enough together, or slowed down sufficiently, some such effects might be detected.'

'How and why?' asked Kron. 'If the forces are there, why should they not be detectable under ordinary conditions?'

'Tiny changes in velocity due to mutual attraction or repulsion would scarcely be noticed, when the atomic speeds are of the order of hundreds of kilometers per second,' returned the Sirian. 'The effects I seek to detect are of a different nature. Consider, please. We know the sizes of the various atoms, from their radiations. We also know that, under normal conditions, a given mass of any particular gas fills a certain volume. If, however, we surround this gas with an impenetrable container and exert pressure, that volume decreases. We would expect that decrease to be proportional to the pressure, except for an easily determined constant due to the size of the atoms, if no interatomic forces existed; to detect such forces, I am making a complete series of pressure-density tests, more delicate than any heretofore, from the level of your cities down to the neutron core of your world.

'If we could reduce the kinetic energy of the atoms—slow down their motions of translation—the task would probably be simpler; but I see no way to accomplish that. Perhaps, if we could negate nearly all of that energy, the interatomic forces would actually hold the atoms in definite relative positions, approximating the solid state. It was that somewhat injudicious and perhaps too imaginative suggestion which caused my whole idea to be ridiculed on Sirius.'

The ship dropped several hundred miles in the few seconds before Kron answered; since gaseous friction is independent of change in density, the high pressures of the regions being penetrated would be no bar to high speed of flight. Unfortunately, the viscosity of a gas does increase directly as the square root of its temperature; and at the lower levels of the sun, travel would be slow.

'Whether or not our scientists will listen to you, I cannot say,' said Kron finally. 'Some of them are a rather imaginative crowd, I guess, and none of them will ignore any data you may produce.

'I do not laugh, either. My reason will certainly interest you, as your theory intrigues me. It is the first time anyone has accounted even partly for the things that happened to us on one of my flights.'

The other members of the crew shifted slightly on their cradles; a ripple of interest passed through them, for all had heard rumours and vague tales of Kron's time in the space carrier fleets. The Sirian settled himself more comfortably; Kron dimmed the central globe of radiance a trifle, for the outside temperature was now considerably higher, and began the tale.

'This happened towards the end of my career in space. I had made many voyages with the merchant and passenger vessels, had been promoted from the lowest ranks, through many rotations, to the post of independent captain. I had my own cruiser —a special long-period explorer, owned by the Solarian government. She was shaped like our modern interstellar carriers, consisting of two cones, bases together, with the field ring just forward of their meeting point. She was larger than most, being designed to carry fuel for exceptionally long flights.

'Another cruiser, similar in every respect, was under the command of a comrade of mine, named Akro; and the two of us were commissioned to transport a party of scientists and explorers to the then newly discovered Fourth System, which lies, as you know, nearly in the plane of the Solar equator, but about half again as distant as Sirius.

'We made good time, averaging nearly half the speed of radiation, and reached the star with a good portion of our hulls still unconsumed. We need not have worried about that, in any case; the star was denser even than the Sirius B twins, and neutronium was very plentiful. I restocked at once, plating my inner walls with the stuff until they had reached their original thickness, although experience indicated that the original supply was ample to carry us either back to Sol, to Sirius, or to Procyon B.

'Akro, at the request of the scientists, did not refuel. Life was present on the star, as it seems to be on all stars where the atomic velocities and the density are high enough; and the biologists wanted to bring back specimens. That meant that room would be needed, and if Akro replated his walls to normal thickness that room would be lacking—as I have mentioned, these were special long-range craft, and a large portion of their volume consisted of available neutronium.

'So it happened that the other ship left the Fourth System with a low, but theoretically sufficient, stock of fuel, and half a dozen compartments filled with specimens of alien life. I kept within detection distance at all times, in case of trouble, for some of those life forms were as dangerous as those of Sol, and, like them, all consumed neutronium. They had to be kept well under control to safeguard the very walls of the ship, and it is surprisingly difficult to make a wild beast, surrounded by food, stay on short rations.

'Some of the creatures proved absolutely unmanageable; they had to be destroyed. Others were calmed by lowering the atomic excitation of their compartments, sending them into a stupor; but the scientists were reluctant to try that in most cases, since not all of the beings could stand such treatment.

'So, for nearly four hundred Solar rotations, Akro practically fought his vessel across space—fought successfully. He managed on his own power until we were within a few hundred diameters of Sol; but I had to help him with the landing—or try to, for the landing was never made.

'It may seem strange, but there is a large volume of space in the neighbourhood of the Sun which is hardly ever traversed. The normal landing orbit arches high over one of the poles of rotation, enters atmosphere almost tangentially somewhere between that pole and the equator, and kills as much as remains of the ship's velocity in the outer atmospheric layers. There is a minimum of magnetic interference that way, since the flier practically coasts along the lines of force of the Solar magnetic field.

'As a result, few ships pass through the space near the plane of the Solar equator. One or two may have done so before us, and I know of several that searched the region later; but none encountered the thing which we found.

'About the time we would normally have started correcting our orbits for a tangential landing. Akro radiated me the information that he could not possibly control his ship any farther with the power still available to him. His walls were already so thin that radiation loss, ordinarily negligible, was becoming a definite menace to his vessel. All his remaining energy would have to be employed in keeping the interior of his ship habitable.

'The only thing I could do was to attach our ships together with an attractor beam, and make a nearly perpendicular drop to Sol. We would have to take our chances with magnetic and electrostatic disturbances in the city-supporting fields which cover so much of the near-equatorial zones, and try to graze the nucleus of the Sun instead of its outer atmosphere, so that Akro could replenish his rapidly failing power.

'Akro's hull was radiating quite perceptibly now; it made an easy target for an attractor. We connected without difficulty, and our slightly different linear velocities caused us to revolve about each other, pivoting on the centre of mass of our two ships. I cut off my driving fields, and we fell spinning towards Sol.

'I was becoming seriously worried about Akro's chances of survival. The now-alarming energy loss through his almost consumed hull threatened to exhaust his supply long before we reached the core; and we were still more than a hundred diameters out. I could not give him any power; we were revolving about each other at a distance of about one tenth of a Solar diameter. To lessen that distance materially would increase our speed of revolution to a point where the attractor could not overcome centrifugal force; and I had neither power nor time to perform the delicate job of exactly neutralizing our rotary momentum without throwing us entirely off course. All we could do was hope.

'We were somewhere between one hundred and one hundred and fifty diameters out when there occurred the most peculiar phenomenon I have ever encountered. The plane of revolution of our two ships passed near Sol, but was nearly perpendicular to the Solar equator; at the time of which I speak, Akro's ship was almost directly between my flier and the Sun. Observations had just shown that we were accelerating Sunward at an unexpectedly high pace, when a call came from Akro.

'"Kron! I am being pulled away from your attractor! There is a large mass somewhere near, for the pull is gravitational, but it emits no radiation that I can detect. Increase your pull, if you can; I cannot possibly free myself alone."

'I did what I could, which was very little. Since we did not know the location of the disturbing dark body, it was impossible to tell just what I should do to avoid bringing my own or Akro's vessel too close. I think now that if I had released him immediately he would have swung clear, for the body was not large, I believe. Unfortunately, I did the opposite, and nearly lost my own ship as well. Two of my crew were throwing as much power as they could convert and handle into the attractor, and trying to hold it on the still easily visible hull of Akro's ship; but the motions of the latter were so peculiar that aiming was a difficult task. They held the ship as long as we could see it; but quite suddenly the radiations by means of which we perceived the vessel faded out, and before we could find a band which would get through, the sudden cessation of our centripetal acceleration told us that the beam had slipped from its target.

'We found that electromagnetic radiations of wave lengths in the octave above H-alpha would penetrate the interference, and Akro's hull was leaking energy enough to radiate in that band. When we found him, however, we could scarcely believe our senses; his velocity was now nearly at right angles to his former course, and his hull radiation had become far weaker. What terrific force had caused this acceleration, and what strange field was blanketing the radiation, were questions none of us could answer.

'Strain as we might, not one of us could pick up an erg of radiant energy that might emanate from the thing that had trapped Akro. We could only watch, and endeavour to plot his course relative to our own, at first. Our ships were nearing each other rapidly and we were attempting to determine the time and distance of closest approach, when we were startled by the impact of a communicator beam. Akro was alive! The beam was weak, very weak, showing what an infinitesimal amount of power he felt he could spare. His words were not encouraging.

'"Kron! You may as well cut your attractor, if you are still trying to catch me. No power that I dare apply seems to move me perceptibly in any direction from this course. We are all badly shocked, for we hit something that felt almost solid. The walls, even, are strained, and may go at any time."

'"Can you perceive anything around you?" I returned. "You seem to us to be alone in space, though something is absorbing most of your radiated energy. There must be energies in the cosmos of which we have never dreamed, simply because they did not affect our senses. What do your scientists say?"

'"Very little," was the answer. "They have made a few tests, but they say that anything they project is absorbed without reradiating anything useful. We seem to be in a sort of energy vacuum—it takes everything, and returns nothing."

'This was the most alarming item yet. Even in free space, we had been doubtful of Akro's chances of survival; now they seemed reduced to the ultimate zero.

'Meanwhile, our ships were rapidly approaching each other. As nearly as my navigators could tell, both vessels were pursuing almost straight lines in space. The lines were nearly perpendicular but did not lie in a common plane; their minimum distance apart was about one one-thousandth of a Solar diameter. His velocity seemed nearly constant, while I was accelerating Sunward. It seemed that we would reach the near-intersection point almost simultaneously, which meant that my ship was certain to approach the energy vacuum much too closely. I did not dare to try to pull Akro free with an attractor; it was only too obvious that such an attempt could end in disaster for both vessels. If he could not free himself, he was lost.

'We could only watch helplessly as the point of light marking the position of Akro's flier swept closer and closer. At first, as I have said, it seemed perfectly free in space; but as we looked, the region around it began to radiate feebly. There was nothing recognizable about the vibrations, simply a continuous spectrum, cut off by some interference just below the H-alpha wave length and, at the other end, some three octaves higher. As the emission grew stronger, the visible region around the stranded ship grew larger, fading into nothingness at the edges.

Brighter and broader the path of radiance grew, as we swept towards it.'

That same radiance was seriously inconveniencing Gordon Aller, who was supposed to be surveying for a geological map of northern Australia. He was camped by the only waterhole in many miles, and had stayed up long after dark preparing his cameras, barometer, soil kit, and other equipment for the morrow's work.

The arrangement of instruments completed, he did not at once retire to his blankets. With his back against a smooth rock and a short, blackened pipe clenched in his teeth, he sat for some time, pondering. The object of his musing does not matter to us; though his eyes were directed heavenward, he was sufficiently accustomed to the southern sky to render it improbable that he was paying much attention to its beauties.

However that may be, his gaze was suddenly attracted to the zenith. He had often seen stars which appeared to move when near the edge of his field of vision—it is a common illusion; but this one continued to shift as he turned his eyes upwards.

Not far from Achernar was a brilliant white point, which brightened as Aller watched it. It was moving slowly northwards, it seemed; but only a moment was needed for the man to realize that the slowness was illusory. The thing was slashing almost vertically downwards at an enormous speed, and must strike Earth not far from his camp.

Aller was not an astronomer, and had no idea of astronomical distances or speeds. He may be forgiven for thinking of the object as travelling perhaps as fast as a modern fighting plane, and first appearing at a height of two or three miles. The natural conclusion from this belief was that the crash would occur within a few hundred feet of the camp. Aller paled; he had seen pictures of the Devil's Pit in Arizona.

Actually, of course, the meteor first presented itself to his gaze at a height of some eighty miles, and was then travelling at a rate of many miles per second relative to Earth. At that speed, the air presented a practically solid obstacle to its flight, and the object was forced to a fairly constant velocity of ten or twelve hundred yards a second while still nearly ten miles from Earth's surface. It was at that point that Aller's eyes caught up with and succeeded in focusing upon the celestial visitor.

The first burst of light had been radiated by the frightfully compressed and heated air in front of the thing; as the original velocity departed, so did the dazzling light. Aller got a clear view of the meteor at a range of less than five miles, for perhaps ten seconds before the impact. It was still incandescent, radiating a bright cherry-red; this must have been due to the loss from within, for so brief a contact even with such highly heated air could not have warmed the Sun ship's neutronium walls a measurable fraction of a degree.

Aller felt the ground tremble as the vessel struck. A geyser of earth, barely visible in the reddish light of the hull, spouted skyward, to fall back seconds later with a long-drawn-out rumble. The man stared at the spot, two miles away, which was still giving off a faint glow. Were 'shooting stars' as regularly shaped as that? He had seen a smooth, slender body, more than a hundred feet in length, apparently composed of two cones of unequal length, joined together at the bases. Around the longer cone, not far from the point of juncture, was a thick bulging ring; no further details were visible at the distance from which he had observed. Aller's vague recollections of meteorites, seen in various museums, brought images of irregular, clinker-like objects before his mind's eye. What, then, could this thing be?

He was not imaginative enough to think for a moment of any possible extraterrestrial source for an aircraft; when it did occur to him that the object was of artificial origin, he thought more of some experimental machine produced by one of the more progressive Earth nations.

At the thought, Aller strapped a first-aid kit to his side and set out towards the crater, in the face of the obvious fact that nothing human could possibly have survived such a crash. He stumbled over the uneven terrain for a quarter of a mile, and then stopped on a small rise of ground to examine more closely the site of the wreck.

The glow should have died by this time, for Aller had taken all of ten minutes to pick his way those few hundred yards; but the dull-red light ahead had changed to a brilliant-orange radiance against which the serrated edges of the pit were clearly silhouetted. No flames were visible; whence came the increasing heat? Aller attempted to get closer, but a wave of frightfully hot air blistered his face and hands, and drove him back. He took up a station near his former camp, and watched.

If the hull of the flier had been anywhere near its normal thickness, the tremendous mass of neutronium would have sunk through the hardest of rocks as though they were liquid. There was, however, scarcely more than a paper thickness of the substance at any part of the walls; and an upthrust of adamantine volcanic rock not far beneath the surface of the desert proved thick enough to absorb the Sun ship's momentum and to support its still enormous weight. Consequently, the ship was covered only by a thin layer of powdered rock which had fallen back into the crater. The disturbances arising from the now extremely rapid loss of energy from Akro's ship were, as a result, decidedly visible from the surface.

The hull, though thin, was still intact; but its temperature was now far above the melting point of the surrounding rocks. The thin layer of pulverized material above the ship melted and flowed away almost instantly, permitting free radiation to the air above; and so enormous is the specific heat of neutronium that no perceptible lowering of hull temperature occurred.

Aller, from his point of observation, saw the brilliant fan of light that sprang from the pit as the flier's hull was exposed—the vessel itself was invisible to him, since he was only slightly above the level of the crater's mouth. He wondered if the impact of the 'meteor' had released some pent-up volcanic energy, and began to doubt, quite justifiably, if he was at a safe distance. His doubts vanished and were replaced by certainty as the edges of the crater began to glow dull-red, then bright-orange, and slowly subsided out of sight. He began packing the most valuable items of his equipment, while a muted, continuous roaring and occasional heavy thuds from the direction of the pit admonished him to hasten.

When he straightened up, with the seventy-pound pack settled on his shoulders, there was simply a lake of lava where the crater had been. The fiery area spread even as he watched; and without further delay he set off on his own back trail. He could see easily, by the light diffused from the inferno behind him; and he made fairly good time, considering his burden and the fact that he had not slept since the preceding night.

The rock beneath Akro's craft was, as we have said, extremely hard. Since there was relatively free escape upward for the constantly liberated energy, the stratum melted very slowly, gradually letting the vessel sink deeper into the earth. What would have happened if Akro's power supply had been greater is problematical; Aller can tell us only that some five hours after the landing, as he was resting for a few moments near the top of a rocky hillock, the phenomenon came to a cataclysmic end.

A quivering of the earth beneath him caused the surveyor to look back towards his erstwhile camp. The lake of lava, which by this time was the better part of a mile in breadth, seemed curiously agitated. Aller, from his rather poor vantage point, could see huge bubbles of pasty lava hump themselves up and burst, releasing brilliant clouds of vapour. Each cloud illuminated Earth and sky before cooling to invisibility, so that the effect was somewhat similar to a series of lightning flashes.

For a short time—certainly no longer than a quarter of a minute—Aller was able to watch as the activity increased. Then a particularly violent shock almost flung him from the hilltop, and at nearly the same instant the entire volume of molten rock fountained skyward. For an instant it seemed to hang there, a white, raging pillar of liquid and gas; then it dissolved, giving way before the savage thrust of the suddenly released energy below. A tongue of radiance, of an intensity indescribable in mere words, stabbed upwards, into and through the lava, volatizing instantly. A dozen square miles of desert glowed white, then an almost invisible violet, and disappeared in superheated gas. Around the edges of this region, great gouts of lava and immense fragments of solid rock were hurled to all points of the compass.

Radiation exerts pressure; at the temperature found in the cores of stars, that pressure must be measured in thousands of tons per square inch. It was this thrust, rather than the by no means negligible gas pressure of the boiling lava, which wrought most of the destruction.

Aller saw little of what occurred. When the lava was hurled upwards, he had flung an arm across his face to protect his eyes from the glare. That act unquestionably saved his eyesight, as the real flash followed; as it was, his body was seared and blistered through the clothing. The second, heavier shock knocked his feet from under him, and he half crawled, half rolled down to the comparative shelter of the little hill. Even here, gusts of hot air almost choked him; only the speed with which the phenomenon ended saved his life.

Within minutes, both the tremblors and hot winds had ceased; and he crawled painfully to the hilltop again to gaze wonderingly at the five-mile-wide crater, ringed by a pile of tumbled, still glowing rock fragments.

Far beneath that pit, shards of neutronium, no more able to remain near the surface than the steel pieces of a wrecked ocean vessel can float on water, were sinking through rock and metal to a final resting place at Earth's heart.

'The glow spread as we watched, still giving no clue to the nature of the substance radiating it,' continued Kron. 'Most of it seemed to originate between us and Akro's ship; Akro himself said that but little energy was being lost on the far side. His messages, during that last brief period as we swept by our point of closest approach, were clear—so clear that we could almost see as he did the tenuous light beyond the ever-thinning walls of his ship; the light that represented but a tiny percentage of the energy being sucked from the hull surface.

'We saw, as though with his own senses, the tiny perforation appear near one end of the ship; saw it extend, with the speed of thought, from one end of the hull to the other, permitting the free escape of all the energy in a single instant; and, from our point of vantage, saw the glowing area where the ship had been suddenly brightened, blazing for a moment almost as brightly as a piece of Sun matter.

'In that moment, every one of us saw the identifying frequencies as the heat from Akro's disrupted ship raised the substance which had trapped him to an energy level which permitted atomic radiation. Every one of us recognized the spectra of iron, of calcium, of carbon and silicon and a score of the other elements—Sirian, I tell you that that "trapping field" was *matter*—matter in such a state that it could not radiate, and could offer resistance to other bodies in exactly the fashion of a solid. I thought, and have always thought, that some strange field of force held the atoms in their "solid" positions; you have convinced me that I was wrong. The "field" was the sum of the interacting atomic forces which you are trying to detect. The energy level of that material body was so low that those forces were able to act without interference. The condition you could not conceive of reaching artificially actually exists in nature!'

'You go too fast, Kron,' responded the Sirian. 'Your first idea is far more likely to be the true one. The idea of unknown radiant or static force fields is easy to grasp; the one you propose in its place defies common sense. My theories called for some such conditions as you described; granted the one premise of a sufficiently low energy level; but a place in the real universe so devoid of energy as to absorb that of a well-insulated interstellar flier is utterly inconceivable. I have assumed your tale to be true as to details, though you offer neither witnesses nor records to support it; but I seem to have heard that you have somewhat of a reputation as an entertainer, and you seem quick-witted enough to have woven such a tale on the spot, purely from the ideas I suggested. I compliment you on the tale, Kron; it was entrancing; but I seriously advise you not to make anything more out of it. Shall we leave it at that, my friend?'

'As you will,' replied Kron.

PROOF

Naturally we associate life with the planet Earth. If we think of life on other planets, we think of it on other worlds something like the Earth. Even if the chemistry of the other worlds are different from that of our planet, at least the other worlds are solid.

Can we really think of life on the Sun?

About 1800 the most renowned astronomer in the world was Sir William Herschel who had discovered the planet Uranus, who had studied double stars and globular clusters, who had even estimated the size and shape of the Galaxy. His opinions, therefore, were to be taken seriously.

Herschel wondered if the sunspots might not be holes in the flaming atmosphere of the Sun and if, through these holes, the cold solid body beneath might not be glimpsed. He wondered if there might not be inhabitants on that solid underpinning.

We now know that is not so; that the atmosphere of the Sun, far from being hotter than the regions beneath, is actually the very coolest part of the Sun and that the Sun's deeper layers are enormously hot.

If, then, life were conceivable on the Sun, it would have to be a life associated with matter in the form of great heat, which, in actual fact is the common state of matter in the Universe. In our Solar system, for instance, 99.85 per cent of all the matter present is hot and gaseous, with a temperature of 6000°C. and up. This is the Sun. All the rest of the Solar system—the planets, satellites, asteroids, comets and so on—is comparatively cool at the surface but makes up only 0.15 per cent of all the matter.

If this represents the general division in the rest of the Universe, we might well say that cold, solid matter represents so small a portion of the total that it might well be ignored.

To imagine structures so complex that they can support

something analogous to what we call life, and even intelligence, under conditions as alien as that of the Sun, and to do so with scientific plausibility, is no easy task. Hal Clement (his real name is Harry Clement Stubbs) is up to it. This was his first published story, appearing when he was barely out of his teens, and he soon became one of the most prominent of the strictly scientific s.f. writers. (He is now science teacher at Milton Academy, with emphasis on astrology.)

Questions and Suggestions

1. Clement speaks of 'neutronium' in the centres of stars, matter made up of neutrons in contact. What are neutrons? Where are they to be found? How and under what conditions would they come together to form neutronium?

2. What is the average width of an atom and the width of a neutron? How would an atom compare with a neutron in volume? If the matter in the Sun were converted into neutronium, how big would the Sun be in diameter?

3. Clement speaks of two small stars, very close together, circling each other and both circling Sirius itself. Actually, Sirius does have a small companion that was discovered before it was seen. How is it possible for this to happen? What kind of a star is this small companion? It is always assumed that the dwarf companion is only a single star; if it were really a closely spaced double star, as Clement suggests, how could we detect the fact?

4. Clement gives distances as such-and-such a multiple of the Sun's diameter. Is that better than giving them as miles or kilometres, or worse? Why?

5. Clement mentions that the cities use up so much energy 'as to lower the Solar temperature considerably for thousands of miles around each city'. This seems to be a reference to sunspots though Clement doesn't say so specifically. Look up the properties of sunspots and decide whether any of them might be consistent with this notion. Is there anything about the behaviour of sunspots in your opinion which is consistent with this far-out suggestion?

6. *Proof* was published in June 1942. When Clement has an

Earthman spot the falling star-vessel he says of the Earthman, 'He was not imaginative enough to think for a moment of any possible extraterrestrial source for an aircraft ...' Would Clement have said this if he had written the story ten years later? What happened in the next decade that would have completely altered human reactions to a strange sight in the sky? What would *you* think if you saw a strange gleaming shape in the sky that looked like a ship?

7. What is the significance of the title of the story?

7. A Subway Named Mobius

A. J. Deutsch

In a complex and ingenious pattern, the subway had spread out from a focus at Park Street. A shunt connected the Lechmere line with the Ashmont for trains southbound, and with the Forest Hills line for those northbound. Harvard and Brookline had been linked with a tunnel that passed through Kenmore Under, and during rush hours every other train was switched through the Kenmore Branch back to Egleston. The Kenmore Branch joined the Maverick Tunnel near Fields Corner. It climbed a hundred feet in two blocks to connect Copley Over with Scollay Square; then it dipped down again to join the Cambridge line at Boylston. The Boylston shuttle had finally tied together the seven principal lines on four different levels. It went into service, you remember, on March 3rd. After that, a train could travel from any one station to any other station in the whole system.

There were two hundred and twenty-seven trains running the subways every weekday, and they carried about a million and a half passengers. The Cambridge-Dorchester train that disappeared on March 4th was Number 86. Nobody missed it at first. During the evening rush, the traffic was a little heavier than usual on that line. But a crowd is a crowd. The ad. posters at the Forest Hills yards looked for 86 about 7.30, but neither of them mentioned its absence until three days later. The controller at the Milk Street Cross-Over called the Harvard checker for an extra train after the hockey game that night, and the Harvard checker relayed the call to the yards. The dispatcher there sent out 87, which had been put to bed at ten o'clock, as usual. He didn't notice that 86 was missing.

It was near the peak of the rush the next morning that Jack O'Brien, at the Park Street Control, called Warren Sweeney at the Forest Hills yards and told him to put another train on the Cambridge run. Sweeney was short, so he went to the board and scanned it for a spare train and crew. Then, for the first time, he noticed that Gallagher had not checked out the night before. He put the tag up and left a note. Gallagher was due on at ten. At ten-thirty, Sweeney was down looking at the board again, and he noticed Gallagher's tag still up, and the note where he had left it. He groused to the checker and asked if Gallagher had come in late. The checker said he hadn't seen Gallagher at all that morning. Then Sweeney wanted to know who was running 86? A few minutes later he found that Dorkin's card was still up, although it was Dorkin's day off. It was 11.30 before he finally realized that he had lost a train.

Sweeney spent the next hour and a half on the phone, and he quizzed every dispatcher, controller, and checker on the whole system. When he finished his lunch at 1.30, he covered the whole net again. At 4.40, just before he left for the day, he reported the matter, with some indignation, to Central Traffic. The phones buzzed through the tunnels and shops until nearly midnight before the general manager was finally notified at his home.

It was the engineer on the main switchbank who, late in the morning on the 6th, first associated the missing train with the newspaper stories about the sudden rash of missing persons. He tipped off the *Transcript*, and by the end of the lunch hour three papers had Extras on the streets. That was the way the story got out.

Kelvin Whyte, the general manager, spent a good part of that afternoon with the police. They checked Gallagher's wife, and Dorkin's. The motorman and the conductor had not been home since the morning of the 4th. By mid-afternoon, it was clear to the police that three hundred and fifty Bostonians, more or less, had been lost with the train. The System buzzed, and Whyte nearly expired with simple exasperation. But the train was not found.

Roger Tupelo, the Harvard mathematician, stepped into the picture the evening of the 6th. He reached Whyte by phone, late, at his home, and told him he had some ideas about the missing train. Then he taxied to Whyte's home in Newton and had the first of many talks with Whyte about Number 86.

Whyte was an intelligent man, a good organizer, and not without imagination. 'But I don't know what you're talking about!' he expostulated.

Tupelo was resolved to be patient. 'This is a very hard thing for *anybody* to understand, Mr. Whyte, he said. 'I can see why you are puzzled. But it's the only explanation. The train has vanished, and the people on it. But the System is closed. Trains are conserved. It's somewhere on the System!'

Whyte's voice grew louder again. 'And I tell you, Dr. Tupelo, that train is *not* on the System! It is *not*! You can't overlook a seven-car train carrying four hundred passengers. The System has been combed. Do you think I'm trying to *hide* the train?'

'Of course not. Now look, let's be reasonable. We know the train was en route to Cambridge at 8.40 a.m. on the 4th. At least twenty of the missing people probably boarded the train a few minutes earlier at Washington, and forty more at Park Street Under. A few got off at both stations. And that's the last. The ones who were going to Kendall, to Central, to Harvard—they never got there. The train did not get to Cambridge.'

'I know that, Dr. Tupelo,' Whyte said savagely. 'In the tunnel under the Charles River, the train turned into a boat. It left the tunnel and sailed for Africa.'

'No, Mr. Whyte. I'm trying to tell you. It hit a node.'

Whyte was livid. 'What is a node?' he exploded. 'The System keeps the tracks clear. Nothing on the tracks but trains, no nodes left lying around—'

'You still don't understand. A node is not an obstruction. It's a singularity. A pole of high order.'

Tupelo's explanations that night did not greatly clarify the situation for Kelvin Whyte. But at two in the morning, the general manager conceded to Tupelo the privilege of examining the master maps of the System. He put in a call first to the police, who could not assist him with his first attempt to master topology, and then, finally, to Central Traffic. Tupelo taxied down there alone, and pored over the maps till morning. He had coffee and a snail, and then went to Whyte's office.

He found the general manager on the telephone. There was a conversation having to do with another, more elaborate inspection of the Dorchester-Cambridge tunnel under the Charles River. When the conversation ended, Whyte slammed the telephone into its cradle and glared at Tupelo. The mathematician spoke first.

'I think probably it's the new shuttle that did this,' he said.

Whyte gripped the edge of his desk and prowled silently through his vocabulary until he had located some civil words. 'Dr. Tupelo,' he said, 'I have been awake all night going over your theory. I don't understand it at all. I don't know what the Boylston shuttle has to do with this.'

'Remember what I was saying last night about the connective properties of networks?' Tupelo asked quietly. 'Remember the Möbius band we made—the surface with one face and one edge? Remember this—?' and he removed a little glass Klein bottle from his pocket and placed it on the desk.

Whyte sat back in his chair and stared wordlessly at the mathematician. Three emotions marched across his face in quick succession—anger, bewilderment, and utter dejection. Tupelo went on.

'Mr. Whyte, the System is a network of amazing topological complexity. It was already complex before the Boylston shuttle was installed, and of a high order of connectivity. But this shuttle makes the network absolutely unique. I don't fully understand it, but the situation seems to be something like this: the shuttle has made the connectivity of the whole System of an order so high that I don't know how to calculate it. I suspect the connectivity has become infinite.'

The general manager listened as though in a daze. He kept

his eyes glued to the little Klein bottle.

'The Möbius band,' Tupelo said, 'has unusual properties because it has a singularity. The Klein bottle, with two singularities, manages to be inside of itself. The topologists know surfaces with as many as a thousand singularities, and they have properties that make the Möbius band and the Klein bottle both look simple. But a network with infinite connectivity must have an infinite number of singularities. Can you imagine what the properties of that network could be?'

After a long pause, Tupelo added: 'I can't either. To tell the truth, the structure of the System, with the Boylston shuttle, is completely beyond me. I can only guess.'

Whyte swivelled his eyes up from the desk at a moment when anger was the dominant feeling within him. 'And you call yourself a mathematician, Professor Tupelo!' he said.

Tupelo almost laughed aloud. The incongruousness, the absolute foolishness of the situation, all but overwhelmed him. He smiled thinly, and said: 'I'm no topologist. Really, Mr. Whyte, I'm a tyro in the field—not much better acquainted with it than you are. Mathematics is a big pasture. I happen to be an algebraist.'

His candour softened Whyte a little. 'Well, then,' he ventured, 'if you don't understand it, maybe we should call in a topologist. Are there any in Boston?'

'Yes and no,' Tupelo answered. 'The best in the world is at Tech.'

Whyte reached for the telephone. 'What's his name?' he asked. 'I'll call him.'

'Merritt Turnbull. He can't be reached. I've tried for three days.'

'Is he out of town?' Whyte asked. 'We'll send for him—emergency.'

'I don't know. Professor Turnbull is a bachelor. He lives alone at the Brattle Club. He has not been seen since the morning of the 4th.'

Whyte was uncommonly perceptive. 'Was he on the train?' he asked tensely.

'I don't know,' the mathematician replied. 'What do you think?'

There was a long silence. Whyte looked alternately at Tupelo and at the glass object on the desk. 'I don't understand it,' he said finally. 'We've looked everywhere on the System. There was no way for the train to get out.'

'The train didn't get out. It's still on the System,' Tupelo said.

'Where?'

Tupelo shrugged. 'The train has no real "where". The whole System is without real "whereness". It's double-valued, or worse.'

'How can we find it?'

'I don't think we can,' Tupelo said.

There was another long silence. Whyte broke it with a loud exclamation. He rose suddenly, and sent the Klein bottle flying across the room. 'You are crazy, professor!' he shouted. 'Between midnight tonight and 6 a.m. tomorrow, we'll get every train out of the tunnels. I'll send in three hundred men, to comb every inch of the tracks—every inch of the one hundred and eighty-three miles. We'll find the train! Now, please excuse me.' He glared at Tupelo.

Tupelo left the office. He felt tired, completely exhausted. Mechanically, he walked along Washington Street towards the Essex Station. Halfway down the stairs, he stopped abruptly, looked around him slowly. Then he ascended again to the street and hailed a taxi. At home, he helped himself to a double shot. He fell into bed.

At 3.30 that afternoon he met his class in 'Algebra of Fields and Rings'. After a quick supper at the Crimson Spa, he went to his apartment and spent the evening in a second attempt to analyse the connective properties of the System. The attempt was vain, but the mathematician came to a few important conclusions. At eleven o'clock he telephoned Whyte at Central Traffic.

'I think you might want to consult me during tonight's search,' he said. 'May I come down?'

The general manager was none too gracious about Tupelo's offer of help. He indicated that the System would solve this little problem without any help from harebrained professors who thought that whole subway trains could jump off into the fourth dimension. Tupelo submitted to Whyte's unkindness, then went to bed. At about 4 a.m. the telephone awakened him. His caller was a contrite Kelvin Whyte.

'Perhaps I was a bit hasty last night, professor,' he stammered. 'You may be able to help us after all. Could you come down to the Milk Street Cross-Over?'

Tupelo agreed readily. He felt none of the satisfaction he had anticipated. He called a taxi, and in less than half an hour he was at the prescribed station. At the foot of the stairs, on the upper level, he saw that the tunnel was brightly lighted, as during normal operation of the System. But the platforms were deserted except for a tight little knot of seven men near the far end. As he walked towards the group, he noticed that two were policemen. He observed a one-car train on the track beside the platform. The forward door was open, the car brightly lit, and empty. Whyte heard his footsteps and greeted him sheepishly.

'Thanks for coming down, professor,' he said, extending his hand. 'Gentlemen, Dr. Roger Tupelo, of Harvard. Dr. Tupelo, Mr. Kennedy, our chief engineer; Mr. Wilson, representing the Mayor; Dr. Gannot, of Mercy Hospital.' Whyte did not bother to introduce the motorman and the two policemen.

'How do you do,' said Tupelo. 'Any results, Mr. Whyte?'

The general manager exchanged embarrassed glances with his companions. 'Well ... yes, Dr. Tupelo,' he finally answered. 'I think we do have some results, of a kind.'

'Has the train been seen?'

'Yes,' said Whyte. 'That is, practically seen. At least, we know it's somewhere in the tunnels.' The six others nodded their agreement.

Tupelo was not surprised to learn that the train was still on the System. After all, the System was closed. 'Would you mind telling me just what happened?' Tupelo insisted.

'I hit a red signal,' the motorman volunteered. 'Just outside the Copley junction.'

'The tracks have been completely cleared of all trains,' Whyte explained, 'except for this one. We've been riding it, all over the System, for four hours now. When Edmunds, here, hit a red light at the Copley junction, he stopped, of course. I thought the light must be defective, and told him to go ahead. But then we heard another train pass the junction.'

'Did you see it?' Tupelo asked.

'We couldn't see it. The light is placed just behind a curve. But we all heard it. There's no doubt the train went through the junction. And it must be Number 86, because our car was the only other one on the tracks.'

'What happened then?'

'Well, then the light changed to yellow, and Edmunds went ahead.'

'Did he follow the other train?'

'No. We couldn't be sure which way it was going. We must have guessed wrong.'

'How long ago did this happen?'

'At 1.38, the first time—'

'Oh,' said Tupelo, 'then it happened again later?'

'Yes. But not at the same spot, of course. We hit another red signal near South Station at 2.15. And then at 3.28—'

Tupelo interrupted the general manager. 'Did you see the train at 2.15?'

'We didn't even hear it, that time. Edmunds tried to catch it, but it must have turned off on to the Boylston shuttle.'

'What happened at 3.28?'

'Another red light. Near Park Street. We heard it up ahead of us.'

'But you didn't see it?'

'No. There is a little slope beyond the light. But we all heard it. The only thing I don't understand, Dr. Tupelo, is how the train could run the tracks for nearly five days without anybody seeing—'

* * *

Whyte's words trailed off into silence, and his right hand went up in a peremptory gesture for quiet. In the distance, the low metallic thunder of a fast-rolling train swelled up suddenly into a sharp, shrill roar of wheels below. The platform vibrated perceptibly as the train passed.

'Now we've got it!' Whyte exclaimed. 'Right past the men on the platform below!' He broke into a run towards the stairs to the lower level. All the others followed him, except Tupelo. He thought he knew what was going to happen. Before Whyte reached the stairs, a policeman bounded up to the top.

'Did you see it, now?' he shouted.

Whyte stopped in his tracks, and the others with him.

'Did you see that train?' the policeman from the lower level asked again, as two more men came running up the stairs.

'What happened?' Wilson wanted to know.

'Didn't *you* see it?' snapped Kennedy.

'Sure not,' the policeman replied. 'It passed through up here.'

'It did *not*,' roared Whyte. 'Down there!'

The six men with Whyte glowered at the three men from the lower level. Tupelo walked to Whyte's elbow. 'The train can't be seen, Mr. Whyte,' he said quietly.

Whyte looked down at him in utter disbelief. 'You heard it yourself. It passed right below—'

'Can we go to the car, Mr. Whyte?' Tupelo asked. 'I think we ought to talk a little.'

Whyte nodded dumbly, then turned to the policeman and the others who had been watching at the lower level. 'You really didn't see it?' he begged them.

'We heard it,' the policeman answered. 'It passed up here, going that way, I think,' and he gestured with his thumb.

'Get back downstairs, Maloney,' one of the policemen with Whyte commanded. Maloney scratched his head, turned, and disappeared below. The two other men followed him. Tupelo led the original group to the car beside the station platform. They went in and took seats, silently. Then they all watched the mathematician and waited.

'You didn't call me down here tonight just to tell me you'd

found the missing train.' Tupelo began, looking at Whyte. 'Has this sort of thing happened before?'

Whyte squirmed in his seat and exchanged glances with the chief engineer. 'Not exactly like this,' he said, evasively, 'but there have been some funny things.'

'Like what?' Tupelo snapped.

'Well, like the red lights. The watchers near Kendall found a red light at the same time we hit the one near South Station.'

'Go on.'

'Mr. Sweeney called me from Forest Hills at Park Street Under. He heard the train just two minutes after we heard it at the Copley junction. Twenty-eight track miles away.'

'As a matter of fact, Dr. Tupelo,' Wilson broke in, 'several dozen men have seen lights go red, or have heard the train, or both, inside of the last four hours. The thing acts as though it can be in several places at once.'

'It can,' Tupelo said.

'We keep getting reports of watchers seeing the thing,' the engineer added. 'Well, not exactly seeing it, either, but everything except that. Sometimes at two or even three places, far apart, at the same time. It's sure to be on the tracks. Maybe the cars are uncoupled.'

'Are you really sure it's on the tracks, Mr. Kennedy?' Tupelo asked.

'Positive,' the engineer said. 'The dynamometers at the power house show that it's drawing power. It's been drawing power all night. So at 3.30 we broke the circuits. Cut the power.'

'What happened?'

'Nothing,' Whyte answered. 'Nothing at all. The power was off for twenty minutes. During that time, not one of the two hundred and fifty men in the tunnels saw a red light or heard a train. But the power wasn't on for five minutes before we had two reports again—one from Arlington, the other from Egleston.'

There was a long silence after Whyte finished speaking. In the tunnel below, one man could be heard calling something to another. Tupelo looked at his watch. The time was 5.20.

'In short, Dr. Tupelo,' the general manager finally said, 'we are compelled to admit that there may be something in your theory.' The others nodded agreement.

'Thank you, gentlemen,' Tupelo said.

The physician cleared his throat. 'Now about the passengers,' he began. 'Have you any idea what—?'

'None,' Tupelo interrupted.

'What should we do, Dr. Tupelo?' the mayor's representative asked.

'I don't know. What can you do?'

'As I understand it from Mr. Whyte,' Wilson continued, 'the train has ... well, it has jumped into another dimension. It isn't really on the System at all. It's just gone. Is that right?'

'In a manner of speaking.'

'And this ... er ... peculiar behaviour has resulted from certain mathematical properties associated with the new Boylston shuttle?'

'Correct.'

'And there is nothing we can do to bring the train back to ... uh ... this dimension?'

'I know of nothing.'

Wilson took the bit in his teeth. 'In this case, gentlemen,' he said, 'our course is clear. First, we must close off the new shuttle, so this fantastic thing can never happen again. Then, since the missing train is really gone, in spite of all these red lights and noises, we can resume normal operation of the System. At least there will be no danger of collision—which has worried you so much, Whyte. As for the missing train and the people on it—' He gestured them into infinity. 'Do you agree, Dr. Tupelo?' he asked the mathematician.

Tupelo shook his head slowly. 'Not entirely, Mr. Wilson,' he responded. 'Now, please keep in mind that I don't fully comprehend what has happened. It's unfortunate that you won't find anybody who can give a good explanation. The one man who might have done so is Professor Turnbull, of Tech, and he was on the train. But in any case, you will want to check my conclusions against those of some competent topologists. I can put you in touch with several.

'Now, with regard to the recovery of the missing train, I can say that I think this is not hopeless. There is a finite probability, as I see it, that the train will eventually pass from the nonspatial part of the network, which it now occupies, back to the spatial part. Since the nonspatial part is wholly inaccessible, there is unfortunately nothing we can do to bring about this transition, or even to predict when or how it will occur. But the possibility of the transition will vanish if the Boylston shuttle is taken out. It is just this section of the track that gives the network its essential singularities. If the singularities are removed, the train can never reappear. Is this clear?'

It was not clear, of course, but the seven listening men nodded agreement. Tupelo continued.

'As for the continued operation of the System while the missing train is in the nonspatial part of the network, I can only give you the facts as I see them and leave to your judgment the difficult decision to be drawn from them. The transition back to the spatial part is unpredictable, as I have already told you. There is no way to know when it will occur, or where. In particular, there is a fifty per cent probability that, if and when the train reappears, it will be running on the wrong track. Then there will be a collision, of course.'

The engineer asked: 'To rule out this possibility, Dr. Tupelo, couldn't we leave the Boylston shuttle open, but send no trains through it? Then, when the missing train reappears on the shuttle, it cannot meet another train.'

'That precaution would be ineffective, Mr. Kennedy,' Tupelo answered. 'You see, the train can reappear anywhere on the System. It is true that the System owes its topological complexity to the new shuttle. But, with the shuttle in the System, it is now the whole System that possesses infinite connectivity. In other words, the relevant topological property is a property *derived* from the shuttle, but *belonging to* the whole System. Remember that the train made its first transition at a point between Park and Kendall, more than three miles away from the shuttle.

'There is one question more you will want answered. If you decide to go on operating the System, with the Boylston shuttle left in until the train reappears, can this happen again, to another train? I am not certain of the answer, but I think it is: No. I believe an exclusion principle operates here, such that only one train at a time can occupy the nonspatial network.'

The physician rose from his seat. 'Dr. Tupelo,' he began, timorously, 'when the train does reappear, will the passengers—?'

'I don't know about the people on the train,' Tupelo cut in. 'The topological theory does not consider such matters.' He looked quickly at each of the seven tired, querulous faces before him. 'I am sorry, gentlemen,' he added, somewhat more gently. 'I simply do not know.' To Whyte, he added: 'I think I can be of no more help tonight. You know where to reach me.' And, turning on his heel, he left the car and climbed the stairs. He found dawn spilling over the street, dissolving the shadows of night.

That impromptu conference in a lonely subway car was never reported in the papers. Nor were the full results of the night-long vigil over the dark and twisted tunnels. During the week that followed, Tupelo participated in four more formal conferences with Kelvin Whyte and certain city officials. At two of these, other topologists were present. Ornstein was imported to Boston from Philadelphia, Kashta from Chicago, and Michaelis from Los Angeles. The mathematicians were unable to reach a consensus. None of the three would fully endorse Tupelo's conclusions, although Kashta indicated that there *might* be something to them. Ornstein averred that a finite network could not possess infinite connectivity, although he could not prove this proposition and could not actually calculate the connectivity of the System. Michaelis expressed his opinion that the affair was a hoax and had nothing whatever to do with the topology of the System. He insisted that if the train could not be found on the System then the System must be open, or at least must once have been open.

But the more deeply Tupelo analysed the problem, the more fully he was convinced of the essential correctness of his first analysis. From the point of view of topology, the System soon suggested whole families of multiple-valued networks, each with an infinite number of infinite discontinuities. But a definite discussion of these new spatio-hyperspatial networks somehow eluded him. He gave the subject his full attention for only a week. Then his other duties compelled him to lay the analysis aside. He resolved to go back to the problem later in the spring, after courses were over.

Meanwhile, the System was operated as though nothing untoward had happened. The general manager and the mayor's representative had somehow managed to forget the night of the search, or at least to reinterpret what they had seen and not seen. The newspapers and the public at large speculated wildly, and they kept continuing pressure on Whyte. A number of suits were filed against the System on behalf of persons who had lost a relative. The State stepped into the affair and prepared its own thorough investigation. Recriminations were sounded in the halls of Congress. A garbled version of Tupelo's theory eventually found its way into the press. He ignored it, and it was soon forgotten.

The weeks passed, and then a month. The State's investigation was completed. The newspaper stories moved from the first page to the second; to the twenty-third; and then stopped. The missing persons did not return. In the large, they were no longer missed.

One day in mid-April, Tupelo travelled by subway again, from Charles Street to Harvard. He sat stiffly in front of the first car, and watched the tracks and grey tunnel walls hurl themselves at the train. Twice the train stopped for a red light, and Tupelo found himself wondering whether the other train was really just ahead, or just beyond space. He half-hoped, out of curiosity, that his exclusion principle was wrong, that the train might make the transition. But he arrived at Harvard on time. Only he among the passengers had found the trip exciting.

The next week he made another trip by subway, and again the next. As experiments, they were unsuccessful, and much less tense than the first ride in mid-April. Tupelo began to doubt his own analysis. Sometime in May, he reverted to the practice of commuting by subway between his Beacon Hill apartment and his office at Harvard. His mind stopped racing down the knotted grey caverns ahead of the train. He read the morning newspaper, or the abstracts in *Reviews of Modern Mathematics*.

Then there was one morning when he looked up from the newspaper and sensed something. He pushed panic back on its stiff, quivering spring, and looked quickly out of the window at his right. The lights of the car showed the black and grey lines of wall-spots streaking by. The tracks ground out their familiar steely dissonance. The train rounded a curve and crossed a junction that he remembered. Swiftly, he recalled boarding the train at Charles, noting the girl on the ice-carnival poster at Kendall, meeting the southbound train going into Central.

He looked at the man sitting beside him, with a lunch pail on his lap. The other seats were filled, and there were a dozen or so straphangers. A mealy-faced youth near the front door smoked a cigarette, in violation of the rules. Two girls behind him across the aisle were discussing a club meeting. In the seat ahead, a young woman was scolding her little son. The man on the aisle, in the seat ahead of that, was reading the paper. The Transit-Ad above him extolled Florida oranges.

He looked again at the man two seats ahead and fought down the terror within. He studied that man. What was it? Brunet, greying hair; a roundish head; wan complexion; rather flat features; a thick neck, with the hairline a little low, a little ragged; a grey, pin-stripe suit. While Tupelo watched, the man waved a fly away from his left ear. He swayed a little with the train. His newspaper was folded vertically down the middle. His *newspaper!* It was last March's!

Tupelo's eyes swivelled to the man beside him. Below his lunch pail was a paper. Today's. He turned in his seat and looked behind him. A young man held the *Transcript* open to the sports pages. The date was March 4th. Tupelo's eyes raced up and down the aisle. There were a dozen passengers carrying papers ten weeks old.

Tupelo lunged out of his seat. The man on the aisle muttered a curse as the mathematician crowded in front of him. He crossed the aisle in a bound and pulled the cord above the windows. The brakes sawed and screeched at the tracks, and the train ground to a stop. The startled passengers eyed Tupelo with hostility. At the rear of the car, the door flew open and a tall, thin man in a blue uniform burst in. Tupelo spoke first.

'Mr. Dorkin?' he called, vehemently.

The conductor stopped short and groped for words.

'There's been a serious accident, Dorkin,' Tupelo said, loudly, to carry over the rising swell of protest from the passengers. 'Get Gallagher back here right away!'

Dorkin reached up and pulled the cord four times. 'What happened?' he asked.

Tupelo ignored the question, and asked one of his own. 'Where have you been, Dorkin?'

The conductor's face was blank. 'In the next car, but—'

Tupelo cut him off. He glanced at his watch, then shouted at the passengers. 'It's ten minutes to nine on May 17th!'

The announcement stilled the rising clamour for a moment. The passengers exchanged bewildered glances.

'Look at your newspapers!' Tupelo shouted. 'Your newspapers!'

The passengers began to buzz. As they discovered each other's papers, the voices rose. Tupelo took Dorkin's arm and led him to the rear of the car. 'What time is it?' he asked.

'8.21,' Dorkin said, looking at his watch.

'Open the door,' said Tupelo, motioning ahead. 'Let me out. Where's the phone?'

Dorkin followed Tupelo's directions. He pointed to a niche in the tunnel wall a hundred yards ahead. Tupelo vaulted to the ground and raced down the narrow lane between the cars and the wall. 'Central Traffic!' he barked at the operator. He waited a few seconds, and saw that a train had stopped at the red signal behind his train. Flashlights were advancing down the tunnel. He saw Gallagher's legs running down the tunnel on the other side of 86. 'Get me Whyte!' he commanded, when Central Traffic answered. 'Emergency!'

There was a delay. He heard voices rising from the train beside him. The sound was mixed—anger, fear, hysteria.

'Hello!' he shouted. 'Hello! Emergency! Get me Whyte!'

'I'll take it,' a man's voice said at the other end of the line. 'Whyte's busy!'

'Number 86 is back,' Tupelo called. 'Between Central and Harvard now. Don't know when it made the jump. I caught it at Charles ten minutes ago, and didn't notice it till a minute ago.'

The man at the other end gulped hard enough to carry over the telephone. 'The passengers?' he croaked.

'All right, the ones that are left,' Tupelo said. 'Some must have got off already at Kendall and Central.'

'Where have they been?'

Tupelo dropped the receiver from his ear and stared at it, his mouth wide open. Then he slammed the receiver on to the hook and ran back to the open door.

Eventually, order was restored, and within a half hour the train proceeded to Harvard. At the station, the police took all passengers into protective custody. Whyte himself arrived at Harvard before the train did. Tupelo found him on the platform.

Whyte motioned weakly towards the passengers. 'They're really all right?' he asked.

'Perfectly,' said Tupelo. 'Don't know they've been gone.'

'Any sign of Professor Turnbull?' asked the general manager.

'I didn't see him. He probably got off at Kendall, as usual.'

'Too bad,' said Whyte. 'I'd like to see him!'

'So would I!' Tupelo answered. 'By the way, now is the time to close the Boylston shuttle.'

'Now is too late,' Whyte said. 'Train 143 vanished twenty-five minutes ago, between Egleston and Dorchester.'

Tupelo stared past Whyte, and down and down the tracks.

'We've got to find Turnbull,' Whyte said.

Tupelo looked at Whyte and smiled thinly.

'Do you really think Turnbull got off this train at Kendall?' he asked.

'Of course!' answered Whyte. 'Where else?'

A SUBWAY NAMED MOBIUS

The germ of the plot of this story rests in the 'Möbius strip' so-called because its properties were first carefully analysed by a German mathematician, August Ferdinand Möbius, in the mid-nineteenth century. (In the story, the name is spelled Mobius, because magazine printers usually don't have type of an 'o' with two dots over it, a symbol that belongs in the German alphabet.)

You can easily construct a Möbius strip for yourself. Take a piece of ordinary note paper about eleven inches long and cut a strip half an inch wide. Bend it in a circle so that the two short edges overlap. Give one of the ends a single twist and then paste them together so that the bottom side of one end adjoins the top side of the other, as overleaf.

The Möbius strip possesses only one side. If you make a pencil mark along the strip anywhere and keep drawing that mark till you return to the starting point, you will find the mark on the side that seems below as well as on that which seems above. The single side is both below and above. For the same reason, the Möbius strip possesses only one edge.

The most startling property of the Möbius strip is revealed when the strip is sliced longwise down its centre. From experience with similar objects of the ordinary type, with two sides and two edges (such as a ring of paper formed by pasting a strip together *without* a twist), you would expect to form two strips just like the original but each one only half as wide. This does not happen with the Möbius strip. Try it and see.

The properties of the Möbius strip are an example of the sort of thing studied in that branch of mathematics called 'topology'. The study of topology leads to the discovery and analysis of all kinds of figures very different from the common ones of everyday life. Their properties are so unusual that it is easy to imagine that you could build a subway network so complicated that its properties would be paradoxical in the fashion of the Möbius strip, only more so.

(The title of the story, by the way, borrows from the famous Tennessee Williams play, *A Streetcar Named Desire* which was produced three years before this story was published.)

Questions and Suggestions

1. Read an introductory book on topology and note some of the unusual properties of odd figures. In particular, what are the properties of the 'Klein bottle' which is briefly mentioned in the story? How did it get its name?

2. In 1950, when Deutsch (who died in 1969) wrote the story, he was in the astronomy department at Harvard. Naturally, then, he wrote the story about the Boston subway system. Get a map of the Boston subway system (which is by no means as complicated as that of New York) and follow the references in the story. Did Deutsch exaggerate the complexity of the system? Could the system, however complex, develop the kind of topological oddness Deutsch describes?

3. There is an odd coincidence in the story that has nothing to do with the story itself and that Deutsch could not have planned. One of the chief characters in the story is Kelvin Whyte. Well, in 1967, Boston elected a man named Kevin White as mayor and he is still in that office as I write this. Another example (and an even stranger one) involves a story called *Merman* written by L. Sprague de Camp in 1940. In that story, de Camp's hero was an ichthyologist named Vernon Brock. Unknown to de Camp there was a real ichthyologist named Vernon Brock, who read science fiction and promptly wrote to de Camp. Fortunately, he was not annoyed. Such coincidences abound everywhere. What do you think of them?

Suppose I said, 'No matter how weird such coincidences may seem, it would be far more weird to have no such coincidences.' Would you agree? There is a branch of mathematics called probability that deals with such things among others, if you are interested.

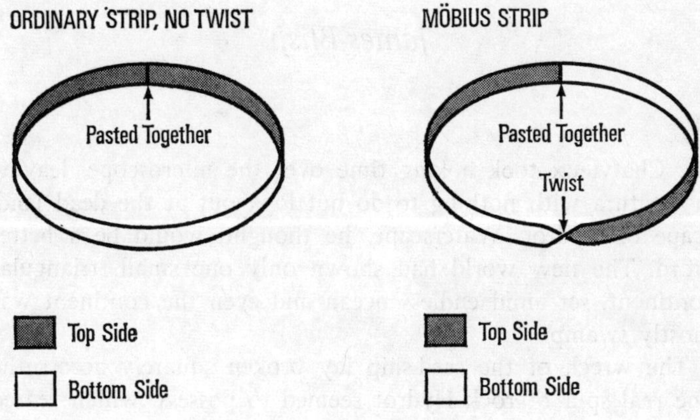

8. Surface Tension

James Blish

Dr. Chatvieux took a long time over the microscope, leaving la Ventura with nothing to do but look out at the dead landscape of Hydrot. Waterscape, he thought, would be a better word. The new world had shown only one small, triangular continent, set amid endless ocean and even the continent was mostly swamp.

The wreck of the seed-ship lay broken squarely across the one real spur of rock Hydrot seemed to possess, which reared a magnificent twenty-one feet above sea-level. From this eminence, la Ventura could see forty miles to the horizon across a flat bed of mud. The red light of the star Tau Ceti, glinting upon thousands of small lakes, pools, ponds, and puddles, made the watery plain look like a mosaic of onyx and ruby.

'If I were a religious man,' the pilot said suddenly, 'I'd call this a plain case of divine vengeance.'

Chatvieux said: 'Hmn?'

'It's as if we've been struck down for—is it *hubris*, arrogant pride?'

'Well, is it?' Chatvieux said, looking up at last. 'I don't feel exactly swollen with pride at the moment. Do you?'

'I'm not exactly proud of my piloting,' la Ventura admitted. 'But that isn't quite what I meant. I was thinking about why we came here in the first place. It takes arrogant pride to think that you can scatter men, or at least things like men, all over the face of the Galaxy. It takes even more pride to do the job—to pack up all the equipment and move from planet to planet and actually make men suitable for every place you touch.'

'I suppose it does,' Chatvieux said. 'But we're only one of several hundred seed-ships in this limb of the Galaxy, so I doubt that the gods picked us out as special sinners.' He smiled drily. 'If they had, maybe they'd have left us our ultraphone, so the Colonization Council could hear about our cropper. Besides, Paul, we try to produce men adapted to Earthlike planets, nothing more. We've sense enough—humility enough, if you like—to know that we can't adapt men to Jupiter or to Tau Ceti.'

'Anyhow, we're here,' la Ventura said grimly. 'And we aren't going to get off. Phil tells me that we don't even have our germ-cell bank any more, so we can't seed this place in the usual way. We've been thrown on to a dead world and dared to adapt it. What are the panatropes going to do—provide built-in waterwings?'

'No,' Chatvieux said calmly. 'You and I and the rest of us are going to die, Paul. Panatropic techniques don't work on the body, only on the inheritance-carrying factors. We can't give you built-in waterwings, any more than we can give you a new set of brains. I think we'll be able to populate this world with men, but we won't live to see it.'

The pilot thought about it, a lump of cold collecting gradually in his stomach. 'How long do you give us?' he said at last.

'Who knows? A month, perhaps.'

The bulkhead leading to the wrecked section of the ship was pushed back, admitting salty, muggy air, heavy with carbon dioxide. Philip Strasvogel, the communications officer, came in, tracking mud. Like la Ventura, he was now a man without a function, but it did not appear to bother him. He unbuckled from around his waist a canvas belt into which plastic vials were stuffed like cartridges.

'More samples, Doc,' he said. 'All alike—water, very wet. I have some quicksand in one boot, too. Find anything?'

'A good deal, Phil. Thanks. Are the others around?'

Strasvogel poked his head out and hallooed. Other voices

rang out over the mudflats. Minutes later, the rest of the survivors were crowding into the panatrope deck: Saltonstall, Chatvieux's senior assistant; Eunice Wagner, the only remaining ecologist; Eleftherios Venezuelos, the delegate from the Colonization Council; and Joan Heath, a midshipman whose duties, like la Ventura's and Strasvogel's, were now without meaning.

Five men and two women—to colonize a planet on which standing room meant treading water.

They came in quietly and found seats or resting places on the deck, on the edges of tables, in corners.

Venezuelos said: 'What's the verdict, Dr. Chatvieux?'

'This place isn't dead,' Chatvieux said. 'There's life in the sea and in the fresh water, both. On the animal side of the ledger, evolution seems to have stopped with the crustacea; the most advanced form I've found is a tiny crayfish, from one of the local rivulets. The ponds and puddles are well-stocked with protozoa and small metazoans, right up to a wonderfully variegated rotifer population—including a castle-building rotifer like Earth's *Floscularidae*. The plants run from simple algae to the thalluslike species.'

'The sea is about the same,' Eunice said, 'I've found some of the larger simple metazoans—jellyfish and so on—and some crayfish almost as big as lobsters. But it's normal to find salt-water species running larger than fresh-water.'

'In short,' Chatvieux said, 'we'll survive here—if we fight.'

'Wait a minute,' la Ventura said. 'You've just finished telling me that we wouldn't survive. And you were talking about us, not about the species, because we don't have our germ-cell banks any more. What's—'

'I'll get to that again in a moment,' Chatvieux said. 'Saltonstall, what would you think of taking to the sea? We came out of it once; maybe we could come out of it again.'

'No good,' Saltonstall said immediately. '*I* like the idea, but I don't think this planet ever heard of Swinburne, or Homer, either. Looking at it as a colonization problem, as if we weren't involved ourselves, I wouldn't give you a credit for *epi oinopa ponton*. The evolutionary pressure there is too high, the competition from other species is prohibitive; seeding the sea should be the last thing we attempt. The colonists wouldn't have a chance to learn a thing before they were destroyed.'

'Why?' la Ventura said. The death in his stomach was becoming hard to placate.

'Eunice, do your sea-going Coelenterates include anything like the Portuguese man-of-war?'

The ecologist nodded.

'There's your answer, Paul,' Saltonstall said. 'The sea is out. It's got to be fresh water, where the competing creatures are less formidable and there are more places to hide.'

'We can't compete with a jellyfish?' la Ventura asked, swallowing.

'No, Paul,' Chatvieux said. 'The panatropes make adaptations, not gods. They take human germ-cells—in this case, our own, since our bank was wiped out in the crash—and modify them towards creatures who can live in any reasonable environment. The result will be manlike and intelligent. It usually shows the donor's personality pattern, too.

'*But we can't transmit memory*. The adapted man is worse than a child in his new environment. He has no history, no techniques, no precedents, not even a language. Ordinarily the seeding teams more or less take him through elementary school before they leave the planet, but we won't survive long enough for that. We'll have to design our colonists with plenty of built-in protections and locate them in the most favourable environment possible, so that at least some of them will survive the learning process.'

The pilot thought about it, but nothing occurred to him which did not make the disaster seem realer and more intimate with each passing second. 'One of the new creatures can have my personality pattern, but it won't be able to remember being me. Is that right?'

'That's it. There may be just the faintest of residuums—panatropy's given us some data which seem to support the old Jungian notion of ancestral memory. But we're all going to die on Hydrot, Paul. There's no avoiding that. Somewhere we'll leave behind people who behave as we would, think and feel as we would, but who won't remember la Ventura, or Chatvieux, or Joan Heath—or Earth.'

The pilot said nothing more. There was a grey taste in his mouth.

'Saltonstall, what do you recommend as a form?'

The panatropist pulled reflectively at his nose. 'Webbed extremities, of course, with thumbs and big toes heavy and thornlike for defence until the creature has had a chance to learn. Book-lungs, like the arachnids, working out of intercostal spiracles—they are gradually adaptable to atmosphere-breathing if it ever decides to come out of the water. Also I'd suggest sporulation. As an aquatic animal, our colonist is going to have an indefinite life-span, but we'll have to give it a breeding cycle of about six weeks to keep its numbers up during the learning period; so there'll have to be a definite break of some duration in its active year. Otherwise it'll hit the population problem before it's learned enough to cope with it.'

'Also, it'll be better if our colonists could winter inside a good hard shell,' Eunice Wagner added in agreement. 'So sporulation's the obvious answer. Most microscopic creatures have it.'

'Microscopic?' Phil said incredulously.

'Certainly,' Chatvieux said, amused. 'We can't very well crowd a six-foot man into a two-foot puddle. But that raises a question. We'll have tough competition from the rotifers, and some of them aren't strictly microscopic. I don't think your average colonist should run under 25 microns, Saltonstall. Give them a chance to slug it out.'

'I was thinking of making them twice that big.'

'Then they'd be the biggest things in their environment,' Eunice Wagner pointed out, 'and won't ever develop any skills. Besides, if you make them about rotifer size, it'll give them an incentive for pushing out the castle-building rotifers.

'They'll be able to take over the castles as dwellings.'

Chatvieux nodded. 'All right, let's get started. While the panatropes are being calibrated, the rest of us can put our heads together on leaving a record for these people. We'll micro-engrave the record on a set of corrosion-proof metal leaves, of a size our colonists can handle conveniently. Some day they may puzzle it out.'

'Question,' Eunice Wagner said. 'Are we going to tell them they're microscopic? I'm opposed to it. It'll saddle their entire early history with a gods-and-demons mythology they'd be better off without.'

'Yes, we are,' Chatvieux said; and la Ventura could tell by the change in the tone of his voice that he was speaking now as their senior. 'These people will be of the race of men, Eunice. We want them to win their way back to the community of men. They are not toys, to be protected from the truth forever in a fresh-water womb.'

'I'll make that official,' Venezuelos said, and that was that.

And then, essentially, it was all over. They went through the motions. Already they were beginning to be hungry. After la Ventura had had his personality pattern recorded, he was out of it. He sat by himself at the far end of the ledge, watching Tau Ceti go redly down, chucking pebbles into the nearest pond, wondering morosely which nameless puddle was to be his Lethe.

He never found out, of course. None of them did.

I

Old Shar set down the heavy metal plate at last, and gazed instead out of the window of the castle, apparently resting his eyes on the glowing green-gold obscurity of the summer waters. In the soft fluorescence which played down upon him, from the Noc dozing impassively in the groined vault of the chamber, Lavon could see that he was in fact a young man. His face was so delicately formed as to suggest that it had not been many seasons since he had first emerged from his spore.

But of course there had been no real reason to expect an

old man. All the Shars had been referred to traditionally as 'old' Shar. The reason, like the reasons for everything else, had been forgotten, but the custom had persisted; the adjective at least gave weight and dignity to the office.

The present Shar belonged to the generation XVI, and hence would have to be at least two seasons younger than Lavon himself. If he was old, it was only in knowledge.

'Lavon, I'm going to have to be honest with you,' Shar said at last, still looking out of the tall, irregular window. 'You've come to me for the secrets on the metal plates, just as your predecessors did to mine. I can give some of them to you—but for the most part, I don't know what they mean.'

'After so many generations?' Lavon asked, surprised. 'Wasn't it Shar III who first found out how to read them? That was a long time ago.'

The young man turned and looked at Lavon with eyes made dark and wide by the depths into which they had been staring. 'I can read what's on the plates, but most of it seems to make no sense. Worst of all, the plates are incomplete. You didn't know that? They are. One of them was lost in a battle during the final war with the Eaters, while these castles were still in their hands.'

'What am I here for, then?' Lavon said. 'Isn't there anything of value on the remaining plates? Do they really contain "the wisdom of the Creators" or is that another myth?'

'No. No, that's true,' Shar said slowly, 'as far as it goes.'

He paused, and both men turned and gazed at the ghostly creature which had appeared suddenly outside the window. Then Shar said gravely, 'Come in, Para.'

The slipper-shaped organism, nearly transparent except for the thousands of black-and-silver granules and frothy bubbles which packed its interior, glided into the chamber and hovered, with a muted whirring of cilia. For a moment it remained silent, probably speaking telepathically to the Noc floating in the vault, after the ceremonious fashion of all the protos. No human had ever intercepted one of these colloquies, but there was no doubt about their reality: humans had used them for long-range communication for generations.

Then the Para's cilia buzzed once more. Each separate hair-like process vibrated at an independent, changing rate; the resulting sound waves spread through the water, intermodulating, reinforcing or cancelling each other. The aggregate wave-front, by the time it reached human ears, was recognizable human speech.

'We are arrived, Shar and Lavon, according to the custom.'

'And welcome,' said Shar. 'Lavon, let's leave this matter of the plates for a while, until you hear what Para has to say; that's a part of the knowledge Lavons must have as they come of age, and it comes before the plates. I can give you some hints of what we are. First Para has to tell you something about what we aren't.'

Lavon nodded, willingly enough, and watched the proto as it settled gently to the surface of the hewn table at which Shar had been sitting. There was in the entity such a perfection and economy of organization, such a grace and surety of movement, that he could hardly believe in his own new-won maturity. Para, like all the protos, made him feel not, perhaps, poorly thought-out, but at least unfinished.

'We know that in this universe there is logically no place for man,' the gleaming, now immobile cylinder upon the table droned abruptly. 'Our memory is the common property to all our races. It reaches back to a time when there were no such creatures as men here. It remembers also that once upon a day there were men here, suddenly, and in some numbers. Their spores littered the bottom; we found the spores only a short time after our season's Awakening, and in them we saw the forms of men slumbering.

'Then men shattered their spores and emerged. They were intelligent, active. And they were gifted with a trait, a character, possessed by no other creature in this world. Not even the savage Eaters had it. Men organized us to exterminate the Eaters and therein lay the difference. Men had initiative. We have the word now, which you gave us, and we apply it, but we still do not know what the thing is that it labels.'

'You fought beside us,' Lavon said.

'Gladly. We would never have thought of that war by ourselves, but it was good and brought good. Yet we wondered. We saw that men were poor swimmers, poor walkers, poor crawlers, poor climbers. We saw that men were formed to make and use tools, a concept we still do not understand, for so wonderful a gift is largely wasted in this universe, and there is no other. What good are tool-useful members such as the hands of men? We do not know. It seems plain that so radical a thing should lead to a much greater rulership over the world than has, in fact, proven to be possible for men.'

Lavon's head was spinning. 'Para, I had no notion that you people were philosophers.'

'The protos are old,' Shar said. He had again turned to look out of the window, his hands locked behind his back. 'They aren't philosophers, Lavon, but they are remorseless logicians. Listen to Para.'

'To this reasoning there could be but one outcome,' the Para said. 'Our strange ally, Man, was like nothing else in this universe. He was and is ill-fitted for it. He does not belong here; he has been—adopted. This drives us to think that there are other universes besides this one, but where these universes might lie, and what their properties might be, it is impossible to imagine. We have no imagination, as men know.'

Was the creature being ironic? Lavon could not tell. He said slowly: 'Other universes? How could that be true?'

'We do not know,' the Para's uninflected voice hummed. Lavon waited, but obviously the proto had nothing more to say.

Shar had resumed sitting on the window sill, clasping his knees, watching the come and go of dim shapes in the lighted gulf. 'It is quite true,' he said. 'What is written on the remaining plates makes it plain. Let me tell you now what they say.

'*We were made*, Lavon. We were made by men who are not

as we are, but men who were our ancestors all the same. They were caught in some disaster, and they made us, and put us here in our universe—so that, even though they had to die, the race of men would live.'

Lavon surged up from the woven spyrogrya mat upon which he had been sitting. 'You must think I'm a fool!' he said sharply.

'No. You're our Lavon; you have a right to know the facts. Make what you like of them.' Shar swung his webbed toes back into the chamber. 'What I've told you may be hard to believe, but it seems to be so; what Para says backs it up. Our unfitness to live here is self-evident. I'll give you some examples:

'The past four Shars discovered that we won't get any further in our studies until we learn how to control heat. We've produced enough heat chemically to show that even the water around us changes when the temperature gets high enough. But there we're stopped.'

'Why?'

'Because heat produced in open water is carried off as rapidly as it's produced. Once we tried to enclose that heat, and we blew up a whole tube of the castle and killed everything in range; the shock was terrible. We measured the pressures that were involved in that explosion, and we discovered that no substance we know could have resisted them. Theory suggests some stronger substance—*but we need heat to form them!*

'Take our chemistry. We live in water. Everything seems to dissolve in water, to some extent. How do we confine a chemical test to the crucible we put it in? How do we maintain a solution at one dilution? I don't know. Every avenue leads me to the same stone door. We're thinking creatures, Lavon, but there's something drastically wrong in the way we think about this universe we live in. It just doesn't seem to lead to results.'

Lavon pushed back his floating hair futilely. 'Maybe you're thinking about the wrong results. We've had no trouble with warfare, or crops, or practical things like that. If we can't create much heat, well, most of us won't miss it; we don't need any. What's the other universe supposed to be like, the one our ancestors lived in? Is it any better than this one?'

'I don't know,' Shar admitted. 'It was so different that it's hard to compare the two. The metal plates tell a story about men who were travelling from one place to another in a container that moved by itself. The only analogy I can think of is the shallops of diatom shells that our youngsters use to sled along the thermocline; but evidently what's meant is something much bigger.

'I picture a huge shallop, closed on all sides, big enough to hold many people—maybe twenty or thirty. It had to travel for generations through some kind of space where there wasn't any water to breathe, so that the people had to carry their own water and renew it constantly. There were no seasons; no yearly turnover; no ice forming on the sky, because there wasn't any sky in a closed shallop; no spore formation.

'Then the shallop was wrecked somehow. The people in it knew they were going to die. They made us, and put us here, as if we were their children. Because they had to die, they wrote their story on the plates, to tell us what had happened. I suppose we'd understand it better if we had the plate Shar III lost during the war, but we don't.'

'The whole thing sounds like a parable,' Lavon said, shrugging. 'Or a song. I can see why you don't understand it. What I can't see is why you bother to try.'

'Because of the plates,' Shar said. 'You've handled them yourself, so you know that we've nothing like them. We have crude, impure metals we've hammered out, metals that last for a while and then decay. But the plates shine on and on, generation after generation. They don't change; our hammers and graving tools break against them; the little heat we can generate leaves them unharmed. Those plates weren't formed in our universe—and that one fact makes every word on them important to me. Someone went to a great deal of trouble to make those plates indestructible to give them to us. Someone to whom the word "stars" was important enough to be worth fourteen repetitions, despite the fact that the word doesn't seem to mean anything. I'm ready to think that if our makers repeated the word even twice on a record that seems likely to last forever, it's important for us to know what it means.'

'All these extra universes and huge shallops and meaningless words—I can't say that they don't exist, but I don't see what difference it makes. The Shars of a few generations ago spent their whole lives breeding better algae crops for us, and showing us how to cultivate them instead of living haphazardly off bacteria. That was work worth doing. The Lavons of those days evidently got along without the metal plates, and saw to it that the Shars did, too: well, as far as I'm concerned, you're welcome to the plates, if you like them better than crop improvement—but I think they ought to be thrown away.'

'All right,' Shar said, shrugging. 'If you don't want them, that ends the traditional interview. We'll go our—'

There was a rising drone from the table-top. The Para was lifting itself, waves of motion passing over its cilia, like the waves which went across the fruiting stalks of the fields of delicate fungi with which the bottom was planted. It had been so silent that Lavon had forgotten it; he could tell from Shar's startlement that Shar had, too.

'This is a great decision,' the waves of sound washing from the creature throbbed. 'Every proto has heard it and agrees with it. We have been afraid of these metal plates for a long time, afraid that men would learn to understand them and to follow what they say to some secret place, leaving the protos behind. Now we are not afraid.'

'There wasn't anything to be afraid of,' Lavon said indulgently.

'No Lavon before you had said so,' Para said. 'We are glad. We will throw the plates away.'

With that, the shining creature swooped towards the embrasure. With it, it bore away the remaining plates, which had been resting under it on the table-top, suspended delicately in the curved tips of its supple cilia. With a cry, Shar plunged through the water towards the opening.

'Stop, Para!'

But Para was already gone, so swiftly that he had not even heard the call. Shar twisted his body and brought up on one shoulder against the tower wall. He said nothing. His face was enough. Lavon could not look at it for more than an instant.

The shadows of the two men moved slowly along the uneven cobbled floor. The Noc descended towards them from the vault, its single thick tentacle stirring the water, its internal light flaring and fading irregularly. It, too, drifted through the window after its cousin, and sank slowly away towards the bottom. Gently its living glow dimmed, flickered, winked out.

II

For many days, Lavon was able to avoid thinking much about the loss. There was always a great deal of work to be done. Maintenance of the castles, which had been built by the now-extinct Eaters rather than by human hands, was a never-ending task. The thousand dichotomously branching wings tended to crumble, especially at their bases where they sprouted from each other, and no Shar had yet come forward with a mortar as good as the rotifer-spittle which had once held them together. In addition, the breaking through of windows and the construction of chambers in the early days had been haphazard and often unsound. The instinctive architecture of the rotifers, after all, had not been meant to meet the needs of human occupants.

And then there were the crops. Men no longer fed precariously upon passing bacteria; now there were the drifting mats of specific water-fungi, rich and nourishing, which had been bred by five generations of Shars. These had to be tended constantly to keep the strains pure, and to keep the older and less intelligent species of the protos from grazing on them. In this latter task, to be sure, the more intricate and far-seeing proto types cooperated, but men were needed to supervise.

There had been a time, after the war with the Eaters, when it had been customary to prey upon the slow-moving and stupid diatoms, whose exquisite and fragile glass shells were so easily burst, and who were unable to learn that a friendly voice did not necessarily mean a friend. There were still people who would crack open a diatom when no one else was looking, but they were regarded as barbarians, to the puzzlement of the protos. The blurred and simple-minded speech of the gorgeously engraved plants had brought them into the category of pets—a concept which the protos were utterly unable to grasp, especially since men admitted that diatoms on the half-frustrule were delicious.

Lavon had had to agree, very early, that the distinction was tiny. After all, humans did eat the desmids, which differed from the diatoms only in three particulars: their shells were flexible, they could not move, and they did not speak. Yet to Lavon, as to most men, there did seem to be some kind of distinction, whether the protos could see it or not, and that was that. Under the circumstance he felt that it was a part of his duty, as a leader of men, to protect the diatoms from the occasional poachers who browsed upon them, in defiance of custom, in the high levels of the sunlit sky.

Yet Lavon found it impossible to keep himself busy enough to forget that moment when the last clues to Man's origin and destination had been seized and borne away into dim space.

It might be possible to ask Para for the return of the plates, explain that a mistake had been made. The protos were creatures of implacable logic, but they respected Man, were used to illogic in Man, and might reverse their decision if pressed—

We are sorry. The plates were carried over the bar and released in the gulf. We will have the bottom there searched, but ...

With a sick feeling he could not repress, Lavon knew that when the protos decided something was worthless, they did not hide it in some chamber like old women. They threw it away—efficiently.

Yet despite the tormenting of his conscience, Lavon was convinced that the plates were well lost. What had they ever done for Man, except to provide Shars with useless things to think about in the late seasons of their lives? What the Shars themselves had done to benefit Man, here, in the water, in the world, in the universe, had been done by direct experimentation. No bit of useful knowledge ever had come from the plates. There had never been anything in the plates but things best left unthought. The protos were right.

Lavon shifted his position on the plant frond, where he had been sitting in order to overlook the harvesting of an experimental crop of blue-green, oil-rich algae drifting in a clotted mass close to the top of the sky, and scratched his back gently against the coarse bole. The protos were seldom wrong, after all. Their lack of creativity, their inability to think an original thought, was a gift as well as a limitation. It allowed them to see and feel things at all times as they were—not as they hoped they might be, for they had no ability to hope, either.

'La-von! Laa-vah-on!'

The long halloo came floating up from the sleepy depths. Propping one hand against the top of the frond, Lavon bent and looked down. One of the harvesters was looking up at him, holding loosely the adze with which he had been splitting free the glutinous tetrads of the algae.

'Up here. What's the matter?'

'We have the ripened quadrant cut free. Shall we tow it away?'

'Tow it away,' Lavon said, with a lazy gesture. He leaned back again. At the same instant, a brilliant reddish glory burst into being above him, and cast itself down towards the depths like mesh after mesh of the finest-drawn gold. The great light which lived above the sky during the day, brightening or dimming according to some pattern no Shar ever had fathomed, was blooming again.

Few men, caught in the warm glow of that light, could resist looking up at it—especially when the top of the sky itself wrinkled and smiled just a moment's climb or swim away. Yet, as always, Lavon's bemused upward look gave him back nothing but his own distorted, bobbling reflection, and a reflection of the plant on which he rested.

Here was the upper limit, the third of the three surfaces of the universe.

The first surface was the bottom, where the water ended.

The second surface was the thermocline, the invisible division between the colder waters of the bottom and the warm, light waters of the sky. During the height of the warm weather, the thermocline was so definite a division as to make for good sledding and for chilly passage. A real interface formed between the cold, denser, bottom waters and the warm reaches above, and maintained itself almost for the whole of the warm season.

The third surface was the sky. One could no more pass through that surface than one could penetrate the bottom, nor was there any better reason to try. There the universe ended. The light which played over it daily, waxing and waning as it chose, seemed to be one of its properties.

Towards the end of the season, the water gradually grew colder and more difficult to breathe, while at the same time the light became duller and stayed for shorter periods between darknesses. Slow currents started to move. The high waters turned chill and began to fall. The bottom mud stirred and smoked away, carrying with it the spores of the fields of fungi. The thermocline tossed, became choppy, and melted away. The sky began to fog with particles of soft silt carried up from the bottom, the walls, the corners of the universe. Before very long, the whole world was cold, inhospitable, flocculent with yellowing, dying creatures.

Then the protos encysted; the bacteria, even most of the plants and, not long afterwards, men, too, curled up in their oil-filled amber shells. The world died until the first tentative current of warm water broke the winter silence.

'La-von!'

Just after the long call, a shining bubble rose past Lavon. He reached out and poked it, but it bounded away from his sharp thumb. The gas-bubbles which rose from the bottom in late summer were almost invulnerable—and when some especially hard blow or edge did penetrate them, they broke into smaller bubbles which nothing could touch, and fled towards the sky, leaving behind a remarkably bad smell.

Gas. There was no water inside a bubble. A man who got inside a bubble would have nothing to breathe.

But, of course, it was impossible to penetrate a bubble. The surface tension was too strong. As strong as Shar's metal plates. As strong as the top of the sky.

As strong as the top of the sky. And above that—once the bubble was broken—a world of gas instead of water? Were all worlds bubbles of water drifting in gas?

If it were so, travel between them would be out of the question, since it would be impossible to pierce the sky to begin with. Nor did the infant cosmology include any provisions for bottoms for the worlds.

And yet some of the local creatures did burrow *into* the bottom, quite deeply, seeking something in those depths which was beyond the reach of Man. Even the surface of the ooze, in high summer, crawled with tiny creatures for which mud was a natural medium. Man, too, passed freely between the two countries of water which were divided by the thermocline, though many of the creatures with which he lived could not pass that line at all, once it had established itself.

And if the new universe of which Shar had spoken existed at all, it had to exist beyond the sky, where the light was. Why could not the sky be passed, after all? The fact that bubbles could be broken showed that the surface skin that formed between water and gas wasn't completely invulnerable. Had it ever been tried?

Lavon did not suppose that one man could butt his way through the top of the sky, any more than he could burrow into the bottom, but there might be ways around the difficulty. Here at his back, for instance, was a plant which gave every appearance of continuing beyond the sky: its uppermost fronds broke off and were bent back only by a trick of reflection.

It had always been assumed that the plants died where they touched the sky. For the most part, they did, for frequently the dead extension could be seen, leached and yellow, the boxes of its component cells empty, floating imbedded in the perfect mirror. But some were simply chopped off, like the one which sheltered him now. Perhaps that was only an illusion, and instead it soared indefinitely into some other place—some place where men might once have been born, and might still live . . .

The plates were gone. There was only one other way to find out.

Determinedly, Lavon began to climb towards the wavering mirror of the sky. His thorn-thumbed feet trampled obliviously upon the clustered sheaves of fragile stippled diatoms. The tulip-heads of Vortae, placid and murmurous cousins of Para, retracted startledly out of his way upon coiling stalks, to make silly gossip behind him.

Lavon did not hear them. He continued to climb doggedly towards the light, his fingers and toes gripping the plant-bole.

'Lavon! Where are you going? Lavon!'

He leaned out and looked down. The man with the adze, a doll-like figure, was beckoning to him from a patch of blue-green retreating over a violet abyss. Dizzily he looked away, clinging to the bole; he had never been so high before. Then he began to climb again.

After a while, he touched the sky with one hand. He stopped to breathe. Curious bacteria gathered about the base of his thumb where blood from a small cut was fogging away, scattered at his gesture, and wriggled mindlessly back towards the dull red lure.

He waited until he no longer felt winded, and resumed climbing. The sky pressed down against the top of his head, against the back of his neck, against his shoulders. It seemed to give slightly, with a tough, frictionless elasticity. The water here was intensely bright, and quite colourless. He climbed another step, driving his shoulders against that enormous weight.

It was fruitless. He might as well have tried to penetrate a cliff.

Again he had to rest. While he panted, he made a curious discovery. All around the bole of the water plant, the steel surface of the sky curved upward, making a kind of sheath. He found that he could insert his hand into it—there was almost enough space to admit his head as well. Clinging closely to the bole, he looked up into the inside of the sheath, probing with his injured hand. The glare was blinding.

There was a kind of soundless explosion. His whole wrist was suddenly encircled in an intense, impersonal grip, as if it were being cut in two. In blind astonishment, he lunged upward.

The ring of pain travelled smoothly down his upflung arm as he rose, was suddenly around his shoulders and chest. Another lunge and his knees were being squeezed in the circular vice. Another—

Something was horribly wrong. He clung to the bole and tried to grasp, but there was—nothing to breathe.

The water came streaming out of his body, from his mouth, his nostrils, the spiracles in his sides, spurting in tangible jets. An intense and fiery itching crawled over the entire surface of his body. At each spasm, long knives ran into him, and from a great distance he heard more water being expelled from his book-lungs in an obscene, frothy sputtering.

Lavon was drowning.

With a final convulsion, he kicked himself away from the splintery bole, and fell. A hard impact shook him; and then the water, which had clung to him so tightly when he had first attempted to leave it, took him back with cold violence.

Sprawling and tumbling grotesquely, he drifted, down and down and down, towards the bottom.

III

For many days, Lavon lay curled insensibly in his spore, as if in the winter sleep. The shock of cold which he had felt on re-entering his native universe had been taken by his body as a sign of coming winter, as it had taken the oxygen-starvation of his brief sojourn above the sky. The spore-forming glands had at once begun to function.

Had it not been for this, Lavon would surely have died. The danger of drowning disappeared even as he fell, as the air bubbled out of his lungs and re-admitted the life-giving water. But for acute desiccation and third degree sunburn, the sunken universe knew no remedy. The healing amnionic fluid generated by the spore-forming glands, after the transparent amber sphere had enclosed him, offered Lavon his only chance.

The brown sphere was spotted after some days by a prowling ameba, quiescent in the eternal winter of the bottom. Down there the temperature was always an even 4°, no matter what the season, but it was unheard of that a spore should be found there while the high epilimnion was still warm and rich in oxygen.

Within an hour, the spore was surrounded by scores of astonished protos, jostling each other to bump their blunt eyeless prows against the shell. Another hour later, a squad of worried men came plunging from the castles far above to press their own noses against the transparent wall. Then swift orders were given.

Four Paras grouped themselves about the amber sphere, and there was a subdued explosion as the trichocysts which lay imbedded at the bases of their cilia, just under the pellicle, burst and cast fine lines of a quickly solidifying liquid into the water. The four Paras thrummed and lifted, tugging.

Lavon's spore swayed gently in the mud and then rose slowly, entangled in the web. Nearby, a Noc cast a cold pulsating glow over the operation—not for the Paras, who did not need the light, but for the baffled knot of men. The sleeping figure of Lavon, head bowed, knees drawn up to its chest, revolved with an absurd solemnity inside the shell as it was moved.

'Take him to Shar, Para.'

The young Shar justified, by minding his own business, the traditional wisdom with which his hereditary office had invested him. He observed at once that there was nothing he could do for the encysted Lavon which would not be classified as simple meddling.

He had the sphere deposited in a high tower room of his castle, where there was plenty of light and the water was warm, which should suggest to the hibernating form that spring was again on the way. Beyond that, he simply sat and watched, and kept his speculations to himself.

Inside the spore, Lavon's body seemed rapidly to be shedding its skin, in long strips and patches. Gradually, his curious shrunkenness disappeared. His withered arms and legs and sunken abdomen filled out again.

The days went by while Shar watched. Finally he could discern no more changes, and, on a hunch, had the spore taken up to the topmost battlements of the tower, into the direct daylight.

An hour later, Lavon moved in his amber prison.

He uncurled and stretched, turned blank eyes up towards the the light. His expression was that of a man who had not yet awakened from a ferocious nightmare. His whole body shone with a strange pink newness.

Shar knocked gently on the wall of the spore. Lavon turned his blind face towards the sound, life coming into his eyes. He smiled tentatively and braced his hands and feet against the inner wall of the shell.

The whole sphere fell abruptly to pieces with a sharp crackling. The amnionic fluid dissipated around him and Shar, carrying away with it the suggestive odour of a bitter struggle against death.

Lavon stood among the bits of shell and looked at Shar silently. At last he said:

'Shar—I've been beyond the sky.'

'I know,' Shar said gently.

Again Lavon was silent. Shar said, 'Don't be humble, Lavon. You've done an epoch-making thing. It nearly cost you your life. You must tell me the rest—all of it.'

'The rest?'

'You taught me a lot while you slept. Or are you still opposed to useless knowledge?'

Lavon could say nothing. He no longer could tell what he knew from what he wanted to know. He had only one question left, but he could not utter it. He could only look dumbly into Shar's delicate face.

'You have answered me,' Shar said, even more gently. 'Come,

my friend; join me at my table. We will plan our journey to the stars.'

It was two winter sleeps after Lavon's disastrous climb beyond the sky that all work on the spaceship stopped. By then, Lavon knew that he had hardened and weathered into that temporarily ageless state a man enters after he has just reached his prime; and he knew also that there were wrinkles engraved upon his brow, to stay and to deepen.

'Old' Shar, too, had changed, his features losing some of their delicacy as he came into his maturity. Though the wedge-shaped bony structure of his face would give him a withdrawn and poetic look for as long as he lived, participation in the plan had given his expression a kind of executive overlay, which at best gave it a masklike rigidity, and at worst coarsened it somehow.

Yet despite the bleeding away of the years, the spaceship was still only a hulk. It lay upon a platform built above the tumbled boulders of the sandbar which stretched out from one wall of the world. It was an immense hull of pegged wood, broken by regularly spaced gaps through which the raw beams of the skeleton could be seen.

Work upon it had progressed fairly rapidly at first, for it was not hard to visualize what kind of vehicle would be needed to crawl through empty space without losing its water. It had been recognized that the sheer size of the machine would enforce a long period of construction, perhaps two full seasons, but neither Shar nor Lavon had anticipated any serious snag.

For that matter, part of the vehicle's apparent incompleteness was an illusion. About a third of its fittings were to consist of living creatures, which could not be expected to install themselves in the vessel much before the actual take-off.

Yet time and time again, work on the ship had had to be halted for long periods. Several times whole sections needed to be ripped out, as it became more and more evident that hardly a single normal, understandable concept could be applied to the problem of space travel.

The lack of the history plates, which the Para steadfastly refused to deliver up, was a double handicap. Immediately upon their loss, Shar had set himself to reproduce them from memory; but unlike the more religious of his people, he had never regarded them as holy writ, and hence had never set himself to memorizing them word by word. Even before the theft, he had accumulated a set of variant translations of passages presenting specific experimental problems, which were stored in his library, carved in wood. But most of these translations tended to contradict each other, and none of them related to spaceship construction, upon which the original had been vague in any case.

No duplicates of the cryptic characters of the original had ever been made, for the simple reason that there was nothing in the sunken universe capable of destroying the originals, nor of duplicating their apparently changeless permanence. Shar remarked too late that through simple caution they should have made a number of verbatim temporary records—but after generations of green-gold peace, simple caution no longer covers preparation against catastrophe. (Nor, for that matter, did a culture which had to dig each letter of its simple alphabet into pulpy waterlogged wood with a flake of stonewort, encourage the keeping of records in triplicate.)

As a result, Shar's imperfect memory of the contents of the history plates, plus the constant and millennial doubt as to the accuracy of the various translations, proved finally to be the worst obstacle to progress on the spaceship itself.

'Men must paddle before they can swim,' Lavon observed belatedly, and Shar was forced to agree with him.

Obviously, whatever the ancients had known about spaceship construction, very little of that knowledge was usable to a people still trying to build its first spaceship from scratch. In retrospect, it was not surprising that the great hulk still rested incomplete upon its platform above the sand boulders, exuding a musty odour of wood steadily losing its strength, two generations after its flat bottom had been laid down.

The fat-faced young man who headed the strike delegation

was Phil XX, a man two generations younger than Lavon, four younger than Shar. There were crow's-feet at the corners of his eyes, which made him look both like a querulous old man and like an infant spoiled in the spore.

'We're calling a halt to this crazy project,' he said bluntly. 'We've slaved our youth away on it, but now that we're our own masters, it's over, that's all. Over.'

'Nobody's compelled you,' Lavon said angrily.

'Society does; our parents do,' a gaunt member of the delegation said. 'But now we're going to start living in the real world. Everybody these days knows that there's no other world but this one. You oldsters can hang on to your superstitions if you like. We don't intend to.'

Baffled, Lavon looked over at Shar. The scientist smiled and said, 'Let them go, Lavon. We have no use for the faint-hearted.'

The fat-faced young man flushed. 'You can't insult us into going back to work. We're through. Build your own ship to no place!'

'All right,' Lavon said evenly. 'Go on, beat it. Don't stand around here orating about it. You've made your decision and we're not interested in your self-justifications. Good-bye.'

The fat-faced young man evidently still had quite a bit of heroism to dramatize which Lavon's dismissal had short-circuited. An examination of Lavon's stony face, however, convinced him that he had to take his victory as he found it. He and the delegation trailed ingloriously out of the archway.

'Now what?' Lavon asked when they had gone. 'I must admit, Shar, that I would have tried to persuade them. We do need the workers, after all.'

'Not as much as they need us,' Shar said tranquilly. 'How many volunteers have you got for the crew of the ship?'

'Hundreds. Every young man of the generation after Phil's wants to go along. Phil's wrong about that segment of the population, at least. The project catches the imagination of the very young.'

'Did you give them any encouragement?'

'Sure,' Lavon said. 'I told them we'd call on them if they were chosen. But you can't take that seriously! We'd do badly to displace our picked group of specialists with youths who have enthusiasm and nothing else.'

'That's not what I had in mind, Lavon. Didn't I see a Noc in your chambers somewhere? Oh, there he is, asleep in the dome. Noc!'

The creature stirred its tentacles lazily.

'Will you give us back the plates?'

'No, Lavon. We have never denied you anything before, but this we must.'

'You're going with us though, Para. Unless you give us the knowledge we need, you'll lose your life if we lose ours.'

'What is one Para?' the creature said. 'We are all alike. This cell will die; but the protos need to know how you fare on this journey. We believe you should make it without the plates.'

'Why?'

The proto was silent. Lavon stared at it a moment, then turned deliberately back to the speaking tubes. 'Everyone hang on,' he said. He felt shaky. 'We're about to start. Tol, is the ship sealed?'

'Noc, I've a message,' Shar called. 'The protos are to tell all men that those who wish to go to the next world with the spaceship must come to the staging area right away. Say that we can't promise to take everyone, but that only those who help us build the ship will be considered at all.'

The Noc curled its tentacles again and appeared to go back to sleep. Actually of course, it was sending its message through the water in all directions.

IV

Lavon turned from the arrangement of speaking-tube megaphones which was his control board and looked at the Para. 'One last try,' he said.

'As far as I can tell, Lavon.'

Lavon shifted to another megaphone. He took a deep breath. Already the water seemed stifling, though the ship hadn't moved.

'Ready with one-quarter power. One, two, three, *go*.'

The whole ship jerked and settled back into place again. The raphe diatoms along the under hull settled into their niches, their jelly treads turning against broad endless belts of crude leather. Wooden gears creaked, stepping up the slow power of the creatures, transmitting it to the sixteen axles of the ship's wheels.

The ship rocked and began to roll slowly along the sandbar. Lavon looked tensely through the mica port. The world flowed painfully past him. The ship canted and began to climb the slope. Behind him, he could feel the electric silence of Shar, Para, the two alternate pilots, as if their gaze were stabbing directly through his body and on out of the port. The world looked different, now that he was leaving it. How had he missed all this beauty before?

The slapping of the endless belts and the squeaking and groaning of the gears and axles grew louder as the slope steepened. The ship continued to climb, lurching. Around it, squadrons of men and protos dipped and wheeled, escorting it towards the sky.

Gradually the sky lowered and pressed down towards the top of the ship.

'A little more work from your diatoms, Tanol,' Lavon said. 'Boulder ahead.' The ship swung ponderously. 'All right, slow them up again. Give us a shove from your side, Than—no, that's too much—there, that's it. Back to normal; you're still turning us! Tanol, give us one burst to line us up again. Good. All right, steady drive on all sides. Won't be long now.'

'How can you think in webs like that?' the Para wondered behind him.

'I just do, that's all. It's the way men think. Overseers, a little more thrust now; the grade's getting steeper.'

The gears groaned. The ship nosed up. The sky brightened in Lavon's face. Despite himself, he began to be frightened. His lungs seemed to burn, and in his mind he felt his long fall through nothingness towards the chill slap of water as if he were experiencing it for the first time. His skin itched and burned.

Could he go up *there* again? Up there into the burning void, the great gasping agony where no life should go?

The sandbar began to level out and the going became a little easier. Up here, the sky was so close that the lumbering motion of the huge ship disturbed it. Shadows of wavelets ran across the sand. Silently, the thick-barrelled bands of blue-green algae drank in the light and converted it to oxygen, writhing in their slow mindless dance just under the long mica skylight which ran along the spine of the ship. In the hold, beneath the latticed corridor and cabin floors, whirring Vortae kept the ship's water in motion, fuelling themselves upon drifting organic particles.

One by one, the figures wheeling about the ship outside waved arms or cilia and fell back, coasting down the slope of the sandbar towards the familiar world, dwindling and disappearing. There was at last only one single Euglena, half-plant cousin of the protos, forging along beside the spaceship into the marches of the shallows. It loved the light, but finally it, too, was driven away into cooler, deeper waters, its single whiplike tentacle undulating placidly as it went. It was not very bright, but Lavon felt deserted when it left.

Where they were going, though, none could follow.

Now the sky was nothing but a thin, resistant skin of water coating the top of the ship. The vessel slowed, and when Lavon called for more power, it began to dig itself in among the sand-grains.

'That's not going to work,' Shar said tensely. 'I think we'd better step down the gear ratio, Lavon, so you can apply stress more slowly.'

'All right,' Lavon agreed. 'Full stop, everybody. Shar, will you supervise gear-changing, please?'

Insane brilliance of empty space looked Lavon full in the face just beyond his big mica bull's-eye. It was maddening to be forced to stop here upon the threshold of infinity; and it was dangerous, too. Lavon could feel building in him the old fear of the outside. A few moments more of inaction, he knew with a gathering coldness at the pit of his stomach, and he would be unable to go through with it.

Surely, he thought, there must be a better way to change gear ratios than the traditional one, which involved dismantling almost the entire gear-box. Why couldn't a number of gears of different sizes be carried on the same shaft, not necessarily all in action all at once, but awaiting use simply by shoving the axle back and forth longitudinally in its sockets? It would still be clumsy, but it could be worked on orders from the bridge and would not involve shutting down the entire machine—and throwing the new pilot into a blue-green funk.

Shar came lunging up through the trap and swam himself to a stop.

'All set,' he said. 'The big reduction gears aren't taking the strain too well, though.'

'Splintering?'

'Yes. I'd go it slow at first.'

Lavon nodded mutely. Without allowing himself to stop, even for a moment, to consider the consequences of his words, he called: 'Half power.'

The ship hunched itself down again and began to move, very slowly indeed, but more smoothly than before. Overhead, the sky thinned to complete transparency. The great light came blasting in. Behind Lavon there was an uneasy stir. The whiteness grew at the front ports.

Again the ship slowed, straining against the blinding barrier. Lavon swallowed and called for more power. The ship groaned like something about to die. It was now almost at a standstill.

'More power,' Lavon ground out.

Once more, with infinite slowness, the ship began to move. Gently, it tilted upward.

Then it lunged forward and every board and beam in it began to squall.

'Lavon! Lavon!'

Lavon started sharply at the shout. The voice was coming at

him from one of the megaphones, the one marked for the port at the rear of the ship.

'Lavon!'

'What is it? Stop your damn yelling.'

'I can see the top of the sky! From the *other* side, from the top side! It's like a big flat sheet of metal. We're going away from it. We're above the sky, Lavon, we're above the sky!'

Another violent start swung Lavon around towards the forward port. On the outside of the mica, the water was evaporating with shocking swiftness, taking with it strange distortions and patterns made of rainbows.

Lavon saw Space.

It was at first like a deserted and cruelly dry version of the bottom. There were enormous boulders, great cliffs, tumbled, split, riven, jagged rocks going up and away in all directions.

But it had a sky of its own—a deep blue dome so far away that he could not believe in, let alone compute, what its distance might be. And in this dome was a ball of white fire that seared his eyeballs.

The wilderness of rock was still a long way away from the ship, which now seemed to be resting upon a level, glistening plain. Beneath the surface-shine, the plain seemed to be made of sand, nothing but familiar sand, the same substance which had heaped up to form a bar in Lavon's own universe, the bar along which the ship had climbed. But the glassy, colourful skin over it—

Suddenly Lavon became conscious of another shout from the megaphone banks. He shook his head savagely and asked, 'What is it now?'

'Lavon, this is Than. What have you got us into? The belts are locked. The diatoms can't move them. They aren't faking, either; we've rapped them hard enough to make them think we were trying to break their shells, but they still can't give us more power.'

'Leave them alone,' Lavon snapped. 'They can't fake; they

haven't enough intelligence. If they say they can't give you more power, they can't.'

'Well, then, you get us out of it,' Than's voice said frightenedly.

Shar came forward to Lavon's elbow. 'We're on a space-water interface, where the surface tension is very high,' he said softly. 'This is why I insisted on our building the ship so that we could lift the wheels off the ground whenever necessary. For a long while I couldn't understand the reference of the history plates to "retractable landing gear", but it finally occurred to me that the tension along a space-water interface—or, to be more exact, a space-mud interface—would hold any large object pretty tightly. If you order the wheels pulled up now, I think we'll make better progress for a while on the belly-treads.'

'Good enough,' Lavon said. 'Hello below—up landing gear. Evidently the ancients knew their business after all, Shar.'

Quite a few minutes later, for shifting power to the belly-treads involved another setting of the gear-box, the ship was crawling along the shore towards the tumbled rock. Anxiously, Lavon scanned the jagged, threatening wall for a break. There was a sort of rivulet off towards the left which might offer a route, though a dubious one, to the next world. After some thought, Lavon ordered his ship turned towards it.

'Do you suppose that thing in the sky is a "star"?' he asked. 'But there were supposed to be lots of them. Only one is up there —and one's plenty for *my* taste.'

'I don't know,' Shar admitted. 'But I'm beginning to get a picture of the way the universe is made, I think. Evidently our world is a sort of cup in the bottom of this huge one. This one has a sky of its own; perhaps it, too, is only a cup in the bottom of a still huger world, and so on and on without end. It's a hard concept to grasp, I'll admit. Maybe it would be more sensible to assume that all the worlds are cups in this one common surface, and that the great light shines on them all impartially.'

'Then what makes it seem to go out every night, and dim even in the day during winter?' Lavon demanded.

'Perhaps it travels in circles, over first one world, then another. How could I know yet?'

'Well, if you're right, it means that all we have to do is crawl along here for a while, until we hit the top of the sky of another world,' Lavon said. 'Then we dive in. Somehow it seems too simple, after all our preparations.'

Shar chuckled, but the sound did not suggest that he had discovered anything funny. 'Simple? Have you noticed the temperature yet?'

Lavon had noticed it, just beneath the surface of awareness, but at Shar's remark he realized that he was gradually being stifled. The oxygen content of the water, luckily, had not dropped, but the temperature suggested the shallows in the last and worst part of the autumn. It was like trying to breathe soup.

'Than, give us more action from the Vortae,' Lavon called. 'This is going to be unbearable unless we get more circulation.'

It was all he could do now to keep his attention on the business of steering the ship.

The cut or defile in the scattered razor-edged rocks was a little closer, but there still seemed to be many miles of rough desert to cross. After a while, the ship settled into a steady, painfully slow crawling, with less pitching and jerking than before, but also with less progress. Under it, there was now a sliding, grinding sound, rasping against the hull of the ship itself, as if it were treadmilling over some coarse lubricant whose particles were each as big as a man's head.

Finally Shar said, 'Lavon, we'll have to stop again. The sand this far up is dry, and we're wasting energy using the treads.'

'Are you sure we can take it?' Lavon asked, gasping for breath. 'At least we are moving. If we stop to lower the wheels and change gears again, we'll boil.'

'We'll boil if we don't,' Shar said calmly. 'Some of our algae are already dead and the rest are withering. That's a pretty good sign that we can't take much more. I don't think we'll make it into the shadows, unless we do change over and put on some speed.'

There was a gulping sound from one of the mechanics. 'We

ought to turn back,' he said raggedly. 'We were never meant to be out here in the first place. We were made for the water, not this hell.'

'We'll stop,' Lavon said, 'but we're not turning back. That's final.'

The words made a brave sound, but the man had upset Lavon more than he dared to admit, even to himself. 'Shar,' he said, 'make it fast, will you?'

The scientist nodded and dived below.

The minutes stretched out. The great white globe in the sky blazed and blazed. It had moved down the sky, far down, so that the light was pouring into the ship directly in Lavon's face, illuminating every floating particle, its rays like long milky streamers. The currents of water passing Lavon's cheek were almost hot.

How could they dare go directly forward into that inferno? The land directly under the 'star' must be even hotter than it was here!

'Lavon! Look at Para!'

Lavon forced himself to turn and look at his proto ally. The great slipper had settled to the deck, where it was lying with only a feeble pulsation of its cilia. Inside, its vacuoles were beginning to swell, to become bloated, pear-shaped bubbles, crowding the granulated protoplasm, pressing upon the dark nuclei.

'This cell is dying,' Para said, as coldly as always. 'But go on—go on. There is much to learn, and you may live, even though we do not. Go on.'

'You're ... for us now?' Lavon whispered.

'We have always been for you. Push your folly to its uttermost. We will benefit in the end, and so will Man.'

The whisper died away. Lavon called the creature again, but it did not respond.

There was a wooden clashing from below, and then Shar's voice came tinnily from one of the megaphones. 'Lavon, go ahead! The diatoms are dying, too, and then we'll be without power. Make it as quickly and directly as you can.'

Grimly, Lavon leaned forward. 'The "star" is directly over the land we're approaching.'

'It is? It may go lower still and the shadows will get longer. That's our only hope.'

Lavon had not thought of that. He rasped into the banked megaphones. Once more, the ship began to move.

It got hotter.

Steadily, with a perceptible motion, the 'star' sank in Lavon's face. Suddenly a new terror struck him. Suppose it should continue to go down until it was gone entirely? Blasting though it was now, it was the only source of heat. Would not space become bitter cold on the instant—and the ship an expanding, bursting block of ice?

The shadows lengthened menacingly, stretched across the desert towards the forward-rolling vessel. There was no talking in the cabin, just the sound of ragged breathing and the creaking of the machinery.

Then the jagged horizon seemed to rush upon them. Stony teeth cut into the lower rim of the ball of fire, devoured it swiftly. It was gone.

They were in the lee of the cliffs. Lavon ordered the ship turned to parallel the rock-line; it responded heavily, sluggishly. Far above, the sky deepened steadily, from blue to indigo.

Shar came silently up through the trap and stood beside Lavon, studying that deepening colour and the lengthening of the shadows down the beach towards their world. He said nothing, but Lavon knew that the same chilling thought was in his mind.

'Lavon.'

Lavon jumped. Shar's voice had iron in it. 'Yes?'

'We'll have to keep moving. We must make the next world, wherever it is, very shortly.'

'How can we dare move when we can't see where we're going? Why not sleep it over—if the cold will let us?'

'It will let us,' Shar said. 'It can't get dangerously cold up here. If it did, the sky—or what we used to think of as the sky—

would have frozen over every night, even in summer. But what I'm thinking about is the water. The plants will go to sleep now. In our world that wouldn't matter; the supply of oxygen is enough to last through the night. But in this confined space, with so many creatures in it and no source of fresh water, we will probably smother.'

Shar seemed hardly to be involved at all, but spoke rather with the voice of implacable physical laws.

'Furthermore,' he said, staring unseeingly out at the raw landscape, 'the diatoms are plants, too. In other words, we must stay on the move for as long as we have oxygen and power—and pray that we make it.'

'Shar, we had quite a few protos on board this ship once. And Para there isn't quite dead yet. If he were, the cabin would be intolerable. The ship is nearly sterile of bacteria, because all the protos have been eating them as a matter of course and there's no outside supply of them, any more than there is for oxygen. But still and all there would have been some decay.'

Shar bent and tested the pellicle of the motionless Para with a probing finger. 'You're right, he's still alive. What does that prove?'

'The Vortae are also alive; I can feel the water circulating. Which proves it wasn't the heat that hurt Para. *It was the light.* Remember how badly my skin was affected after I climbed beyond the sky? Undiluted starlight is deadly. We should add that to the information on the plates.'

'I still don't see the point.'

'It's this. We've got three or four Noc down below. They were shielded from the light, and so must be alive. If we concentrate them in the diatom galleys, the dumb diatoms will think it's still daylight and will go on working. Or we can concentrate them up along the spine of the ship, and keep the algae putting out oxygen. So the question is: which do we need more, oxygen or power? Or can we split the difference?'

Shar actually grinned. 'A brilliant piece of thinking. We'll make a Shar of you yet, Lavon. No, I'd say that we can't split the difference. There's something about daylight, some quality, that the light Noc emits doesn't have. You and I can't detect it, but the green plants can, and without it they don't make oxygen. So we'll have to settle for the diatoms—for power.'

Lavon brought the vessel away from the rocky lee of the cliff, out on to the smoother sand. All trace of direct light was gone now, although there was still a soft, general glow on the sky.

'Now, then,' Shar said thoughtfully, 'I would guess that there's water over there in the canyon, if we can reach it. I'll go below and arrange—'

Lavon gasped, 'What's the matter?'

Silently, Lavon pointed, his heart pounding.

The entire dome of indigo above them was spangled with tiny, incredibly brilliant lights. There were hundreds of them, and more and more were becoming visible as the darkness deepened. And far away, over the ultimate edge of the rocks, was a dim red globe, crescented with ghostly silver. Near the zenith was another such body, much smaller, and silvered all over . . .

Under the two moons of Hydrot, and under the eternal stars, the two-inch wooden spaceship and its microscopic cargo toiled down the slope towards the drying little rivulet.

V

The ship rested on the bottom of the canyon for the rest of the night. The great square doors were thrown open to admit the raw, irradiated, life-giving water from outside—and the wriggling bacteria which were fresh food.

No other creatures approached them, either with curiosity or with predatory intent, while they slept, though Lavon had posted guards at the doors. Evidently, even up here on the very floor of space, highly organized creatures were quiescent at night.

But when the first flush of light filtered through the water, trouble threatened.

First of all, there was the bug-eyed monster. The thing was green and had two snapping claws, either one of which could have broken the ship in two like a spyrogyra straw. Its eyes were black and globular, on the ends of short columns, and its long feelers were as thick as a plant-bole. It passed in a kicking fury of motion, however, never noticing the ship at all.

'Is that—a sample of the kind of life we can expect in the next world?' Lavon whispered. Nobody answered, for the very good reason that nobody knew.

After a while, Lavon risked moving the ship forward against the current, which was slow but heavy. Enormous writhing worms whipped past them. One struck the hull a heavy blow, then thrashed on obliviously.

'They don't notice us,' Shar said. 'We're too small. Lavon, the ancients warned us of the immensity of space, but even when you see it, it's impossible to grasp. And all those stars—can they mean what I think they mean? It's beyond thought, beyond belief!'

'The bottom's sloping,' Lavon said, looking ahead intently. 'The walls of the canyon are retreating, and the water's becoming rather silty. Let the stars wait, Shar; we're coming towards the entrance of our new world.'

Shar subsided moodily. His vision of space had disturbed him, perhaps seriously. He took little notice of the great thing that was happening, but instead huddled worriedly over his own expanding speculations. Lavon felt the old gap between their two minds widening once more.

Now the bottom was tilting upward again. Lavon had no experience with delta-formation, for no rivulets left his own world, and the phenomenon worried him. But his worries were swept away in wonder as the ship topped the rise and nosed over.

Ahead, the bottom sloped away again, indefinitely, into glimmering depths. A proper sky was over them once more, and Lavon could see small rafts of plankton floating placidly beneath it. Almost at once, too, he saw several of the smaller kinds of protos, a few of which were already approaching the ship—

Then the girl came darting out of the depths, her features

distorted with terror. At first she did not see the ship at all. She came twisting and turning lithely through the water, obviously hoping only to throw herself over the ridge of the delta and into the savage streamlet beyond.

Lavon was stunned. Not that there were men here—he had hoped for that—but the girl's single-minded flight towards suicide.

'What—'

Then a dim buzzing began to grow in his ears, and he understood.

'Shar! Than! Tanol!' he bawled. 'Break out crossbows and spears! Knock out all the windows!' He lifted a foot and kicked through the big port in front of him. Someone thrust a crossbow into his hand.

'Eh? What's happening?' Shar blurted.

'Rotifers!'

The cry went through the ship like a galvanic shock. The rotifers back in Lavon's own world were virtually extinct, but everyone knew thoroughly the grim history of the long battle Man and proto had waged against them.

The girl spotted the ship suddenly and paused, stricken by despair at the sight of the new monster. She drifted with her own momentum, her eyes alternately fixed hypnotically upon the ship and glancing back over her shoulder, towards where the buzzing snarled louder and louder in the dimness.

'Don't stop!' Lavon shouted. 'This way, this way! We're friends! We'll help!'

Three great semi-transparent trumpets of smooth flesh bored over the rise, the thick cilia of their coronas whirring greedily. Dicrans—the most predacious of the entire tribe of Eaters. They were quarrelling thickly among themselves as they moved, with the few blurred, pre-symbolic noises which made up their 'language'.

Carefully, Lavon wound the crossbow, brought it to his shoulder, and fired. The bolt sang away through the water. It lost momentum rapidly, and was caught by a stray current which brought it closer to the girl than to the Eater at which Lavon had aimed.

He bit his lip, lowered the weapon, wound it up again. It did not pay to underestimate the range; he would have to wait until he could fire with effect. Another bolt, cutting through the water from a side port, made him issue orders to cease firing.

The sudden irruption of the rotifers decided the girl. The motionless wooden monster was strange to her and had not yet menaced her—but she must have known what it would be like to have three Dicrans over her, each trying to grab away from the other the biggest share. She threw herself towards the big port. The Eaters screamed with fury and greed and bored after her.

She probably would not have made it, had not the dull vision of the lead Dicran made out the wooden shape of the ship at the last instant. It backed off, buzzing, and the other two sheered away to avoid colliding with it. After that they had another argument, though they could hardly have formulated what it was that they were fighting about. They were incapable of saying anything much more complicated than the equivalent of 'Yaah', 'Drop dead', and 'You're another'.

While they were still snarling at each other, Lavon pierced the nearest one all the way through with an arablast bolt. It disintegrated promptly—rotifers are delicately organized creatures despite their ferocity—and the remaining two were at once involved in a lethal battle over the remains.

'Than, take a party out and spear me those two Eaters while they're still fighting,' Lavon ordered. 'Don't forget to destroy their eggs, too. I can see that this world needs a little taming.'

The girl shot through the port and brought up against the far wall of the cabin, flailing in terror. Lavon tried to approach her, but from somewhere she produced a flake of stonewort chipped to a nasty point. He sat down on the stool before his control board and waited while she took in the cabin, Lavon, Shar, the pilot, the senescent Para.

At last she said: 'Are—you—the gods from beyond the sky?'

'We're from beyond the sky, all right,' Lavon said. 'But we're not gods. We're human beings, like yourself. Are there many humans here?'

The girl seemed to assess the situation very rapidly, savage though she was. Lavon had the odd and impossible impression that he should recognize her. She tucked the knife back into her matted hair—ah, Lavon thought, that's a trick I may need to remember—and shook her head.

'We are few. The Eaters are everywhere. Soon they will have the last of us.'

Her fatalism was so complete that she actually did not seem to care.

'And you've never cooperated against them? Or asked the protos to help?'

'The protos?' She shrugged. 'They are as helpless as we are against the Eaters. We have no weapons which kill at a distance, like yours. And it is too late now for such weapons to do any good. We are too few, the Eaters too many.'

Lavon shook his head emphatically. 'You've had one weapon that counts, all along. Against it, numbers mean nothing. We'll show you how we've used it. You may be able to use it even better than we did, once you've given it a try.'

The girl shrugged again. 'We have dreamed of such a weapon now and then, but never found it. I do not think that what you say is true. What is this weapon?'

'Brains,' Lavon said. 'Not just one brain, but brains. Working together. Cooperation.'

'Lavon speaks the truth,' a weak voice said from the deck.

The Para stirred feebly. The girl watched it with wide eyes. The sound of the Para using human speech seemed to impress her more than the ship or anything else it contained.'

'The Eaters can be conquered,' the thin, buzzing voice said. 'The protos will help, as they helped in the world from which we came. They fought this flight through space, and deprived Man of his records; but Man made the trip without the records. The protos will never oppose men again. I have already spoken to the protos of this world and have told them what Man can dream, Man can do, whether the protos wish it or not.

'Shar, your metal records are with you. They were hidden in the ship. My brothers will lead you to them.

'This organism dies now. It dies in confidence of knowledge, as an intelligent creature dies. Man has taught us this. There is nothing that knowledge ... cannot do. With it, men ... have crossed ... have crossed space ...'

The voice whispered away. The shining slipper did not change, but something about it was gone. Lavon looked at the girl; their eyes met.

'We have crossed space,' Lavon repeated softly.

Shar's voice came to him across a great distance. The young-old man was whispering: 'But *have* we?'

'As far as I'm concerned, yes,' said Lavon.

SURFACE TENSION

A common type of science fiction plot is that which deals with men the size of microorganisms, or the size of atoms. The basic assumption is that men can somehow be shrunk to tiny size yet remain men.

But how could this be done? Is the tiny man made up of fewer atoms, or are the atoms themselves miniaturized? If the atoms themselves are miniaturized, how could men live on food containing unminiaturized atoms, make use of unminiaturized oxygen to breathe? If the miniature man is made up of fewer atoms, are there sufficient atoms to keep him as complex as he is now; to give him a brain sufficiently complex to be intelligent?

I think we can safely say that by today's understanding of science the miniaturization of human beings, while keeping them alive and intelligent, is quite impossible.

Nevertheless, James Blish has a thorough understanding of science and it can be assumed that he is aware of the impossibility of his basic assumption. Why, then, did he do it?

Well, by doing so, he was able to give a fascinating picture of a world in which the plants and animals surrounding man were microorganisms. He could also describe the difficulties and heroism involved in the conquest of space, in terms of a tiny wooden vessel, making its way from one puddle to another.

Notice, too, that, having made his one basic impossible assumption, he does everything he can to make all else plausible. (It is sometimes said that a good science fiction writer makes one assumption—even if an impossible one—to start his story and then, no more.)

Questions and Suggestions

1. Blish makes use of microorganisms to substitute for machine technology. Noc supplies illumination, the Vortae supply water circulation and so on. Find information on the microorganisms called 'noctiluca' and 'vorticella' and see if this sounds reasonable. What are the rotifera (the 'eaters' of the story)? How would they seem to one-celled animals?

2. The most intelligent of the microorganisms is Para. Check the description with that of the 'paramecium'. Notice that Para talks by the careful manipulation of its cilia. How do the cilia of the paramecium work and do you think that Para's ciliar manipulation is possible? Do you think it is possible for any organism at the level of complexity of the paramecium to be intelligent? Blish implies that there is a bond of union between all the Paras; that there is a multi-cellular organism built up of them although the individual cells are not in contact. Do you think that men might evolve in the direction of a multi-organismic creature, with each man being part of a total society with a superconsciousness? How might such a living society conduct itself? Would you like to be part of it?

3. Blish places the planet Hydrot (why the name?) in the Tau Ceti system. Tau Ceti is a real star. Where is it located and why does it have that name? What else can you find out about it? Why did Blish choose this star rather than Sirius, Rigel, or any of the other bright, familiar ones?

4. What is surface tension and why was it so difficult for the microscopic men to get out of the water and into the air?

Does surface tension exist in our world and if it does, why are we not bothered by it? What other facts of the environment might bother a miniature man but does not bother us? What facts of the environment which are a greater danger to ourselves would not bother a miniature man?

9. Country Doctor

William Morrison

He had long resigned himself to thinking that opportunity had passed him by for life. Now, when it struck so unexpectedly and so belatedly, he wasn't sure that it was welcome.

He had gone to sleep early, after an unusually hectic day. As if the need for immunizing against the threat of an epidemic hadn't been enough, he had also had to treat the usual aches and pains, and to deliver one baby, plus two premature Marsopolis calves. Even as he pulled the covers over himself, the phone was ringing, but he let Maida answer it. Nothing short of a genuine first-class emergency was going to drag him out of the house again before morning if he could help it. Evidently the call wasn't that important, for Maida hadn't come in to bother him about it, and his last feeling, before dropping off to sleep, was one of gratitude for her common sense.

He wasn't feeling grateful when the phone rang again. He awoke with a start. The dark of night still lay around the house, and from alongside him came the sound of his wife's slow breathing. In the next room, one of the kids, he couldn't tell which, said drowsily, 'Turn off the alarm.' Evidently the sound of the ringing hadn't produced complete wakefulness.

While he lay there, feeling too heavy to move, Maida moaned slightly in her sleep, and he said to himself, 'If that's old Bender, calling about his constipation again, I'll feed him dynamite pills.' Then he reached over to the night table and forced himself to pick up the phone. 'Who is it?'

'Doctor Meltzer?' He recognized the hoarse and excited tones of Tom Linton, the city peace officer. 'You better get over here right away!'

'What is it, Tom? And where am I supposed to get?'

'Over at the space port. Ship out of control—almost ran into Phobos coming down—and it landed with a crash. They need you fast.'

'I'm coming.'

The sleep was out of his eyes now. He grabbed his emergency equipment, taking along a plentiful supply of antibiotics and adjustable bandages. There was no way of knowing how many men had been hurt, and he had better be ready to treat an entire crew.

Outside the house, his bicar was waiting for him. He tossed in his equipment and hopped in after it. A throw of the switch brought in full broadcast power, and a fraction of a second later he had begun to skim over the smooth path that led over the farmland reclaimed from the desert.

The space port was less than twenty miles away, and it took him no more than ten minutes to get there. As he approached, the light blinked green at an intersection. Ah, he thought, one advantage of being a country doctor with a privileged road is that you always have the right of way. Are there any other advantages? None that you can think of offhand. You go through college with a brilliant record, you dream of helping humanity, of doing research in medicine, of making discoveries that will lengthen human life and lend it a little added happiness. And then, somehow, you find yourself trapped. The frontier outpost that's supposed to be the steppingstone to bigger things turns out to be a lifetime job. You find that your most important patients are not people, but food-animals. On Mars there are plenty of men and women, but few cows and sheep. Learn to treat *them*, and you really amount to something. Save a cow, and the news gets around faster than if you saved a man. And so, gradually, the animals begin to take more and more of your time, and you become known and liked in the community. You marry, you have children, you slip into a routine that dulls the meaning of the fast-hurrying days. You reach fifty—and you realize suddenly that life has passed you by. Half your allotted hundred years are gone, you can't tell where. The opportunities that once beckoned so brightly have faded in the distance.

What do you have to show for what the years have taken? One wife, one boy, one girl—

A surge of braking-power caught him from the direction of the space port. The sudden deceleration brought him out of his musings to realize that the entire area was brightly lit up. A huge ship lay across the middle of the field. Its length was at least a thousand feet, and he knew that there must be more than two dozen men in its crew. He hoped that none had been killed.

'Doc!'

Tom was rushing over to him. 'How many hurt, Tom?'

'Our injuries are all minor, Doctor,' said a sharp voice. 'Nothing that I can't handle well enough myself.'

As he stared at the man in the gold-trimmed uniform who was standing alongside Tom, he had a feeling of disappointment. If there were no serious injuries, what was the rush all about? Why hadn't they telephoned him while he was riding over, told him there was no need of him, let him get back to bed?

'I thought there was a serious crash.'

'The crash was nothing, Doctor. Linton, here, was excited by our near-miss of Phobos. But we've no time to waste discussing that. I understand, Doctor Meltzer, that you're a first-class vet.'

He flushed. 'I hope you didn't drag me out of bed to treat a sick dog. I'm not sentimental about ship's pets—'

'This is no pet. Come along, and I'll show you.'

He followed silently as the Captain led the way up the ramp and into the ship. Inside the vessel, there were no indications of any disorder caused by the crash. One or two of the men were bandaged around the head, but they seemed perfectly capable of getting around and doing their work.

He and the Captain were on a moving walkway now, and for three hundred feet they rode swiftly along it together, towards the back of the ship. Then the Captain stepped off, and Dr. Meltzer followed suit. When he caught sight of the thing that was waiting for him, his jaw dropped.

Almost the entire stern of the ship, about one third its length, was occupied by a great reddish creature that lay there quietly like an overgrown lump of flesh taken from some giant's butcher shop. A transparent panel walled it off from the rest of the ship. Through the panel Dr. Meltzer could see the thirty-foot-wide slit that marked the mouth. Above that was a cluster of breathing pores, looking like gopher holes, and above these was a semicircle of six great eyes, half closed and dulled as if with pain.

He had never seen anything like it before. 'My God, what is it?'

'For lack of a better name, we call it a space-cow. Actually, it doesn't inhabit free space—we picked it up on Ganymede as a matter of fact—and as you can see, it doesn't resemble a cow in the least.'

'Is that supposed to be my patient?'

'That's it, Doctor.'

He laughed, with more anger than amusement. 'I haven't the slightest idea what that behemoth is like and what's wrong with it. How do you expect me to treat it?'

'That's up to you. Now, wait a minute, Doctor, before you blow up. This thing is sick. It isn't eating. It hardly moves. And it's been getting worse almost from the time we left Ganymede. We meant to land at Marsopolis and have it treated there, but we overshot the place and then something went wrong with our drive so we had no choice but to come down here.'

'Don't they have any doctors to spare from town?'

'They're no better than you are. I mean that, Doctor. The vets they have in Marsopolis are used to treating pets for a standard series of diseases, and they don't handle animals as big as the ones you do. And they don't meet the kind of emergencies you do, either. You're as good a man as we can get.'

'And I tell you, I don't know a thing about this overgrown hunk of protein.'

'Then you'll just have to find out about it. We've radioed Earth, and hope to be getting some information soon from some of their zoo directors. Meanwhile—'

The crewmen were bringing over what appeared to be a diver's uniform. 'What's this?' he asked suspiciously.

'Something for you to wear. You're going to go down into this animal.'

'Into that mass of flesh?' For a moment horror left him with his mouth open. Then anger took over. 'Like hell I am.'

'Look, Doctor, it's necessary. We want to keep this beast alive—for scientific purposes, as well as possible value as a food animal. And how can we keep it alive unless we learn something about it?'

'There's plenty we can learn without going into it. Plenty of tests we can make first. Plenty of—'

He caught himself abruptly because he was talking nonsense and he knew it. You could take the thing's temperature—but what would the figure you got tell you? What was normal temperature for a space-cow? What was normal blood pressure—provided the creature had blood? What was normal heartbeat—assuming there was a heart? Presumably the thing had teeth, a bony skeleton—but how to learn where and what they were? You couldn't X-ray a mass of flesh like this—not with any equipment he had ever seen, even in the best-equipped office.

There were other, even more disquieting ways in which he was ignorant. What kind of digestive juices did the thing have? Suppose he did go down in a diver's uniform—would the juices dissolve it? Would they dissolve the oxygen lines, the instruments he used to look around and probe the vast inside of the beast?

He expressed his doubts to the Captain, and the latter said, 'These suits have been tested, and so have the lines. We know that they can stand a half hour inside without being dissolved away. If they start to go, you'll radio up to us, and we'll pull you up.'

'Thanks. How do I know that once the suit starts to go, it won't rip? How do I know that the juices simply won't eat my skin away?'

There was no answer to that. You just didn't know, and you had to accept your ignorance.

Even while he was objecting, Dr. Meltzer began putting on

the suit. It was thin and light, strong enough to withstand several atmospheres of pressure, and at the same time not so clumsy as to hamper his movements considerably. Sealed pockets carried an assortment of instruments and supplies. Perfect two-way communication would make the exchange of ideas—such as they might be—as easy as if the person he was talking to were face to face with him. With the suit came a pair of fragile-looking gloves that left his hands almost as free as if they were bare. But the apparent fragility was misleading. Mechanical strength was there.

But what about resistance to biological action? The question kept nagging him. You can't know, he told himself. About things like that you take a chance. You take a chance and hope that if anything goes wrong, they'll pull you up before the juices have time to get working on you.

They had everything in readiness. Two of the other men were also wearing uniforms like his own, and when he had put his on, and tested it, the Captain gave the signal, and they all went into a small airlock. They were in the chamber where the great beast lay and quivered dully as if in giant pain.

They tied strong thin plastic cords around Doctor Meltzer's waist, tested the oxygen lines. Then they put a ladder up in front of the beast's face. Doctor Meltzer had a little trouble breathing, but it was not because of anything wrong with the oxygen supply. That was at the right pressure and humidity, and it was mixed with the correct amount of inert gases. It was merely the thought of going down into the creature's belly that constricted his throat, the idea of going into a strange and terrible world so different from his own, of submitting to unimaginable dangers.

He said hoarsely into the radio speaker, 'How do I get in anyway, knock? The mouth's at least forty feet off the ground. And it's closed. You've got to open it, Captain. Or do you expect me to pry it open myself?'

The two men with him stretched out a plastic ladder. In the low gravity of Mars, climbing forty feet was no problem. Dr. Meltzer began to pull his way up. As he went higher, he noticed that the great mouth was slowly opening. One of the men had poked the creature with an electric prod.

Dr. Meltzer reached the level of the lower jaw, and with the fascinated fear of a bird staring at a snake, gazed at the great opening that was going to devour him. Inside there was a grey and slippery surface which caught the beam of his flashlight and reflected it back and forth until the rays faded away. Fifty feet beyond the opening, the passage made a slow turn to one side. What lay ahead, he couldn't guess.

The sensible thing was to go in at once, but he couldn't help hesitating. Suppose the jaws closed just as he got between them? He'd be crushed like an eggshell. Suppose the throat constricted with the irritation he caused it? That would crush him too. He recalled suddenly an ancient fable about a man who had gone down into a whale's belly. What was the man's name, now? Daniel—no, he had only gone into a den of lions. Job—wrong again. Job had been afflicted with boils, the victim of staphylococci at the other end of the scale of size. Jonah, that was it. Jonah, the man whose name was a symbol among the superstitious for bad luck.

But a scientist had no time for superstition. A scientist just thrust himself forward—

He stepped off the ladder into the great mouth. Beneath him, the jaw was slippery. His feet slid out from under him, and then his momentum carried him forward, and he glided smoothly down the yawning gullet. It was like going down a Martian hillside on a greased sled, the low gravity making the descent nice and easy. He noticed that the cords around his waist, as well as the oxygen lines, were descending smoothly after him. He reached the turn, threw his body away from the grey wall, and continued sliding. Another fifty feet, and he landed with a small splash in a pool of liquid.

The stomach? Never mind what you called it, this was probably the beginning of a digestive tract. He'd have a chance now to see how resistant his suit was.

He was immersed in the liquid now, and he sank slowly until his feet touched more solid flesh again. By the beam from his flashlight, he saw that the liquid around him was a light green. The portion of the digestive tract on which he stood was slate grey, with bright emerald streaks.

A voice spoke anxiously in his ears. 'Doctor Meltzer! Are you safe?'

'Fine, Captain. Having a wonderful time. Wish you were here.'

'What's it like in there?'

'I'm standing at the bottom of a pool of greenish liquid. I'm fascinated, but not greatly instructed.'

'See anything that might be wrong?'

'How the devil would I tell right from wrong in here? I've never been in one of these beasts before. I've got sample bottles, and I'm going to fill them in various places. This is going to be sample one. You can analyse it later.'

'Fine, Doctor. You just keep on going.'

He flashed the beam around him. The liquid was churning gently, possibly because of the splash he himself had made. The grey-green walls themselves were quiet, and the portion underfoot yielded slightly as he put his weight upon it, but was otherwise apparently undisturbed by his presence.

He moved ahead. The liquid grew shallower, came to an end. He climbed out and stepped cautiously forward.

'Doctor, what's happening?'

'Nothing's happening. I'm just looking around.'

'Keep us informed. I don't think there's any danger, but—'

'But in case there is, you want the next man to know what to watch out for? All right, Captain.'

'Lines all right?'

'They're fine.' He took another step forward. 'The ground—I suppose I can call it the ground—is getting less slippery. Easier to walk on. Walls about twenty feet apart here. No sign of macroscopic flora or fauna. No artifacts to indicate intelligent life.'

The Captain's voice sounded pained. 'Don't let your sense of humour carry you away, Doctor. This is important. Maybe you don't realize exactly how important, but—'

He interrupted. 'Hold it, Captain, here's something interesting.

A big reddish bump, about three feet across, in the grey-green wall.'

'What is it?'

'Might be a tumour. I'll slice some tissue from the wall itself. That's sample number two. Tissue from the tumour, sample number three.'

The wall quivered almost imperceptibly as he sliced into it. The fresh-cut surface was purple, but it slowly turned red again as the internal atmosphere of the beast got at it.

'Here's another tumour, like the first, this time on the other side of the wall. And here are a couple more. I'm leaving them alone. The walls are getting narrower. There's still plenty of room to walk, but—wait a minute, I take that back. There's some kind of valve ahead of me. It's opening and closing spasmodically.'

'Can you get through?'

'I'd hate to take a chance. And even if I did make it while it was open, it could crush the oxygen lines when it closed.'

'Then that's the end of the road?'

'I don't know. Let me think.'

He stared at the great valve. It moved rapidly, opening and closing in a two-second rhythm. Probably a valve separating one part of the digestive system from another, he thought, like the human pylorus. The green-streaked grey flesh seemed totally unlike human muscle, but all the same it appeared to serve a similar function. Maybe the right kind of drug would cause muscular relaxation.

He pulled a large hypodermic syringe from one of the sealed pockets of his diver's uniform. He plunged the needle quickly into the edge of the valve as it paused for a fraction of a second before closing, shot a pint of drug solution into the flesh, and ripped the needle out again. The valve closed once more, but more slowly. It opened, closed again, opened once more—and stayed open.

How long before it recovered, and shut off his retreat? He didn't know. But if he wanted to find out what was on the other side, he'd have to work fast. He plunged forward, almost slipping in his eagerness, and leaped through the motionless valve.

Then he called up to tell the Captain what he had done.

The Captain's voice was anxious. 'I don't know whether you ought to risk it, Doctor.'

'I'm down here to learn things. I haven't learned much yet. By the way, the walls are widening out again. And there's another pool of liquid ahead. Blue liquid, this time.'

'Are you taking a sample?'

'I'm a sampler from way back, Captain.'

He waded into the blue pond, filled his sample bottle, and put it into one of his pockets. Suddenly, in front of him something broke the surface of the pond, then dived down again.

He came to a full stop. 'Hold it, Captain. There seems to be fauna.'

'What? Something alive?'

'Very much alive.'

'Be careful, Doctor. I think there's a gun in one of the pockets of that uniform. Use it if necessary.'

'A gun? Don't be cruel, Captain. How'd you like to have somebody shooting off guns inside you?'

'Be careful, man!'

'I'll use my hypodermic as a weapon.'

But the creature, whatever it was, did not approach him again, and he waded further into the blue pond. When his eyes were below the surface of the liquid, he saw the thing moving again.

'Looks like an overgrown tadpole, about two feet long.'

'Is it coming close?'

'No, it's darting away from me. And there's another one. I think the light bothers it.'

'Any signs that the thing is dangerous?'

'I can't tell. It may be a parasite of the big creature, or it may be something that lives in symbiosis with it.'

'Stay away from it, Doctor. No use risking your life for nothing.'

A trembling voice said, 'Larry! Are you all right?'

'Maida! What are you doing here?'

'I woke up when you left. And then I had trouble going to sleep again.'

'But why did you come to the space port?'

'Ships began to flash by overhead, and I began to wonder what had happened. So I called up—and they told me.'

'Ships overhead?'

The Captain's voice cut in again. 'The news services, Doctor. This case has aroused great interest. I didn't want to tell you before, but don't be surprised if you come up to find yourself famous.'

'Never mind the news services. Have you heard from Earth yet?'

'No messages from Earth. We did hear from the curator of the Marsopolis Zoo.'

'What did he say?'

'He never even heard of a space-cow, and he has no suggestions to make.'

'That's fine. By the way, Captain, are there any photographers around from those news services?'

'Half a dozen. Still, motion picture, television—'

'How about sending them down inside to take a few pictures?'

There was a moment of silence. Then the Captain's voice again: 'I don't think they can go down for a while yet. Maybe later.'

'Why can't they go down now? I'd like to have some company. If the beast's mouth is open—' A disquieting thought struck him. 'Say, it is open, isn't it?'

The Captain's voice sounded tense. 'Now, don't get upset, Doctor, we're doing all we can!'

'You mean it's closed?'

'Yes, it's closed. I didn't want to tell you this, but the mouth closed unexpectedly, and then, when we did have the idea of sending a photographer down inside, we couldn't get it open again. Apparently the creature has adapted to the effects of the electric shock.'

'There must be some way of getting it open again.'

'Of course there's a way. There's always a way. Don't worry, Doctor, we're working on it. We'll find it.'

'But the oxygen—'

'The lines are strong, and the mouth isn't closed tight enough to pinch them off. You can breathe all right, can't you?'

'Now that I think of it, I can. Thanks for telling me.'

'You see, Doctor, it isn't so bad.'

'It's perfectly lovely. But what happens if my uniform or the oxygen lines start to dissolve?'

'We'll pull you out. We'll do something to open the mouth. Just don't get caught behind that valve, Doctor.'

'Thanks for the advice. I don't know what I'd do without it, Captain.'

He felt a sudden surge of anger. If there was one thing he hated, it was good advice, given smugly when the giver could stand off to one side, without sharing the danger of the person he was helping. Don't let this happen, don't get caught here, take care of yourself. But you were down here to do a job, and so far you hadn't done it. You hadn't learned a thing about what made this monstrous creature tick.

And the chances were that you wouldn't learn, either. The way to examine a beast was from the outside, not from within. You watched it eat, you studied the transfer of the food from one part of the body to another, you checked on the circulation of the body fluids, using radioactive tracers if no other methods offered, you dissected specimens of typical individuals. The Captain should have had a few scientists aboard, and they should have done a few of these things instead of just sitting there staring at the beast. But that would have made things too easy. No, they had to wait for you to come aboard, and then send you deliberately sliding down into the guts of an animal you didn't know anything about, in the hope of having a miracle happen to you. Maybe they thought a loop of intestine or some gland of internal secretion would come over to you and say, 'I'm not working right. Fix me, and everything will be fine.'

Another of the tadpole-like creatures was swimming over towards him, approaching slowly, the forepart twitching like the nose of a curious dog. Then, like the others, the creature turned and darted away. 'Maybe that's the cause,' he thought. 'Maybe that's the parasite that's causing the trouble.'

Only—it might just as well be a creature necessary to the larger creature's health. Again and again you were faced with the same problem. Down here you were in a world you knew nothing about. And when everything was so strange to you—what was normal, and what wasn't?

When in doubt, he decided, move on. He moved.

The blue pool was shallow, and once more he came up on what he decided to call dry ground. Once more the walls grew narrow again. After a time he could reach out and touch the walls on either side of him at the same time.

He flashed his light into the narrow passage, and saw that a dozen yards ahead of him it seemed to come to an end. 'Blind alley,' he thought. 'Time to turn back.'

The Captain's voice came to him again. 'Doctor, is everything all right?'

'Beautiful. I've had a most interesting tour. By the way, did you get the creature's mouth open yet?'

'We're still working on it.'

'I wish you luck. Maybe when those reports from Earth come in—'

'They've come. None of the curators knows anything about space-cows. For some reason, the electric-shock method doesn't work any more, and we're trying all sorts of other stimuli.'

'I take it that nothing is effective.'

'Not yet. One of the photo service men suggested we use a powerful mechanical clamp to pull the jaws open. We're having one flown over.'

'Use anything,' he said fervently. 'But for God's sake, get that *mouth* open!'

Dr. Meltzer cursed the photo service people, to whom he meant nothing more than a series of coloured lines in space. Then he added an unkind word or two for the Captain, who had got him into this mess, and started back.

The tadpole creatures seemed to be interested in his progress. They came swarming around him, and now he could see that there were almost a dozen of them. They moved with quick flips of their tails, like the minnows he had once seen back on Earth, where he had attended medical school. Between each pair of flips there was a momentary pause, and when they came close he was able to get a reasonably good look at them. He was surprised to see that they had two rows of eyes each.

Were the eyes functional or vestigial? In the former case, they must spend some part of their life cycle outside the host creature, in places where they had need of the sense of sight. In the latter case, they were at least descended from outside creatures. Maybe I'll try to catch one of them, he thought. Once I get it outside I can give it a real examination.

Once I get it outside, he repeated. Provided I get outside myself.

He waded through the pond again. As he reached the shallow part of the blue liquid, a voice came to him—this time his wife's voice. 'Larry, are you all right?'

'Doing fine. How are the kids?'

'They're with me. They woke up during the excitement, and I brought them along.'

'You didn't tell me that before!'

'I didn't want to upset you.'

'Oh, it doesn't upset me in the least. Nothing like a nice family picnic. But how do you expect them to go to school in the morning?'

'Oh, Larry, what difference does it make if they miss school for once? A chance to be in on something like this happens once in a lifetime.'

'That's a little too often to suit me. Well, now that I know they're here, let me talk to them.'

Evidently they had been waiting for the chance, for Jerry's voice came at once. 'Hiya, Dad.'

'Hiya, Jerry. Having a good time?'

'Swell. You oughtta be out here, Dad. There are a lot of people. They're treatin' us swell.'

Martia cut in. 'Mom, he isn't letting me talk. I want to talk to Daddy too.'

'Let her talk, Jerry. Go ahead, Martia. Say something to Daddy.'

A sudden blast almost knocked out his eardrum. 'Dad, can you hear me?' Martia screamed. 'Can you hear me Dad?'

'I can hear you, and so can these animals. Not so loud, sweetheart.'

'Gee, Dad, you oughtta see all the people. They took pictures of me and Mom. Oh, we're so thrilled!'

'They took pictures of me too, Dad,' said Jerry.

'They're sending the pictures all over. To Earth and Venus, and everywhere. We're gonna be on television too, Dad. Isn't it exciting?'

'It's terrific, Martia. You don't know what this does for my morale.'

'Aw, all she thinks about is pictures. Mom, make her get away from the microphone, or I'll push her away.'

'You've had your chance, Martia. Let Jerry talk again.'

'You know what, Dad? Everybody says you're gonna be famous. They say this is the only animal of its kind ever discovered. And you're the only person ever went into it. Can I go down there too, Dad?'

'No!' he yelled.

'Okay, okay. Say, Dad, know what? If you bring it back alive, they're gonna take it to Earth, and put it in a special zoo of its own.'

'Thank them for me. Look, Jerry, did they get the animal's mouth open yet?'

'Not yet, Dad, but they're bringing in a great big machine.'

The Captain's voice again: 'We'll have the mouth open soon. Doctor. Where are you now?'

'Approaching the valve again. Have you heard anything that could be useful? Maybe some explorer or hunter might be able to tell you something about space-cows—'

'Sorry, Doctor. Nobody knows anything about space-cows.'

'That's what you said before. All right, Captain, stand by for further news. I've got a shoal of these tadpole beasts in attendance. Let's see what happens now.'

'They're not attacking, are they?'

'Not yet.'

'You feel all right otherwise?'

'Fine. A little short of breath, though. That may be the result of tension. And a little hungry. I wonder how this beast would taste raw—my God!'

The Captain asked anxiously, 'What is it?'

'That valve I paralysed. It's working normally once more!'

'You mean it's opening and closing?'

'The same rhythm as before. And every time it closes, it squeezes those oxygen tubes. That's why I sometimes feel short of breath. I have to get out of here!'

'Do you have enough drug to paralyse the valve again?'

'No, I don't. Keep quiet, Captain, let me figure this out.'

The valve was almost impassable. If he had found a good place to take off from, he might have dived safely through the opening during the near-second when the muscles were far apart. But there was no place for a take-off. He had to approach up a slippery slope, hampered by uniform and lines. And if he misjudged the right moment to go through, he'd be caught when the valve closed again.

He stood there motionless for a moment, sweat pouring down his forehead and into his eyes. Damn it, he thought, I can't even wipe it away. I've got to tackle this thing half blind.

Through one partially fogged eyeplate he noticed the tadpole creatures approaching more closely. Were they vicious after all? Were they coming closer because they sensed that he was in danger? Were they closing in for the kill?

One of them plunged straight at him, and involuntarily he ducked. The thing turned barely aside at the last moment, raced past him, slithered out of the blue liquid, and squirmed up the slope towards the valve.

Unexpectedly, the valve opened to twice its previous width, and the creature plunged through without trouble.

'Doctor Meltzer? Are you still all right?'

'I'm alive, if that interests you. Listen, Captain, I'm going to try getting through that valve. One of the tadpole beasts just did it, and the valve opened a lot wider to let it through.'

'Just how do you expect to manage?'

'I'll try grabbing one of the beasts and hitch-hike through. I just hope it isn't vicious, and doesn't turn on me.'

But the tadpole creatures wouldn't let themselves be grabbed. In this, their home territory, they moved a great deal faster than he did, and even though they didn't seem to be using their eyes to see with, they evaded his grasp with great skill.

At last he gave up the attempt and climbed out of the blue pool. The creatures followed him.

One of the biggest of them suddenly dashed forward. Sensing what the thing was going to do, Dr. Meltzer hurried after it. It scurried up the slope, and plunged through the valve. The valve opened wide. Dr. Meltzer, racing desperately forward, threw himself into the opening. The valve paused, then snapped at him. He felt it hit his heel.

The next moment he was gasping for breath. The oxygen lines had become tangled.

He fought frenziedly to untwist them, and failed. Then he realized that he was trying to do too much. All he needed to do was loosen the knot and straighten out the kinks. By the time he finally succeeded, he was seeing black spots in front of his eyes.

'Doctor Meltzer, Doctor Meltzer!'

The sound had been in his ears for some time. 'Still alive,' he gasped.

'Thank God! We're going to try to open the mouth now, Doctor. If you hurry forward, you'll be in a position to be pulled out.'

'I'm hurrying. By the way, those tadpoles are still with me. They're trailing along as if they'd found a long-lost friend. I feel like a pie-eyed piper.'

'I just hope they don't attack.'

'You're not hoping any harder than I am.'

He could catch his breath now, and with the oxygen lines free, the perspiration that had dimmed his sight slowly evaporated. He caught sight of one of the reddish tumours he had noticed on his forward passage.

'May as well be hung for a sheep as a lamb,' he murmured. 'It would take an axe really to chop that tumour out, but I may as well slice into it and see what I can learn.'

From one of his pockets he took a sharp oversize scalpel, and began to cut around the edges.

The tumour throbbed convulsively.

'Well, well, I may have something here,' he said, with a surgeon's pleasure. He dug deeper.

The tumour erupted. Great blobs of reddish liquid spurted out, and with one of them came another of the tadpole creatures, a small one, half the average size of those he had first encountered.

'Glory be,' he muttered. 'So that's the way they grow.'

The creature sensed him and darted aside, in the direction of the valve. As it approached, the open valve froze in place, and let the small creature through, further into the host, without enlarging. Then the valve began to close again.

They're adapted to each other, he thought. Probably symbiosis, rather than a one-side parasitism.

He moved upwards, towards the greenish liquid.

An earthquake struck.

The flesh heaved up beneath his feet, tossing him head over heels into the pool. The first shock was followed by a second and a third. A tidal wave hit him, and carried him to the side of the pool. He landed with a thud against the hard side and bounced back.

The sides began to constrict, hemming him in.

'Captain!' he yelled. 'What's going on out there? What are you doing to the beast?'

'Trying to pry open its mouth. It doesn't seem to like the idea. It's threshing around against the walls of the ship.'

'For God's sake, cut it out! It's giving me a beating in here.'

They must have halted their efforts at once, for immediately afterwards the beast's movements became less convulsive. But it was some time before the spasmodic quivering of the side walls came to an end.

Dr. Meltzer climbed out of the pool of liquid, making an automatic and entirely useless gesture to wipe the new perspiration from his forehead.

'Is it better in there, Doctor?'

'It's better. Don't try that again,' he panted.

'We have to get the mouth open some way.'

'Try a bigger electric shock.'

'If you want us to. But it may mean another beating for you, Doctor.'

'Then wait a minute. Wait till I get near the upper part of the gullet.'

'Whenever you say. Just tell us when you're ready.'

Better be ready soon, he thought. My light's beginning to dim. When it goes out altogether. I'll probably be in a real panic. I'll be yelling for him to do anything, just to get me out of there.

And what about the suit and the oxygen lines? I think the digestive fluid's beginning to affect them. It's hard to be sure, now that the light's weakening, but they don't have the clear transparent look they had at first. And when they finally go, I go with them.

He tried to move forward faster, but the surface underfoot was slimy, and when he moved too hastily, he slipped. The lines were getting tangled too. Now that the creature's mouth was closed, it was no use tugging at the cord around his waist. That wouldn't get him up.

'Doctor Meltzer!'

He didn't answer. Instead, he pulled out his lancet and cut the useless cords away. The oxygen lines too were a nuisance, in constant danger of kinking and tangling, now that they were no longer taut. But at least the gas was still flowing through them and would continue to flow—until the digestive fluid ate through.

The tadpole creatures seemed to have developed a positive affection for him. They were all around him, not close enough for him to grab them, but still too close for comfort. At any moment they might decide to take a nip out of his suit or an oxygen line. And with the plastic already weakened, even a slight tear might be fatal.

He reached the sharp slope that signified the gullet. 'Dr. Meltzer?'

'What do you want?'

'Why didn't you answer?'

'I was busy. I cut the cord away from around my waist. Now I'm going to try climbing up inside this thing's throat.'

'Shall we try that sharp electric shock?'

'Go ahead.'

He had a pair of small surgical clamps, and he took one in each hand. The flashlight he put in a holder at his waist. Then, getting down on all fours, he began to crawl up, digging each pair of clamps into the flesh in turn to give him a grip. A slow wave ran away in both directions every time he inserted one of the pairs of clamps into the flesh, but otherwise the beast didn't seem to mind too much.

He was about halfway up, when the earthquakes began again. The first one sent him tumbling head over heels down the slope. The others added some slight injury to the insult, knocking him painfully against the walls. They must have used a powerful electric jolt, for some of it was transmitted through the creature to him, making his skin tingle. He hadn't lost his flashlight, but by now it was exceedingly dim, and shed only a feeble circle of light. Far ahead of him, where the mouth was to open, was blackness.

'No luck, Captain?'

'No luck, Doctor. We'll try again.'

'Don't. You just make things worse.'

'Larry, were you hurt? Larry—'

'Don't bother me now, Maida,' he said roughly. 'I have to figure out a way to get out.'

A faint hiss came from the oxygen line. A leak. Time was growing short.

The tadpole creatures were swimming around faster now. They too must have been upset by the shock. One of them darted ahead of him, and wriggled ahead until it was lost in blackness.

That seems to be trying to get out too, he told himself. Maybe we can work this together. There must be some way, something to get this creature to open its mouth. Maybe the Captain can't do it from outside, but I'm in here, where the beast's most sensitive. I can hit it, slash at it, tickle it—

There's a thought. Tickle it. It's a monster, and it'll take some monstrous tickling, but sooner or later, something should affect it.

He stamped hard with his foot. No effect. He took his large lancet from his pocket and slashed viciously with it. A shudder ran through the flesh, but that was all.

And then he had an idea. That green liquid undoubtedly contained hormones. Hormones, enzymes, co-enzymes, antibiotics, biological chemicals of all kinds. Stuff to which some tissues would be adapted and some would not. And those that weren't would react violently.

He turned back, filled his hypodermic syringe with the greenish liquid, and ran forward again. The light was almost gone by now, and the hissing from the oxygen line was growing ominously, but he climbed forward as far as he could, before plunging the hypodermic in and injecting its contents.

The creature heaved. He dropped hypodermic, light, and clamps, and let the huge shuddering take him where it would. First it lifted him high. Then it let him fall suddenly—not backwards, but in the same place. Two of the tadpole beasts were thrown against him. Then he was lifted way up again, and this time forward. A huge cavern opened before him. Light bathed the grey surface and he was vomited out.

The light began to flicker, and he had time for one last thought. Oxygen lack, he told himself. My suit's ripped, the lines have finally torn.

And then blackness.

When he came to, Maida was at his side. He could see that

she had been crying. The Captain stood a little further off, his face drawn, but relieved.

'Larry, dear, are you all right? We thought you'd never get out.'

'I'm fine.' He sat up and saw his two children, standing anxious and awe-stricken on the other side of the bed. Their silence showed how strongly they had been affected. 'I hope you kids didn't worry too much about me.'

'Of course I didn't worry,' said Jerry bravely. 'I knew you were smart, Dad. I knew you'd think of a way to get out.'

'While we're on the subject,' interposed the Captain, 'what *was* the way out?'

'I'll tell you later. How's the patient?'

'Doing fine. Seems to have recovered completely.'

'How many of the tadpoles came out with me?'

'About six. We're keeping them in the same low-oxygen atmosphere as the creature itself. We're going to study them. We figure that if they're parasites—'

'They're not parasites. I finally came to a conclusion about them. They're the young.'

'What?'

'The young. If you take good care of them, they'll eventually grow to be as big as the mother-monster you've got in the ship.'

'Good God, where will we keep them?'

'That's your worry. Maybe you'd better expand that zoo you're preparing. What you'll do for money to feed them, though, I don't know.'

'But what—'

'The trouble with that monster—its "illness"—was merely that it was gravid.'

'Gravid?'

'That means pregnant,' exclaimed Jerry.

'I know what it means.' The Captain flushed. 'Look, do we have to have these kids in here while we discuss this?'

'Why not? They're a doctor's children. They know what it's all about. They've seen calves and other animals being born.'

'Lots of times,' said Martia.

'Confined as it was on the ship, your beast couldn't get the exercise it needed. And the young couldn't get themselves born.'

'But that was the digestive tract you went down—'

'What of it? Are all animals born the same way? Ask the average kid where a baby grows, and he'll tell you that it's in the stomach.'

'Some kids are dopes,' said Jerry.

'They wouldn't be in this case. What better place to get a chance at the food the mother eats, in all stages from raw to completely digested? All that beast needed to give birth was a little exercise. You gave it some from the outside, but not enough. I finished the job by injecting some of its own digestive fluid into the flesh. That caused a pretty little reaction.'

The Captain scratched his head. 'Doctor, you did a good job. How would you like to take care of that beast permanently? I could recommend you—'

'To go down inside that monster again? No, thanks. From now on, I treat nothing but small monsters. Sheep, cows—and human beings.'

There was a pounding of feet in the hallway. Then the door swung in, violently. Flashbulbs that gave invisible light began to pop with inaudible bursts of high-frequency sound. Cameras pointed menacingly at him and sent his image winging to Earth and far-off planets. Reporters began to fire their questions.

'My God,' he muttered wearily, 'who let these animals in here? They're worse than the ones I met inside the blue pool.'

'Be nice to them, dear,' chided Maida gently. 'They're turning you into a great man.'

Then Maida and Jerry and Martia grouped themselves around him, and the cameras caught them too. The proud look on their faces was something to see. And he realized that he was glad for their sake.

Opportunity had knocked, and when he had opened the door to it, it had proved to be an exacting guest. Still, he hadn't been a bad host—not a bad host at all, he thought. And slowly his features relaxed into a tired and immediately famous grin.

COUNTRY DOCTOR

The 'space-cow' in this story is by no means as odd a creature as the pyramid-beings in *A Martian Odyssey* or the star-intelligences of *Proof*. The space-cow is at least made up of protein.

The problem set in the story is a very realistic one, given the premise. If we do ever locate advanced forms of life outside the Earth, forms that are not intelligent, how do we handle them? To keep them in zoos, or to exploit them as food, would require us to understand something about their physiology, if only to keep them alive and healthy.

Aside from such purely materialistic considerations, there would be considerable advance in our understanding of life if we could learn details concerning the physiology and biochemistry of such creatures.

The most remarkable characteristic of the space-cow is, of course, its sheer size. It nearly fills the spaceship and it is large enough to allow a human being to tramp about its interior. (The realism of that invasion of the animal's gut may be accounted for by the fact that the author, whose real name is Joseph Samachson, has a Ph.D. in chemistry.) The space-cow's mouth is forty feet from the ground and is thirty feet wide and fifty feet deep, so that it ought to be considerably larger than even the largest whale. Yet it would seem to be a land creature.

On Earth, so large a creature would be quite impossible outside the oceans. Without the support of the buoyancy of the ocean, its own weight would crush it. However, it comes from Ganymede, Jupiter's largest satellite, which has a considerably smaller gravitational pull at its surface than Earth has. To be sure, there are many other reasons for supposing Ganymede cannot support a creature such as the space-cow, but here, as in *Surface Tension*, we have an impossible assumption designed merely to start the story.

Questions and Suggestions

1. Investigate the matter of size of living creatures in relation to gravity. What are the most massive land organisms that ever existed? How would their mass compare with that of the largest whale living today?

2. A sperm-whale has a head about a third the length of its body. Assuming the sea-cow is similarly proportioned, estimate its length and its mass. (You might be interested in discovering the size and mass of a large whale's organs; its heart, its tongue; and how its physiology is organized.)

3. What is the gravitational intensity at the surface of Ganymede compared to that on the surface of the Earth? What else is known about Ganymede? What do you think the chances are of finding any kind of life on that world?

4. Do you think there are forms of life on Earth itself as strange as the space-cow, if not as large? When the duck-billed platypus was first discovered in Australia, it was difficult to get biologists back in Europe to believe the descriptions were of real animals and not of hoaxes. What was so strange about the platypus? What other earthly creatures have to be seen to be believed? What about the Venus's-flytrap? the flying-fox? the mandrill? If you were familiar with all the forms of life on Earth except for *Homo sapiens*, do you think you would be able to predict the existence of man? What in man, if anything, might seem unpredictable?

10. The Holes Around Mars

Jerome Bixby

Spaceship crews should be selected on the basis of their non-irritating qualities as individuals. No chronic complainers, no hypochondriacs, no bugs on cleanliness—particularly no one-man parties. I speak from bitter experience.

Because on the first expedition to Mars, Hugh Allenby damned near drove us nuts with his puns. We finally got so we just ignored them.

But no one can ignore that classic last one—it's written right into the annals of astronomy, and it's there to stay.

Allenby, in command of the expedition, was first to set foot outside the ship. As he stepped down from the airlock of the *Mars I,* he placed that foot on a convenient rock, caught the toe of his weighted boot in a hole in the rock, wrenched his ankle and smote the ground with his pants.

Sitting there, eyes pained behind the transparent shield of his oxygen-mask, he stared at the rock.

It was about five feet high. Ordinary granite—no special shape. Several inches below its summit, running straight through it in a north-easterly direction, was a neat round four-inch hole.

'I'm *upset* by the *hole* thing,' he grunted.

The rest of us scrambled out of the ship and gathered around his plump form.

'Break anything, Hugh?' asked Burton, our pilot, kneeling beside him.

'Get out of my way, Burton,' said Allenby. 'You're obstructing my view.'

Burton blinked. A man constructed of long bones and caution, he angled out of the way, looking around to see what he was obstructing view *of*.

He saw the rock and the round hole through it. He stood very still, staring. So did the rest of us.

'Well, I'll be damned,' said Janus, our photographer. 'A hole.'

'In a rock,' added Gonzales, our botanist.

'Round,' said Randolph, our biologist.

'An *artifact*,' finished Allenby softly.

Burton helped him to his feet. Silently we gathered around the rock.

Janus bent down and put an eye to one end of the hole. I bent down and looked through the other end. We squinted at each other.

As mineralogist, I was expected to opinionate. 'Not drilled,' I said slowly. 'Not chipped. Not melted. Certainly not eroded.'

I heard a rasping sound by my ear and straightened. Burton was scratching a thumbnail along the rim of the hole. 'Weathered,' he said. 'Plenty old. But I'll bet it's a perfect circle, if we measure.'

Janus was already fiddling with his camera, testing the cooperation of the tiny distant sun with a light-meter.

'Let us see *weather* it is or not,' Allenby said.

Burton brought out a steel tape-measure. The hole was four and three-eighths inches across. It was perfectly circular and about sixteen inches long. And four feet above the ground.

'But why?' said Randolph. 'Why should anyone bore a four-inch tunnel through a rock way out in the middle of the desert?'

'Religious symbol,' said Janus. He looked around, one hand on his gun. 'We'd better keep an eye out—maybe we've landed on sacred ground or something.'

'A totem *hole*, perhaps,' Allenby suggested.

'Oh, I don't know,' Randolph said—to Janus, not Allenby. As I've mentioned, we always ignored Allenby's puns. 'Note the lack of ornamentation. Not at all typical of religious articles.'

'On Earth,' Gonzales reminded him. 'Besides, it might be utilitarian, not symbolic.'

'Utilitarian how?' asked Janus.

'An altar for snakes,' Burton said drily.

'Well,' said Allenby, 'you can't deny that it has its *holy* aspects.'

'Get your hand away, will you, Peters?' asked Janus.

I did. When Janus's camera had clicked, I bent again and peered through the hole. 'It sights on that low ridge over there,' I said. 'Maybe it's some kind of surveying setup. I'm going to take a look.'

'Careful,' warned Janus. 'Remember, it may be sacred.'

As I walked away, I heard Allenby say, 'Take some scrapings from the inside of the hole, Gonzales. We might be able to determine if anything is kept in it ...'

One of the stumpy, purplish, barrel-type cacti on the ridge had a long vertical bite out of it ... as if someone had carefully carved out a narrow U-shaped section from the top down, finishing the bottom of the U in a neat semicircle. It was as flat and cleancut as the inside surface of a horseshoe magnet.

I hollered. The others came running. I pointed.

'Oh, my God!' said Allenby. 'Another one.'

The pulp of the cactus in and around the U-hole was dried and dead-looking.

Silently Burton used his tape-measure. The hole measured four and three-eighths inches across. It was eleven inches deep. The semicircular bottom was about a foot above the ground.

'This ridge,' I said, 'is about three feet higher than where we landed the ship. I bet the hole in the rock and the hole in this cactus are on the same level.'

Gonzales said slowly, 'This was not done all at once. It is a result of periodic attacks. Look here and here. These overlapping depressions along the outer edges of the hole—' he pointed—'on this side of the cactus. They are the signs of repeated impact. And the scallop effect on *this* side, where whatever made the hole emerged. There are juices still oozing—not at the point of impact, where the plant is desiccated, but below, where the shock was transmitted—'

A distant shout turned us around. Burton was at the rock, beside the ship. He was bending down, his eye to the far side of the mysterious hole.

He looked for another second, then straightened and came towards us at a lope.

'They line up,' he said when he reached us. 'The bottom of the hole in the cactus is right in the middle when you sight through the hole in the rock.'

'As if somebody came around and whacked the cactus regularly,' Janus said, looking around warily.

'To keep the line of sight through the holes clear?' I wondered. 'Why not just remove the cactus?'

'Religious,' Janus explained.

We went on past the ridge towards an outcropping of rock about a hundred yards farther on. We walked silently, each of us wondering if what we half-expected would really be there.

It was. In one of the tall, weathered spires in the outcropping, some ten feet below its peak and four feet above the ground, was a round four-inch hole.

Allenby sat down on a rock, nursing his ankle, and remarked that anybody who believed this crazy business was really happening must have holes in the rocks in his head.

Burton put his eye to the hole and whistled. 'Sixty feet long if it's an inch,' he said. 'The other end's just a pinpoint. But you can see it. The damn thing's perfectly straight.'

I looked back the way we had come. The cactus stood on the ridge, with its U-shaped bite, and beyond was the ship, and beside it the perforated rock.

'If we surveyed,' I said, 'I bet the holes would all line up, right to the last millimetre.'

'But,' Randolph complained, 'why would anybody go out and bore holes in things all along a line through the desert?'

'Religious,' Janus muttered. 'It doesn't *have* to make sense.'

We stood there by the outcropping and looked out along

the wide, red desert beyond. It stretched flatly for miles from this point, south towards Mars's equator—dead sandy wastes, crisscrossed by the 'canals', which we had observed while landing to be great straggly patches of vegetation, probably strung along underground waterflows.

BLONG-G-G-G- ... st-st-st ...

We jumped half out of our skins. Ozone bit at our nostrils. Our hair stirred in the electrical uproar.

'L-look,' Janus chattered, lowering his smoking gun.

About forty feet to our left, a small rabbity creature poked its head from behind a rock and stared at us in utter horror.

Janus raised his gun again.

'Don't bother,' said Allenby tiredly. 'I don't think it intends to attack.'

'But—'

'I'm sure it isn't a Martian with religious convictions.'

Janus wet his lips and looked a little shamefaced. 'I guess I'm kind of tense.'

'That's what I *taut*,' said Allenby.

The creature darted from behind its rock and, looking at us over its shoulder, employed six legs to make small but very fast tracks.

We turned our attention again to the desert. Far out, black against Mars's azure horizon, was a line of low hills.

'Shall we go look?' asked Burton, eyes gleaming at the mystery.

Janus lifted his gun nervously. It was still crackling faintly from the discharge. 'I say let's get back to the ship!'

Allenby sighed. 'My leg hurts.' He studied the hills. 'Give me the field-glasses.'

Randolph handed them over. Allenby put them to the shield of his mask and adjusted them.

After a moment he sighed again. 'There's a hole. On a plane surface that catches the Sun. A lousy damned round little impossible hole.'

'Those hills,' Burton observed, 'must be thousands of feet thick.'

* * *

The argument lasted all the way back to the ship.

Janus, holding out for his belief that the whole thing was of religious origin, kept looking around for Martians as if he expected them to pour screaming from the hills.

Burton came up with the suggestion that perhaps the holes had been made by a disintegrator-ray.

'It's possible,' Allenby admitted. 'This might have been the scene of some great battle—'

'With only one such weapon?' I objected.

Allenby swore as he stumbled. 'What do you mean?'

'I haven't seen any other lines of holes—only the one. In a battle, the whole joint should be cut up.'

That was good for a few moments' silent thought. Then Allenby said, 'It might have been brought out by one side as a last resort. Sort of an ace in the hole.'

I resisted the temptation to mutiny. 'But would even *one* such weapon, in battle, make only *one* line of holes? Wouldn't it be played in an arc against the enemy? You know it would.'

'Well—'

'Wouldn't it cut slices out of the landscape, instead of boring holes? And wouldn't it sway or vibrate enough to make the holes miles away from it something less than perfect circles?'

'It could have been very firmly mounted.'

'Hugh, does that sound like a practical weapon to you?'

Two seconds of silence. 'On the other hand,' he said, 'instead of a war, the whole thing might have been designed to frighten some primitive race—or even some kind of beast—the *hole* out of here. A demonstration—'

'Religious,' Janus grumbled, still looking around.

We walked on, passing the cactus on the low ridge.

'Interesting,' said Gonzales. 'The evidence that whatever causes the phenomenon has happened again and again. I'm afraid that the war theory—'

'Oh, my God!' gasped Burton.

We stared at him.

'The ship,' he whispered. 'It's right in line with the holes! If whatever made them is still in operation ...'

'Run!' yelled Allenby, and we ran like fiends.

We got the ship into the air, out of line with the holes to what we fervently hoped was safety, and then we realized we were admitting our fear that the mysterious hole-maker might still be lurking around.

Well, the evidence was all for it, as Gonzales had reminded us—that cactus had been oozing.

We cruised at twenty thousand feet and thought it over.

Janus, whose only training was in photography, said, 'Some kind of omniverous animal? Or bird? Eats rocks and everything?'

'I will not totally discount the notion of such an animal,' Randolph said. 'But I will resist to the death the suggestion that it forages with geometric precision.'

After a while, Allenby said, 'Land, Burton. By that "canal". Lots of plant life—fauna, too. We'll do a little collecting.'

Burton set us down feather-light at the very edge of the sprawling flat expanse of vegetation, commenting that the scene reminded him of his native Texas pear-flats.

We wandered in the chilly air, each of us except Burton pursuing his speciality. Randolph relentlessly stalked another of the rabbity creatures. Gonzales was carefully digging up plants and stowing them in jars. Janus was busy with his cameras, recording every aspect of Mars transferable to film. Allenby walked around, helping anybody who needed it. An astronomer, he'd done half his work on the way to Mars and would do the other half on the return trip. Burton lounged in the sun, his back against a ship's fin, and played chess with Allenby, calling out his moves in a bull roar. I grubbed for rocks.

My search took me farther and farther away from the others—all I could find around the 'canal' was gravel, and I wanted to chip at some big stuff. I walked towards a long rise a half-mile or so away, beyond which rose an enticing array of house-sized boulders.

As I moved out of earshot, I heard Randolph snarl, 'Burton,

will you stop yelling, "Kt to B-2 and check?" Every time you open your yap, this critter takes off on me.'

Then I saw the groove.

It started right where the ground began to rise—a thin, shallow, curve-bottomed groove in the dirt at my feet, about half an inch across, running off straight towards higher ground.

With my eyes glued to it, I walked. The ground slowly rose. The groove deepened, widened—now it was about three inches deep.

The ground rose some more. Four and three-eighths inches wide. I didn't have to measure it—I *knew*.

Now, as the ground rose, the edges of the groove began to curve inwards over the groove. They touched. No more groove.

The ground had risen, the groove had stayed level and gone underground.

Except that now it wasn't a groove. It was a round tunnel.

A hole.

A few paces farther on, I thumped the ground with my heel where the hole ought to be. The dirt crumbled, and there was the little dark tunnel, running straight in both directions.

I walked on, the ground falling away gradually again. The entire process was repeated in reverse. A hairline appeared in the dirt—widened—became lips that drew slowly apart to reveal the neat straight four-inch groove—which shrank as slowly to a shallow line of the ground—and vanished.

I looked ahead of me. There was one low ridge of ground between me and the enormous boulders. A neat four-inch semicircle was bitten out of the very top of the ridge. In the house-sized boulder directly beyond was a four-inch hole.

Allenby called the others when I came back and reported. 'The mystery *deepens*,' he told them. He turned to me. 'Lead on, Peters, you're temporary *drill* leader.'

Thank God he didn't say *Fall in*.

The holes went straight through the nest of boulders—there'd be a hole in one and, ten or twenty feet farther on in the next boulder, another hole. And then another, and another—right through the nest in a line. About thirty holes in all.

Burton, standing by the boulder I'd first seen, flashed his flashlight into the hole. Randolph, clear on the other side of the jumbled nest, eye to hole, saw it.

Straight as a string.

The ground sloped away on the far side of the nest—no holes were visible in that direction—just miles of desert. So, after we'd stared at the holes for a while and they didn't go away, we headed back for the canal.

'Is there any possibility,' asked Janus, as we walked, 'that it could be a natural phenomenon?'

'There are no straight lines in nature,' Randolph said, a little shortly. 'That goes for a bunch of circles in a straight line. And for perfect circles, too.'

'A planet is a circle,' objected Janus.

'An oblate spheroid,' Allenby corrected.

'A planet's orbit—'

'An ellipse.'

Janus walked a few steps, frowning. Then he said, 'I remember reading that there *is* something darned near a perfect circle in nature.' He paused a moment. 'Potholes.' And he looked at me, as mineralogist, to corroborate.

'What kind of potholes?' I asked cautiously. 'Do you mean where part of a limestone deposit has dissol—'

'No. I once read that when a glacier passes over a hard rock that's lying on some softer rock, it grinds the hard rock down into the softer, and both of them sort of wear down to fit together, and it all ends up with a round hole in the soft rock.'

'Probably neither stone,' I told Janus, 'would be homogenous. The softer parts would abrade faster in the soft stone. The end result wouldn't be a perfect circle.'

Janus's face fell.

'Now,' I said, 'would anyone care to define this term "perfect circle" we're throwing around so blithely? Because such holes as Janus describes are often pretty damned round.'

Randolph said, 'Well ...'

'It is settled, then,' Gonzales said, a little sarcastically. 'Your discussion, gentlemen, has established that the long, horizontal holes we have found were caused by glacial action.'

'Oh, no,' Janus argued seriously. 'I once read that Mars never had any glaciers.'

All of us shuddered.

Half an hour later, we spotted more holes, about a mile down the 'canal', still on a line, marching along the desert, through cacti, rocks, hills, even through one edge of the low vegetation of the 'canal' for thirty feet or so. It was the damnedest thing to bend down and look straight through all that curling, twisting growth ... a round tunnel from end to end.

We followed the holes for about a mile, to the rim of an enormous saucerlike valley that sank gradually before us until, miles away, it was thousands of feet deep. We stared out across it, wondering about the other side.

Allenby said determinedly, 'We'll get to the *bottom* of these holes, once and for all. Back to the ship, men!'

We hiked back, climbed in and took off.

At an altitude of fifty feet, Burton lined the nose of the ship on the most recent line of holes and we flew out over the valley.

On the other side was a range of hefty hills. The holes went through them. Straight through. We would approach one hill —Burton would manipulate the front viewscreen until we spotted the hole—we would pass over the hill and spot the other end of the hole in the rear screen.

One hole was two hundred and eighty miles long.

Four hours later, we were halfway around Mars.

Randolph was sitting by a side port, chin on one hand, his eyes unbelieving. 'All around the planet,' he kept repeating. 'All around the planet ...'

'Halfway at least,' Allenby mused. 'And we can assume that it continues in a straight line, through anything and everything that gets in its way ...' He gazed out of the front port at the uneven blue-green haze of a 'canal' off to our left. 'For the love of Heaven, *why?*'

Then Allenby fell down. We all did.

Burton had suddenly slapped at the control board, and the ship braked and sank like a plugged duck. At the last second, Burton propped up the nose with a short burst, the ten-foot wheels hit desert sand, and in five hundred yards we had jounced to a stop.

Allenby got up from the floor. 'Why did you do that?' he asked Burton politely, nursing a bruised elbow.

Burton's nose was almost touching the front port. 'Look!' he said, and pointed.

About two miles away, the Martian village looked like a handful of yellow marbles flung on the desert.

We checked our guns. We put on our oxygen-masks. We checked our guns again. We got out of the ship and made damned sure the airlock was locked.

An hour later, we crawled inch by painstaking inch up a high sand dune and poked our heads over the top.

The Martians were runts—the tallest of them less than five feet tall—and skinny as a pencil. Dried-up and brown, they wore loincloths of woven fibre.

They stood among the dusty-looking inverted-bowl buildings of their village, and every one of them was looking straight up at us with unblinking brown eyes.

The six safeties of our six guns clicked off like a rattle of dice. The Martians stood there and gawped.

'Probably a highly developed sense of hearing in this thin atmosphere,' Allenby murmured. 'Heard us coming.'

'They thought that landing of Burton's was an earthquake,' Randolph said sourly.

'Marsquake,' corrected Janus. One look at the village's scrawny occupants seemed to have convinced him that his life was in no danger.

Holding the Martians covered, we examined the village from atop the thirty-foot dune.

The domelike buildings were constructed of something that looked like adobe. No windows—probably built with sandstorms in mind. The doors were about halfway up the sloping sides, and from each door a stone ramp wound down around the house to the ground—again with sandstorms in mind, no doubt, so drifting dunes wouldn't block the entrances.

The centre of the village was a wide street, a long sandy area some thirty feet wide. On either side of it, the houses were scattered at random, as if each Martian had simply hunted for a comfortable place to sit and then built a house around it.

'Look,' whispered Randolph.

One Martian had stepped from a group on the far side of the street from us. He started to cross the street, his round brown eyes on us, his small bare feet plodding sand, and we saw that in addition to a loincloth he wore jewellery—a hammered metal ring, a bracelet on one skinny ankle. The Sun caught a copperish gleam on his bald narrow head, and we saw a band of metal there, just above where his eyebrows should have been.

'The super-chief,' Allenby murmured. 'Oh, *shaman* me!'

As the bejewelled Martian approached the centre of the street, he glanced briefly at the ground at his feet. Then he raised his head, stepped with dignity across the exact centre of the street and came on towards us, passing the dusty-looking buildings of his realm and the dusty-looking groups of his subjects.

He reached the slope of the dune we lay on—paused—and raised small hands over his head, palms towards us.

'I think,' Allenby said, 'that an anthropologist would give odds on that gesture meaning peace.'

He stood up, holstered his gun—without buttoning the flap—and raised his own hands over his head. We all did.

The Martian language consisted of squeaks.

We made friendly noises, the chief squeaked, and pretty soon we were the centre of a group of wide-eyed Martians, none of whom made a sound. Evidently no one dared peep while the chief spoke—very likely the most articulate Martians simply squeaked themselves into the job. Allenby, of course, said they just *squeaked by*.

He was going through the business of drawing concentric circles in the sand, pointing at the third orbit away from the Sun and thumping his chest. The crowd around us kept growing as more Martians emerged from the dome buildings to see what was going on. Down the winding ramps of the buildings on our side of the wide, sandy street they came—and from the buildings on the other side of the street, plodding through the sand, blinking brown eyes at us, not making a sound.

Allenby pointed at the third orbit and thumped his chest. The chief squeaked and thumped his own chest and pointed at the copperish band around his head. Then he pointed at Allenby.

'I seem to have conveyed to him,' Allenby said drily, 'the fact that I'm chief of our party. Well, let's try again.'

He started over on the orbits. He didn't seem to be getting anyplace, so the rest of us watched the Martians instead. A last handful was struggling across the wide street.

'Curious,' said Gonzales. 'Note what happens when they reach the centre of the street.'

Each Martian, upon reaching the centre of the street, glanced at his feet—just for a moment—without even breaking stride. And then came on.

'What can they be looking at?' Gonzales wondered.

'The chief did it too,' Burton mused. 'Remember when he first came towards us?'

We all stared intently at the middle of the street. We saw absolutely nothing but sand.

The Martians milled around us and watched Allenby and his orbits. A Martian child appeared from between two buildings across the street. On six-inch legs, it started across, got halfway, glanced downward—and came on.

'I don't get it,' Burton said. 'What in hell are they *looking* at?'

The child reached the crowd and squeaked a thin, high note.

A number of things happened at once.

Several members of the group around us glanced down, and along the edge of the crowd nearest the centre of the street there was a mild stir as individuals drifted off to either side. Quite casually—nothing at all urgent about it. They just moved concertedly to get farther away from the centre of the street, not taking their interested gaze off us for one second in the process.

Even the chief glanced up from Allenby's concentric circles at the child's squeak. And Randolph, who had been fidgeting uncomfortably and paying very little attention to our conversation, decided that he must answer nature's call. He moved off into the dunes surrounding the village. Or rather, he started to move.

The moment he set off across the wide street, the little Martian chief was in front of him, brown eyes wide, hands out before him as if to thrust Randolph back.

Again six safeties clicked. The Martians didn't even blink at the sudden appearance of our guns. Probably the only weapon they recognized was a club, or maybe a rock.

'What can the matter be?' Randolph said.

He took another step forward. The chief squeaked and stood his ground. Randolph had to stop or bump into him. Randolph stopped.

The chief squeaked, looking right into the bore of Randolph's gun.

'Hold still,' Allenby told Randolph, 'till we know what's up.'

Allenby made an interrogative sound at the chief. The chief squeaked and pointed at the ground. We looked. He was pointing at his shadow.

Randolph stirred uncomfortably.

'Hold still,' Allenby warned him, and again he made the questioning sound.

The chief pointed up the street. Then he pointed down the street. He bent to touch his shadow, thumping it with thin fingers. Then he pointed at the wall of a house nearby.

We all looked.

Straight lines had been painted on the curved brick-coloured wall, up and down and across, to form many small squares about four inches across. In each square was a bit of squiggly writing, in blackish paint, and a small wooden peg jutting out from the wall.

Burton said, 'Looks like a damn crossword puzzle.'

'Look,' said Janus. 'In the lower right corner—a metal ring hanging from one of the pegs.'

And that was all we saw on the wall. Hundreds of squares with figures in them—a small peg set in each—and a ring hanging on one of the pegs.

'You know what?' Allenby said slowly. 'I think it's a calendar! Just a second—thirty squares wide by twenty-two high—that's six hundred and sixty. And that bottom line has twenty-six—twenty-*seven* squares. Six hundred and eighty-seven squares in all. That's how many days there are in the Martian year!'

He looked thoughtfully at the metal ring. 'I'll bet that ring is hanging from the peg in the square that represents *today*. They must move it along every day, to keep track ...'

'What's a calendar got to do with my crossing the street?' Randolph asked in a pained tone.

He started to take another step. The chief squeaked as if it were a matter of desperate concern that he make us understand. Randolph stopped again and swore impatiently.

Allenby made his questioning sound again.

The chief pointed emphatically at his shadow, then at the communal calendar—and we could see now that he was pointing at the metal ring.

Burton said slowly, 'I think he's trying to tell us that this is *today*. And such-and-such a *time* of day. I bet he's using his shadow as a sundial.'

'Perhaps,' Allenby granted.

Randolph said, 'If this monkey doesn't let me go in another minute—'

The chief squeaked, eyes concerned.

'Stand still,' Allenby ordered. 'He's trying to warn you of some danger.'

The chief pointed down the street again and, instead of squealing, revealed that there was another sound at his command. He said, 'Whoooooosh!'

We all stared at the end of the street.

Nothing! Just the wide avenue between the houses, and the high sand dune down at the end of it, from which we had first looked upon the village.

The chief described a large circle with one hand, sweeping the hand above his head, down to his knees, up again, as fast as he could. He pursed his monkey-lips and said, 'Whooooooosh!' And made the circle again.

A Martian emerged from the door in the side of a house across the avenue and blinked again, this time in interest. He made his way down around the winding ramp and started to cross the street.

About halfway, he paused, eyed the calendar on the house wall, glanced at his shadow. Then he got down on his hands and knees and *crawled* across the middle of the street. Once past the middle, he rose, walked the rest of the way to join one of the groups and calmly stared at us along with the rest of them.

'They're all crazy,' Randolph said disgustedly. 'I'm going to cross that street!'

'Shut up. So it's a certain time of a certain day,' Allenby mused. 'And from the way the chief is acting, he's afraid for you to cross the street. And that other one just *crawled*. By God, do you know what this might tie in with?'

We were silent for a moment. Then Gonzales said, 'Of course!'

And Burton said, 'The *holes*!'

'Exactly,' said Allenby. 'Maybe whatever made—or makes—the holes comes right down the centre of the street here. Maybe that's why they built the village this way—to make room for—'

'For what?' Randolph asked unhappily, shifting his feet.

'I don't know,' Allenby said. He looked thoughtfully at the chief. 'That circular motion he made—could he have been describing something that went around and around the planet? Something like—oh, no!' Allenby's eyes glazed. 'I wouldn't believe it in a million years.'

His gaze went to the far end of the street, to the high sand dune that rose there. The chief seemed to be waiting for something to happen.

'I'm going to crawl,' Randolph stated. He got to his hands and knees and began to creep across the centre of the avenue.

The chief let him go.

The sand dune at the end of the street suddenly erupted. A forty-foot spout of dust shot straight out from the sloping side, as if a bullet had emerged. Powdered sand hazed the air, yellowed it almost the full length of the avenue. Grains of sand stung the skin and rattled minutely on the houses.

WhoooSSSHHHHH!

Randolph dropped flat on his belly. He didn't have to continue his trip. He had made other arrangements.

That night in the ship, while we all sat around, still shaking our heads every once in a while, Allenby talked with Earth. He sat there, wearing the headphones, trying to make himself understood above the godawful static.

'... an exceedingly small body,' he repeated wearily to his unbelieving audience, 'about four inches in diameter. It travels at a mean distance of four feet above the surface of the planet, a velocity yet to be calculated. Its unique nature results in many hitherto unobserved—I might say even unimagined—phenomena.' He stared blankly in front of him for a moment, then delivered the understatement of his life. 'The discovery may necessitate a re-examination of many of our basic postulates in the physical sciences.'

The headphones squawked.

Patiently, Allenby assured Earth that he was entirely serious, and reiterated the results of his observations. I suppose that he, an astronomer, was twice as flabbergasted as the rest of us. On the other hand, perhaps he was better equipped to adjust to the evidence.

'Evidently,' he said, 'when the body was formed, it travelled at such fantastic velocity as to enable it to'—his voice was almost a whisper—'to punch holes in things.'

The headphones squawked.

'In rocks,' Allenby said, 'in mountains, in anything that got in its way. And now the holes form a large portion of its fixed orbit.'

Squawk.

'Its mass must be on the order of—'

Squawk.

'—process of making the holes slowed it, so that now it travels just fast enough—'

Squawk.

'—maintain its orbit and penetrate occasional objects such as—'

Squawk.

'—and sand dunes—'

Squawk.

'My God, I *know* it's a mathematical monstrosity,' Allenby snarled. '*I* didn't put it there!'

Squawk.

Allenby was silent for a moment. Then he said slowly, 'A name?'

Squawk.

'H'm,' said Allenby. 'Well, well.' He appeared to brighten just a little. 'So it's up to me, as leader of the expedition, to name it?'

Squawk.

'Well, well,' he said.

That chop-licking tone was in his voice. We'd heard it all too often before. We shuddered, waiting.

'Inasmuch as Mars's outermost moon is called Deimos, and the next Phobos,' he said, 'I think I shall name the third moon of Mars—*Bottomos*.'

THE HOLES AROUND MARS

Jerome Bixby, although an excellent piano player, is not an author usually associated with 'scientific' s.f. *The Holes Around*

Mars is entertaining and fascinating, but it has many scientific flaws.

Mars has two known moons: Deimos, the outer, which is 12,500 miles above the Martian surface, and Phobos, the inner, which is 3,700 miles above that surface. Bixby postulates a third satellite, which circles Mars a few feet above its surface.

Bixby supposes this third satellite has the energy to punch holes through any Martian object rising more than those few feet above the surface. But where does the energy to punch holes, sometimes hundreds of miles long, come from?

The kinetic energy of motion depends on the mass and on the square of the velocity of the moving object, and Bixby blames the holes on the vast velocity of the satellite. However, a relatively small object travelling in an orbit about a planet has only one possible velocity, and this depends on the mass of the planet and the distance of the orbiting object from the centre of that planet. If the satellite were to move faster than that, its orbit would curve downward. To maintain a perfectly circular orbit, neither rising further above the surface nor dropping towards it, requires an orbital velocity that, in the case of Mars, is not enormously high. It is certainly not high enough to make those holes.

The energy might be due to mass rather than velocity. Suppose that the third satellite were neutronium (see *Proof*). It would then be enormously heavy for its size and it might bore those holes for that reason, but it seems quite certain that a four-inch-across ball of neutronium could not exist by itself. It would explode into ordinary matter as soon as it formed.

Questions and Suggestions

1. What is the orbital velocity of the two known Martian satellites? If you divide the escape velocity from the Martian surface by the square root of two you would obtain the orbital velocity for a satellite revolving in a circular orbit in the neighbourhood of the Martian surface. How much is that in miles per hour? If the satellite were of ordinary granite, what

would its kinetic energy be in comparison with that of a .45 bullet shot out of a revolver?

2. If the third satellite were neutronium, how much would it weigh? What would be its kinetic energy at the orbital velocity?

3. Our explorers in *The Holes Around Mars* find that the holes are in a straight line; that is, if you sight through a hole in one place you would see another hole in another place far away. But could you? Is the third satellite travelling in a true straight line or is it following the curvature of the Martian surface? How much does the Martian surface curve; that is, in the space of one mile, how far does the Martian surface drop? Calculate how far apart two holes must be so that when sighting through one you can no longer see the other?

4. According to the story, it would seem that the third satellite follows precisely the same path each time it circles the planet. Yet if the orbit were at an angle to the Martian equator, it would follow a different path each time around, for Mars will have rotated part-way during the time of one orbit. What would the orbit look like on a flat map of the Martian surface?

5. If the third satellite were following a path exactly along the Martian equator, the rotation of the planet wouldn't matter and the little satellite would follow its own track each rotation. (Why?) Is it likely, though, that its orbit would be lined up exactly with the Martian equator? What about the orbits of Phobos and Deimos in this respect. Suppose the third satellite's orbit varied from the line of the equator so slightly that it moved four inches north of the equator at one extreme of its orbit and four inches south at another. What would that do to the holes?

11. The Deep Range

Arthur C. Clarke

There was a killer loose on the range. A copter patrol, five hundred miles off Greenland, had seen the great corpse staining the sea crimson as it wallowed in the waves. Within seconds, the intricate warning system had been alerted; men were plotting circles and moving counters on the North Atlantic chart—and Don Burley was still rubbing the sleep from his eyes as he dropped silently down to the twenty-fathom line.

The pattern of green lights on the tell-tale was a glowing symbol of security. As long as that pattern was unchanged, as long as none of those emerald stars winked to red, all was well with Don and his tiny craft. Air—fuel—power—this was the triumvirate which ruled his life. If any of them failed, he would be sinking in a steel coffin down towards the pelagic ooze, as Johnnie Tyndall had done the season before last. But there was no reason why they should fail; the accidents one foresaw, Don told himself reassuringly, were never the ones that happened.

He leaned across the tiny control board and spoke into the mike. Sub 5 was still close enough to the mother ship for radio to work, but before long he'd have to switch to the sonics.

'Setting course 255, speed 50 knots, depth 20 fathoms, full sonar coverage.... Estimated time to target area, 70 minutes. Will report at 10-minute intervals. That is all.... Out.'

The acknowledgment, already weakening with range, came back at once from the *Herman Melville*.

'Message received and understood. Good hunting. What about the hounds?'

Don chewed his lower lip thoughtfully. This might be a job he'd have to handle alone. He had no idea, to within fifty miles either way, where Benj and Susan were at the moment. They'd certainly follow if he signalled for them, but they couldn't maintain his speed and would soon have to drop behind. Besides, he might be heading for a pack of killers, and the last thing he wanted to do was to lead his carefully trained porpoises into trouble. That was common sense and good business. He was also very fond of Susan and Benj.

'It's too far, and I don't know what I'm running into,' he replied. 'If they're in the interception area when I get there, I may whistle them up.'

The acknowledgment from the mother ship was barely audible, and Don switched off the set. It was time to look around.

He dimmed the cabin lights so that he could see the scanner screen more clearly, pulled the polaroid glasses down over his eyes, and peered into the depths. This was the moment when Don felt like a god, able to hold within his hands a circle of the Atlantic twenty miles across, and to see clear down to the still-unexplored deeps, three thousand fathoms below. The slowly rotating beam of inaudible sound was searching the world in which he floated, seeking out friend and foe in the eternal darkness where light could never penetrate. The pattern of soundless shrieks, too shrill even for the hearing of the bats, who had invented sonar a million years before man, pulsed out into the watery night; the faint echoes came tingling back as floating, blue-green flecks on the screen.

Through long practice, Don could read their message with effortless ease. A thousand feet below, stretching out to his submerged horizon, was the scattering layer—the blanket of life that covered half the world. The sunken meadow of the sea, it rose and fell with the passage of the sun, hovering always at the edge of darkness. But the ultimate depths were no concern of his. The flocks he guarded, and the enemies who ravaged them, belonged to the upper levels of the sea.

Don flicked the switch of the depth-selector, and his sonar

beam concentrated itself into the horizontal plane. The glimmering echoes from the abyss vanished, but he could see more clearly what lay around him here in the ocean's stratospheric heights. That glowing cloud two miles ahead was a school of fish; he wondered if Base knew about it, and made an entry in his log. There were some larger, isolated *blips* at the edge of the school—the carnivores pursuing the cattle insuring that the endlessly turning wheel of life and death would never lose momentum. But this conflict was no affair of Don's; he was after bigger game.

Sub 5 drove on towards the west, a steel needle swifter and more deadly than any other creature that roamed the seas. The tiny cabin, lit only by the flicker of lights from the instrument board, pulsed with power as the spinning turbines thrust the water aside. Don glanced at the chart and wondered how the enemy had broken through this time. There were still many weak points, for fencing the oceans of the world had been a gigantic task. The tenuous electric fields, fanning out between generators many miles apart, could not always hold at bay the starving monsters of the deep. They were learning, too. When the fences were opened, they would sometimes slip through with the whales and wreak havoc before they were discovered.

The long-range receiver bleeped plaintively, and Don switched over to TRANSCRIBE. It wasn't practical to send speech any distance over an ultrasonic beam, and code had come back into its own. Don had never learned to read it by ear, but the ribbon of paper emerging from the slot saved him the trouble.

COPTER REPORTS SCHOOL 50—100 WHALES HEADING 95 DEGREES GRID REF X186475 Y438034 STOP. MOVING AT SPEED. STOP. MELVILLE. OUT.

Don started to set the coordinates on the plotting grid, then saw that it was no longer necessary. At the extreme edge of his screen, a flotilla of faint stars had appeared. He altered course slightly, and drove head-on towards the approaching herd.

The copter was right; they were moving fast. Don felt a mounting excitement, for this could mean that they were on the run and luring the killers towards him. At the rate at which they were travelling he would be among them in five minutes. He cut the motors and felt the backward tug of water bringing him swiftly to rest.

Don Burley, a knight in armour, sat in his tiny dim-lit room fifty feet below the bright Atlantic waves, testing his weapons for the conflict that lay ahead. In these moments of poised suspense, before action began, his racing brain often explored such fantasies. He felt a kinship with all shepherds who had guarded their flocks back to the dawn of time. He was David, among ancient Palestinian hills, alert for the mountain lions that would prey upon his father's sheep. But far nearer in time, and far closer in spirit, were the men who had marshalled the great herds of cattle on the American plains, only a few lifetimes ago. They would have understood his work, though his implements would have been magic to them. The pattern was the same; only the scale had altered. It made no fundamental difference that the beasts Don herded weighed almost a hundred tons, and browsed on the endless savannahs of the sea.

The school was now less than two miles away, and Don checked his scanner's continuous circling to concentrate on the sector ahead. The picture on the screen altered to a fan-shaped wedge as the sonar beam started to flick from side to side; now he could count every whale in the school, and even make a good estimate of its size. With a practised eye, he began to look for stragglers.

Don could never have explained what drew him at once towards those four echoes at the southern fringe of the school. It was true that they were a little apart from the rest, but others had fallen as far behind. There is some sixth sense that a man acquires when he has stared long enough into a sonar screen—some hunch which enables him to extract more from the moving flecks than he has any right to do. Without conscious thought, Don reached for the control which would start the turbines whirling into life. Sub 5 was just getting under way when three laden thuds reverberated through the hull, as if someone was knocking on the front door and wanted to come in.

'Well, I'm damned,' said Don. 'How did you get here?' He did not bother to switch on the TV; he'd know Benj's signal anywhere. The porpoises must have been in the neighbourhood and had spotted him before he'd even switched on the hunting call. For the thousandth time, he marvelled at their intelligence and loyalty. It was strange that Nature had played the same trick twice—on land with the dog, in the ocean with the porpoise. Why were these graceful sea-beasts so fond of man, to whom they owed so little? It made one feel that the human race was worth something after all, if it could inspire such unselfish devotion.

It had been known for centuries that the porpoise was at least as intelligent as the dog, and could obey quite complex verbal commands. The experiment was still in progress, but if it succeeded, then the ancient partnership between shepherd and sheep-dog would have a new lease on life.

Don switched on the speakers recessed into the sub's hull and began to talk to his escorts. Most of the sounds he uttered would have been meaningless to other human ears; they were the product of long research by the animal psychologists of the World Food Administration. He gave his orders twice to make sure that they were understood, then checked with the sonar screen to see that Benj and Susan were following astern as he had told them to.

The four echoes that had attracted his attention were clearer and closer now, and the main body of the whale pack had swept past him to the east. He had no fear of a collision; the great animals, even in their panic, could sense his presence as easily as he could detect theirs, and by similar means. Don wondered if he should switch on his beacon. They might recognize its sound pattern, and it would reassure them. But the still unknown enemy might recognize it, too.

He closed for an interception, and hunched low over the screen as if to drag from it by sheer will power every scrap of information the scanner could give. There were two large echoes, some distance apart, and one was accompanied by a pair of smaller satellites. Don wondered if he was already too late. In his mind's eye, he could picture the death struggle taking place in the water less than a mile ahead. Those two fainter *blips* would be the enemy—either shark or grampus—worrying a whale while one of its companions stood by in helpless terror, with no weapons of defense except its mighty flukes.

Now he was almost close enough for vision. The TV camera in Sub 5's prow strained through the gloom, but at first could show nothing but the fog of plankton. Then a vast shadowy shape began to form in the centre of the screen, with two smaller companions below it. Don was seeing, with the greater precision but hopelessly limited range of ordinary light, what the sonar scanners had already told him.

Almost at once he saw his mistake. The two satellites were calves, not sharks. It was the first time he had ever met a whale with twins; although multiple births were not unknown, a cow could suckle only two young at once and usually only the stronger would survive. He choked down his disappointment; this error had cost him many minutes and he must begin the search again.

Then came the frantic tattoo on the hull that meant danger. It wasn't easy to scare Benj, and Don shouted his reassurance as he swung Sub 5 round so that the camera could search the turgid waters. Automatically, he had turned towards the fourth *blip* on the sonar screen—the echo he had assumed, from its size, to be another adult whale. And he saw that, after all, he had come to the right place.

'Jesus!' he said softly. 'I didn't know they came that big.' He'd seen larger sharks before, but they had all been harmless vegetarians. This, he could tell at a glance, was a Greenland shark, the killer of the northern seas. It was supposed to grow up to thirty feet long, but this specimen was bigger than Sub 5. It was every inch of forty feet from snout to tail, and when he spotted it, it was already turning in towards the kill. Like the coward it was, it had launched its attack at one of the calves.

Don yelled to Benj and Susan, and saw them racing ahead

into his field of vision. He wondered fleetingly why porpoises had such an overwhelming hatred of sharks; then he loosed his hands from the controls as the autopilot locked on to the target. Twisting and turning as agilely as any other sea-creature of its size, Sub 5 began to close in on the shark, leaving Don free to concentrate on his armament.

The killer had been so intent upon his prey that Benj caught him completely unaware, ramming him just behind the left eye. It must have been a painful blow; an iron-hard snout, backed by a quarter-ton of muscle moving at fifty miles an hour is something not to be laughed at, even by the largest fish. The shark jerked round in an impossibly tight curve, and Don was almost jolted out of his seat as the sub snapped on to a new course. If this kept up, he'd find it hard to use his Sting. But at least the killer was too busy now to bother about his intended victims.

Benj and Susan were worrying the giant like dogs snapping at the heels of an angry bear. They were too agile to be caught in those ferocious jaws, and Don marvelled at the coordination with which they worked. When either had to surface for air, the other would hold off for a minute until the attack could be resumed in strength.

There was no evidence that the shark realized that a far more dangerous adversary was closing in upon it, and that the porpoises were merely a distraction. That suited Don very nicely; the next operation was going to be difficult unless he could hold a steady course for at least fifteen seconds. At a pinch he could use the tiny rocket torps to make a kill. If he'd been alone, and faced with a pack of sharks he would certainly have done so. But it was messy, and there was a better way. He preferred the technique of the rapier to that of the hand-grenade.

Now he was only fifty feet away, and closing in rapidly. There might never be a better chance. He punched the launching stud.

From beneath the belly of the sub, something that looked like a sting-ray hurtled forward. Don had checked the speed of his own craft; there was no need to come any closer now. The tiny, arrow-shaped hydrofoil, only a couple of feet across, could move far faster than his vessel and would close the gap in seconds. As it raced forward, it spun out the thin line of the control wire, like some underwater spider laying its thread. Along that wire passed the energy that powered the Sting, and the signals that steered it to its goal. Don had completely ignored his own larger craft in the effort of guiding this underwater missile. It responded to his touch so swiftly that he felt he was controlling some sensitive high-spirited steed.

The shark saw the danger less than a second before impact. The resemblance of the Sting to an ordinary ray confused it, as the designers had intended. Before the tiny brain could realize that no ray behaved like this, the missile had struck. The steel hypodermic, rammed forward by an exploding cartridge, drove through the shark's horny skin, and the great fish erupted in a frenzy of terror. Don backed rapidly away, for a blow from that tail would rattle him around like a pea in a can and might even cause damage to the sub. There was nothing more for him to do, except to speak into the microphone and call off his hounds.

The doomed killer was trying to arch its body so that it could snap at the poisoned dart. Don had now reeled the Sting back into its hiding place, pleased that he had been able to retrieve the missile undamaged. He watched without pity as the great fish succumbed to its paralysis.

Its struggles were weakening. It was swimming aimlessly back and forth, and once Don had to sidestep smartly to avoid a collision. As it lost control of buoyancy, the dying shark drifted up to the surface. Don did not bother to follow; that could wait until he had attended to more important business.

He found the cow and her two calves less than a mile away, and inspected them carefully. They were uninjured, so there was no need to call the vet in his highly specialized two-man sub which could handle any cetalogical crisis from a stomach-ache to a Caesarean. Don made a note of the mother's number, stencilled just behind the flippers. The calves, as was obvious from their size, were this season's and had not yet been branded.

Don watched for a little while. They were no longer in the least alarmed, and a check on the sonar had shown that the whole school had ceased its panicky flight. He wondered how they knew what had happened; much had been learned about communication among whales, but much was still a mystery.

'I hope you appreciate what I've done for you, old lady,' he muttered. Then, reflecting that fifty tons of mother love was a slightly awe-inspiring sight, he blew his tanks and surfaced.

It was calm, so he cracked the airlock and popped his head out of the tiny conning tower. The water was only inches below his chin, and from time to time a wave made a determined effort to swamp him. There was little danger of this happening, for he fitted the hatch so closely that he was quite an effective plug.

Fifty feet away, a long slate-coloured mound, like an overturned boat, was rolling on the surface. Don looked at it thoughtfully and did some mental calculations. A brute this size should be valuable; with any luck, there was a chance of a double bonus. In a few minutes he'd radio his report, but for the moment it was pleasant to drink the fresh Atlantic air and to feel the open sky above his head.

A grey thunderbolt shot up out of the depths and smashed back on to the surface of the water, smothering Don with spray. It was just Benj's modest way of drawing attention to himself; a moment later the porpoise had swum up to the conning tower, so that Don could reach down and tickle its head. The great, intelligent eyes stared back into his; was it pure imagination, or did an almost human sense of fun also lurk in their depths?

Susan, as usual, circled shyly at a distance until jealousy overpowered her and she butted Benj out of the way. Don distributed caresses impartially, and apologized because he had nothing to give them. He undertook to make up for the omission as soon as he returned to the *Herman Melville*.

'I'll go for another swim with you, too,' he promised, 'as long as you behave yourselves next time.' He rubbed thoughtfully at a large bruise caused by Benj's playfulness, and wondered if he was not getting a little too old for rough games like this.

'Time to go home,' Don said firmly, sliding down into the cabin and slamming the hatch. He suddenly realized that he was very hungry, and had better do something about the breakfast he had missed. There were not many men on earth who had earned a better right to eat their morning meal. He had saved for humanity more tons of meat, oil, and milk than could easily be estimated.

Don Burley was the happy warrior coming home from one battle that man would always have to fight. He was holding at bay the spectre of famine which had confronted all earlier ages, but which would never threaten the world again while the great plankton farms harvested their millions of tons of protein, and the whale herds obeyed their new masters. Man had come back to the sea after aeons of exile; until the oceans froze, he would never be hungry again....

Don glanced at the scanner as he set his course. He smiled as he saw the two echoes keeping pace with the central splash of light that marked his vessel. 'Hang around,' he said. 'We mammals must stick together.' Then, as the auto-pilot took over, he lay back in his chair.

And presently Benj and Susan heard a most peculiar noise, rising and falling against the drone of the turbines. It had filtered faintly through the thick walls of Sub 5, and only the sensitive ears of the porpoises could have detected it. But intelligent beasts though they were, they could hardly be expected to understand why Don Burley was announcing, in a highly unmusical voice, that he was Heading for the Last Round-up....

THE DEEP RANGE

The Deep Range might be considered a science-fiction Western. For cattle, we have whales; for cougars, we have killer sharks; for dogs, we have porpoises; for a cowboy on a horse, we have what we might call a 'whaleboy' in a submarine.

The story ends on a very optimistic note, for it states that once whales are herded for food, man will never starve again. This optimism may not be justified.

There are food chains in which Animal A eats Animal B which eats Animal C which eats Animal D and so on. Usually, we finally reach an animal which lives on plants, and the plants get their energy out of sunlight and their building blocks out of the inanimate environment. Thus, we eat cattle which eats grass or we might eat polar bears, which eat seals which eat fish, which eat minnows, which eat insect larvae, which eat one-celled plants.

At each step of feeding there is considerable waste so that only 10 per cent of the living matter of the creature fed upon is converted into the living matter of the creature who is feeding. The total weight of the polar bears cannot be more than 10 per cent of the total weight of the seals it feeds on which in turn cannot be more than 10 per cent of the fish *it* feeds on, and so on.

Thus, the polar bears weigh only a tenth of a tenth, or one hundredth of the fish the seals feed on. If the polar bears fed on the fish directly, they could weigh, altogether, one tenth the weight of the fish. There would be ten times as many fish-feeding polar bears as seal-feeding polar bears. By cutting out items in the food chain, then, a feeder can do better in terms of its own numbers and mass.

The largest creatures, huge whales and sharks, live on tiny creatures and cut out all the steps in the food chain in between.

Whales can grow larger and more numerous living on tiny shrimp called krill, than they could by living on large fish that lived on smaller fish that lived on krill. If men learned to live on whales, they would have a valuable source of good protein, but suppose they cut out one step of the food chain and learned to harvest and process krill, making it tasty and nourishing. They would then have a food supply ten times as great.

(Clarke, one of the best of the 'scientific' s.f. writers, is best known now for his writing of the screen play of the motion picture *2001*.)

Questions and Suggestions

1. The plant life in the ocean is about four times as great in quantity as the plant life on land. Man's present food supply is based chiefly on land plants and animals. If men could exploit the sea to the same extent as the land, the total food supply would increase fivefold. But man is doubling his numbers every forty-seven years. At the present rate of doubling, how long would it be before the human population increases fivefold? By that time, the amount of food per capita, land and sea, would be no greater than it is now. Is Clarke, in your opinion, right to be so optimistic over man's food supply? What is needed to make the optimism realistic?

2. The question of the intelligence of porpoises is of great interest to biologists now. Look up some of the work being done with them. If porpoises (and how do they differ from dolphins and from whales, by the way?) are as intelligent as man, as some think, why have they not developed a civilization?

3. If mankind learns to harvest and process krill, what would happen to the great whales?

4. Why has Clarke named the whale-herding ship the *Herman Melville*?

12. The Cave of Night

James E. Gunn

The phrase was first used by a poet disguised in the cynical hide of a newspaper reporter. It appeared on the first day and was widely reprinted. He wrote:

'At eight o'clock, after the Sun has set and the sky is darkening, look up! There's a man up there where no man has ever been.

'He is lost in the cave of night ...'

The headlines demanded something short, vigorous and descriptive. That was it. It was inaccurate, but it stuck.

If anybody was in a cave, it was the rest of humanity. Painfully, triumphantly, one man had climbed out. Now he couldn't find his way back in to the cave with the rest of us.

What goes up doesn't always come back down.

That was the first day. After it came twenty-nine days of agonized suspense.

The cave of night. I wish the phrase had been mine.

That was it, the tag, the symbol. It was the first thing a man saw when he glanced at the newspaper. It was the way people talked about it: 'What's the latest about the cave?' It summed it all up, the drama, the anxiety, the hope.

Maybe it was the Floyd Collins influence. The papers dug up their files on that old tragedy, reminiscing, comparing; and they remembered the little girl—Kathy Fiscus, wasn't it?—who was trapped in that abandoned California drain pipe; and a number of others.

Periodically, it happens, a sequence of events so accidentally dramatic that men lose their hatreds, their terrors, their shynesses, their inadequacies, and the human race momentarily recognizes its kinship.

The essential ingredients are these: a person must be in unusual and desperate peril. The peril must have duration. There must be proof that the person is still alive. Rescue attempts must be made. Publicity must be widespread.

One could probably be constructed artificially, but if the world ever discovered the fraud, it would never forgive.

Like many others, I have tried to analyse what makes a niggling, squabbling, callous race of beings suddenly share that most human emotion of sympathy, and, like them, I have not succeeded. Suddenly a distant stranger will mean more than their own comfort. Every waking moment, they pray: Live, Floyd! Live, Kathy! Live, Rev!

We pass on the street, we who would not have nodded, and ask, 'Will they get there in time?'

Optimists and pessimists alike, we hope so. We all hope so.

In a sense, this one was different. This was purposeful. Knowing the risk, accepting it because there was no other way to do what had to be done, Rev had gone into the cave of night. The accident was that he could not return.

The news came out of nowhere—literally—to an unsuspecting world. The earliest mention the historians have been able to locate was an item about a ham radio operator in Davenport, Iowa. He picked up a distress signal on a sticky-hot June evening.

The message, he said later, seemed to fade in, reach a peak, and fade out:

'... and fuel tanks empty —ceiver broke ... transmitting in clear so someone can pick this up, and ... no way to get back ... stuck ...'

A small enough beginning.

The next message was received by a military base radio watch near Fairbanks, Alaska. That was early in the morning.

Half an hour later, a night-shift worker in Boston heard something on his short-wave set that sent him rushing to the telephone.

That morning, the whole world learned the story. It broke over them, a wave of excitement and concern. Orbiting 1,075 miles above their heads was a man, an officer of the United States Air Force, in a fuelless spaceship.

All by itself, the spaceship part would have captured the world's attention. It was achievement as monumental as anything Man has ever done and far more spectacular. It was liberation from the tyranny of Earth, this jealous mother who had bound her children tight with the apron strings of gravity.

Man was free. It was a symbol that nothing is completely and finally impossible if Man wants it hard enough and long enough.

There are regions that humanity finds peculiarly congenial. Like all Earth's creatures, Man is a product and a victim of environment. His triumph is that the slave became the master. Unlike more specialized animals, he distributed himself across the entire surface of the Earth, from the frozen Antarctic continent to the Arctic icecap.

Man became an equatorial animal, a temperate zone animal, an artic animal. He became a plain dweller, a valley dweller, a mountain dweller. The swamp and the desert became equally his home.

Man made his own environment.

With his inventive mind and his dexterous hands, he fashioned it, conquered cold and heat, dampness, aridness, land, sea, air. Now, with his science, he had conquered everything. He had become independent of the world that bore him.

It was a birthday cake for all mankind, celebrating its coming of age.

Brutally, the disaster was icing on the cake.

But it was more, too. When everything is considered, perhaps it was the aspect that, for a few, brief days, united humanity and made possible what we did.

It was a sign: Man is never completely independent of Earth; he carries with him his environment; he is always and forever a part of humanity. It was a conquest mellowed by a confession of mortality and error.

It was a statement: Man has within him the qualities of greatness that will never accept the restraints of circumstance, and yet he carries, too, the seeds of fallibility that we all recognize in ourselves.

Rev was one of us. His triumph was our triumph; his peril—more fully and finely—was our peril.

Reverdy L. McMillen, III, first lieutenant, U.S.A.F. Pilot. Rocket jockey. Man. Rev. He was only a thousand miles away, calling for help, but those miles were straight up. We got to know him as well as any member of our own family.

The news came as a great personal shock to me. I knew Rev. We had become good friends in college, and fortune had thrown us together in the Air Force, a writer and a pilot. I had got out as soon as possible, but Rev had stayed in. I knew, vaguely, that he had been testing rocket-powered aeroplanes with Chuck Yeager. But I had no idea that the rocket programme was that close to space.

Nobody did. It was a better-kept secret than the Manhattan Project.

I remember staring at Rev's picture in the evening newspaper—the straight black hair, the thin, rakish moustache, the Clark Gable ears, the reckless, rueful grin—and I felt again, like a physical thing, his great joy in living. It expressed itself in a hundred ways. He loved widely, but with discrimination. He ate well, drank heartily, revelled in expert jazz and artistic inventiveness, and talked incessantly.

Now he was alone and soon all that might be extinguished. I told myself that I would help.

That was a time of wild enthusiasm. Men mobbed the Air Force Proving Grounds at Cocoa, Florida, wildly volunteering their services. But I was no engineer. I wasn't even a welder or a riveter. At best, I was only a poor word mechanic.

But words, at least, I could contribute.

I made a hasty verbal agreement with a local paper and caught the first plane to Washington, D.C. For a long time, I liked to think that what I wrote during the next few days had something to do with subsequent events, for many of my articles were picked up for reprint by other newspapers.

The Washington fiasco was the responsibility of the Senate Investigating Committee. It subpoenaed everybody in sight—which effectively removed them from the vital work they were doing. But within a day, the Committee realized that it had bitten off a bite it could neither swallow nor spit out.

General Beauregard Finch, head of the research and development programme, was the tough morsel the Committee gagged on. Coldly, accurately, he described the development of the project, the scientific and technical research, the tests, the building of the ship, the training of the prospective crewmen, and the winnowing of the volunteers down to one man.

In words more eloquent because of their clipped precision, he described the take-off of the giant three-stage ship, shoved upward on a lengthening arm of combining hydrazine and nitric acid. Within fifty-six minutes, the remaining third stage had reached its orbital height of 1,075 miles.

It had coasted there. In order to maintain that orbit, the motors had to flicker on for fifteen seconds.

At that moment, disaster laughed at Man's careful calculations.

Before Rev could override the automatics, the motors had flamed for almost half a minute. The fuel he had depended upon to slow the ship so that it would drop, re-enter the atmosphere and be reclaimed by Earth was almost gone. His efforts to counteract the excess speed resulted only in an approximation of the original orbit.

The fact was this: Rev was up there. He would stay there until someone came and got him.

And there was no way to get there.

The Committee took that as an admission of guilt and incompetence; they tried to lever themselves free with it, but

General Finch was not to be intimidated. A manned ship had been sent up because no mechanical or electronic computer could contain the vast possibilities for decision and action built into a human being.

The original computer was still the best all-purpose computer.

There had been only one ship built, true. But there was good reason for that, a completely practical reason—money.

Leaders are, by definition, ahead of the people. But this wasn't a field in which they could show the way and wait for the people to follow. This was no expedition in ancient ships, no light exploring party, no pilot-plant operation. Like a parachute jump, it had to be successful the first time.

This was an enterprise into new, expensive fields. It demanded money (billions of dollars), brains (the best available), and the hard, dedicated labour of men (thousands of them).

General Finch became a national hero that afternoon. He said, in bold words, 'With the limited funds you gave us, we have done what we set out to do. We have demonstrated that space flight is possible, that a space platform is feasible.

'If there is any inefficiency, if there is any blame for what has happened, it lies at the door of those who lacked confidence in the courage and ability of their countrymen to fight free of Earth to the greatest glory. Senator, how did you vote on that?'

But I am not writing a history. The shelves are full of them. I will touch on the international repercussions only enough to show that the event was no more a respecter of national boundaries than was Rev's orbiting ship.

The orbit was almost perpendicular to the equator. The ship travelled as far north as Nome, as far south as Little America on the Antarctic continent. It completed one giant circle every two hours. Meanwhile, the Earth rotated beneath. If the ship had been equipped with adequate optical instruments, Rev could have observed every spot on Earth within twenty-four hours. He could have seen fleets and their dispositions, aircraft carriers and the planes taking off their decks, troop manoeuvres.

In the General Assembly of the United Nations, the Russian ambassador protested this unwarranted and illegal violation of its national boundaries. He hinted darkly that it would not be allowed to continue. The U.S.S.R. had not been caught unprepared, he said. If the violation went on—*'every few hours!'*—drastic steps would be taken.

World opinion reared up in indignation. The U.S.S.R. immediately retreated and pretended, as only it could, that its belligerence had been an unwarranted inference and that it had never said anything of the sort, anyway.

This was not a military observer above our heads. It was a man who would soon be dead unless help reached him.

A world offered what it had. Even the U.S.S.R. announced that it was outfitting a rescue ship, since its space programme was already on the verge of success. And the American public responded with more than a billion dollars within a week. Congress appropriated another billion. Thousands of men and women volunteered.

The race began.

Would the rescue party reach the ship in time? The world prayed.

And it listened daily to the voice of a man it hoped to buy back from death.

The problem shaped up like this:

The trip had been planned to last for only a few days. By careful rationing, the food and water might be stretched out for more than a month, but the oxygen, by cutting down activity to conserve it, couldn't possibly last more than thirty days. That was the absolute outside limit.

I remember reading the carefully detailed calculations in the paper and studying them for some hopeful error. There was none.

Within a few hours, the discarded first stage of the ship had been located floating in the Atlantic Ocean. It was towed back to Cocoa, Florida. Almost a week was needed to find and return to the Proving Grounds the second stage, which had landed 906 miles away.

Both sections were practically undamaged; their fall had been cushioned by ribbon parachute. They could be cleaned, repaired and used again. The trouble was the vital third stage—the nose section. A new one had to be designed and built within a month.

Space-madness became a new form of hysteria. We read statistics, we memorized insignificant details, we studied diagrams, we learned the risks and the dangers and how they would be met and conquered. It all became part of us. We watched the slow progress of the second ship and silently, tautly, urged it upward.

The schedule overhead became part of everyone's daily life. Work stopped while people rushed to windows or outside or to their television sets, hoping for a glimpse, a glint from the high, swift ship, so near, so untouchably far.

And we listened to the voice from the cave of night:

'I've been staring out the portholes. I never tire of that. Through the one on the right, I see what looks like a black velvet curtain with a strong light behind it. There are pinpoint holes in the curtain and the light shines through, not winking the way stars do, but steady. There's no air up here. That's the reason. The mind can understand and still misinterpret.

'My air is holding out better than I expected. By my figures, it should last twenty-seven days more. I shouldn't use so much of it talking all the time, but it's hard to stop. Talking, I feel as if I'm still in touch with Earth, still one of you, even if I am way up here.

'Through the left-hand window is San Francisco Bay, looking like a dark, wandering arm extended by the ocean octopus. The city itself looks like a heap of diamonds with trails scattered from it. It glitters up cheerfully, an old friend. It misses me, it says. Hurry home, it says. It's gone now, out of sight. Good-bye, Frisco!

'Do you hear me down there? Sometimes I wonder. You can't see me now. I'm in the Earth's shadow. You'll have to wait for the dawn. I'll have mine in a few minutes.

'You're all busy down there. I know that. If I know you, you're all worrying about me, working to get me down, forgetting everything else. You don't know what a feeling that is. I hope to Heaven you never have to, wonderful though it is.

'Too bad the receiver was broken, but if it had to be one or the other, I'm glad it was the transmitter that came through. There's only one of me. There are billions of you to talk to.

'I wish there were some way I could be sure you were hearing me. Just that one thing might keep me from going crazy.'

Rev, you were one in millions. We read all about your selection, your training. You were our representative, picked with our greatest skill.

Out of a thousand who passed the initial rigid requirements for education, physical and emotional condition and age, only five could qualify for space. They couldn't be too tall, too stout, too young, too old. Medical and psychiatric tests weeded them out.

One of the training machines—Lord, how we studied this—reproduces the acceleration strains of a blasting rocket. Another trains men for manoeuvring in the weightlessness of space. A third duplicates the cramped, sealed conditions of a spaceship cabin. Out of the final five, you were the only one who qualified.

No, Rev, if any of us could stay sane, it was you.

There were thousands of suggestions, almost all of them useless. Psychologists suggested self-hypnotism; cultists suggested yoga. One man sent a detailed sketch of a giant electromagnet with which Rev's ship could be drawn back to Earth.

General Finch had the only practical idea. He outlined a plan for letting Rev know that we were listening. He picked out Kansas City and set the time. 'Midnight,' he said. 'On the dot. Not a minute earlier or later. At that moment, he'll be right overhead.'

And at midnight, every light in the city went out and came back on and went out and came back on again.

For a few awful moments, we wondered if the man up there in the cave of night had seen. Then came the voice we knew now so well that it seemed it had always been with us, a part of us, our dreams and our waking.

The voice was husky with emotion:

'Thanks ... Thanks for listening. Thanks, Kansas City. I saw you winking at me. I'm not alone. I know that now. I'll never forget. Thanks.'

And silence then as the ship fell below the horizon. We pictured it to ourselves sometimes, continually circling the Earth, its trajectory exactly matching the curvature of the globe beneath it. We wondered if it would ever stop.

Like the Moon, would it be a satellite of the Earth forever?

We went through our daily chores like automatons while we watched the third stage of the rocket take shape. We raced against a dwindling air supply, and death raced to catch a ship moving at 15,800 miles per hour.

We watched the ship grow. On our television screens, we saw the construction of the cellular fuel tanks, the rocket motors, and the fantastic multitude of pumps, valves, gauges, switches, circuits, transistors, and tubes.

The personnel space was built to carry five men instead of one man. We watched it develop, a Spartan simplicity in the middle of the great complex, and it was as if we ourselves would live there, would watch those dials and instruments, would grip those chair-arm controls for the infinitesimal sign that the automatic pilot had faltered, would feel the soft flesh and the softer internal organs being wrenched away from the unyielding bone, and would hurtle upward into the cave of night.

We watched the plating wrap itself protectively around the vitals of the nose section. The wings were attached; they would make the ship a huge, metal glider in its unpowered descent to Earth after the job was done.

We met the men who would man the ship. We grew to know them as we watched them train, saw them fighting artificial gravities, testing spacesuits in simulated vacuums, practising manoeuvres in the weightless condition of free fall.

That was what we lived for.

And we listened to the voice that came to us out of the night:

'Twenty-one days. Three weeks. Seems like more. Feel a little sluggish, but there's no room for exercise in a coffin. The concentrated foods I've been eating are fine, but not for a steady diet. Oh, what I'd give for a piece of home-baked apple-pie!

'The weightlessness got me at first. Felt I was sitting on a ball that was spinning in all directions at once. Lost my breakfast a couple of times before I learned to stare at one thing. As long as you don't let your eyes roam, you're okay.

'There's Lake Michigan! My God, but it's blue today! Dazzles the eyes! There's Milwaukee, and how are the Braves doing? It must be a hot day in Chicago. It's a little muggy up here, too. The water absorbers must be overloaded.

'The air smells funny, but I'm not surprised. I must smell funny, too, after twenty-one days without a bath. Wish I could have one. There are an awful lot of things I used to take for granted and suddenly want more than—

'Forget that, will you? Don't worry about me. I'm fine. I know you're working to get me down. If you don't succeed, that's okay with me. My life wouldn't just be wasted. I've done what I've always wanted to do. I'd do it again.

'Too bad, though, that we only had the money for one ship.'

And again: 'An hour ago, I saw the Sun rise over Russia. It looks like any other land from here, green where it should be green, farther north a sort of mud colour, and then white where the snow is still deep.

'Up here, you wonder why we're so different when the land is the same. You think: we're all children of the same mother planet. Who says we're different?

'Think I'm crazy. Maybe you're right. It doesn't matter much what I say as long as I say something. This is one time I won't be interrupted. Did any man ever have such an audience?'

No, Rev. Never.

The voice from above, historical now, preserved:

'I guess the gadgets are all right. You slide-rule mechanics!

You test-tube artists! You finding what you want? Getting the dope on cosmic rays, meteoric dust, those islands you could never map, the cloud formations, wind movements, all the weather data? Hope the telemetering gauges are working. They're more important than my voice.'

I don't think so, Rev. But we got the data. We built some of it into the new ships. *Ships*, not *ship*, for we didn't stop with one. Before we were finished, we had two complete three-stages and a dozen nose sections.

The voice: 'Air's bad tonight. Can't seem to get a full breath. Sticks in the lungs. Doesn't matter, though. I wish you could all see what I have seen, the vast-spreading universe around Earth, like a bride in a soft veil. You'd know, then, that we belong out here.'

We know, Rev. You led us out. You showed us the way.

We listened and we watched. It seems to me now that we held our breath for thirty days.

At last we watched the fuel pumping into the ship—nitric acid and hydrazine. A month ago, we did not know their names; now we recognize them as the very substances of life itself. It flowed through the long special hoses, dangerous, cautiously grounded, over half a million dollars' worth of rocket fuel.

Statisticians estimate that more than a hundred million Americans were watching their television sets that day. Watching and praying.

Suddenly the view switched to the ship fleeing south above us. The technicians were expert now. The telescopes picked it up instantly, the focus perfect the first time, and tracked it across the sky until it dropped beyond the horizon. It looked no different now than when we had seen it first.

But the voice that came from our speakers was different. It was weak. It coughed frequently and paused for breath.

'Air very bad. Better hurry. Can't last much longer ... Silly! ... Of course you'll hurry.

'Don't want anyone feeling sorry for me.... I've been living fast ... Thirty days? I've seen 360 sunrises, 360 sunsets ... I've seen what no man has ever seen before ... I was the first. That's something ... worth dying for ...

'I've seen the stars, clear and undiminished. They look cold, but there's warmth to them and life. They have families of planets like our own Sun, some of them ... They must. God wouldn't put them there for no purpose ... They can be homes to our future generations. Or, if they have inhabitants, we can trade with them: goods, ideas, the love of creation ...

'But—more than this—I have seen the Earth. I have seen it—as no man has ever seen it—turning below me like a fantastic ball, the seas like blue glass in the Sun ... or lashed into grey storm-peaks ... and the land green with life ... the cities of the world in the night, sparkling ... and the people ...

'I have seen the Earth—there where I have lived and loved ... I have known it better than any man and loved it better and known its children better ... It has been good ...

'Good-bye ... I have a better tomb than the greatest conqueror Earth ever bore ... Do not disturb ...'

We wept. How could we help it?

Rescue was so close and we could not hurry it. We watched impotently. The crew were hoisted far up into the nose section of the three-stage rocket. It stood as tall as a 24-storey building. *Hurry*! we urged. But they could not hurry. The interception of a swiftly moving target is precision business. The takeoff was all calculated and impressed on the metal and glass and free electrons of an electronic computer.

The ship was tightened down methodically. The spectators scurried back from the base of the ship. We waited. The ship waited. Tall and slim as it was, it seemed to crouch. Someone counted off the seconds to a breathless world: ten—nine—eight ... five, four, three ... one—*fire*!

There was no flame, and then we saw it spurting into the air from the exhaust tunnel several hundred feet away. The ship balanced, unmoving, on a squat column of incandescence; the column stretched itself, grew tall; the huge ship picked up speed and dwindled into a point of brightness.

The telescopic lenses found it, lost it, found it again. It

arched over on its side and thrust itself seaward. At the end of 84 seconds, the rear jets faltered, and our hearts faltered with them. Then we saw that the first stage had been dropped. The rest of the ship moved off on a new fiery trail. A ring-shaped ribbon parachute blossomed out of the third stage and slowed it rapidly.

The second stage dropped away 124 seconds later. The nose section, with its human cargo, its rescue equipment, went on alone. At 63 miles altitude, the flaring exhaust cut out. The third stage would coast up the gravitational hill more than a thousand miles.

Our stomachs were knotted with dread as the rescue ship disappeared beyond the horizon of the farthest television camera. By this time, it was on the other side of the world, speeding towards a carefully planned rendezvous with its sister.

Hang on, Rev! Don't give up!

Fifty-six minutes. That was how long we had to wait. Fifty-six minutes from the take-off until the ship was in its orbit. After that, the party would need time to match speeds, to send a space-suited crewman drifting across the emptiness between, over the vast, eerily turning sphere of the Earth beneath.

In imagination, we followed them.

Minutes would be lost while the rescuer clung to the ship, opened the airlock cautiously so that none of the precious remnants of air would be lost, and passed into the ship where one man had known utter loneliness.

We waited. We hoped.

Fifty-six minutes. They passed. An hour. Thirty minutes more. We reminded ourselves—and were reminded—that the first concern was Rev. It might be hours before we would get any real news.

The tension mounted unbearably. We waited—a nation, a world—for relief.

At eighteen minutes less than two hours—*too soon,* we told ourselves, lest we hope too much—we heard the voice of

Captain Frank Pickrell, who was later to become the first commander of the *Doughnut.*

'I have just entered the ship,' he said slowly. 'The airlock was open.' He paused. The implication stunned our emotions; we listened mutely. 'Lieutenant McMillen is dead. He died heroically, waiting until all hope was gone, until every oxygen gauge stood at zero. And then—well, the airlock was open when we arrived.

'In accordance with his own wishes, his body will be left here in its eternal orbit. This ship will be his tomb for all men to see when they look up towards the stars. As long as there are men on Earth, it will circle above them, an everlasting reminder of what men have done and what men can do.

'That was Lieutenant McMillen's hope. This he did not only as an American, but as a man, dying for all humanity, and all humanity can glory for it.

'From this moment, let this be his shrine, sacred to all the generations of spacemen, inviolate. And let it be a symbol that Man's dreams can be realized, but sometimes the price is steep.

'I am going to leave here now. My feet will be the last to touch this deck. The oxygen I released is almost used up. Lieutenant McMillen is in his control chair, staring out towards the stars. I will leave the airlock doors open behind me. Let the airless, frigid arms of space protect and preserve for all eternity the man they would not let go.'

Good-bye, Rev! Farewell! Good night!

Rev was not long alone. He was the first, but not the last to receive a space burial and a hero's farewell.

This, as I said, is no history of the conquest of space. Every child knows the story as well as I and can identify the make of a spaceship more swiftly.

The story of the combined efforts that built the orbital platform irreverently called the *Doughnut* has been told by others. We have learned at length the political triumph that placed it under United Nations control.

Its contribution to our daily lives has received the accolade of the commonplace. It is an observatory, a laboratory, and a guardian. Startling discoveries have come out of that weightless, airless, heatless place. It has learned how weather is made and predicted it with incredible accuracy. It has observed the stars clear of the veil of the atmosphere. And it has insured our peace ...

It has paid its way. No one can question that. It and its smaller relay stations made possible today's worldwide television and radio network. There is no place on Earth where a free voice cannot be heard or the face of freedom be seen. Sometimes we find ourselves wondering how it could have been any other way.

And we have had adventure. We have travelled to the dead gypsum seas of the Moon with the first exploration party. This year, we will solve the mysteries of Mars. From our armchairs, we will thrill to the discoveries of our pioneers—our stand-ins, so to speak. It has given us a common heritage, a common goal, and for the first time we are united.

This I mention only for background; no one will argue that the conquest of space was not of incalculable benefit to all mankind.

The whole thing came back to me recently, an overpowering flood of memory. I was skirting Times Square, where every face is a stranger's, and suddenly I stopped, incredulous.

'Rev!' I shouted.

The man kept on walking. He passed me without a glance. I turned around and stared after him. I started to run. I grabbed him by the arm. 'Rev!' I said huskily, swinging him around. 'Is it really you?'

The man smiled politely. 'You must have mistaken me for someone else.' He unclamped my fingers easily and moved away. I realized then that there were two men with him, one on each side. I felt their eyes on my face, memorizing it.

Probably it didn't mean anything. We all have our doubles. I could have been mistaken.

But it started me remembering and thinking.

The first thing the rocket experts had to consider was expense.

They didn't have the money. The second thing was weight. Even a medium-sized man is heavy when rocket payloads are reckoned, and the stores and equipment essential to his survival are many times heavier.

If Rev had escaped alive, why had they announced that he was dead? But I knew the question was all wrong.

If my speculations were right, Rev had never been up there at all. The essential payload was only a thirty-day recording and a transmitter. Even if the major feat of sending up a manned rocket was beyond their means and their techniques, they could send up that much.

Then they got the money; they got the volunteers and the techniques.

I suppose the telemetered reports from the rocket helped. But what they accomplished in thirty days was an unparalleled miracle.

The timing of the recording must have taken months of work; but the vital part of the scheme was secrecy. General Finch had to know and Captain—now Colonel—Pickrell. A few others—workmen, administrators—and Rev ...

What could they do with him? Disguise him? Yes. And then hide him in the biggest city in the world. They would have done it that way.

It gave me a funny, sick kind of feeling, thinking about it. Like everybody else, I don't like to be taken in by a phony plea. And this was a fraud perpetrated on all humanity.

Yet it had led us to the planets. Perhaps it would lead us beyond, even to the stars. I asked myself: could they have done it any other way?

I would like to think I was mistaken. This myth has become part of us. We lived through it ourselves, helped make it. Someday, I tell myself, a spaceman whose reverence is greater than his obedience will make a pilgrimage to that swift shrine and find only an empty shell.

I shudder then.

This pulled us together. In a sense, it keeps us together. Nothing is more important than that.

I try to convince myself that I was mistaken. The straight black hair was grey at the temples now and cut much shorter. The moustache was gone. The Clark Gable ears were flat to the head; that's a simple operation, I understand.

But grins are hard to change. And anyone who lived through those thirty days will never forget that voice.

I think about Rev and the life he must have now, the things he loved and can never enjoy again, and I realize perhaps he made the greater sacrifice.

I think sometimes he must wish he were really in the cave of night, seated in that icy control chair, 1,075 miles above, staring out at the stars.

THE CAVE OF NIGHT

This story was first published in February 1955, two and a half years before the first satellite was orbited, and six and a half years before the first man was put into orbit.

It is interesting to see in what ways James Gunn (who now works in an administrative position at the University of Kansas) foresaw events correctly, and in what ways he did not.

Gunn felt, as science fiction writers had always felt, that it was logical for a man to be inside the first object orbited. Actually, this proved not to be the case. All sorts of objects (including animals) were placed in orbit before the men in charge of the space programmes in either the U.S.A. or the U.S.S.R. would trust men to ride a spaceship safely.

Gunn's final twist has a recording orbited before a man after all (and that is much more nearly correct) and he uses that recording as a device to force mankind of all nations to be willing to invest in a space programme. This was, actually, a remarkable piece of prophecy. The first orbiting vehicle, even though it was very simple, transmitted only a bleep, and did not represent a human life in danger, did arouse enough interest to bring about the spending of billions.

The space effort that resulted, however, was not a united

drive aimed at an errand of mercy, but was a nationalistic push on the part of two competing nations, each determined to pull prestige-coups over the other. (This no science fiction writer foresaw.)

Gunn assumed (as all American science fiction writers did) that the American effort would be the first to succeed. He does say the U.S.S.R. announced 'its space programme was already on the verge of success' but Gunn may have intended this ironically as the sort of thing the vainglorious Russians would be bound to say for propaganda reasons. He must have been surprised (as I was) when, in 1957, it was the Russians, after all, who managed to put up a satellite first.

Gunn had the centre of the effort at Cocoa, Florida, which is only fifteen miles west of Cape Canaveral (later Cape Kennedy) where the launchings eventually did take place. On the other hand, his picture of Earth as seen from space seems to envisage a planet with all its land and ocean clearly in view. As it turned out, the most prominent feature visible from space is Earth's cloud cover and very little of its land features can be made out easily at any given moment.

Questions and Suggestions

1. Actually no astronaut or cosmonaut has yet died by being marooned in space. A cosmonaut has died in the process of landing in the U.S.S.R. and three astronauts have died on the ground while testing a capsule in the U.S.A. Do you think that the world would react to a marooned astronaut as described? Or do you think national rivalries would overcome human sympathy? How about world reaction to starvation in Biafra or in India? What about people in crowds who yell 'Jump! Jump!' when someone teeters on a high building ledge? How would *you* feel if it were a Russian who was marooned?

2. Gunn has the rescue vessels designed, built, and launched in the space of thirty days. Do you think this is practical? Look up data on the space programme and find out how long such things take.

3. Gunn, like all science fiction writers of the time, takes the

value of the space effort for granted. He says: 'No one will argue that the conquest of space was not of incalculable benefit to all mankind.' Yet, at the present time, after the Moon has actually been reached, many do argue against the value of the space effort. Look into the matter and assemble points to be made in favour of the space effort and against it.

13. Dust Rag

Hal Clement

'Checking out.'

'Checked, Ridge. See you soon.'

Ridging glanced over his shoulder at Beacon Peak, as the point where the relay station had been mounted was known. The gleaming dome of its leaden meteor shield was visible as a spark; most of the lower peaks of Harpalus were already below the horizon, and with them the last territory with which Ridging or Shandara could claim familiarity. The humming turbine tractor that carried them was the only sign of humanity except each other's faces—the thin crescent of their home world was too close to the sun to be seen easily, and Earth doesn't look very 'human' from outside in any case.

The prospect ahead was not exactly strange, of course, Shandara had remarked several times in the last four weeks that a man who had seen any of the moon had seen all of it. A good many others had agreed with him. Even Ridging, whose temperament kept him normally expecting something new to happen, was beginning to get a trifle bored with the place. It wasn't even dangerous; he knew perfectly well what exposure to vacuum would mean, but checking spacesuit and air-lock valves had become a matter of habit long before.

Cosmic rays went through plastic suits and living bodies like glass, for the most part ineffective because unabsorbed; meteors blew microscopic holes through thin metal, but scarcely marked spacesuits or hulls, as far as current experiences went; the 'dust-hidden crevasses' which they had expected to catch unwary men or vehicles simply didn't exist—the dust was too dry to cover any sort of hole, except by filling it completely. The closest approach to a casualty suffered so far had occurred when a man had missed his footing on the ladder outside the *Albireo*'s air lock and narrowly avoided a hundred and fifty foot fall.

Still, Shandara was being cautious. His eyes swept the ground ahead of their tracks, and his gauntleted hands rested lightly on brake and steering controls as the tractor glided ahead.

Harpalus and the relay station were out of sight now. Another glance behind assured Ridging of that. For the first time in weeks he was out of touch with the rest of the group, and for the first time he wondered whether it was such a good idea. Orders had been strict; the radius of exploration settled on long before was not to be exceeded. Ridging had been completely in favour of this; but it was his own instruments which had triggered the change of schedule.

One question about the moon to which no one could more than guess an answer in advance was that of its magnetic field. Once the group was on the surface it had immediately become evident that there was one, and comparative readings had indicated that the south magnetic pole—or *a* south magnetic pole —lay a few hundred miles away. It had been decided to modify the programme to check the region, since the last forlorn chance of finding any trace of a gaseous envelope around the moon seemed to lie in auroral investigation. Ridging found himself, to his intense astonishment, wondering why he had volunteered for the trip and then wondering how such thoughts could cross his mind. He had never considered himself a coward, and certainly had no one but himself to blame for being in the tractor. No one had made him volunteer, and any technician could have set up and operated the equipment.

'Come out of it, Ridge. Anyone would think you were worried.' Shandara's careless tones cut into his thoughts. 'How about running this buggy for a while? I've had her for a hundred kilos.'

'Right.' Ridging slipped into the driver's seat as his companion left it without slowing the tractor. He did not need to find their location on the photographic map clipped beside the panel; he had been keeping a running check almost unconsciously between the features it showed and the landmarks appearing over the horizon. A course had been marked on it, and navigation was not expected to be a problem even without a magnetic compass.

The course was far from straight, though it led over what passed for fairly smooth territory on the moon. Even back on Sinus Roris the tractor had had to weave its way around numerous obstacles; now well on to the Mare Frigoris the situation was no better, and according to the map it was nearly time to turn south through the mountains, which would be infinitely worse. According to the photos taken during the original landing approach the journey would be possible, however, and would lead through the range at its narrowest part out on to Mare Imbrium. From that point to the vicinity of Plato, where the region to be investigated lay, there should be no trouble at all.

Oddly enough, there wasn't. Ridging was moderately surprised; Shandara seemed to take it as a matter of course. The cartographer had eaten, slept, and taken his turn at driving with only an occasional remark. Ridging was beginning to believe by the time they reached their goal that his companion was actually as bored with the moon as he claimed to be. The thought, however, was fleeting; there was work to be done.

About six hundred pounds of assorted instruments were attached to the trailer which had been improvised from discarded fuel tanks. The tractor itself could not carry them; its entire cargo space was occupied by another improvisation—an auxiliary fuel tank which had been needed to make the present journey possible. The instruments had to be removed, set up in various spots, and permitted to make their records for the next thirty hours. This would have been a minor task, and possibly even justified a little boredom, had it not been for the fact that some of the 'spots' were supposed to be as high as possible. Both men had climbed Lunar mountains in the last four weeks, and neither was worried about the task; but there was some question as to which mountain would best suit their needs.

They had stopped on fairly level ground south and somewhat west of Plato—'sunset' west, that is, not astronomical. There were a number of fairly prominent elevations in sight. None seemed more than a thousand metres or so in height, however, and the men knew that Plato in one direction and the Teneriffe Mountains in the other had peaks fully twice as high. The problem was which to choose.

'We can't take the tractor either way,' pointed out Shandara. 'We're cutting things pretty fine on the fuel question as it is. We are going to have to pack the instruments ourselves, and it's fifty or sixty kilometres to Teneriffe before we even start climbing. Plato's a lot closer.'

'The *near side* of Plato's a lot closer,' admitted Ridging, 'but the measured peaks in its rim must be on the east and west sides, where they can cast shadows across the crater floor. We might have to go as far for a really good peak as we would if we headed south.'

'That's not quite right. Look at the map. The near rim of the crater is fairly straight, and doesn't run straight east and west; it must cast shadows that they could measure from Earth. Why can't it contain some of those two thousand metre humps mentioned in the atlas?'

'No reason why it *can't;* but we don't know that it *does*. This map doesn't show.'

'It doesn't show for Teneriffe, either.'

'That's true, but there isn't much choice there, and we know that there's at least one high peak in a fairly small area. Plato is well over three hundred kilometres around.'

'It's still a closer walk, and I don't see why, if there are high peaks at any part of the rim, they shouldn't be fairly common all around the circumference.'

'I don't see *why* either,' retorted Ridging, 'but I've seen several craters for which that wasn't true. So have you.' Shandara had no immediate answer to this, but he had no intention of exposing himself to an unnecessarily long walk if he could help it. The instruments to be carried were admittedly light, at least on the moon; but there would be no chance of opening space-suits until the men got back to the tractor, and spacesuits got quite uncomfortable after a while.

It was the magnetometer that won Shandara's point for him. This pleased him greatly at the time, though he was heard to express a different opinion later. The meter itself did not attract attention until the men were about ready to start, and he had resigned himself to the long walk after a good deal more argument; but a final check of the recorders already operating made Ridging stop and think.

'Say, Shan, have you noticed any sunspots lately?'

'Haven't looked at the sun, and don't plan to.'

'I know. I mean, have any of the astronomers mentioned anything of the sort?'

'I didn't hear them, and we'll never be able to ask until we get back. Why?'

'I'd say there was a magnetic storm of some sort going on. The intensity, dip, and azimuth readings have all changed quite a bit in the last hour.'

'I thought dip was near vertical anyway.'

'It is, but that doesn't keep it from changing. You know, Shan, maybe it would be better if we went to Plato, instead.'

'That's what I've been saying all along. What's changed your mind?'

'This magnetic business. On Earth, such storms are caused by charged particles from the sun, deflected by the planet's magnetic field and forming what amounts to tremendous electric currents which naturally produce fields of their own. If that's what is happening here, it would be nice to get even closer to the local magnetic vertical, if we can; and that seems to be in, or at least near, Plato.'

'That suits me. I've been arguing that way all along. I'm with you.'

'There's one other thing—'

'What?'

'This magnetometer ought to go along with us, as well as the stuff we were taking anyway. Do you mind helping with the extra weight?' Shandara had not considered this aspect of the matter, but since his arguments had been founded on the question of time rather than effort he agreed readily to the additional labour.

'All right. Just a few minutes while I dismount and repack this gadget, and we'll be on our way.' Ridging set to work, and was ready in the specified time, since the apparatus had been designed to be handled by spacesuited men. The carrying racks that took the place of regular packs made the travellers look top-heavy, but they had long since learned to keep their balance under such loads. They turned until the nearly motionless sun was behind them and to their right, and set out for the hills ahead.

These elevations were not the peaks they expected to use; the moon's near horizon made those still invisible. They did, however, represent the outer reaches of the area which had been disturbed by whatever monstrous explosion had blown the ring of Plato in the moon's crust. As far as the men were concerned, these hills simply meant that very little of their journey would be across level ground, which pleased them just as well. Level ground was sometimes an inch or two deep in dust; and while dust could not hide deep cracks it could and sometimes did fill broader hollows and cover irregularities where one could trip. For a top-heavy man, this could be a serious nuisance. Relatively little dust had been encountered by any of the expedition up to this point, since most of their work had involved slopes or peaks; but a few annoying lessons had been learned.

Shandara and Ridging stuck to the relatively dust-free slopes, therefore. The going was easy enough for experienced men, and they travelled at pretty fair speed—some ten or twelve miles per hour, they judged. The tractor soon disappeared, and compasses were useless, but both men had a good eye for country, and were used enough to the Lunar landscape to have no particular difficulty in finding distinctive features. They said little, except to call each other's attention to particularly good landmarks.

The general ground level was going up after the first hour and a half, though there was still plenty of downhill travel. A relatively near line of peaks ahead was presumably the crater rim; there was little difficulty in deciding on the most suitable one and heading for it. Naturally the footing became worse and the slopes steeper as they approached, but nothing was dangerous even yet. Such crevasses as existed were easy both to see and to jump, and there are few loose rocks on the moon.

It was only about three and a half hours after leaving the tractor, therefore, that the two men reached the peak they had selected, and looked out over the great malled plain of Plato. They couldn't see all of it, of course; Plato is a hundred kilometres across, and even from a height of two thousand metres the farther side of the floor lies below the horizon. The opposite rim could be seen, of course, but there was no easy way to tell whether any of the peaks visible there were as high as the one from which the men saw them. It didn't really matter; this one was high enough for their purposes.

The instruments were unloaded and set up in half an hour. Ridging did most of the work, with a professional single-mindedness which Shandara made no attempt to emulate. The geophysicist scarcely glanced at the crater floor after his first look around upon their arrival, while Shandara did little else. Ridging was not surprised; he had been reasonably sure that his friend had had ulterior reasons for wanting to come this way.

'All right,' he said, as he straightened up after closing the last switch, 'when do we go down, and how long do we take?'

'Go down where?' asked Shandara innocently.

'Down to the crater floor, I suppose. I'm sure you don't see enough to satisfy you from here. It's just an ordinary crater, of course, but it's three times the diameter of Harpalus even if the walls are less than half as high, and you'll surely want to see every square metre of the floor.'

'I'll want to see *some* of the floor, anyway.' Shandara's tone carried feeling even through the suit radios. 'It's nice of you to realize that we have to go down. I wish you realized why.'

'You mean ... you mean you really expect to climb down there?' Ridging, in spite of his knowledge of the other's interests, was startled. 'I didn't really mean—'

'I didn't think you did. You haven't looked over the edge once.'

Ridging repaired the omission, letting his gaze sweep carefully over the greyish plain at the foot of the slope. He knew that the floor of Plato was one of the darker areas on the moon, but had never supposed that this fact constituted a major problem.

'I don't get it,' he said at last. 'I don't see anything. The floor is smoother than that of Harpalus, I'd say, but I'm not really sure even of that, from this distance. It's a couple of kilos down and I don't know how far over.'

'You brought the map.' It was not a question.

'Of course.'

'Look at it. It's a good one.' Ridging obeyed, bewildered. The map was good, as Shandara had said; its scale was sufficient to show Plato some fifteen centimetres across, with plenty of detail. It was basically an enlargement of a map published on Earth, from telescopic observations; but a good deal of detail had been added from photographs taken during the approach and landing of the expedition. Shandara knew that; it was largely his own work.

As a result, Ridging was not long in seeing what his companion meant. The map showed five fairly large craterlets *within* Plato, and nearly a hundred smaller features.

Ridging could see none of them from where he stood.

He looked thoughtfully down the slope, then at the other man.

'I begin to see what you mean. Did you expect something like this? Is that why you wanted to come here? Why didn't you tell me?'

'I didn't expect it, though I had a vague hope. A good many

times in the past, observers have reported that the features on the floor of this crater were obscured. Dr. Pickering, at the beginning of the century, thought of it as an active volcanic area; others have blamed the business on clouds—and others, of course, have assumed the observers themselves were at fault, though that is pretty hard to justify. I didn't really expect to get a chance to check up on the phenomenon, but I'm sure you don't expect me to stay up here now.'

'I suppose not.' Ridging spoke in a tone of mock resignation. The problem did not seem to concern his field directly, but he judged rightly that the present situation affected Shandara the way an offer of a genuine fragment of Terrestrial core material would influence Ridging himself. 'What do you plan to take down? I suppose you want to get measures of some sort.'

'Well, there isn't too much here that will apply, I'm afraid. I have my own camera and some filters, which may do some good. I can't see that the magnetic stuff will be any use down there. We don't have any pressure measuring or gas collecting gadgetry; I suppose if we'd brought a spare water container from the tractor we could dump it, but we didn't and I'd bet that nothing would be found in it but water vapour if we did. We'll just have to go down and see what our eyes will tell us, and record anything that seems recordable on film. Are you ready?'

'Ready as I ever will be.' Ridging knew the remark was neither original nor brilliant, but nothing else seemed to fit.

The inner wall of the crater was a good deal steeper than the one they had climbed, but still did not present a serious obstacle. The principal trouble was that much of the way led through clefts where the sun did not shine, and the only light was reflected from distant slopes. There wasn't much of it, and the men had to be careful of their footings—there was an occasional loose fragment here, and a thousand-metre fall is no joke even on the moon. The way did not lead directly towards the crater floor; the serrated rim offered better ways between its peaks, hairpinning back and forth so that sometimes the central plain was not visible at all. No floor details appeared as they descended, but whatever covered them was still below; the stars, whenever the mountains cut off enough sidelight, were clear as ever. Time and again Shandara stopped to look over the great plain, which seemed limitless now that the peaks on the farther side had dropped below the horizon, but nothing in the way of information rewarded the effort.

It was the last few hundred metres of descent that began to furnish something of interest. Shandara was picking his way down an unusually uninviting bit of slope when Ridging, who had already negotiated it, spoke up sharply.

'Shan! Look at the stars over the northern horizon! Isn't there some sort of haze? The sky around them looks a bit lighter.' The other paused and looked.

'You're right. But how could that be? There couldn't suddenly be enough air at this level—gases don't behave that way. Van Maanen's star might have an atmosphere twenty metres deep, but the moon doesn't and never could have.'

'There's *something* between us and the sky.'

'That I admit; but I still say it isn't gas. Maybe dust—'

'What would hold it up? Dust is just as impossible as air.'

'I don't know. The floor's only a few yards down—let's not stand here guessing.' They resumed their descent.

The crater floor was fairly level, and sharply distinguished from the inner slope of the crater wall. Something had certainly filled, partly at least, the vast pit after the original explosion; but neither man was disposed to renew the argument about the origin of Lunar craters just then. They scrambled down the remaining few yards of the journey and stopped where they were, silently.

There *was* something blocking vision; the horizon was no longer visible, nor could the stars be seen for a few degrees above where it should have been. Neither man would have had the slightest doubt about the nature of the obscuring matter had he been on Earth; it bore every resemblance to dust. It *had* to be dust.

But it couldn't be. Granted that dust can be fine enough to remain suspended for weeks or months in Earth's atmosphere when a volcano like Krakatoa hurls a few cubic miles of it aloft, the moon had not enough gas molecules around it to interfere with the trajectory of a healthy virus particle—and no seismometer in the last four weeks had registered crustal activity even approaching the scale of vulcanism. There was nothing on the moon to throw the dust up, and even less to keep it there.

'Meteor splash?' Shandara made the suggestion hesitantly, fully aware that while a meteor might raise dust it could never keep it aloft. Ridging did not bother to answer, and his friend did not repeat the suggestion.

The sky straight overhead seemed clear as ever; whatever the absorbing material was it apparently took more than the few feet above them to show much effect. That could not be right, though, Ridging reflected, if this stuff were responsible for hiding the features which should have been visible from the crater rim. Maybe it was thicker farther in. If so, they'd better go on—there might be some chance of collecting samples after all.

He put this to Shandara, who agreed; and the two started out across the hundred kilometre plain.

The surface *was* fairly smooth, though a pattern of minute cracks suggestive of the joints formed in cooling basalt covered it almost completely. These were not wide enough even to constitute a tripping danger, and the men ignored them for the time being, though Ridging made a mental note to get a sample of the rock if he could detach one.

The obscuration did thicken as they progressed, and by the time they had gone half a dozen kilometres it was difficult to see the crater wall behind them. Looking up, they saw that all but the brighter stars had faded from view even when the men shaded their eyes from the sunlit rock around them.

'Maybe gas is coming from these cracks, carrying dust up with it?' Shandara was no geologist, but had an imagination.

He had also read most of the serious articles which had ever been published about the moon.

'We could check. If that were the case, it should be possible to see currents coming from them; the dust would be thicker just above a crack than a few centimetres away. If we had something light, like a piece of paper, it might be picked up.'

'Worth trying. We have the map,' Shandara pointed out. 'That should do for paper; the plastic is thin enough.' Ridging agreed. With some difficulty—spacesuit gloves were not designed for that purpose—he tore a tiny corner off the sheet on which the map was printed, knelt down, and held the fragment over one of the numerous cracks. It showed no tendency to flutter in his grasp, and when he let go it dropped as rapidly as anything ever did on the moon, to lie quietly directly across the crack he had been testing. He tried to pick it up, but could not get a grip on it with his stiff gloves.

'That one didn't seem to pan out,' he remarked, standing up once more.

'Maybe the paper was too heavy—this stuff must be awfully fine—or else it's coming from only a few of the cracks.'

'Possibly; but I don't think it's practical to try them all. It would be smarter to figure some way to get a sample of this stuff, and let people with better lab facilities figure out what it is and what holds it off the surface.'

'I've been trying to think of a way to do that. If we laid the map out on the ground, some of the material might settle on it.'

'Worth trying. If it does, though, we'll have another question—why does it settle there and yet remain suspended long enough to do what is being done? We've been more than an hour coming down the slope, and I'll bet your astronomical friends of the past have reported obscurations longer lasting even than that.'

'They have. Well, even if it does raise more problems it's worth trying. Spread out the map, and we'll wait a few minutes.' Ridging obeyed; then, to keep the score even, came up with an idea of his own.

'Why don't you lay your camera on the ground pointing up and make a couple of time exposures of the stars? You could repeat them after we get back in the clear, and maybe get some data on the obscuring power of this material.'

'Good enough.' Shandara removed the camera from its case, clipped a sun shade over its lense, and looked up to find a section of sky with a good selection of stars. As usual, he had to shield his eyes both from sunlight and from the glare of the nearby hills; but even then he did not seem satisfied.

'This stuff is getting thicker, I think,' he said. 'It's scattering enough light so that it's hard to see any stars at all—harder than it was a few minutes ago, I'd say.' Ridging imitated his manoeuvre, and agreed.

'That's worth recording, too,' he pointed out. 'Better stay here a while and get several shots at different times.' He looked down again. 'It certainly *is* getting thicker. I'm having trouble seeing you, now.'

Human instincts being what they are, the solution to the mystery followed automatically and immediately. A man who fails, for any reason, to see as clearly as he expects usually rubs his eyes—if he can get at them. A man wearing goggles or a space helmet may just possibly control this impulse, but he follows the practically identical one of wiping the panes through which he looks. Ridging did not have a handkerchief within reach, of course, and the gauntlet of a spacesuit is not one of the best windshield wipers imaginable; but without giving a single thought to the action, he wiped his face plate with his gauntlet.

Had there been no results he would not have been surprised; he had no reason to expect any. He would probably have dismissed the matter, perhaps with a faint hope that his companion might not have noticed the futile gesture. However, there were results. Very marked ones.

The points where the plastic of the gauntlet actually touched the face plate were few; but they left trails all the way across—opaque trails. Surprised and still not thinking, Ridging repeated the gesture in an automatic effort to wipe the smears of whatever it was from his helmet; he only made matters worse. He did not quite cover the supposedly transparent area with glove trails—but in the few seconds after he got control of his hand the streaks spread and merged until nothing whatever was possible. He was not quite in darkness; sunlight penetrated the obscuring layer, but he could not see any details.

'Shan!' The cry contained almost a note of panic. 'I can't see at all. Something's covering my helmet!' The cartographer straightened up from his camera and turned towards his friend.

'How come? You look all right from here. I can't see too clearly, though—'

Reflexes are wonderful. It took about five seconds to blind Shandara as thoroughly as Ridging. He couldn't even find his camera to close the shutter.

'You know,' said Ridging thoughtfully after two or three minutes of heavy silence, 'we should have been able to figure all this out without coming down here.'

'Why?'

'Oh, it's plain as anything—'

'Nothing, and I mean *nothing*, is plain right now.'

'I suppose a map maker would joke while he was surveying Gehenna. Look, Shan, we have reason to believe there's a magnetic storm going on, which strongly suggests charged particles from the sun. We are standing, for practical purposes, on the moon's south magnetic pole. Most level parts of the moon are covered with dust—but we walked over bare rock from the foot of the rim to here. Don't those items add up to something?'

'Not to me.'

'Well, then, add the fact that electrical attraction and repulsion are inverse square forces like gravity, but involve a vastly bigger proportionality constant.'

'If you're talking about scale I know all about it, but you still don't paint me a picture.'

'All right. There are, at a guess, protons coming from the sun. They are reaching the moon's surface here—virtually all of them, since the moon has a magnetic field but no atmosphere. The surface material is one of the lousiest imaginable electrical conductors, so the dust normally on the surface picks up *and keeps* a charge. And what, dear student, happens to particles carrying like electrical charges?'

'They are repelled from each other.'

'Head of the class. And if a hundred-kilometre circle with a rim a couple of kilos high is charged all over, what happens to the dust lying on it?'

Shandara did not answer; the question was too obviously rhetorical. He thought for a moment or two, instead, then asked, 'How about our face plates?'

Ridging shrugged—a rather useless gesture, but the time for fighting bad habits had passed some minutes before.

'Bad luck. Whenever two materials rub against each other, electrons come loose. Remember your rubber-and-cat-fur demonstrations in grade school. Unless the materials are of identical electron make-up, which for practical purposes means unless they are the same substance, one of them will hang on to the electrons a little—or a lot—better than the other, so one will have a negative net charge and the other a positive one. It's our misfortune that the difference between the plastic in our face plates and that in the rest of the suits is the wrong way; when we rubbed the two, the face plates picked up a charge opposite to that of the surrounding dust—probably negative, since I suppose the dust is positive and a transparent material should have a good grip on its electrons.'

'Then the rest of our suits, and the gloves we wiped with in particular, ought to be clean.'

'Ought to be. I'd like nothing better than a chance to check the point.'

'Well, the old cat's fur didn't stay charged very long, as I remember. How long will it take this to leak off, do you think?'

'Why should it leak off at all?'

'What? Why, I should think— Hm-m-m.' Shandara was silent

for a moment. 'Water *is* pretty wonderful stuff, isn't it?'

'Yep. And air has its uses, too.'

'Then we're ... Ridge, we've got to *do* something. Our air will last indefinitely, but you still can't stay in a spacesuit too long.'

'I agree that we should do something; I just haven't figured out what. Incidentally, just how sure are you that our air will last? The windows of the regenerators are made, as far as I know, of the same plastic our face plates are. What'll you bet you're not using emergency oxygen right now?'

'I don't know—I haven't checked the gauges.'

'I'll say you haven't. You won't, either; they're outside your helmet.'

'But if we're on emergency now, we could hardly get back to the tractor starting this minute. We've got to get going.'

'Which way?'

'Towards the rim!'

'Be specific, son. Just which way is that? And please don't point; it's rude, and I can't see you anyway.'

'All right, don't rub it in. But Ridge, what *can* we do?'

'While this stuff is on our helmets, and possibly our air windows, nothing. We couldn't climb even if we knew which way the hills were. The only thing which will do us the least good is to get this dust off us; and that will do the trick. As my mathematical friends would say, it is necessary and sufficient.'

'All right, I'll go along with that. We know that the material the suits are made of is worse than useless for wiping, but wiping and electrical discharge seem to be the only methods possible. What do we have which by any stretch of the imagination might do either job?'

'What is your camera case made of?' asked Ridging.

'As far as I know, same as the suits. It's a regular clip-on carrier, the sort that came with the suits—remember Tazewell's remarks about the dividends AirTight must have paid when they sold the suits to the Project? It reminded me of the old days when you had to buy a lot of accessories with your automobile whether you wanted them or not—'

'All right, you've made your point. The case is the same plastic. It would be a pretty poor wiper anyway; it's a box rather than a bag, as I remember. What else is there?'

The silence following this question was rather lengthy. The sad fact is that spacesuits don't have outside pockets for handkerchiefs. It did occur to Ridging after a time that he was carrying a set of geological specimen bags; but when he finally did think of these and took one out to use as a wiper, the unfortunate fact developed that it, too, left the wrong charge on the face plate of his helmet. He could see the clear, smooth plastic of the bag as it passed across the plate, but the dust collected so fast behind it that he saw nothing of his surroundings. He reflected ruefully that the charge to be removed was now greater than ever. He also thought of using the map, until he remembered that he had put it on the ground and could never find it by touch.

'I never thought,' Shandara remarked after another lengthy silence, 'that I'd ever miss a damp rag so badly. Blast it, Ridge, there must be *something*.'

'Why? We've both been thinking without any result that I can see. Don't tell me you're one of those fellows who think there's an answer to every problem.'

'I am. It may not be the answer we want, but there is one. Come on, Ridge, you're the physicist; I'm just a high-priced picture-copier. Whatever answer there is, you're going to have to furnish it; all my ideas deal with maps, and we've done about all we can with those at the moment.'

'Hm-m-m. The more I think, the more I remember that there isn't enough fuel on the moon to get a rescue tractor out here, even if anyone knew we were in trouble and could make the trip in time. Still—wait a minute; you said something just then. What was it?'

'I said all my ideas dealt with maps, but—'

'No; before that.'

'I don't recall, unless it was that crack about damp rags, which we don't have.'

'That was it. That's it, Shan; we don't have any rags, but we do have *water*.'

'Yes—inside our spacesuits. Which of us opens up to save the other?'

'Neither one. Be sensible. You know as well as I do that the amount of water in a closed system containing a living person is constantly increasing; we produce it, oxidizing hydrogen in the food we eat. The suits have dryers in the air cycler or we couldn't last two hours in them.'

'That's right; but how do you get the water out? You can't open your air system.'

'You can shut it off, and the check valve will keep air in your suit—remember, there's always the chance someone will have to change emergency tanks. It'll be a job, because we won't be able to see what we're doing, and working by touch through spacesuit gauntlets will be awkward as anything I've ever done. Still, I don't see anything else.'

'That means you'll have to work on my suit, then, since I don't know what to do after the line is disconnected. How long can I last before you reconnect? And what do you do, anyway? You don't mean there's a reservoir of liquid water there, do you?'

'No, it's a calcium chloride dryer; and it should be fairly moist by now— You've been in the suit for several hours. It's in several sections, and I can take out one and leave you the others, so you won't suffer from its lack. The air in your suit should do you for four or five minutes, and if I can't make the disconnection and disassembly in that time I can't do it at all. Still, it's your suit, and if I do make a mistake it's your life; do you want to take the chance?'

'What have I to lose? Besides, you always were a pretty good mechanic—or if you weren't, please don't tell me. Get to work.'

'All right.'

As it happened, the job was not started right away, for there was the minor problem of finding Shandara to be solved first. The two men had been perhaps five yards apart when their face plates were first blanked out, but neither could now be sure that he hadn't moved in the meantime, or at least shifted around to face a new direction. After some discussion of the problem, it was agreed that Shandara should stand still, while Ridging walked in what he hoped was the right direction for what he hoped was five yards and then start from wherever he found himself to quarter the area as well as he could by length of stride. He would have to guess at his turns since even the sun no longer could penetrate the layer of dust on the helmets.

It took a full ten minutes to bump into his companion, and even then he felt undeservedly lucky.

Shandara lay down, so as to use a minimum of energy while the work was being done. Ridging felt over the connections several times until he was sure he had them right—they were of course, designed to be handled by spacesuit gauntlets, though not by a blindfolded operator. Then he warned the cartographer, closed the main cutoffs at helmet and emergency tanks to isolate the renewer mechanism, and opened the latter. It was a simple device, designed in throw away units like a piece of electronic gear, with each unit automatically sealing as it was removed—a fortunate fact if the alga culture on which Shandara's life for the next few hours depended was to survive the operation.

The calcium chloride cells were easy to locate; Ridging removed two of the half dozen to be on the safe side, replaced and reassembled the renewer, tightened the connections and reopened the valves.

Ridging now had two cans of calcium chloride. He could not tell whether it had yet absorbed enough water actually to go into solution, though he doubted it; but he took no chances. Holding one of the little containers carefully right side up, he opened its perforated top, took a specimen bag and pushed it into the contents. The plastic was not, of course, absorptive—it was not the first time in the past hour he had regretted the change from cloth bags—but the damp crystals should adhere, and the solution if there was any would wet it. He pulled out the material and applied it to his face plate.

It was not until much later that he became sure whether there was any liquid. For the moment it worked, and he found that he could see; he asked no more. Hastily he repeated the process on Shandara's helmet, and the two set out rapidly for the rim. They did not stop to pick up camera or map.

Travel is fast on the moon, but they made less than four hundred metres. Then the face plates were covered again. With a feeling of annoyance they stopped, and Ridging repeated the treatment.

This time it didn't work.

'I supposed you emptied the can while you were jumping,' Shandara remarked in an annoyed tone. 'Try the other one.'

'I didn't empty anything; but I'll try.' The contents of the other container proved equally useless, and the cartographer's morale took another slump.

'What happened?' he asked. 'And please don't tell me it's obvious, because you certainly didn't foresee it.'

'I didn't, but it is. The chloride dried out again.'

'I thought it held on to water.'

'It does, under certain conditions. Unfortunately its equilibrium vapour pressure at this temperature is higher than the local barometer reading. I don't suppose that every last molecule of water has gone, but what's left isn't sufficient to make a conductor. Our face plates are holding charge again—maybe better than before; there must be some calcium chloride dust on them now, though I don't know offhand what effect it would have.'

'There are more chloride cartridges in the cyclers.'

'You have four left, which would get us maybe two kilos at the present rate. We can't use mine, since you can't get them out; and if we use all yours you'd never get up the rim. Drying your air isn't just a matter of comfort, you know; that suit has no temperature controls—it depends on radiation balance and insulation. If your perspiration stops evaporating, your inner insulation is done; and in any case, the cartridges won't get us to the rim.'

'In other words you think we're done—again.'

'I certainly don't have any more ideas.'

'Then I suppose I'll have to do some more pointless chattering. If it gave you the last idea, maybe it will work again.'

'Go ahead. It won't bother me. I'm going to spend my last hours cursing the character who used a different plastic for the face plate than he did for the rest of these suits.'

'All right,' Tazewell snapped as the geophysicist paused. 'I'm supposed to ask you what you did then. You've just told me that that handkerchief of yours is a good windshield wiper; I'll admit I don't see how. I'll even admit I'm curious, if it'll make you happy.'

'It's not a handkerchief, as I said. It's a specimen bag.'

'I thought you tried those and found they didn't work—left a charge on your face plate like the glove.'

'It did. But a remark I made myself about different kinds of plastic in the suits gave me another idea. It occurred to me that if the dust was, say, positively charged—'

'Probably was. Protons from the sun.'

'All right. Then my face plate picked up a negative, and my suit glove a positive, so the dust was attracted to the plate.

'Then when we first tried the specimen bag, it also charged positively and left negative on the face plate.

'Then it occurred to me that the specimen bag *rubbed by the suit* might go negative; and since it was fairly transparent, I could—'

'I get it! You could tie it over your face plate and have a windshield you could see through which would repel the dust.'

'That was the idea. Of course, I had nothing to tie it with; I had to hold it.'

'Good enough. So you got a good idea out of an idle remark.'

'Two of them. The moisture one came from Shan the same way.'

'But yours worked.' Ridging grinned.

'Sorry. It didn't. The specimen bag still came out negative when rubbed on the suit plastic—at least it didn't do the face plate any good.'

Tazewell stared blankly, then looked as though he were about to use violence.

'*All right!* Let's have it, once and for all.'

'Oh, it was simple enough. I worked the specimen bag—I tore it open so it would cover more area across my face plate, pressing tight so there wouldn't be any dust under it.'

'What good would that do? You must have collected more over it right away.'

'Sure. Then I rubbed my face plate, dust rag and all, against Shandara's. We couldn't lose; one of them was bound to go positive. I won, and led him up the rim until the ground charge dropped enough to let the dust stick to the surface instead of us. I'm glad no one was there to take pictures, though; I'd hate to have a photo around which could be interpreted as my kissing Shandara's ugly face—even through a space helmet.'

DUST RAG

During the 1940s and 1950s there was considerable discussion as to whether the Moon was covered by dust and if so, by how much. It seemed that the surface temperature of the Moon dropped very quickly during Lunar eclipses and this meant a large heat loss from the surface. The heat loss wouldn't have been that great if additional heat could only have leaked upwards to the surface from below. Something apparently stopped that leakage, which meant that the material composing the surface of the Earth was a good insulator.

Vacuum is an excellent insulator, so it might be that the Moon's surface consisted of dust particles, touching each other at odd points with vacuum between. There were even speculations that the dust might be very deep and that spaceships trying to land would sink into the dust layer completely.

Even if the dust were not deep, there might be enough to stir up by any disturbance, such as a ship landing, or even the footsteps of a walking man. If that happened, however, the problem would not be a serious one as, in the absence of air, the dust would rise and fall like so many pebbles.

As it happened, close range studies of the Moon's surface, soft-landings of instrument satellites, and finally manned landings on the Moon, showed the dust was not dangerously deep. The footing underneath was crunchy, but firm.

Clement's story written in 1956, over a decade before the close-range studies, predicted that accurately. However, he did want to make the dust dangerous at least under some conditions by having it hover above the Moon's surface even in the absence of air. To do this, he assumed the Moon had a magnetic field and that over the magnetic poles, the dust particles would tend to become charged and to repel each other. In this respect, though, Clement's vision failed. It turned out that the Moon had no magnetic field to speak of.

He did turn out to be correct in supposing that the Moon was bombarded by the Solar wind; that it was continually being struck by charged particles from the Sun. The surface rocks of the Moon contain helium that could have originated only in this fashion.

Questions and Suggestions

1. Most theories of Earth's magnetic field involve the presence of an iron core at its centre. Do you think the Moon has an iron core? Why or why not? If it lacks an iron core, would that fact be known in 1956? Do you suppose Clement might have suspected the Moon did not have a magnetic field, even while he used one for the purposes of the story?

2. It is likely that Venus has an iron core, yet it has no magnetic field to speak of. How do we know it has none? Why should it not have one despite the iron core? What about other planets: Mars, Jupiter, Saturn? How do we know?

3. Look up the reports on the manned landings on the Moon. What do these have to say about dust?

14. Pâté de Foie Gras

Isaac Asimov

I couldn't tell you my real name if I wanted to and, under the circumstances, I don't want to.

I'm not much of a writer myself, unless you count the kind of stuff that passes muster in a scientific paper, so I'm having Isaac Asimov write this up for me.

I've picked him for several reasons. First, he's a biochemist, so he understands what I tell him; some of it, anyway. Secondly, he can write; or at least he has published considerable fiction, which may not, of course, be the same thing.

But most important of all, he can get what he writes published in science-fiction magazines and he has written two articles on thiotimoline, and that is exactly what I need for reasons that will become clear as we proceed.

I was not the first person to have the honour of meeting The Goose. That belongs to a Texas cotton-farmer named Ian Angus MacGregor, who owned it before it became government property. (The names, places and dates I use are deliberately synthetic. None of you will be able to trace anything through them. Don't bother trying.)

MacGregor apparently kept geese about the place because they ate weeds, but not cotton. In this way, he had automatic weeders that were self-fuelling and, in addition, produced eggs, down, and, at judicious intervals, roast goose.

By summer of 1955, he had sent an even dozen of letters to

the Department of Agriculture requesting information on the hatching of goose eggs. The department sent him all the booklets on hand that were anywhere near the subject, but his letters simply got more impassioned and freer in their references to his 'friend', the local congressman.

My connection with this is that I am in the employ of the Department of Agriculture. I have considerable training in agricultural chemistry, plus a smattering of vertebrate physiology. (This won't help you. If you think you can pin my identity out of this, you are mistaken.)

Since I was attending a convention at San Antonio in July of 1955, my boss asked me to stop off at MacGregor's place and see what I could do to help him. We're servants of the public and besides we had finally received a letter from MacGregor's congressman.

On July 17, 1955, I met The Goose.

I met MacGregor first. He was in his fifties, a tall man with a lined face full of suspicion. I went over all the information he had been given, explained about incubators, the values of trace minerals in the diet, plus some late information on Vitamin E, the cobalamins and the use of antibiotic additives.

He shook his head. He had tried it all and still the eggs wouldn't hatch.

What could I do? I'm a Civil Service employee and not the archangel, Gabriel. I'd told him all I could and if the eggs still wouldn't hatch, they wouldn't and that was that. I asked politely if I might see his geese, just so no one could say afterwards I hadn't done all I possibly could.

He said, 'It's not geese, mister; it's one goose.'

I said, 'May I see the one goose?'

'Rather not.'

'Well, then, I can't help you any further. If it's only one goose, then there's just something wrong with it. Why worry about one goose? Eat it.'

I got up and reached for my hat.

He said, 'Wait!' and I stood there while his lips tightened and his eyes wrinkled and he had a quiet fight with himself.

He said, 'If I show you something, will you swear to keep it secret?'

He didn't seem like the type of man to rely on another's vow of secrecy, but it was as though he had reached such a pit of desperation that he had no other way out.

I said, 'If it isn't anything criminal—'

'Nothing like that,' he snapped.

And then I went out with him to a pen near the house, surrounded by barbed wire, with a locked gate to it, and holding one goose—The Goose.

'That's The Goose,' he said. The way he said it, I could hear the capitals.

I stared at it. It looked like any other goose, Heaven help me, fat, self-satisfied and short-tempered. I said, 'Hm-m-m' in my best professional manner.

MacGregor said, 'And here's one of its eggs. It's been in the incubator. Nothing happens.' He produced it from a capacious overall pocket. There was a queer strain about his manner of holding it.

I frowned. There was something wrong with the egg. It was smaller and more spherical than normal.

MacGregor said, 'Take it.'

I reached out and took it. Or tried to. I gave it the amount of heft an egg like that ought to deserve and it just sat where it was. I had to try harder and then up it came.

Now I knew what was queer about the way MacGregor held it. It weighed nearly two pounds. (To be exact, when we weighed it later, we found its mass to be 852.6 grammes.)

I stared at it as it lay there, pressing down the palm of my hand, and MacGregor grinned sourly. 'Drop it,' he said.

I just looked at him, so he took it out of my hand and dropped it himself.

It hit soggy. It didn't smash. There was no spray of white and yolk. It just lay where it fell with the bottom caved in.

I picked it up again. The white eggshell had shattered where the egg had struck. Pieces of it had flaked away and what shone through was a dull yellow in colour.

My hands trembled. It was all I could do to make my fingers work, but I got some of the rest of the shell flaked away, and stared at the yellow.

I didn't have to run any analyses. My heart told me.

I was face to face with The Goose!

The Goose That Laid The Golden Eggs!

You don't believe me. I'm sure of that. You've got this tabbed as another thiotimoline article.

Good! I'm *counting* on your thinking that. I'll explain later.

Meanwhile, my first problem was to get MacGregor to give up that golden egg. I was almost hysterical about it. I was almost ready to clobber him and make off with the egg by force if I had to.

I said, 'I'll give you a receipt. I'll guarantee you payment. I'll do anything in reason. You can't cash the gold unless you can explain how it came into your possession. Holding gold is illegal. And how do you expect to explain? If the government—'

'I don't want the government butting in,' he said, stubbornly.

But I was twice as stubborn. I followed him about. I pleaded. I yelled. I threatened. It took me hours. Literally. In the end, I signed a receipt and he dogged me out to my car and stood in the road as I drove away, following me with his eyes.

He never saw that egg again. Of course, he was compensated for the value of the gold—$656.47 after taxes had been subtracted—but that was a bargain for the government.

When one considers the potential value of that egg—

The *potential* value! That's the irony of it. That's the reason for this article.

The head of my section at the Department of Agriculture is Louis P. Bronstein. (Don't bother looking him up. The 'P.' stands for Pittfield if you want more misdirection.)

He and I are on good terms and I felt I could explain things without being placed under immediate observation. Even so, I took no chances. I had the egg with me and when I got to the tricky part, I just laid it on the desk between us.

Finally, he touched it with his finger as though it were hot.

I said, 'Pick it up.'

It took him a long time, but he did, and I watched him take two tries at it as I had.

I said, 'It's a yellow metal and it could be brass only it isn't because it's inert to concentrated nitric acid. I've tried that already. There's only a shell of gold because it can be bent with moderate pressure. Besides, if it were solid gold, the egg would weigh over ten pounds.'

Bronstein said, 'It's some sort of hoax. It *must* be.'

'A hoax that uses real gold? Remember, when I first saw this thing, it was covered completely with authentic unbroken egg-shell. It's been easy to check a piece of the eggshell. Calcium carbonate. That's a hard thing to gimmick. And if we look inside the egg—I didn't want to do that on my own, chief—and find real egg, then we've got it, because that would be impossible to gimmick. Surely, this is worth an official project.'

'How can I approach the Secretary with—' He stared at the egg.

But he did in the end. He made phone calls and sweated out most of a day. One or two of the department brass came to look at the egg.

Project Goose was started. That was July 20, 1955.

I was the responsible investigator to begin with and remained in titular charge throughout, though matters quickly got beyond me.

We began with one egg. Its average radius was 35 millimetres (major axis, 72 millimetres; minor axis, 68 millimetres). The gold shell was 2·45 millimetres in thickness. Studying other eggs later on, we found this value to be rather high. The average thickness turned out to be 2·1 millimetres.

Inside *was* egg. It looked like egg and it smelled like egg.

Aliquots were analysed and the organic constituents were reasonably normal. The white was 9·7 per cent albumin. The yolk had the normal complement of vitellin, cholesterol, phospholipid and carotenoid. We lacked enough material to test for trace constituents but later on with more eggs at our disposal we did and nothing unusual showed up as far as the contents of vitamins, co-enzymes, nucleotides, sulfhydryl groups, et cetera, et cetera were concerned.

One important gross abnormality that showed was the egg's behaviour on heating. A small portion of the yolk, heated, 'hard-boiled' almost at once. We fed a portion of the hard-boiled egg to a mouse. It survived.

I nibbled at another bit of it. Too small a quantity to taste, really, but it made me sick. Purely psychosomatic, I'm sure.

Boris W. Finley, of the Department of Biochemistry of Temple University—a department consultant—supervised these tests.

He said, referring to the hard-boiling, 'The ease with which the egg-proteins are heat-denatured indicates a partial denaturation to begin with and, considering the nature of the shell, the obvious guilt would lie at the door of heavy-metal contamination.'

So a portion of the yolk was analysed for inorganic constituents, and it was found to be high in chloraurate ion, which is a singly-charged ion containing an atom of gold and four of chlorine, the symbol for which is $AuCl_4$. (The 'Au' symbol for gold comes from the fact that the Latin word for gold is 'aurum'.) When I say the chloraurate ion content was high, I mean it was 3·2 parts per thousand, or 0·32 per cent. That's high enough to form insoluble complexes of 'gold-protein' which would coagulate easily.

Finley said, 'It's obvious this egg cannot hatch. Nor can any other such egg. It is heavy-metal poisoned. Gold may be more glamorous than lead but it is just as poisonous to proteins.'

I agreed gloomily, 'At least it's safe from decay, too.'

'Quite right. No self-respecting bug would live in this chlorauriferous soup.'

The final spectrographic analysis of the gold of the shell came in. Virtually pure. The only detectable impurity was iron which amounted to 0·23 per cent of the whole. The iron content of the egg yolk had been twice normal, also. At the moment, however, the matter of the iron was neglected.

* * *

One week after Project Goose was begun, an expedition was sent into Texas. Five biochemists went—the accent was still on biochemistry, you see—along with three truckloads of equipment, and a squadron of army personnel. I went along, too, of course.

As soon as we arrived, we cut MacGregor's farm off from the world.

That was a lucky thing, you know—the security measures we took right from the start. The reasoning was wrong at first, but the results were good.

The Department wanted Project Goose kept quiet at the start simply because there was always the thought that this might still be an elaborate hoax and we couldn't risk the bad publicity, if it were. And if it weren't a hoax, we couldn't risk the newspaper hounding that would definitely result over any goose-and-golden-egg story.

It was only well after the start of Project Goose, well after our arrival at MacGregor's farm, that the real implications of the matter became clear.

Naturally, MacGregor didn't like the men and equipment settling down all about him. He didn't like being told The Goose was government property. He didn't like having his eggs impounded.

He didn't like it but he agreed to it—if you can call it agreeing when negotiations are being carried on while a machine gun is being assembled in a man's barnyard and ten men, with bayonets fixed, are marching past while the arguing is going on.

He was compensated, of course. What's money to the government?

The Goose didn't like a few things, either—like having blood samples taken. We didn't dare anaesthetize it for fear of doing anything to alter its metabolism, and it took two men to hold it each time. Ever try to hold an angry goose?

The Goose was put under a twenty-four hour guard with the threat of summary court-martial to any man who let anything happen to it. If any of those soldiers read this article, they may get a sudden glimmering of what was going on. If so, they will probably have the sense to keep shut about it. At least, if they know what's good for them, they will.

The blood of The Goose was put through every test conceivable.

It carried 2 parts per hundred thousand (0·002 per cent) of chloraurate ion. Blood taken from the hepatic vein was richer than the rest, almost 4 parts per hundred thousand.

Finley grunted. 'The liver,' he said.

We took X-rays. On the X-ray negative, the liver was a cloudy mass of light grey, lighter than the viscera in its neighbourhood, because it stopped more of the X-rays, because it contained more gold. The blood vessels showed up lighter than the liver proper and the ovaries were pure white. No X-rays got through the ovaries at all.

It made sense and in an early report, Finley stated it as bluntly as possible. Paraphrasing the report, it went, in part:

'The chloraurate ion is secreted by the liver into the blood stream. The ovaries act as a trap for the ion, which is there reduced to metallic gold and deposited as a shell about the developing egg. Relatively high concentrations of unreduced chloraurate ion penetrate the contents of the developing egg.

'There is little doubt that The Goose finds this process useful as a means of getting rid of the gold atoms which, if allowed to accumulate, would undoubtedly poison it. Excretion by egg-shell may be novel in the animal kingdom, even unique, but there is no denying that it is keeping The Goose alive.

'Unfortunately, however, the ovary is being locally poisoned to such an extent that few eggs are laid, probably not more than will suffice to get rid of the accumulating gold, and those few eggs are definitely unhatchable.'

That was all he said in writing, but to the rest of us, he said, 'That leaves one peculiarly embarrassing question.'

I knew what it was. We all did.

Where was the gold coming from?

No answer to that for a while, except for some negative evidence. There was no perceptible gold in The Goose's feed, nor were there any gold-bearing pebbles about that it might have swallowed. There was no trace of gold anywhere in the soil of the area and a search of the house and grounds revealed nothing. There were no gold coins, gold jewellery, gold plate, gold watches or gold anything. No one on the farm even had as much as gold fillings in his teeth.

There was Mrs. MacGregor's wedding ring, of course, but she had only had one in her life and she was wearing that one.

So where was the gold coming from?

The beginnings of the answer came on August 16, 1955.

Albert Nevis, of Purdue, was forcing gastric tubes into The Goose—another procedure to which the bird objected strenuously—with the idea of testing the contents of its alimentary canal. It was one of our routine searches for exogenous gold.

Gold *was* found, but only in traces and there was every reason to suppose those traces had accompanied the digestive secretions and were, therefore, endogenous—from within, that is—in origin.

However, something else showed up, or the lack of it, anyway.

I was there when Nevis came into Finley's office in the temporary building we had put up overnight—almost—near the goosepen.

Nevis said, 'The Goose is low in bile pigment. Duodenal contents show about none.'

Finley frowned and said, 'Liver function is probably knocked loop-the-loop because of its gold concentration. It probably isn't secreting bile at all.'

'It *is* secreting bile,' said Nevis. 'Bile acids are present in normal quanity. Near normal, anyway. It's just the bile pigments that are missing. I did a faecal analysis and that was confirmed. No bile pigments.'

Let me explain something at this point. Bile acids are steroids secreted by the liver into the bile and *via* that are poured into the upper end of the small intestine. These bile acids are detergentlike molecules which help to emulsify the fat in our diet—or The Goose's—and distribute them in the form of tiny bubbles through the watery intestinal contents. This distribution, or homogenization, if you'd rather, makes it easier for the fat to be digested.

Bile pigments, the substances that were missing in The Goose, are something entirely different. The liver makes them out of haemoglobin, the red oxygen-carrying protein of the blood. Worn out haemoglobin is broken up in the liver, the haeme part being split away. The haeme is made up of a squarish molecule—called a 'porphyrin'—with an iron atom in the centre. The liver takes the iron out and stores it for future use, then breaks the squarish molecule that is left. This broken porphyrin is bile pigment. It is coloured brownish or greenish—depending on further chemical changes—and is secreted into the bile.

The bile pigments are of no use to the body. They are poured into the bile as waste products. They pass through the intestines and come out with the faeces. In fact, the bile pigments are responsible for the colour of the faeces.

Finley's eyes began to glitter.

Nevis said, 'It looks as though porphyrin catabolism isn't following the proper course in the liver. Doesn't it to you?'

It surely did. To me, too.

There was tremendous excitement after that. This was the first metabolic abnormality, not directly involving gold, that had been found in The Goose!

We took a liver biopsy (which means we punched a cylindrical sliver out of The Goose reaching down into the liver). It hurt The Goose but didn't harm it. We took more blood samples, too.

This time, we isolated haemoglobin from the blood and small quantities of the cytochromes from our liver samples. (The cytochromes are oxidizing enzymes that also contain haeme.) We separated out the haeme and in acid solution some of it precipitated in the form of a brilliant orange substance. By August 22, 1955, we had 5 microgrammes of the compound.

The orange compound was similar to haeme, but it was not haeme. The iron in haeme can be in the form of a doubly charged ferrous ion (Fe^{++}) or a triply charged ferric ion (Fe^{+++}), in which latter case, the compound is called haematin. (Ferrous and ferric, by the way, come from the Latin word for iron, which is 'ferrum'.)

The orange compound we had separated from haeme had the porphyrin portion of the molecule all right, but the metal in the centre was gold, to be specific, a triply charged auric ion (Au+ + +). We called this compound 'auraeme', which is simply short for 'auric haeme'.

Auraeme was the first naturally-occurring gold-containing organic compound ever discovered. Ordinarily, it would rate headline news in the world of biochemistry. But now it was nothing; nothing at all in comparison to the further horizons its mere existence opened up.

The liver, it seemed, was not breaking up the haeme to bile pigment. Instead it was converting it to auraeme; it was replacing iron with gold. The auraeme, in equilibrium with chloraurate ion, entered the blood stream and was carried to the ovaries where the gold was separated out and the porphyrin portion of the molecule disposed of by some as yet unidentified mechanism.

Further analyses showed that 29 per cent of the gold in the blood of The Goose was carried in the plasma in the form of chloraurate ion. The remaining 71 per cent was carried in the red blood corpuscles in the form of 'auraemoglobin'. An attempt was made to feed The Goose traces of radioactive gold so that we could pick up radioactivity in plasma and corpuscles and see how readily the auraemoglobin molecules were handled in the ovaries. It seemed to us the auraemoglobin should be much more slowly disposed of than the dissolved chloraurate ion in the plasma.

The experiment failed, however, since we detected no radioactivity. We put it down to inexperience since none of us were isotopes men which was too bad since the failure was highly significant, really, and by not realizing it, we lost several weeks.

The auraemoglobin was, of course, useless as far as carrying oxygen was concerned, but it only made up about 0·1 per cent of the total haemoglobin of the red blood cells so there was no interference with the respiration of The Goose.

This still left us with the question of where the gold came

from and it was Nevis who first made the crucial suggestion.

'Maybe,' he said, at a meeting of the group held on the evening of August 25, 1955, 'The Goose doesn't replace the iron with gold. Maybe it *changes* the iron to gold.'

Before I met Nevis personally that summer, I had known him through his publications—his field is bile chemistry and liver function—and had always considered him a cautious, clear-thinking person. Almost overcautious. One wouldn't consider him capable for a minute of making any such completely ridiculous statement.

It just shows the desperation and demoralization involved in Project Goose.

The desperation was the fact that there was nowhere, literally nowhere, that the gold could come from. The Goose was excreting gold at the rate of 38·9 grammes of gold a day and had been doing it over a period of months. That gold had to come from somewhere and, failing that—absolutely failing that—it had to be made from something.

The demoralization that led us to consider the second alternative was due to the mere fact that we were face to face with The Goose That Laid The Golden Eggs; the undeniable GOOSE. With that, everything became possible. All of us were living in a fairy-tale world and all of us reacted to it by losing all sense of reality.

Finley considered the possibility seriously. 'Haemoglobin,' he said, 'enters the liver and a bit of auraemoglobin comes out. The gold shell of the eggs has iron as its only impurity. The egg yolk is high in only two things; in gold, of course, and also, somewhat, in iron. It all makes a horrible kind of distorted sense. We're going to need help, men.'

We did and it meant a third stage of the investigation. The first stage had consisted of myself alone. The second was the biochemical task-force. The third, the greatest, the most important of all, involved the invasion of the nuclear physicists.

On September 5, 1955, John L. Billings of the University of

California arrived. He had some equipment with him and more arrived in the following weeks. More temporary structures were going up. I could see that within a year we would have a whole research institution built about The Goose.

Billings joined our conference the evening of the 5th.

Finley brought him up to date and said, 'There are a great many serious problems involved in this iron-to-gold idea. For one thing, the total quantity of iron in The Goose can only be of the order of half a gramme, yet nearly 40 grammes of gold a day are being manufactured.'

Billings had a clear, high-pitched voice. He said, 'There's a worse problem than that. Iron is about at the bottom of the packing fraction curve. Gold is much higher up. To convert a gramme of iron to a gramme of gold takes just about as much energy as is produced by the fissioning of one gramme of U-235.'

Finley shrugged. 'I'll leave the problem to you.'

Billings said, 'Let me think about it.'

He did more than think. One of the things done was to isolate fresh samples of haeme from The Goose, ash it and send the iron oxide to Brookhaven for isotopic analysis. There was no particular reason to do that particular thing. It was just one of a number of individual investigations, but it was the one that brought results.

When the figures came back, Billings choked on them. He said, 'There's no Fe^{56}.'

'What about the other isotopes?' asked Finley at once.

'All present,' said Billings, 'in the appropriate relative ratios, but no detectable Fe^{56}.'

I'll have to explain again: iron, as it occurs naturally, is made up of four different isotopes. These isotopes are varieties of atoms that differ from one another in atomic weight. Iron atoms with an atomic weight of 56, or Fe^{56}, makes up 91·6 per cent of all the atoms in iron. The other atoms have atomic weights of 54, 57 and 58.

The iron from the haeme of The Goose was made up only of Fe^{54}, Fe^{57} and Fe^{58}. The implication was obvious. Fe^{56} was disappearing while the other isotopes weren't and this meant a nuclear reaction was taking place. A nuclear reaction could take one isotope and leave others be. An ordinary chemical reaction, any chemical reaction at all, would have to dispose of all isotopes equally.

'But it's energically impossible,' said Finley.

He was only saying that in mild sarcasm with Billings's initial remark in mind. As biochemists, we knew well enough that many reactions went on in the body which required an input of energy and that this was taken care of by coupling the energy-demanding reaction with an energy-producing reaction.

However, chemical reactions gave off or took up a few kilocalories per mole. Nuclear reactions gave off or took up millions. To supply energy for an energy-demanding nuclear reaction required, therefore, a second, and energy-producing, nuclear reaction.

We didn't see Billings for two days.

When he did come back, it was to say, 'See here. The energy-producing reaction must produce just as much energy per nucleon involved as the energy-demanding reaction uses up. If it produces even slightly less, then the overall reaction won't go. If it produces even slightly more, then considering the astronomical number of nucleons involved, the excess energy produced would vapourize The Goose in a fraction of a second.'

'So?' said Finley.

'So the number of reactions possible is very limited. I have been able to find only one plausible system. Oxygen-18, if converted to iron-56 will produce enough energy to drive the iron-56 on to gold-197. It's like going down one side of a roller-coaster and then up the other. We'll have to test this.'

'How?'

'First, suppose we check the isotopic composition of the oxygen in The Goose.'

Oxygen is made up of three stable isotopes, almost all of it O^{16}. O^{18} makes up only one oxygen atom out of 250.

Another blood sample. The water content was distilled off in vacuum and some of it put through a mass spectograph. There was O^{18} there but only one oxygen atom out of 1300. Fully 80 per cent of the O^{18} we expected wasn't there.

Billings said, 'That's corroborative evidence. Oxygen-18 is being used up. It is being supplied constantly in the food and water fed to The Goose, but it is still being used up. Gold-197 is being produced. Iron-56 is one intermediate and since the reaction that uses up iron-56 is faster than the one that produces it, it has no chance to reach significant concentration and isotopic analysis shows its absence.'

We weren't satisfied, so we tried again. We kept The Goose on water that had been enriched with O^{18} for a week. Gold production went up almost at once. At the end of a week, it was producing 45·8 grammes while the O^{18} content of its body water was no higher than before.

'There's no doubt about it,' said Billings.

He snapped his pencil and stood up. 'That Goose is a living nuclear reactor.'

The Goose was obviously a mutation.

A mutation suggested radiation among other things and radiation brought up the thought of nuclear tests conducted in 1952 and 1953 several hundred miles away from the site of MacGregor's farm. (If it occurs to you that no nuclear tests have been conducted in Texas, it just shows two things; I'm not telling you everything and you don't know everything.)

I doubt that at any time in the history of the atomic era was background radiation so thoroughly analysed and the radioactive content of the soil so rigidly sifted.

Back records were studied. It didn't matter how top-secret they were. By this time, Project Goose had the highest priority that had ever existed.

Even weather records were checked in order to follow the behaviour of the winds at the time of the nuclear tests.

Two things turned up.

One: The background radiation at the farm was a bit higher than normal. Nothing that could possibly do harm, I hasten to add. There were indications, however, that at the time of the birth of The Goose, the farm had been subjected to the drifting edge of at least two fallouts. Nothing really harmful, I again hasten to add.

Second: The Goose, alone of all geese on the farm, in fact, alone of all living creatures on the farm that could be tested, including the humans, showed no radioactivity at all. Look at it this way: *everything* shows traces of radioactivity; that's what is meant by background radiation. But The Goose showed none.

Finley sent one report on December 6, 1955, which I can paraphrase as follows:

'The Goose is a most extraordinary mutation, born of a high-level radioactivity environment which at once encouraged mutations in general and which made this particular mutation a beneficial one.

'The Goose has enzyme systems capable of catalysing various nuclear reactions. Whether the enzyme system consists of one enzyme or more than one is not known. Nor is anything known of the nature of the enzymes in question. Nor can any theory be yet advanced as to how an enzyme can catalyse a nuclear reaction, since these involve particular interactions with forces five orders of magnitude higher than those involved in the ordinary chemical reactions commonly catalysed by enzymes.

'The overall nuclear change is from oxygen-18 to gold-197. The oxygen-18 is plentiful in its environment, being present in significant amount in water and all organic foodstuffs. The gold-197 is excreted via the ovaries. One known intermediate is iron-56 and the fact that auraemoglobin is formed in the process leads us to suspect that the enzyme or enzymes involved may have haeme as a prosthetic group.

'There has been considerable thought devoted to the value this overall nuclear change might have to the goose. The oxygen-18 does it no harm and the gold-197 is troublesome to be rid of, potentially poisonous, and a cause of its sterility. Its formation might possibly be a means of avoiding greater danger. This danger—'

But just reading it in the report, friend, makes it all seem so quiet, almost pensive. Actually, I never saw a man come closer to apoplexy and survive than Billings did when he found out about our own radioactive gold experiments which I told you about earlier—the ones in which we detected no radioactivity in the goose, so that we discarded the results as meaningless.

Many times over he asked how we could possibly consider it unimportant that we had lost radioactivity.

'You're like the cub reporter,' he said, 'who was sent to cover a society wedding and on returning said there was no story because the groom hadn't shown up.

'You fed The Goose radioactive gold and lost it. Not only that, you failed to detect any natural radioactivity about The Goose. Any carbon-14. Any potassium-40. And you called it failure.'

We started feeding The Goose radioactive isotopes. Cautiously, at first, but before the end of January of 1956 we were shovelling it in.

The Goose remained nonradioactive.

'What it amounts to,' said Billings, 'is that this enzyme-catalysed nuclear process of The Goose manages to convert any unstable isotope into a stable isotope.'

'Useful,' I said.

'Useful? It's a thing of beauty. It's the perfect defence against the atomic age. Listen, the conversion of oxygen-18 to gold-197 should liberate eight and a fraction positrons per oxygen atom. That means eight and a fraction gamma rays as soon as each positron combines with an electron. No gamma rays either. The Goose must be able to absorb gamma rays harmlessly.'

We irradiated The Goose with gamma rays. As the level rose, The Goose developed a slight fever and we quit in panic. It was just fever, though, not radiation sickness. A day passed, the fever subsided, and The Goose was as good as new.

'Do you see what we've got?' demanded Billings.

'A scientific marvel,' said Finley.

'Man, don't you see the practical applications? If we could find out the mechanism and duplicate it in the test tube, we've got a perfect method of radioactive ash disposal. The most important drawback preventing us from going ahead with a full-scale atomic economy is the headache of what to do with the radioactive isotopes manufactured in the process. Sift them through an enzyme preparation in large vats and that would be it.

'Find out the mechanism, gentlemen, and you can stop worrying about fallouts. We would find a protection against radiation sickness.

'Alter the mechanism somehow and we can have Geese excreting any element needed. How about uranium-235 eggshells?

'The mechanism! The mechanism!'

We sat there, all of us, staring at The Goose.

If only the eggs would hatch. If only we could get a tribe of nuclear-reactor Geese.

'It must have happened before,' said Finley. 'The legends of such Geese must have started somehow.'

'Do you want to wait?' asked Billings.

If we had a gaggle of such Geese, we could begin taking a few apart. We could study its ovaries. We could prepare tissue slices and tissue homogenates.

That might not do any good. The tissue of a liver biopsy did not react with oxygen-18 under any conditions we tried.

But then we might perfuse an intact liver. We might study intact embryos, watch for one to develop the mechanism.

But with only one Goose, we could do none of that.

We don't dare kill The Goose That Lays The Golden Eggs.

The secret was in the liver of that fat Goose.

Liver of fat goose! *Pâté de foie gras!* No delicacy to us!

Nevis said, thoughtfully, 'We need an idea. Some radical departure. Some crucial thought.'

'Saying it won't bring it,' said Billings despondently.

And in a miserable attempt at a joke, I said, 'We could advertise in the newspapers,' and that gave *me* an idea.

'Science fiction!' I said.

'What?' said Finley.

'Look, science-fiction magazines print gag articles. The readers consider it fun. They're interested.' I told them about the thiotimoline articles Asimov wrote and which I had once read.

The atmosphere was cold with disapproval.

'We won't even be breaking security regulations,' I said, 'because no one will believe it.' I told them about the time in 1944 when Cleve Cartmill wrote a story describing the atom bomb one year early and the F.B.I. kept its temper.

'And science-fiction readers have ideas. Don't underrate them. Even if they think it's a gag article, they'll send their notions in to the editor. And since we have no ideas of our own; since we're up a dead-end street, what can we lose?'

They still didn't buy it.

So I said, 'And you know—The Goose won't live forever.'

That did it, somehow.

We had to convince Washington; then I got in touch with John Campbell and he got in touch with Asimov.

Now the article is done. I've read it, I approve, and I urge you all not to believe it. Please don't.

Only—

Any ideas?

PÂTÉ DE FOIE GRAS

Since this story is my own, I can tell you how it originated. It began with a deliberate attempt to pick something utterly unscientific and surround it with the trappings of science in so plausible a manner as to make it legitimate science fiction.

The fantasy I chose was that of the goose that lays the golden eggs. The question was how such a goose, which has no gold in its diet, can produce golden eggs. Gold must be produced out of other elements and that requires nuclear reactions in quantity. But nuclear reactions do not take place in living tissue in quantity, the assumption that it does is the impossible point that starts the story.

This impossible assumption must be surrounded with a wealth of quite authentic chemical and biochemical reasoning, and with an accurate picture of what scientific research is like. And since

I have a Ph.D. in chemistry and spent years teaching biochemistry at a medical school, I could manage it—and have little to add here to what I said in the story.

Questions and Suggestions

1. How are nuclear reactions different from ordinary chemical reactions? What arguments can you bring forward against (or for) the possibility of nuclear reactions in living tissue? Cosmic rays and other hard radiation can indeed bring about nuclear reactions in living tissue (with what effects?) but how does this differ from the sort of thing dealt with in *Pâté de Foie Gras*?

2. Have you any suggestions that may help answer the problem posed at the end of the story?

15. Omnilingual

H. Beam Piper

Martha Dane paused, looking up at the purple-tinged copper sky. The wind had shifted since noon, while she had been inside, and the dust storm that was sweeping the high deserts to the east was now blowing out over Syrtis. The sun, magnified by the haze, was a gorgeous magenta ball, as large as the sun of Terra, at which she could look directly. Tonight, some of that dust would come sifting down from the upper atmosphere to add another film to what had been burying the city for the last fifty thousand years.

The red loess lay over everything, covering the streets and the open spaces of park and plaza, hiding the small houses that had been crushed and pressed flat under it and the rubble that had come down from the tall buildings when roofs had caved in and walls had toppled outward. Here where she stood, the ancient streets were a hundred to a hundred and fifty feet below the surface; the breach they had made in the wall of the building behind her had opened into the sixth storey. She could look down on the cluster of prefabricated huts and sheds, on the brush-grown flat that had been the waterfront when this place had been a seaport on the ocean that was now Syrtis Depression; already, the bright metal was thinly coated with red dust. She thought, again, of what clearing this city would mean, in terms of time and labour, of people and supplies and equipment brought across fifty million miles of space. They'd have to use machinery; there was no other way it could be done.

Bulldozers and power shovels and draglines; they were fast, but they were rough and indiscriminate. She remembered the digs around Harappa and Mohenjo-Daro, in the Indus Valley, and the careful, patient native labourers—the painstaking foremen, the pickmen and spademen, the long files of basketmen carrying away the earth. Slow and primitive as the civilization whose ruins they were uncovering, yes, but she could count on the fingers of one hand the times one of her pickmen had damaged a valuable object in the ground. If it hadn't been for the underpaid and uncomplaining native labourer, archaeology would still be back where Wincklemann had found it. But on Mars there was no native labour; the last Martian had died five hundred centuries ago.

Something started banging like a machine gun, four or five hundred yards to her left. A solenoid jack-hammer; Tony Lattimer must have decided which building he wanted to break into next. She became conscious, then, of the awkward weight of her equipment, and began redistributing it, shifting the straps of her oxy-tank pack, slinging the camera from one shoulder and the board and drafting tools from the other, gathering the notebooks and sketchbooks under her left arm. She started walking down the road, over hillocks of buried rubble, around snags of wall jutting up out of the loess, past buildings still standing, some of them already breached and explored, and across the brush-grown flat to the huts.

There were ten people in the main office room of Hut One when she entered. As soon as she had disposed of her oxygen equipment, she lit a cigarette, her first since noon, then looked from one to another of them. Old Selim von Ohlmhorst, the Turco-German, one of her two fellow archaeologists, sitting at the end of the long table against the farther wall, smoking his big curved pipe and going through a looseleaf notebook. The girl ordnance officer, Sachiko Koremitsu, between two droplights at the other end of the table, her head bent over her work. Colonel Hubert Penrose, the Space Force CO, and Captain Field, the intelligence officer, listening to the report of one of the airdyne pilots, returned from his afternoon survey flight. A couple of girl lieutenants from Signals, going over the script of the evening telecast, to be transmitted to the *Cyrano*, on orbit five thousand miles off planet and relayed from thence to Terra via Lunar. Sid Chamberlain, the Trans-Space News Service man, was with them. Like Selim and herself, he was a civilian; he was advertising the fact with a white shirt and a sleeveless blue sweater. And Major Lindemann, the engineer officer, and one of his assistants, arguing over some plans on a drafting board. She hoped, drawing a pint of hot water to wash her hands and sponge off her face, that they were doing something about the pipeline.

She started to carry the notebooks and sketchbooks over to where Selim von Ohlmhorst was sitting, and then, as she always did, she turned aside and stopped to watch Sachiko. The Japanese girl was restoring what had been a book, fifty thousand years ago; her eyes were masked by a binocular loup, the black headband invisible against her glossy black hair, and she was picking delicately at the crumpled page with a hair-fine wire set in a handle of copper tubing. Finally, loosening a particle as tiny as a snowflake, she grasped it with tweezers, placed it on the sheet of transparent plastic on which she was reconstructing the page, and set it with a mist of fixative from a little spraygun. It was a sheer joy to watch her; every movement was as graceful and precise as though done to music after being rehearsed a hundred times.

'Hello, Martha. It isn't cocktail-time yet, is it?' The girl at the table spoke without raising her head, almost without moving her lips, as though she were afraid that the slightest breath would disturb the flaky stuff in front of her.

'No, it's only fifteen-thirty. I finished my work, over there. I didn't find any more books, if that's good news for you.'

Sachiko took off the loup and leaned back in her chair, her palms cupped over her eyes.

'No, I like doing this. I call it micro-jigsaw puzzles. This book, here, really is a mess. Selim found it lying open, with some heavy stuff on top of it; the pages were simply crushed.'

She hesitated briefly. 'If only it would mean something, after I did it.'

There could be a faintly critical overtone to that. As she replied, Martha realized that she was being defensive.

'It will, some day. Look how long it took to read Egyptian hieroglyphics, even after they had the Rosetta Stone.'

Sachiko smiled. 'Yes, I know. But they did have the Rosetta Stone.'

'And we don't. There is no Rosetta Stone, not anywhere on Mars. A whole race, a whole species, died while the first Cro-Magnon cave-artist was daubing pictures of reindeer and bison, and across fifty thousand years and fifty million miles there was no bridge of understanding.

'We'll find one. There must be something, somewhere, that will give us the meaning of a few words, and we'll use them to pry meaning out of more words, and so on. We may not live to learn this language, but we'll make a start, and some day somebody will.'

Sachiko took her hands from her eyes, being careful not to look towards the unshaded lights, and smiled again. This time Martha was sure that it was not the Japanese smile of politeness, but the universally human smile of friendship.

'I hope so, Martha; really I do. It would be wonderful for you to be the first to do it, and it would be wonderful for all of us to be able to read what these people wrote. It would really bring this dead city to life again.' The smile faded slowly. 'But it seems so hopeless.'

'You haven't found any more pictures?'

Sachiko shook her head. Not that it would have meant much if she had. They had found hundreds of pictures with captions; they had never been able to establish a positive relationship between any pictured object and any printed word. Neither of them said anything more, and after a moment Sachiko replaced the loup and bent her head forward over the book.

Selim von Ohlmhorst looked up from his notebook, taking his pipe out of his mouth.

'Everything finished, over there?' he asked, releasing a puff of smoke.

'Such as it was.' She laid the notebooks and sketches on the table. 'Captain Gicquel's started airsealing the building from the fifth floor down, with an entrance on the sixth; he'll start putting in oxygen generators as soon as that's done. I have everything cleared up where he'll be working.'

Colonel Penrose looked up quickly, as though making a mental note to attend to something later. Then he returned his attention to the pilot, who was pointing something out on a map.

Von Ohlmhorst nodded. 'There wasn't much to it, at that,' he agreed. 'Do you know which building Tony has decided to enter next?'

'The tall one with the conical thing like a candle extinguisher on top, I think. I heard him drilling for the blasting shots over that way.'

'Well, I hope it turns out to be one that was occupied up to the end.'

The last one hadn't. It had been stripped of its contents and fittings, a piece of this and a bit of that, haphazardly, apparently over a long period of time, until it had been almost gutted. For centuries, as it had died, this city had been consuming itself by a process of autocannibalism. She said something to that effect.

'Yes. We always find that—except, of course, at places like Pompeii. Have you seen any of the other Roman cities in Italy?' he asked. 'Minturnae, for instance? First the inhabitants tore down this to repair that, and then, after they had vacated the city, other people came along and tore down what was left, and burned the stones for lime, or crushed them to mend roads, till there was nothing left but the foundation traces. That's where we are fortunate; this is one of the places where the Martian race perished, and there were no barbarians to come later and destroy what they had left.' He puffed slowly at his pipe. 'Some of these days, Martha, we are going to break into one of these buildings and find that it was one in which the last of these people died. Then we will learn the story of the end of this civilization.'

And if we learn to read their language, we'll learn the whole story, not just the obituary. She hesitated, not putting the thought into words. 'We'll find that, some time, Selim,' she said, then looked at her watch. 'I'm going to get some more work done on my lists, before dinner.'

For an instant, the old man's face stiffened in disapproval; he started to say something, thought better of it, and put his pipe back into his mouth. The brief wrinkling around his mouth and the twitch of his white moustache had been enough, however; she knew what he was thinking. She was wasting time and effort, he believed; time and effort belonging not to herself but to the expedition. He could be right, too, she realized. But he had to be wrong; there had to be a way to do it. She turned from him silently and went to her own packing case seat, at the middle of the table.

Photographs, and photostats of restored pages of books, and transcripts of inscriptions, were piled in front of her, and the notebooks in which she was compiling her lists. She sat down, lighting a fresh cigarette, and reached over to a stack of unexamined material, taking off the top sheet. It was a photostat of what looked like the title page and contents of some sort of a periodical. She remembered it; she had found it herself, two days before, in a closet in the basement of the building she had just finished examining.

She sat for a moment, looking at it. It was readable, in the sense that she had set up a purely arbitrary but consistently pronouncable system of phonetic values for the letters. The long vertical symbols were vowels. There were only ten of them; not too many, allowing separate characters for long and short sounds. There were twenty of the short horizontal letters, which meant that sounds like -ng or -ch or -sh were single letters. The odds were millions to one against her system being anything like the original sound of the language, but she had listed several thousand Martian words, and she could pronounce all of them.

And that was as far as it went. She could pronounce between three and four thousand Martian words, and she couldn't assign a meaning to one of them. Selim von Ohlmhorst believed that she never would. So did Tony Lattimer, and he was a great deal less reticent about saying so. So, she was sure, did Sachiko Koremitsu. There were times, now and then, when she began to be afraid that they were right.

The letters on the page in front of her began squirming and dancing, slender vowels with fat little consonants. They did that, now, every night in her dreams. And there were other dreams, in which she read them as easily as English; waking, she would try desperately and vainly to remember. She blinked, and looked away from the photostated page; when she looked back, the letters were behaving themselves again. There were three words at the top of the page, over-and-underlined, which seemed to be the Martian method of capitalization. *Mastharnorvod Tadavas Sornhulva.* She pronounced them mentally, leafing through her notebooks to see if she had encountered them before, and in what contexts. All three were listed. In addition, *masthar* was a fairly common word, and so was *norvod,* and so was *nor,* but *-vod* was a suffix and nothing but a suffix. *Davas,* was a word, too, and *ta-* was a common prefix; *sorn* and *hulva* were both common words. This language, she had long ago decided, must be something like German; when the Martians had needed a new word, they had just pasted a couple of existing words together. It would probably turn out to be a grammatical horror. Well, they had published magazines, and one of them had been called *Mastharnorvod Tadavas Sornhulva.* She wondered if it had been something like the *Quarterly Archaeological Review,* or something more on the order of *Sexy Stories.*

A smaller line, under the title, was plainly the issue number and date; enough things had been found numbered in series to enable her to identify the numerals and determine that a decimal system of numeration had been used. This was the one thousand and seven hundred and fifty-fourth issue, for Doma, 14837; then Doma must be the name of one of the Martian months. The word had turned up several times before. She found herself puffing furiously on her cigarette as she leafed through notebooks and piles of already examined material.

Sachiko was speaking to somebody, and a chair scraped at the end of the table. She raised her head, to see a big man with red hair and a red face, in Space Force green, with the single star of a major on his shoulder, sitting down. Ivan Fitzgerald, the medic. He was lifting weights from a book similar to the one the girl ordnance officer was restoring.

'Haven't had time, lately,' he was saying, in reply to Sachiko's question. 'The Finchley girl's still down with whatever it is she has, and it's something I haven't been able to diagnose yet. And I've been checking on bacteria cultures, and in what spare time I have, I've been dissecting specimens for Bill Chandler. Bill's finally found a mammal. Looks like a lizard, and it's only four inches long, but it's a real warm-blooded, gamogenetic, placental, viviparous mammal. Burrows, and seems to live on what pass for insects here.'

'Is there enough oxygen for anything like that?' Sachiko was asking.

'Seems to be, close to the ground.' Fitzgerald got the head-band of his loup adjusted, and pulled it down over his eyes. 'He found this thing in a ravine down on the sea bottom— Ha, this page seems to be intact; now, if I can get it out all in one piece—'

He went on talking inaudibly to himself, lifting the page a little at a time and sliding one of the transparent plastic sheets under it, working with minute delicacy. Not the delicacy of the Japanese girl's small hands, moving like the paws of a cat washing her face, but like a steam-hammer cracking a peanut. Field archaeology requires a certain delicacy of touch, too, but Martha watched the pair of them with envious admiration. Then she turned back to her own work, finishing the table of contents.

The next page was the beginning of the first article listed; many of the words were unfamiliar. She had the impression that this must be some kind of scientific or technical journal; that could be because such publications made up the bulk of her own periodical reading. She doubted if it were fiction; the paragraphs had a solid, factual look.

At length, Ivan Fitzgerald gave a short, explosive grunt. 'Ha! Got it!'

She looked up. He had detached the page and was cementing another plastic sheet on to it.

'Any pictures?' she asked.

'None on this side. Wait a moment.' He turned the sheet. 'None on this side, either.' He sprayed another sheet of plastic to sandwich the page, then picked up his pipe and relighted it.

'I get fun out of this, and it's good practice for my hands, so don't think I'm complaining,' he said, 'but, Martha, do you honestly think anybody's ever going to get anything out of this?'

Sachiko held up a scrap of the silicone plastic the Martians had used for paper with her tweezers. It was almost an inch square.

'Look; three whole words on this piece,' she crowed. 'Ivan, you took the easy book.'

Fitzgerald wasn't being sidetracked. 'This stuff's absolutely meaningless,' he continued. 'It had a meaning fifty thousand years ago, when it was written, but it has none at all now.'

She shook her head. 'Meaning isn't something that evaporates with time,' she argued. 'It has just as much meaning now as it ever had. We just haven't learned how to decipher it.'

'That seems like a pretty pointless distinction,' Selim von Ohlmhorst joined the conversation. 'There no longer exists a means of deciphering it.'

'We'll find one.' She was speaking, she realized, more in self-encouragement than in controversy.

'How? From pictures and captions? We've found captioned pictures, and what have they given us? A caption is intended to explain the picture, not the picture to explain the caption. Suppose some alien to our culture found a picture of a man with a white beard and moustache sawing a billet from a log. He would think the caption meant, "Man Sawing Wood." How would he know that it was really, "Wilhelm II in Exile at Doorn"?'

Sachiko had taken off her loup and was lighting a cigarette.

'I can think of pictures intended to explain their captions,' she said. 'These picture-language books, the sort we use in the Service—little line drawings, with a word or phrase under them.'

'Well, of course, if we found something like that,' von Ohlmhorst began.

'Michael Ventris found something like that, back in the Fifties,' Hubert Penrose's voice broke in from directly behind her.

She turned her head. The colonel was standing by the archaeologists' table; Captain Field and the airdyne pilot had gone out.

'He found a lot of Greek inventories of military stores,' Penrose continued. 'They were in Cretan Linear B script, and at the head of each list was a little picture, a sword or a helmet or a cooking tripod or a chariot wheel. That's what gave him the key to the script.'

'Colonel's getting to be quite an archaeologist,' Fitzgerald commented. 'We're all learning each other's specialities, on this expedition.'

'I heard about that long before this expedition was even contemplated.' Penrose was tapping a cigarette on his gold case. 'I heard about that back before the Thirty Days' War, at Intelligence School, when I was a lieutenant. As a feat of cryptanalysis, not an archaeological discovery.'

'Yes, cryptanalysis,' von Ohlmhorst pounced. 'The reading of a known language in an unknown form of writing. Ventris's lists were in the known language, Greek. Neither he nor anybody else ever read a word of the Cretan language until the finding of the Greek-Cretan bilingual in 1963, because only with a bilingual text, one language already known, can an unknown ancient language be learned. And what hope, I ask you, have we of finding anything like that here? Martha, you've been working on these Martian texts ever since we landed here—for the last six months. Tell me, have you found a single word to which you can positively assign a meaning?'

'Yes, I think I have one.' She was trying hard not to sound too exultant. '*Doma*. It's the name of one of the months of the Martian calendar.'

'Where did you find that?' von Ohlmhorst asked. 'And how did you establish—'

'Here.' She picked up the photostat and handed it along the table to him. 'I'd call this the title page of a magazine.'

He was silent for a moment, looking at it. 'Yes, I would say so, too. Have you any of the rest of it?'

'I'm working on the first page of the first article, listed there. Wait till I see; yes, here's all I found, together, here.' She told him where she had got it. 'I just gathered it up, at the time, and gave it to Geoffrey and Rosita to photostat; this is the first time I've really examined it.'

The old man got to his feet, brushing tobacco ashes from the front of his jacket, and came to where she was sitting, laying the title page on the table and leafing quickly through the stack of photostats.

'Yes, and here is the second article, on page eight, and here's the next one.' He finished the pile of photostats. 'A couple of pages missing at the end of the last article. This is remarkable; surprising that a thing like a magazine would have survived so long.'

'Well, this silicone stuff the Martians used for paper is pretty durable,' Hubert Penrose said. 'There doesn't seem to have been any water or any other fluid in it originally, so it wouldn't dry out with time.'

'Oh, it's not remarkable that the material would have survived. We've found a good many books and papers in excellent condition. But only a really vital culture, an organized culture, will publish magazines, and this civilization had been dying for hundreds of years before the end. It might have been a thousand years before the time they died out completely that such activities as publishing ended.'

'Well, look where I found it; in a closet in a cellar. Tossed in there and forgotten, and then ignored when they were stripping the building. Things like that happen.'

Penrose had picked up the title page and was looking at it. 'I don't think there's any doubt about this being a magazine, at all.' He looked again at the title, his lips moving silently. '*Mastharnorvod Tadavas Sornhulva.* Wonder what it means. But you're right about the date—*Doma* seems to be the name of a month. Yes, you have a word, Dr. Dane.'

Sid Chamberlain, seeing that something unusual was going on, had come over from the table at which he was working. After examining the title page and some of the inside pages, he began whispering into the stenophone he had taken from his belt.

'Don't try to blow this up to anything big, Sid,' she cautioned. 'All we have is the name of a month, and Lord only knows how long it'll be till we even find out which month it was.'

'Well, it's a start, isn't it?' Penrose argued. 'Grotefend only had the word for "king" when he started reading Persian cuneiform.'

'But I don't have the word for month; just the name of a month. Everybody knew the names of the Persian kings, long before Grotefend.'

'That's not the story,' Chamberlain said. 'What the public back on Terra will be interested in is finding out that the Martians published magazines, just like we do. Something familiar; make the Martians seem more real. More human.'

Three men had come in, and were removing their masks and helmets and oxy-tanks, and peeling out of their quilted coveralls. Two were Space Force lieutenants; the third was a youngish civilian with close-cropped blond hair in a checked woollen shirt. Tony Lattimer and his helpers.

'Don't tell me Martha finally got something out of that stuff?' he asked, approaching the table. He might have been commenting on the antics of the village half-wit, from his tone.

'Yes; the name of one of the Martian months,' Hubert Penrose went on to explain, showing the photostat.

Tony Lattimer took it, glanced at it, and dropped it on the table.

'Sounds plausible, of course, but just an assumption. That word may not be the name of a month, at all—could mean "published" or "authorized" or "copyrighted" or anything like that. Fact is, I don't think it's more than a wild guess that that thing's anything like a periodical.' He dismissed the subject and turned to Penrose. 'I picked out the next building to enter; that tall one with the conical thing on top. It ought to be in pretty good shape inside; the conical top wouldn't allow dust to accumulate, and from the outside nothing seems to be caved in or crushed. Ground level's higher than the other one, about the seventh floor. I found a good place and drilled for the shots; tomorrow I'll blast a hole in it, and if you can spare some people to help, we can start exploring it right away.'

'Yes, of course, Dr. Lattimer. I can spare about a dozen, and I suppose you can find a few civilian volunteers,' Penrose told him. 'What will you need in the way of equipment?'

'Oh, about six demolition-packets; they can all be shot together. And the usual thing in the way of lights, and breaking and digging tools, and climbing equipment in case we run into broken or doubtful stairways. We'll divide into two parties. Nothing ought to be entered for the first time without a qualified archaeologist along. Three parties, if Martha can tear herself away from this catalogue of systematized incomprehensibilities she's making long enough to do some real work.'

She felt her chest tighten and her face become stiff. She was pressing her lips together to lock in a furious retort when Hubert Penrose answered for her.

'Dr. Dane's been doing as much work, and as important work, as you have,' he said brusquely. 'More important work, I'd be inclined to say.'

Von Ohlmhorst was visibly distressed; he glanced once towards Sid Chamberlain, then looked hastily away from him. Afraid of a story of dissension among archaeologists getting out.

'Working out a system of pronunciation by which the Martian

language could be translated was a most important contribution,' he said. 'And Martha did that almost unassisted.'

'Unassisted by Dr. Lattimer, anyway,' Penrose added. 'Captain Field and Lieutenant Koremitsu did some work, and I helped out a little, but nine-tenths of it she did herself.'

'Purely arbitrary,' Lattimer disdained. 'Why, we don't even know that the Martians could make the same kind of vocal sounds we do.'

'Oh, yes, we do,' Ivan Fitzgerald contradicted, safe on his own ground. 'I haven't seen any actual Martian skulls—these people seem to have been very tidy about disposing of their dead—but from statues and busts and pictures I've seen, I'd say that their vocal organs were identical with our own.'

'Well, grant that. And grant that it's going to be impressive to rattle off the names of Martian notables whose statues we find, and that if we're ever to attribute any place-names, they'll sound a lot better than this horse-doctors' Latin the old astronomers splashed all over the map of Mars,' Lattimer said. 'What I object to is her wasting time on this stuff, of which nobody will ever be able to read a word if she fiddles around with those lists till there's another hundred feet of loess on this city, when there's so much real work to be done and we're as shorthanded as we are.'

That was the first time that had come out in just so many words. She was glad Lattimer had said it and not Selim von Ohlmhorst.

'What you mean,' she retorted, 'is that it doesn't have the publicity value that digging up statues has.'

For an instant, she could see that the shot had scored. Then Lattimer, with a side glance at Chamberlain, answered:

'What I mean is that you're trying to find something that any archaeologist, yourself included, should know doesn't exist. I don't object to your gambling your professional reputation and making a laughingstock of yourself; what I object to is that the blunders of one archaeologist discredit the whole subject in the eyes of the public.'

That seemed to be what worried Lattimer most. She was

framing a reply when the communication-outlet whistled shrilly, and then squawked: 'Cocktail time! One hour to dinner; cocktails in the library, Hut Four!'

The library, which was also lounge, recreation room, and general gathering-place, was already crowded; most of the crowd was at the long table topped with sheets of glasslike plastic that had been wall panels out of one of the ruined buildings. She poured herself what passed, here, for a martini, and carried it over to where Selim von Ohlmhorst was sitting alone.

For a while, they talked about the building they had just finished exploring, then drifted into reminiscences of their work on Terra—von Ohlmhorst's in Asia Minor, with the Hittite Empire, and hers in Pakistan, excavating the cities of the Harappa civilization. They finished their drinks—the ingredients were plentiful; alcohol and flavouring extracts synthesized from Martian vegetation—and von Ohlmhorst took the two glasses to the table for refills.

'You know, Martha,' he said, when he returned, 'Tony was right about one thing. You are gambling your professional standing and reputation. It's against all archaeological experience that a language so completely dead as this one could be deciphered. There was a continuity between all the other ancient languages—by knowing Greek, Champollion learned to read Egyptian; by knowing Egyptian, Hittite was learned. That's why you and your colleagues have never been able to translate the Harappa hieroglyphics; no such continuity exists there. If you insist that this utterly dead language can be read, your reputation will suffer for it.'

'I heard Colonel Penrose say, once, that an officer who's afraid to risk his military reputation seldom makes much of a reputation. It's the same with us. If we really want to find things out, we have to risk making mistakes. And I'm a lot more interested in finding things out than I am in my reputation.'

She glanced across the room, to where Tony Lattimer was sitting with Gloria Standish, talking earnestly, while Gloria sipped one of the counterfeit Martinis and listened. Gloria was the leading contender for the title of Miss Mars, 1996, if you liked big bosomy blondes, but Tony would have been just as attentive to her if she'd looked like the Wicked Witch in the *Wizard of Oz*, because Gloria was the Pan-Federation Telecast System commentator with the expedition.

'I know you are,' the old Turco-German was saying. 'That's why, when they asked me to name another archaeologist for this expedition, I named you.'

He hadn't named Tony Lattimer; Lattimer had been pushed on to the expedition by his university. There'd been a lot of high-level string-pulling to that; she wished she knew the whole story. She'd managed to keep clear of universities and university politics; all her digs had been sponsored by non-academic foundations or art museums.

'You have an excellent standing; much better than my own, at your age. That's why it disturbs me to see you jeopardizing it by this insistence that the Martian language can be translated. I can't, really, see how you can hope to succeed.'

She shrugged and drank some more of her cocktail, then lit another cigarette. It was getting tiresome to try to verbalize something she only felt.

'Neither do I, now, but I will. Maybe I'll find something like the picture-books Sachiko was talking about. A child's primer, maybe; surely they had things like that. And if I don't, I'll find something else. We've only been here six months. I can wait the rest of my life, if I have to, but I'll do it some time.'

'I can't wait so long,' von Ohlmhorst said. 'The rest of my life will only be a few years, and when the *Schiaparelli* orbits in, I'll be going back to Terra on the *Cyrano*.'

'I wish you wouldn't. This is a whole new world of archaeology. Literally.'

'Yes.' He finished the cocktail and looked at his pipe as though wondering whether to re-light it so soon before dinner, then put it in his pocket. 'A whole new world—but I've grown old, and it isn't for me. I've spent my life studying the Hittites. I can speak the Hittite language, though maybe King Muwatallis wouldn't be able to understand my modern Turkish accent. But the things I'd have to learn, here—chemistry, physics, engineering, how to run analytic tests on steel girders and beryllo-silver alloys and plastics and silicones. I'm more at home with a civilization that rode in chariots and fought with swords and was just learning how to work iron. Mars is for young people. This expedition is a cadre of leadership—not only the Space Force people, who'll be the commanders of the main expedition, but us scientists, too. And I'm just an old cavalry general who can't learn to command tanks and aircraft. You'll have time to learn about Mars. I won't.'

His reputation as the dean of Hittitologists was solid and secure, too, she added mentally. Then she felt ashamed of the thought. He wasn't to be classed with Tony Lattimer.

'All I came for was to get the work started,' he was continuing. 'The Federation Government felt that an old hand should do that. Well, it's started, now; you and Tony and whoever come out on the *Schiaparelli* must carry it on. You said it, yourself; you have a whole new world. This is only one city, of the last Martian civilization. Behind this, you have the Late Upland Culture, and the Canal Builders, and all the civilizations and races and empires before them, clear back to the Martian Stone Age.' He hesitated for a moment. 'You have no idea what you have to learn, Martha. This isn't the time to start specializing too narrowly.'

They all got out of the truck and stretched their legs and looked up the road to the tall building with the queer conical cap askew on its top. The four little figures that had been busy against its wall climbed into the jeep and started back slowly, the smallest of them, Sachiko Koremitsu, paying out an electric cable behind. When it pulled up beside the truck, they climbed out; Sachiko attached the free end of the cable to a nuclear-electric battery. At once, dirty grey smoke and orange dust puffed out from the wall of the building, and, a second later, the multiple explosion banged.

She and Tony Lattimer and Major Lindemann climbed on to the truck, leaving the jeep standing by the road. When they reached the building, a satisfying wide breach had been blown in the wall. Lattimer had placed his shots between two of the windows; they were both blown out along with the wall between, and lay unbroken on the ground. Martha remembered the first building they had entered. A Space Force officer had picked up a stone and thrown it at one of the windows, thinking that would be all they'd need to do. It had bounced back. He had drawn his pistol—they'd all carried guns, then, on the principle that what they didn't know about Mars might easily hurt them—and fired four shots. The bullets had ricochetted, screaming thinly; there were four coppery smears of jacket-metal on the window, and a little surface spalling. Somebody tried a rifle; the 4000-f.s. bullet had cracked the glasslike pane without penetrating. An oxy-acetylene torch had taken an hour to cut the window out; the lab crew, aboard the ship, were still trying to find out just what the stuff was.

Tony Lattimer had gone forward and was sweeping his flashlight back and forth, swearing petulantly, his voice harshened and amplified by his helmet-speaker.

'I thought I was blasting into a hallway; this lets us into a room. Careful; there's about a two-foot drop to the floor, and a lot of rubble from the blast just inside.'

He stepped down through the breach; the others began dragging equipment out of the trucks—shovels and picks and crowbars and sledges, portable floodlights, cameras, sketching materials, an extension ladder, even Alpinists' ropes and crampons and pickaxes. Hubert Penrose was shouldering something that looked like a surrealist machine gun but which was really a nuclear-electric jack-hammer. Martha selected one of the spike-shod mountaineer's ice axes, with which she could dig or chop or poke or pry or help herself over rough footing.

The windows, grimed and crusted with fifty millennia of dust, filtered in a dim twilight; even the breach in the wall, in the morning shade, lighted only a small patch of floor. Somebody snapped on a floodlight, aiming it at the ceiling. The big room was empty and bare; dust lay thick on the floor and reddened the once-white walls. It could have been a large office, but there was nothing left in it to indicate its use.

'This one's been stripped up to the seventh floor!' Lattimer exclaimed. 'Street level'll be cleaned out, completely.'

'Do for living quarters and shops, then,' Lindemann said. 'Added to the others, this'll take care of everybody on the *Schiaparelli*.'

'Seem to have been a lot of electric or electronic apparatus over along this wall,' one of the Space Force officers commented. 'Ten or twelve electric outlets.' He brushed the dusty wall with his glove, then scraped on the floor with his foot. 'I can see where things were pried loose.'

The door, one of the double sliding things the Martians had used, was closed. Selim von Ohlmhorst tried it, but it was stuck fast. The metal latch-parts had frozen together, molecule bonding itself to molecule, since the door had last been closed. Hubert Penrose came over with the jack-hammer, fitting a spear-point chisel into place. He set the chisel in the joint between the doors, braced the hammer against his hip, and squeezed the trigger-switch. The hammer banged briefly like the weapon it resembled, and the doors popped a few inches apart, then stuck. Enough dust had worked into the recesses into which it was supposed to slide to block it on both sides.

That was old stuff; they ran into that every time they had to force a door, and they were prepared for it. Somebody went outside and brought in a power-jack and finally one of the doors inched back to the doorjamb. That was enough to get the lights and equipment through; they all passed from the room to the hallway beyond. About half the other doors were open; each had a number and a single word, *Darfhulva*, over it.

One of the civilian volunteers, a woman professor of natural ecology from Penn State University, was looking up and down the hall.

'You know,' she said, 'I feel at home here. I think this was a college of some sort, and these were classrooms. That word, up there; that was the subject taught, or the department. And those electronic devices, all where the class would face them; audio-visual teaching aids.'

'A twenty-five-storey university?' Lattimer scoffed. 'Why, a building like this would handle thirty thousand students.'

'Maybe there were that many. This was a big city, in its prime,' Martha said, moved chiefly by a desire to oppose Lattimer.

'Yes, but think of the snafu in the halls, every time they changed classes. It'd take half an hour to get everybody back and forth from one floor to another.' He turned to von Ohlmhorst. 'I'm going up above this floor. This place has been looted clean up to here, but there's a chance there may be something above,' he said.

'I'll stay on this floor, at present,' the Turco-German replied. 'There will be much coming and going, and dragging things in and out. We should get this completely examined and recorded first. Then Major Lindemann's people can do there worst, here.'

'Well, if nobody else wants it, I'll take the downstairs,' Martha said.

'I'll go along with you,' Hubert Penrose told her. 'If the lower floors have no archaeological value, we'll turn them into living quarters. I like this building; it'll give everybody room to keep out from under everybody else's feet.' He looked down the hall. 'We ought to find escalators at the middle.'

The hallway, too, was thick underfoot with dust. Most of the open rooms were empty, but a few contained furniture, including small seat-desks. The original proponent of the university theory pointed these out as just what might be found in classrooms. There were escalators, up and down, on either side of the hall, and more on the intersecting passage to the right.

'That's how they handled the students, between classes,' Martha commented. 'And I'll bet there are more ahead, there.'

They came to a stop where the hallway ended at a great square central hall. There were elevators, there, on two of the sides, and four escalators, still usable as stairways. But it was the walls, and the paintings on them, that brought them up short and staring.

They were clouded with dirt—she was trying to imagine what they must have looked like originally, and at the same time estimating the labour that would be involved in cleaning them—but they were still distinguishable, as was the word, *Darfhulva,* in golden letters above each of the four sides. It was a moment before she realized, from the murals, that she had at last found a meaningful Martian word. They were a vast historical panorama, clockwise around the room. A group of skin-clad savages squatting around a fire. Hunters with bows and spears, carrying the carcass of an animal slightly like a pig. Nomads riding long-legged, graceful mounts like hornless deer. Peasants sowing and reaping; mud-walled hut villages, and cities; processions of priests and warriors; battles with swords and bows, and with cannon and muskets; galleys, and ships with sails, and ships without visible means of propulsion, and aircraft. Changing costumes and weapons and machines and styles of architecture. A richly fertile landscape, gradually merging into barren deserts and bushlands—the time of the great planet-wide drought. The Canal Builders—men with machines recognizable as steam-shovels and derricks, digging and quarrying and driving across the empty plains with aquaducts. More cities—seaports on the shrinking oceans; dwindling, half-deserted cities; an abandoned city, with four tiny humanoid figures and a thing like a combat-car in the middle of a brush-grown plaza, they and their vehicle dwarfed by the huge lifeless buildings around them. She had not the least doubt; *Darfhulva* was History.

'Wonderful!' von Ohlmhorst was saying. 'The entire history of this race. Why, if the painter depicted appropriate costumes and weapons and machines for each period, and got the architecture right, we can break the history of this planet into eras and periods and civilizations.'

'You can assume they're authentic. The faculty of this university would insist on authenticity in the *Darfhulva*—History—Department,' she said.

'Yes! *Darfhulva*—History! And your magazine was a journal

of *Sornhulva!*' Penrose exclaimed. 'You have a word, Martha!' It took her an instant to realize that he had called her by her first name, and not Dr. Dane. She wasn't sure if that weren't a bigger triumph than learning a word of the Martian language. Or a more auspicious start. 'Alone, I suppose that *hulva* means something like science or knowledge, or study; combined, it would be equivalent to our 'ology. And *darf* would mean something like past, or old times, or human events, or chronicles.'

'That gives you three words, Martha!' Sachiko jubilated. 'You did it.'

'Let's don't go too fast,' Lattimer said, for once not derisively. 'I'll admit that *darfhulva* is the Martian word for history as a subject of study; I'll admit that *hulva* is the general word and *darf* modifies it and tells us which subject is meant. But as for assigning specific meanings, we can't do that because we don't know just how the Martians thought, scientifically or otherwise.'

He stopped short, startled by the blue-white light that blazed as Sid Chamberlain's Kliegettes went on. When the whirring of the camera stopped, it was Chamberlain who was speaking:

'This is the biggest thing yet; the whole history of Mars, Stone Age to the end, all on four walls. I'm taking this with the fast shutter, but we'll telecast it in slow motion, from the beginning to the end. Tony, I want you to do the voice for it—running commentary, interpretation of each scene as it's shown. Would you do that?'

Would he do that! Martha thought. If he had a tail, he'd be wagging it at the very thought.

'Well, there ought to be more murals on the other floors,' she said. 'Who wants to come downstairs with us?'

Sachiko did; immediately, Ivan Fitzgerald volunteered. Sid decided to go upstairs with Tony Lattimer and Gloria Standish decided to go upstairs, too. Most of the party would remain on the seventh floor, to help Selim von Ohlmhorst get it finished. After poking tentatively at the escalator with the spike of her ice axe, Martha led the way downward.

* * *

The sixth floor was *Darfhulva*, too; military and technological history, from the character of the murals. They looked around the central hall, and went down to the fifth; it was like the floors above except that the big quadrangle was stacked with dusty furniture and boxes. Ivan Fitzgerald, who was carrying the floodlight, swung it slowly around. Here the murals were of heroic-sized Martians, so human in appearance as to seem members of her own race, each holding some object—a book, or a test tube, or some bit of scientific apparatus, and behind them were scenes of laboratories and factories, flame and smoke, lightning-flashes. The word at the top of each of the four walls was one with which she was already familiar—*Sornhulva*.

'Hey, Martha; there's that word,' Ivan Fitzgerald exclaimed. 'The one in the title of your magazine.' He looked at the paintings. 'Chemistry, or physics.'

'Both,' Hubert Penrose considered. 'I don't think the Martians made any sharp distinction between them. See, the old fellow with the scraggly whiskers must be the inventor of the spectroscope; he has one in his hands, and he has a rainbow behind him. And the woman in the blue smock, beside him, worked in organic chemistry; see the diagrams of long-chain molecules behind her. What word would convey the idea of chemistry and physics taken as one subject?'

'*Sornhulva*,' Sachiko suggested. 'If *hulva's* something like science, *sorn* must mean matter, or substance, or physical object. You were right, all along, Martha. A civilization like this would certainly leave something like this, that would be self-explanatory.'

'This'll wipe a little more of that superior grin off Tony Lattimer's face,' Fitzgerald was saying, as they went down the motionless escalator to the floor below. 'Tony wants to be a big shot. When you want to be a big shot, you can't bear the possibility of anybody else being a bigger big shot, and whoever makes a start on reading this language will be the biggest big shot archaeology ever saw.'

That was true. She hadn't thought of it, in that way, before, and now she tried not to think about it. She didn't want to be a big shot. She wanted to be able to read the Martian language, and find things out about the Martians.

Two escalators down, they came out on a mezzanine around a wide central hall on the street level, the floor forty feet below them and the ceiling forty feet above. Their lights picked out object after object below—a huge group of sculptured figures in the middle; some kind of a motor vehicle jacked up on trestles for repairs; things that looked like machine guns and auto-cannon; long tables, tops littered with a dust-covered miscellany; machinery; boxes and crates and containers.

They made their way down and walked among the clutter, missing a hundred things for every one they saw, until they found an escalator to the basement. There were three basements, one under another, until at last they stood at the bottom of the last escalator, on a bare concrete floor, swinging the portable floodlight over stacks of boxes and barrels and drums, and heaps of powdery dust. The boxes were plastic—nobody had ever found anything made of wood in the city—and the barrels and drums were of metal or glass or some glasslike substance. They were outwardly intact. The powdery heaps might have been anything organic, or anything containing fluid. Down here, where wind and dust could not reach, evaporation had been the only force of destruction after the minute life that caused putrefaction had vanished.

They found refrigeration rooms, too, and using Martha's ice axe and the pistol-like vibratool Sachiko carried on her belt, they pounded and pried one open, to find desiccated piles of what had been vegetables, and leathery chunks of meat. Samples of that stuff, rocketed up to the ship, would give a reliable estimate, by radio-carbon dating, of how long ago this building had been occupied. The refrigeration unit, radically different from anything their own culture had produced, had been electrically powered. Sachiko and Penrose, poking into it, found the switches still on; the machine had only ceased to function when the power-source, whatever that had been, had failed.

The middle basement had also been used, at least towards

the end, for storage; it was cut in half by a partition pierced by but one door. They took half an hour to force this, and were on the point of sending above for heavy equipment when it yielded enough for them to squeeze through. Fitzgerald, in the lead with the light, stopped short, looked around, and then gave a groan that came through his helmet-speaker like a foghorn.

'Oh, no! *No!*'

'What's the matter, Ivan?' Sachiko, entering behind him, asked anxiously.

He stepped aside. 'Look at it, Sachi! Are we going to have to do all that?'

Martha crowded through behind her friend and looked around, then stood motionless, dizzy with excitement. Books. Case on case of books, half an acre of cases, fifteen feet to the ceiling. Fitzgerald, and Penrose, who had pushed in behind her, were talking in rapid excitement; she only heard the sound of their voices, not their words. This must be the main stacks of the university library—the entire literature of the vanished race of Mars. In the centre, down an aisle between the cases, she could see the hollow square of the librarian's desk, and stairs and a dumb-waiter to the floor above.

She realized that she was walking forward, with the others, towards this. Sachiko was saying: 'I'm the lightest; let me go first.' She must be talking about the spidery metal stairs.

'I'd say they were safe,' Penrose answered. 'The trouble we've had with doors around here shows that the metal hasn't deteriorated.'

In the end, the Japanese girl led the way, more catlike than ever in her caution. The stairs were quite sound, in spite of their fragile appearance, and they all followed her. The floor above was a duplicate of the room they had entered, and seemed to contain about as many books. Rather than waste time forcing the door here, they returned to the middle basement and came up by the escalator down which they had originally descended.

The upper basement contained kitchens—electric stoves, some with pots and pans still on them—and a big room that must have been, originally, the students' dining room, though when last used it had been a workshop. As they expected, the library reading room was on the street-level floor, directly above the stacks. It seemed to have been converted into a sort of common living room for the building's last occupants. An adjoining auditorium had been made into a chemical works; there were vats and distillation apparatus, and a metal fractionating tower that extended through a hole knocked in the ceiling seventy feet above. A good deal of plastic furniture of the sort they had been finding everywhere in the city was stacked about, some of it broken up, apparently for reprocessing. The other rooms on the street floor seemed also to have been devoted to manufacturing and repair work; a considerable industry, along a number of lines, must have been carried on here for a long time after the university had ceased to function as such.

On the second floor, they found a museum; many of the exhibits remained, tantalizingly half-visible in grimed glass cases. There had been administrative offices there, too. The doors of most of them were closed, and they did not waste time trying to force them, but those that were open had been turned into living quarters. They made notes, and rough floor-plans, to guide them in future more thorough examination; it was almost noon before they had worked their way back to the seventh floor.

Selim von Ohlmhorst was in a room on the north side of the building, sketching the position of things before examining them and collecting them for removal. He had the floor checker-boarded with a grid of chalked lines, each numbered.

'We have everything on this floor photographed,' he said. 'I have three gangs—all the floodlights I have—sketching and making measurements. At the rate we're going, with time out for lunch, we'll be finished by the middle of the afternoon.'

'You've been working fast. Evidently you aren't being high-church about a "qualified archaeologist" entering rooms first,' Penrose commented.

'Ach, childishness!' the old man exclaimed impatiently. 'These officers of yours aren't fools. All of them have been to Intelligence School and Criminal Investigation School. Some of the most careful amateur archaeologists I ever knew were retired soldiers or policemen. But there isn't much work to be done. Most of the rooms are either empty or like this one—a few bits of furniture and broken trash and scraps of paper. Did you find anything down on the lower floors?'

'Well, yes,' Penrose said, a hint of mirth in his voice. 'What would you say, Martha?'

She started to tell Selim. The others, unable to restrain their excitement, broke in with interruptions. Von Ohlmhorst was staring in incredulous amazement.

'But this floor was looted almost clean, and the buildings we've entered before were all looted from the street level up,' he said, at length.

'The people who looted this one lived here,' Penrose replied. 'They had electric power to the last; we found refrigerators full of food, and stoves with the dinner still on them. They must have used the elevators to haul things down from the upper floor. The whole first floor was converted into workshops and laboratories. I think that this place must have been something like a monastery in the Dark Ages in Europe, or what such a monastery would have been like if the Dark Ages had followed the fall of a highly developed scientific civilization. For one thing, we found a lot of machine guns and light auto-cannon on the street level, and all the doors were barricaded. The people here were trying to keep a civilization running after the rest of the planet had gone back to barbarism; I suppose they'd have to fight off raids by the barbarians now and then.'

'You're not going to insist on making this building into expedition quarters, I hope, colonel?' von Ohlmhorst asked anxiously.

'Oh, no! This place is an archaeological treasure-house. More than that; from what I saw, our technicians can learn a lot, here. But you'd better get this floor cleaned up as soon as you can, though. I'll have the subsurface part, from the sixth floor down, airsealed. Then we'll put in oxygen generators and power units, and get a couple of elevators into service. For the floors above, we can use temporary airsealing floor by floor, and portable equipment; when we have things atmosphered and lighted and heated, you and Martha and Tony Lattimer can go to work systematically and in comfort, and I'll give you all the help I can spare from the other work. This is one of the biggest things we've found yet.'

Tony Lattimer and his companions came down to the seventh floor a little later.

'I don't get this, at all,' he began, as soon as he joined them. 'This building wasn't stripped the way the others were. Always, the procedure seems to have been to strip from the bottom up, but they seem to have stripped the top floors first, here. All but the very top. I found out what that conical thing is, by the way. It's a wind-rotor, and under it there's an electric generator. This building generated its own power.'

'What sort of condition are the generators in?' Penrose asked.

'Well, everything's full of dust that blew in under the rotor, of course, but it looks to be in pretty good shape. Hey, I'll bet that's it! They had power, so they used the elevators to haul stuff down. That's just what they did. Some of the floors above here don't seem to have been touched, though.' He paused momentarily; back of his oxy-mask, he seemed to be grinning. 'I don't know that I ought to mention this in front of Martha, but two floors above we hit a room—it must have been the reference library for one of the departments—that had close to five hundred books in it.'

The noise that interrupted him, like the squawking of a Brobdingnagian parrot, was only Ivan Fitzgerald laughing through his helmet-speaker.

Lunch at the huts was a hasty meal, with a gabble of full-mouthed and excited talking. Hubert Penrose and his chief subordinates snatched their food in a huddled consultation at one end of the table; in the afternoon, work was suspended on everything else and the fifty-odd men and women of the expedition concentrated their efforts on the university. By the middle of the afternoon, the seventh floor had been completely examined, photographed and sketched, and the murals in the square central hall covered with protective tarpaulins, and Laurent Gicquel and his airsealing crew had moved in and were at work. It had been decided to seal the central hall at the entrances. It took the French-Canadian engineer most of the afternoon to find all the ventilation-ducts and plug them. An elevator-shaft on the north side was found reaching clear to the twenty-fifth floor; this would give access to the top of the building; another shaft, from the centre, would take care of the floors below. Nobody seemed willing to trust the ancient elevators, themselves; it was the next evening before a couple of cars and the necessary machinery could be fabricated in the machine shops aboard the ship and sent down by landing-rocket. By that time, the airsealing was finished, the nuclear-electric energy-converters were in place, and the oxygen generators set up.

Martha was in the lower basement, an hour or so before lunch the day after, when a couple of Space Force officers came out of the elevator, bringing extra lights with them. She was still using oxygen-equipment; it was a moment before she realized that the newcomers had no masks, and that one of them was smoking. She took off her own helmet-speaker, throat-mike and mask and unslung her tank-pack, breathing cautiously. The air was chilly, and musty-acrid with the odour of antiquity—the first Martian odour she had smelled—but when she lit a cigarette, the lighter flamed clear and steady and the tobacco caught and burned evenly.

The archaeologists, many of the other civilian scientists, a few of the Space Force officers and the two news-correspondents, Sid Chamberlain and Gloria Standish, moved in that evening, setting up cots in vacant rooms. They installed electric stoves and a refrigerator in the old library reading room, and put in a bar and lunch counter. For a few days, the place was full of noise and activity, then, gradually, the Space Force people and all but a few of the civilians returned to their own work. There was still the business of airsealing the more habitable of the buildings already explored, and fitting them up in readiness for the arrival, in a year and a half, of the five hundred members of the main expedition. There was work to be done enlarging the landing field for the ship's rocket craft, and building new chemical-fuel tanks.

There was the work of getting the city's ancient reservoirs cleared of silt before the next spring thaw brought more water down the underground aquaducts everybody called canals in mistranslation of Schiaparelli's Italian word, though this was proving considerably easier than anticipated. The ancient Canal Builders must have anticipated a time when their descendants would no longer be capable of maintenance work, and had prepared against it. By the day after the university had been made completely habitable, the actual work there was being done by Selim, Tony Lattimer and herself, with half a dozen Space Force officers, mostly girls, and four or five civilians, helping.

They worked up from the bottom, dividing the floor-surfaces into numbered squares, measuring and listing and sketching and photographing. They packaged samples of organic matter and sent them up to the ship for carbon-14 dating and analysis; they opened cans and jars and bottles, and found that everything fluid in them had evaporated, through the porosity of glass and metal and plastic if there were no other way. Wherever they looked, they found evidence of activity suddenly suspended and never resumed. A vice with a bar of metal in it, half cut through and the hacksaw beside it. Pots and pans with hardened remains of food in them; a leathery cut of meat on a table, with the knife ready at hand. Toilet articles on washstands; unmade beds, the bedding ready to crumble at a touch but still retaining the impress of the sleeper's body; papers and writing materials on desks, as though the writer had got up, meaning to return and finish in a fifty-thousand-year-ago moment.

It worried her. Irrationally, she began to feel that the Martians had never left this place; that they were still around her, watching disapprovingly every time she picked up something they had laid down. They haunted her dreams, now, instead of their enigmatic writing. At first, everybody who had moved into the university had taken a separate room, happy to escape the crowding and lack of privacy of the huts. After a few nights, she was glad when Gloria Standish moved in with her, and accepted the newswoman's excuse that she felt lonely without somebody to talk to before falling asleep. Sachiko Koremitsu joined them the next evening, and before going to bed, the girl officer cleaned and oiled her pistol, remarking that she was afraid some rust may have got into it.

The others felt it, too. Selim von Ohlmhorst developed the habit of turning quickly and looking behind him, as though trying to surprise somebody or something that was stalking him. Tony Lattimer, having a drink at the bar that had been improvised from the librarian's desk in the reading room, set down his glass and swore.

'You know what this place is? It's an archaeological *Marie Celeste*!' he declared. 'It was occupied right up to the end—we've all seen the shifts these people used to keep a civilization going here—but what was the end? What happened to them? Where did they go?'

'You didn't expect them to be waiting out front, with a red carpet and a big banner, *Welcome Terrans*, did you, Tony?' Gloria Standish asked.

'No, of course not; they've all been dead for fifty thousand years. But if they were the last of the Martians, why haven't we found their bones, at least? Who buried them, after they were dead?' He looked at the glass, a bubble-thin goblet, found, with hundreds of others like it, in a closet above, as though debating with himself whether to have another drink. Then he voted in the affirmative and reached for the cocktail pitcher. 'And every door on the old ground level is either barred or barricaded from the inside. How did they get out? And why did they leave?'

The next day, at lunch, Sachiko Koremitsu had the answer to the second question. Four or five electrical engineers had come down by rocket from the ship, and she had been spending the morning with them, in oxy-masks, at the top of the building.

'Tony, I thought you said those generators were in good shape,' she began, catching sight of Lattimer. 'They aren't. They're in the most unholy mess I ever saw. What happened, up there, was that the supports of the wind-rotor gave way, and weight snapped the main shaft, and smashed everything under it.'

'Well, after fifty thousand years, you can expect something like that,' Lattimer retorted. 'When an archaeologist says something's in good shape, he doesn't necessarily mean it'll start as soon as you shove a switch in.'

'You didn't notice that it happened when the power was on, did you,' one of the engineers asked, nettled at Lattimer's tone. 'Well, it was. Everything's burned out or shorted or fused together; I saw one busbar eight inches across melted clean in two. It's a pity we didn't find things in good shape, even archaeologically speaking. I saw a lot of interesting things, things in advance of what we're using now. But it'll take a couple of years to get everything sorted out and figure what it looked like originally.'

'Did it look as though anybody'd made any attempt to fix it?' Martha asked.

Sachiko shook her head. 'They must have taken one look at it and given up. I don't believe there would have been any possible way to repair anything.'

'Well, that explains why they left. They needed electricity for lighting, and heating, and all their industrial equipment was electrical. They had a good life, here, with power; without it, this place wouldn't have been habitable.'

'Then why did they barricade everything from the inside, and how did they get out?' Lattimer wanted to know.

'To keep other people from breaking in and looting. Last man out probably barred the last door and slid down a rope from upstairs,' von Ohlmhorst suggested. 'This Houdini-trick doesn't worry me too much. We'll find about it eventually.'

'Yes, about the time Martha starts reading Martian,' Lattimer scoffed.

'That may be just when we'll find out,' von Ohlmhorst

replied seriously. 'It wouldn't surprise me if they left something in writing when they evacuated this place.'

'Are you really beginning to treat this pipe dream of hers as a serious possibility, Selim?' Lattimer demanded. 'I know, it would be a wonderful thing, but wonderful things don't happen just because they're wonderful. Only because they're possible, and this isn't. Let me quote that distinguished Hittitologist, Johannes Friedrich: "Nothing can be translated out of nothing." Or that later but not less distinguished Hittitologist, Selim von Ohlmhorst: "Where are you going to get your bilingual?"'

'Friedrich lived to see the Hittite language deciphered and read,' von Ohlmhorst reminded him.

'Yes, when they found Hittite-Assyrian bilinguals.' Lattimer measured a spoonful of coffee-powder into his cup and added hot water. 'Martha, you ought to know, better than anybody, how little chance you have. You've been working for years in the Indus Valley; how many words of Harappa have you or anybody else ever been able to read?'

'We never found a university, with a half-million-volume library, at Harappa or Mohenjo-Daro.'

'And, the first day we entered this building, we established meaning for several words,' Selim von Ohlmhorst added.

'And you've never found another meaningful word since,' Lattimer added. 'And you're only sure of general meaning, not specific meaning of word-elements, and you have a dozen different interpretations for each word.'

'We made a start,' von Ohlmhorst maintained. 'We have Grotefend's word for "king". But I'm going to be able to read some of those books, over there, if it takes me the rest of my life here. It probably will, anyhow.'

'You mean you've changed your mind about going home on the *Cyrano*?' Martha asked. 'You'll stay on here?'

The old man nodded. 'I can't leave this. There's too much to discover. The old dog will have to learn a lot of new tricks, but this is where my work will be, from now on.'

Lattimer was shocked. 'You're nuts!' he cried. 'You mean

you're going to throw away everything you've accomplished in Hittitology and start all over again here on Mars? Martha, if you've talked him into his crazy decision, you're a criminal!'

'Nobody talked me into anything,' von Ohlmhorst said roughly. 'And as for throwing away what I've accomplished in Hittitology, I don't know what the devil you're talking about. Everything I know about the Hittite Empire is published and available to anybody. Hittitology's like Egyptology; it's stopped being research and archaeology and become scholarship and history. And I'm not a scholar or a historian; I'm a pick-and-shovel field archaeologist—a highly skilled and specialized grave-robber and junk-picker—and there's more pick-and-shovel work on this planet than I could do in a hundred lifetimes. This is something new; I was a fool to think I could turn my back on it and go back to scribbling footnotes about Hittite kings.'

'You could have anything you wanted, in Hittitology. There are a dozen universities that'd sooner have you than a winning football team. But no! You have to be the top man in Martiology, too. You can't leave that for anybody else—' Lattimer shoved his chair back and got to his feet, leaving the table with an oath that was almost a sob of exasperation.

Maybe his feelings were too much for him. Maybe he realized, as Martha did, what he had betrayed. She sat, avoiding the eyes of the others, looking at the ceiling, as embarrassed as though Lattimer had flung something dirty on the table in front of them. Tony Lattimer had, desperately, wanted Selim to go home on the *Cyrano*. Martiology was a new field; if Selim entered it, he would bring with him the reputation he had already built in Hittitology, automatically stepping into the leading role that Lattimer had coveted for himself. Ivan Fitzgerald's words echoed back to her—when you want to be a big shot, you can't bear the possibility of anybody else being a bigger big shot. His derision of her own efforts became comprehensible, too. It wasn't that he was convinced that she would never learn to read the Martian language. He had been afraid that she would.

* * *

Ivan Fitzgerald finally isolated the germ that had caused the Finchley girl's undiagnosed illness. Shortly afterwards, the malady turned into a mild fever, from which she recovered. Nobody else seemed to have caught it. Fitzgerald was still trying to find out how the germ had been transmitted.

They found a globe of Mars, made when the city had been a seaport. They located the city, and learned that its name had been Kukan—or something with a similar vowel-consonant ratio. Immediately, Sid Chamberlain and Gloria Standish began giving their telecasts a Kukan dateline, and Hubert Penrose used the name in his official reports. They also found a Martian calendar; the year had been divided into ten more or less equal months, and one of them had been Doma. Another month was Nor, and that was a part of the name of the scientific journal Martha had found.

Bill Chandler, the zoologist, had been going deeper and deeper into the old sea bottom of Syrtis. Four hundred miles from Kukan, and at fifteen thousand feet lower altitude, he shot a bird. At least, it was a something with wings and what were almost but not quite feathers, though it was more reptilian than avian in general characteristics. He and Ivan Fitzgerald skinned and mounted it, and then dissected the carcass almost tissue by tissue. About seven-eighths of its body capacity was lungs; it certainly breathed air containing at least half enough oxygen to support human life, or five times as much as the air around Kukan.

That took the centre of interest away from archaeology, and started a new burst of activity. All the expedition's aircraft—four jetticopters and three wingless airdyne reconnaisance fighters—were thrown into intensified exploration of the lower sea bottoms, and the bio-science boys and girls were wild with excitement and making new discoveries on each flight.

The university was left to Selim and Martha and Tony Lattimer, the latter keeping to himself while she and the old Turco-German worked together. The civilian specialists in other fields, and the Space Force people who had been holding tape lines and making sketches and snapping cameras, were all flying to lower Syrtis to find out how much oxygen there was and what kind of life it supported.

Sometimes Sachiko dropped in; most of the time she was busy helping Ivan Fitzgerald dissect specimens. They had four or five species of what might loosely be called birds, and something that could easily be classed as a reptile, and a carnivorous mammal the size of a cat with birdlike claws, and a herbivore almost identical with the piglike thing in the big *Darfhulva* mural, and another like a gazelle with a single horn in the middle of its forehead.

The high point came when one party, at thirty thousand feet below the level of Kukan, found breathable air. One of them had a mild attack of *sorroche* and had to be flown back for treatment in a hurry, but the others showed no ill effects.

The daily newscasts from Terra showed a corresponding shift in interest at home. The discovery of the university had focused attention on the dead past of Mars; now the public was interested in Mars as a possible home for humanity. It was Tony Lattimer who brought archaeology back into the activities of the expedition and the news at home.

Martha and Selim were working in the museum on the second floor, scrubbing the grime from the glass cases, noting contents, and grease-pencilling numbers; Lattimer and a couple of Space Force officers were going through what had been the administrative offices on the other side. It was one of these, a young second lieutenant, who came hurrying in from the mezzanine, almost bursting with excitement.

'Hey, Martha! Dr. von Ohlmhorst!' he was shouting. 'Where are you? Tony's found the Martians!'

Selim dropped his rag back in the bucket; she laid her clipboard on top of the case beside her.

'Where?' they asked together.

'Over on the north side.' The lieutenant took hold of himself and spoke more deliberately. 'Little room, back of one of the old faculty offices—conference room. It was locked from the inside, and we had to burn it down with a torch. That's where they are. Eighteen of them, around a long table—'

Gloria Standish, who had dropped in for lunch, was on the mezzanine, fairly screaming into a radio-phone extension:

'... Dozen and a half of them! Well, of course they're dead. What a question! They look like skeletons covered with leather. No, I do not know what they died of. Well, forget it; I don't care if Bill Chandler's found a three-headed hippopotamus. Sid, don't you get it? We've found the *Martians*!'

She slammed the phone back on its hook, rushing away ahead of them.

Martha remembered the closed door; on the first survey, they hadn't attempted opening it. Now it was burned away at both sides and lay, still hot along the edges, on the floor of the big office room in front. A floodlight was on in the room inside, and Lattimer was going around looking at things while a Space Force officer stood by the door. The centre of the room was filled by a long table; in armchairs around it sat the eighteen men and women who had occupied the room for the last fifty millennia. There were bottles and glasses on the table in front of them, and, had she seen them in a dimmer light, she would have thought that they were merely dozing over their drinks. One had a knee hooked over his chair-arm and was curled in foetus-like sleep. Another had fallen forward on to the table, arms extended, the emerald set of a ring twinkling dully on one finger. Skeletons covered with leather, Gloria Standish had called them, and so they were—faces like skulls, arms and legs like sticks, the flesh shrunken on to the bones under it.

'Isn't this something!' Lattimer was exulting. 'Mass suicide, that's what it was. Notice what's in the corners?'

Braziers, made of perforated two-gallon-odd metal cans, the white walls smudged with smoke above them. Von Ohlmhorst had noticed them at once, and was poking into one of them with his flashlight.

'Yes; charcoal. I noticed a quantity of it around a couple of hand-forges in the shop on the first floor. That's why you had so much trouble breaking in; they'd sealed the room on the inside.' He straightened and went around the room, until he found a ventilator, and peered into it. 'Stuffed with rags. They must have been all that were left, here. Their power was gone, and they were old and tired, and all around them their world was dying. So they just came in here and lit the charcoal, and sat drinking together till they all fell asleep. Well, we know what became of them, now, anyhow.'

Sid and Gloria made the most of it. The Terran public wanted to hear about Martians, and if live Martians couldn't be found, a room full of dead ones was the next best thing. Maybe an even better thing; it had been only sixty-odd years since the Orson Welles invasion-scare. Tony Lattimer, the discoverer, was beginning to cash in on his attentions to Gloria and his ingratiation with Sid; he was always either making voice-and-image talks for telecast or listening to the news from the home planet. Without question, he had become, overnight, the most widely known archaeologist in history.

'Not that I'm interested in all this, for myself,' he disclaimed, after listening to the telecast from Terra two days after his discovery. 'But this is going to be a big thing for Martian archaeology. Bring it to the public attention; dramatize it. Selim, can you remember when Lord Carnarvon and Howard Carter found the tomb of Tutankhamen?'

'In 1923? I was two years old, then,' von Ohlmhorst chuckled. 'I really don't know how much that publicity ever did for Egyptology. Oh, the museums did devote more space to Egyptian exhibits, and after a museum department head gets a few extra showcases, you know how hard it is to make him give them up. And, for a while, it was easier to get financial support for new excavations. But I don't know how much good all this public excitement really does, in the long run.'

'Well, I think one of us should go back on the *Cyrano*, when the *Schiaparelli* orbits in,' Lattimer said. 'I'd hoped it would be you; your voice would carry the most weight. But I think it's important that one of us go back, to present the story of our work, and what we have accomplished and what we hope to accomplish, to the public and to the universities and the learned societies, and to the Federation Government. There will be a great deal of work that will have to be done. We must not allow the other scientific fields and the so-called practical interests to monopolize public and academic support. So, I believe I shall go back at least for a while, and see what I can do—'

Lectures. The organization of a Society of Martian Archaeology, with Anthony Lattimer, Ph.D., the logical candidate for the chair. Degrees, honours; the deference of the learned, and the adulation of the lay public. Positions, with impressive titles and salaries. Sweet are the uses of publicity.

She crushed out her cigarette and got to her feet. 'Well, I still have the final lists of what we found in *Halvhulva*—Biology—Department to check over. I'm starting on Sornhulva tomorrow, and I want that stuff in shape for expert evaluation.'

That was the sort of thing Tony Lattimer wanted to get away from, the detail-work and the drudgery. Let the infantry do the slogging through the mud; the brass-hats got the medals.

She was halfway through the fifth floor, a week later, and was having midday lunch in the reading room on the first floor when Hubert Penrose came over and sat down beside her, asking her what she was doing. She told him.

'I wonder if you could find me a couple of men, for an hour or so,' she added. 'I'm stopped by a couple of jammed doors at the central hall. Lecture room and library, if the layout of that floor's anything like the ones below it.'

'Yes. I'm a pretty fair door-buster, myself.' He looked around the room. 'There's Jeff Miles; he isn't doing much of anything. And we'll put Sid Chamberlain to work, for a change, too. The four of us ought to get your doors open.' He called to Chamberlain, who was carrying his tray over to the dishwasher. 'Oh, Sid; you doing anything for the next hour or so?'

'I was going up to the fourth floor, to see what Tony's doing.'

'Forget it. Tony's bagged his season limit of Martians. I'm going to help Martha bust in a couple of doors; we'll probably find a whole cemetery full of Martians.'

Chamberlain shrugged. 'Why not. A jammed door can have

anything back of it, and I know what Tony's doing—just routine stuff.'

Jeff Miles, the Space Force captain, came over, accompanied by one of the lab-crew from the ship who had come down on the rocket the day before.

'This ought to be up your alley, Mort,' he was saying to his companion. 'Chemistry and Physics Department. Want to come along?'

The lab man, Mort Tranter, was willing. Seeing the sights was what he'd come down from the ship for. She finished her coffee and cigarette, and they went out into the hall together, gathered equipment and rode the elevator to the fifth floor.

The lecture hall door was the nearest; they attacked it first. With proper equipment and help, it was no problem and in ten minutes they had it open wide enough to squeeze through with the floodlights. The room inside was quite empty, and, like most of the rooms behind closed doors, comparatively free from dust. The students, it appeared, had sat with their backs to the door, facing a low platform, but their seats and the lecturer's table and equipment had been removed. The two side walls bore inscriptions: on the right, a pattern of concentric circles which she recognized as a diagram of atomic structure, and on the left a complicated table of numbers and words, in two columns. Tranter was pointing at the diagram on the right.

'They got as far as the Bohr atom, anyhow,' he said. 'Well, not quite. They knew about electron shells, but they have the nucleus pictured as a solid mass. No indication of proton-and-neutron structure. I'll bet, when you come to translate their scientific books, you'll find that they taught that the atom was the ultimate and indivisible particle. That explains why you people never found any evidence that the Martians used nuclear energy.'

'That's a uranium atom,' Captain Miles mentioned.

'It is?' Sid Chamberlain asked, excitedly. 'Then they did know about atomic energy. Just because we haven't found any pictures of A-bomb mushrooms doesn't mean—'

She turned to look at the other wall. Sid's signal reactions were getting away from him again; uranium meant nuclear power to him, and the two words were interchangeable. As she studied the arrangement of the numbers and words, she could hear Tranter saying:

'Nuts, Sid. We knew about uranium a long time before anybody found out what could be done with it. Uranium was discovered on Terra in 1789, by Klaproth.'

There was something familiar about the table on the left wall. She tried to remember what she had been taught in school about physics, and what she had picked up by accident afterwards. The second column was a continuation of the first: there were forty-six items in each, each item numbered consecutively—

'Probably used uranium because it's the largest of the natural atoms,' Penrose was saying. 'The fact that there's nothing beyond it there shows that they hadn't created any of the transuranics. A student could go to that thing and point out the outer electron of any of the ninety-two elements.'

Ninety-two! That was it: there were ninety-two items in the table on the left wall! Hydrogen was Number One, she knew; One, *Sarfaldsorn*. Helium was Two; that was *Tirfaldsorn*. She couldn't remember which element came next, but in Martian it was *Sarfalddavas*. *Sorn* must mean matter, or substance, then. And *davas*; she was trying to think of what it could be. She turned quickly to the others, catching hold of Hubert Penrose's arm with one hand and waving her clipboard with the other.

'Look at this thing, over here,' she was clamouring excitedly. 'Tell me what you think it is. Could it be a table of the elements?'

They all turned to look. Mort Tranter stared at it for a moment.

'Could be. If I only knew what those squiggles meant—'

That was right; he'd spent his time aboard the ship.

'If you could read the numbers, would that help?' she asked, beginning to set down the Arabic digits and their Martian equivalents. 'It's decimal system, the same as we use.'

'Sure. If that's a table of elements, all I'd need would be the numbers. Thanks,’ he added as she tore off the sheet and gave it to him.

Penrose knew the numbers, and was ahead of him. ‘Ninety-two items, numbered consecutively. The first number would be the atomic number. Then a single word, the name of the element. Then the atomic weight—’

She began reading off the names of the elements. ‘I know hydrogen and helium; what’s *tirfalddavas*, the third one?’

‘Lithium,’ Tranter said. ‘The atomic weights aren’t run out past the decimal point. Hydrogen’s one plus, if that double-hook dingus is a plus sign; Helium’s four-plus, that’s right. And lithium’s given as seven, that isn’t right. It’s six-point-nine-four-oh. Or is that thing a Martian minus sign?’

‘Of course! Look! A plus sign is a hook, to hang things together; a minus sign is a knife, to cut something off from something—see, the little loop is the handle and the long pointed loop is the blade. Stylized, of course, but that’s what it is. And the fourth element, *kiradavas*; what’s that?’

‘Beryllium. Atomic weight given as nine-and-a-hook; actually it’s nine-point-oh-two.’

Sid Chamberlain had been disgruntled because he couldn’t get a story about the Martians having developed atomic energy. It took him a few minutes to understand the newest development, but finally it dawned on him.

‘Hey! You’re reading that!’ he cried. ‘You’re reading Martian!’

‘That’s right,’ Penrose told him. ‘Just reading it right off. I don’t get the two items after the atomic weight, though. They look like months of the Martian calendar. What ought they to be, Mort?’

Tranter hesitated. ‘Well, the next information after the atomic weight ought to be the period and group numbers. But those are words.’

‘What would the numbers be for the first one, hydrogen?’

‘Period One, Group One. One electron shell, one electron in the outer shell,’ Tranter told her. ‘Helium’s period one, too, but it has the outer—only—electron shell full, so it's in the group of inert elements.'

'*Trav, Trav. Trav's* the first month of the year. And helium's *Trav, Yenth; Yenth* is the eighth month.'

'The inert elements could be called Group Eight, yes. And the third element, lithium, is Period Two, Group One. That check?'

'It certainly does. *Sanv, Trav; Sanv's* the second month. What's the first element in Period Three?'

'Sodium, Number Eleven.'

'That's right; it's *Krav, Trav*. Why, the names of the months are simply numbers, one to ten, spelled out.'

'*Doma's* the fifth month. That was your first Martian word, Martha,' Penrose told her. 'The word for five. And if *davas* is the word for metal, and *sornhulva* is chemistry and/or physics, I'll bet *Tadavas Sornhulva* is literally translated as: 'Of-Metal Matter-Knowledge.' Metallurgy, in other words. I wonder what *Mastharnorvod* means.' It surprised her that, after so long and with so much happening in the meantime, he could remember that. 'Something like "Journal", or "Review", or maybe "Quarterly".'

'We'll work that out, too,' she said confidently. After this, nothing seemed impossible. 'Maybe we can find—' Then she stopped short. 'You said "Quarterly", I think it was "Monthly", instead. It was dated for a specific month, the fifth one. And if *nor* is ten, *Mastharnorvod* could be "Year-Tenth". And I'll bet we'll find that *masthar* is the word for year.' She looked at the table on the wall again. 'Well, let's get all these words down, with translations for as many as we can.'

'Let's take a break for a minute,' Penrose suggested, getting out his cigarettes. 'And then, let's do this in comfort. Jeff, suppose you and Sid go across the hall and see what you find in the other room in the way of a desk or something like that, and a few chairs. There'll be a lot of work to do on this.'

Sid Chamberlain had been squirming as though he were afflicted with ants, trying to contain himself. Now he let go with an excited jabber.

'This is really it! *The* it, not just it-of-the-week, like finding the reservoirs or those statues or this building, or even the animals and the dead Martians! Wait till Selim and Tony see this! Wait till Tony sees it; I want to see his face! And when I get this on telecast, all Terra's going to go nuts about it!' He turned to Captain Miles. 'Jeff, suppose you take a look at that other door, while I find somebody to send to tell Selim and Tony. And Gloria; wait till she sees this—'

'Take it easy, Sid,' Martha cautioned. 'You'd better let me have a look at your script, before you go too far overboard on the telecast. This is just a beginning; it'll take years and years before we're able to read any of those books downstairs.'

'It'll go faster than you think, Martha,' Hubert Penrose told her. 'We'll all work on it, and we'll teleprint material to Terra, and people there will work on it. We'll send them everything we can ... everything we work out, and copies of books, and copies of your word-lists—'

And there would be other tables—astronomical tables, tables in physics and mechanics, for instance—in which words and numbers were equivalent. The library stacks, below, would be full of them. Transliterate them into Roman alphabet spellings and Arabic numerals, and somewhere, somebody would spot each numerical significance, as Hubert Penrose and Mort Tranter and she had done with the table of elements. And pick out all the chemistry textbooks in the library; new words would take on meaning from contexts in which the names of elements appeared. She'd have to start studying chemistry and physics, herself—

Sachiko Koremitsu peeped in through the door, then stepped inside.

'Is there anything I can do—?' she began. 'What's happened? Something important?'

'Important?' Sid Chamberlain exploded. 'Look at that, Sachi! We're reading it! Martha's found out how to read Martian!' He grabbed Captain Miles by the arm. 'Come on, Jeff; let's go.

I want to call the others—' He was still babbling as he hurried from the room.

Sachi looked at the inscription. 'Is it true?' she asked, and then, before Martha could more than begin to explain, flung her arms around her. 'Oh, it really is! You are reading it! I'm so happy!'

She had to start explaining again when Selim von Ohlmhorst entered. This time, she was able to finish.

'But, Martha, can you be really sure? You know, by now, that learning to read this language is as important to me as it is to you, but how can you be so sure that those words really mean things like hydrogen and helium and boron and oxygen? How do you know that their table of elements was anything like ours?'

Tranter and Penrose and Sachiko all looked at him in amazement.

'That isn't just the Martian table of elements; that's *the* table of elements. It's the only one there is,' Mort Tranter almost exploded. 'Look, hydrogen has one proton and one electron. If it had more of either, it wouldn't be hydrogen, it'd be something else. And the same with all the rest of the elements. And hydrogen on Mars is the same as hydrogen on Terra, or on Alpha Centauri, or in the next galaxy—'

'You just set up those numbers, in that order, and any first-year chemistry student could tell you what elements they represented,' Penrose said. 'Could if he expected to make a passing grade, that is.'

The old man shook his head, slowly, smiling. 'I'm afraid I wouldn't make a passing grade. I didn't know, or at least didn't realize, that. One of the things I'm going to place an order for, to be brought on the *Schiaparelli,* will be a set of primers in chemistry and physics, of the sort intended for a bright child of ten or twelve. It seems that a Martiologist has to learn a lot of things the Hittites and the Assyrians never heard about.'

Tony Lattimer, coming in, caught the last part of the explanation. He looked quickly at the walls and, having found out just what had happened, advanced and caught Martha by the hand.

'You really did it, Martha! You found your bilingual! I never believed that it would be possible; let me congratulate you!'

He probably expected that to erase all the jibes and sneers of the past. If he did, he could have it that way. His friendship would mean as little to her as his derision—except that his friends had to watch their backs and his knife. But he was going home on the *Cyrano*, to be a big shot. Or had this changed his mind for him again?

'This is something we can show the world, to justify any expenditure of time and money on Martian archaeological work. When I get back to Terra, I'll see that you're given full credit for this achievement—'

On Terra, her back and his knife would be out of her watchfulness.

'We won't need to wait that long,' Hubert Penrose told him dryly. 'I'm sending off an official report, tomorrow; you can be sure Dr. Dane will be given full credit, not only for this but for her previous work, which made it possible to exploit this discovery.'

'And you might add, work done in spite of the doubts and discouragements of her colleagues,' Selim von Ohlmhorst said. 'To which I am ashamed to have to confess my own share.'

'You said we had to find a bilingual,' she said. 'You were right, too.'

'This is better than a bilingual, Martha,' Hubert Penrose said. 'Physical science expresses universal facts; necessarily it is a universal language. Heretofore archaeologists have dealt only with pre-scientific cultures.'

OMNILINGUAL

In the 1870s, thin, long markings were observed on Mars which, from their straightness, seemed sure to be artificial. They were called 'canals' and many people (including professional astronomers) felt they were the artifacts of a high civilization trying to survive the gradual desiccation of the small planet.

Science fiction writers seized upon this and for half a century there were innumerable stories of civilizations on Mars, usually slowly dying, sometimes malevolent.

Twentieth-century studies of Mars made this all seem increasingly unlikely. Few astronomers could actually make out the canals and the opinion grew more common that they were optical illusions; that the eye made straight lines out of barely visible irregular markings. The atmosphere seemed very thin indeed and it was difficult to detect water or free oxygen.

Even so, as late as 1957, when *Omnilingual* was published there was still some faint reason to hope for life on Mars.

Since then, however, unmanned probes have skimmed past Mars and taken photographs and made measurements. The atmosphere is thinner than the most pessimistic earlier estimates had made it appear and there are no canals. There are numerous craters and the state of weathering would seem to indicate that the atmosphere has been this thin for many millions of years. What's more, there is no free oxygen and the atmosphere, what there is of it, seems to be entirely or almost entirely carbon dioxide.

Then, too, the temperature seems lower than had been thought and the polar ice caps on Mars, which had been thought to be frozen water, now seem more likely to be frozen carbon dioxide.

It seems quite unlikely, therefore, that there is, or ever was, intelligent life on Mars; and it is even increasingly doubtful that there is life of any sort.

Piper's speculations would seem to be quite wrong, therefore. He not only assumed intelligent life almost at the level of our own but had it existing as late as 50,000 years ago. What's more, he had the Martian atmosphere dense enough to support a flying creature, and had it contain enough oxygen to support it chemically as well as mechanically. (He did, however, make its internal organs mostly lung.)

But then, one unlikely, or even impossible assumption, is allowed to start a science fiction story, and Piper's purpose was to tackle the problem of an unknown language—as unknown as possible—and its decipherment. That intention he fulfilled admirably.

Questions and Suggestions

1. The decipherment of numerous unknown languages are mentioned in the story. Look up the story of the decipherment of Egyptian hieroglyphics and Babylonian cuneiform and decide what made the decipherment possible.

2. Why are the two ships in the story named *Schiaparelli* and *Cyrano*?

3. What is the meaning of *Omnilingual*? Is it reasonable to use that adjective to describe the periodic table of the elements? If so, why? Could any ancient languages have been deciphered through omnilingual inscriptions? Can omnilingual situations arise in a non-technological civilization?

4. Do you think a civilization can develop and reach a high state of technology, yet do so without duplicating any of our theories, and without ever working out the periodic table of the elements, for instance? Or, having worked it out, might an alien civilization represent the table in such a way as to have it unrecognizable? In other words, is intelligence intelligence, or are there different kinds that can be mutually incomprehensible?

5. What is the periodic table of the elements, by the way?

16. The Big Bounce

Walter S. Tevis

'Let me show you something,' Farnsworth said. He set his near-empty drink—a Bacardi Martini—on the mantel and waddled out of the room towards the basement.

I sat in my big leather chair, feeling very peaceful with the world, watching the fire. Whatever Farnsworth would have to show tonight would be far more entertaining than watching TV—my custom on other evenings. Farnsworth, with his four labs in the house and his very tricky mind, never failed to provide my best night of the week.

When he returned, after a moment, he had with him a small box, about three inches square. He held this carefully in one hand and stood by the fireplace dramatically—or as dramatically as a very small, very fat man with pink cheeks can stand by a fireplace of the sort that seems to demand a big man with tweeds, pipe and, perhaps, a sabre wound.

Anyway, he held the box dramatically and he said, 'Last week, I was playing around in the chem lab, trying to make a new kind of rubber eraser. Did quite well with the other drafting equipment, you know, especially the dimensional curve and the photo-sensitive ink. Well, I approached the job by trying for a material that would absorb graphite without abrading paper.'

I was a little disappointed with this; it sounded pretty tame. But I said, 'How did it come out?'

He screwed his pudgy face up thoughtfully. 'Synthesized the material, all right, and it seems to work, but the interesting thing is that it has a certain—ah—secondary property that would make it quite awkward to use. Interesting property, though. Unique, I am inclined to believe.'

This began to sound more like it. 'And what property is that?' I poured myself a shot of straight rum from the bottle sitting on the table beside me. I did not like straight rum, but I preferred it to Farnsworth's rather imaginative cocktails.

'I'll show you, John,' he said. He opened the box and I could see that it was packed with some kind of batting. He fished in this and withdrew a grey ball about the size of a golfball and set the box on the mantel.

'And that's the—eraser?' I asked.

'Yes,' he said. Then he squatted down, held the ball about a half inch from the floor, dropped it.

It bounced, naturally enough. Then it bounced again. And again. Only this was not natural, for on the second bounce the ball went higher in the air than on the first, and on the third bounce higher still. After a half minute, my eyes were bugging out and the little ball was bouncing four feet in the air and going higher each time.

I grabbed my glass. 'What the hell!' I said.

Farnsworth caught the ball in a pudgy hand and held it. He was smiling a little sheepishly. 'Interesting effect, isn't it?'

'Now wait a minute,' I said, beginning to think about it. 'What's the gimmick? What kind of motor do you have in that thing?'

His eyes were wide and a little hurt. 'No gimmick, John. None at all. Just a very peculiar molecular structure.'

'Structure!' I said. 'Bouncing balls just don't pick up energy out of nowhere, I don't care how their molecules are put together. And you don't get energy out without putting energy in.'

'Oh,' he said, 'that's the really interesting thing. Of course you're right; energy *does* go into the ball. Here, I'll show you.'

He let the ball drop again and it began bouncing, higher and higher, until it was hitting the ceiling. Farnsworth reached out to catch it, but he fumbled and the thing glanced off his hand, hit the mantelpiece and zipped across the room. It banged into the far wall, ricocheted, banked off three other walls, picking up speed all the time.

When it whizzed by me like a rifle bullet, I began to get worried, but it hit against one of the heavy draperies by the window and this damped its motion enough so that it fell to the floor.

It started bouncing again immediately, but Farnsworth scrambled across the room and grabbed it. He was perspiring a little and he began instantly to transfer the ball from one hand to another and back again as if it were hot.

'Here,' he said, and handed it to me.

I almost dropped it.

'It's like a ball of ice!' I said. 'Have you been keeping it in the refrigerator?'

'No. As a matter of fact, it was at room temperature a few minutes ago.'

'Now wait a minute,' I said. 'I only teach physics in high school, but I know better than that. Moving around in warm air doesn't make anything cold except by evaporation.'

'Well, there's your input and output, John,' he said. 'The ball lost heat and took on motion. Simple conversion.'

My jaw must have dropped to my waist. 'Do you mean that that little thing is converting heat to kinetic energy?'

'Apparently.'

'But that's impossible!'

He was beginning to smile thoughtfully. The ball was not as cold now as it had been and I was holding it in my lap.

'A steam engine does it,' he said, 'and a steam turbine. Of course, they're not very efficient.'

'They work mechanically, too, and only because water expands when it turns to steam.'

'This seems to do it differently,' he said, sipping thoughtfully at his dark-brown Martini. 'I don't know exactly how—maybe something piezo-electric about the way its molecules slide about. I ran some tests—measured its impact energy in foot pounds and compared that with the heat loss in BTUs. Seemed to be about 98 per cent efficient, as close as I could tell. Apparently it converts heat into bounce very well. Interesting, isn't it?'

'*Interesting?*' I almost came flying out of my chair. My mind was beginning to spin like crazy. 'If you're not pulling my leg with this thing, Farnsworth, you've got something by the tail there that's just a little bit bigger than the discovery of fire.'

He blushed modestly. 'I'd rather thought that myself,' he admitted.

'Good Lord, look at the heat that's available!' I said, getting really excited now.

Farnsworth was still smiling, very pleased with himself. 'I suppose you could put this thing in a box, with convection fins, and let it bounce around inside—'

'I'm away ahead of you,' I said. 'But that wouldn't work. All your kinetic energy would go right back to heat, on impact—and eventually that little ball would build up enough speed to blast its way through any box you could build.'

'Then how would you work it?'

'Well,' I said, choking down the rest of my rum, 'you'd seal the ball in a big steel cylinder, attach the cylinder to a crankshaft and flywheel, give the thing a shake to start the ball bouncing back and forth, and let it run like a gasoline engine or something. It would get all the heat it needed from the air in a normal room. Mount the apparatus in your house and it would pump your water, operate a generator and keep you cool at the same time!'

I sat down again, shakily, and began pouring myself another drink.

Farnsworth had taken the ball from me and was carefully putting it back in its padded box. He was visibly showing excitement, too; I could see that his cheeks were ruddier and his eyes even brighter than normal. 'But what if you want the cooling and don't have any work to be done?'

'Simple,' I said. 'You just let the machine turn a flywheel or lift weights and drop them, or something like that, outside your house. You have an air intake inside. And if in the winter, you don't want to lose heat, you just mount the thing in an outside building, attach it to your generator and use the power to do whatever you want—heat your house, say. There's plenty of heat in the outside air even in December.'

'John,' said Farnsworth, 'you are very ingenious. It might work.'

'Of course it'll work.' Pictures were beginning to light up in my head. 'And don't you realize that this is the answer to the solar power problem? Why, mirrors and selenium are, at best, ten per cent efficient! Think of big pumping stations on the Sahara! All that heat, all that need for power, for irrigation!' I paused a moment for effect. 'Farnsworth, this can change the very shape of the Earth!'

Farnsworth seemed to be lost in thought. Finally he looked at me strangely and said, 'Perhaps we had better try to build a model.'

I was so excited by the thing that I couldn't sleep that night. I kept dreaming of power stations, ocean liners, even automobiles, being operated by balls bouncing back and forth in cylinders.

I even worked out a spaceship in my mind, a bullet-shaped affair with a huge rubber ball on its end, gyrscopes to keep it oriented properly, the ball serving as solution to that biggest of missile-engineering problems, excess heat. You'd built a huge concrete launching field, supported all the way down to bedrock, hop in the ship and start bouncing. Of course it would be kind of a rough ride ...

In the morning, I called my superintendent and told him to get a substitute for the rest of the week; I was going to be busy.

Then I started working in the machine shop in Farnsworth's basement, trying to turn out a working model of a device that, by means of a crankshaft, oleo dampers and a reciprocating cylinder, would pick up some of that random kinetic energy from the bouncing ball and do something useful with it, like turning a drive shaft. I was just working out a convection-and-air-pump system for circulating hot air around the ball when Farnsworth came in.

He had tucked carefully under his arm a sphere of about the size of a basketball and, if he had made it to my specifications, weighing thirty-five pounds. He had a worried frown on his forehead.

'It looks good,' I said. 'What's the trouble?'

'There seems to be a slight hitch,' he said. 'I've been testing for conductivity. It seems to be quite low.'

'That's what I'm working on now. It's just a mechanical problem of pumping enough warm air back to the ball. We can do it with no more than a twenty per cent efficiency loss. In an engine, that's nothing.'

'Maybe you're right. But this material conducts heat even less than rubber does.'

'The little ball yesterday didn't seem to have any trouble,' I said.

'Naturally not. It had had plenty of time to warm up before I started it. And its mass-surface area relationship was pretty low—the larger you make a sphere, of course, the more mass inside in proportion to the outside area.'

'You're right, but I think we can whip it. We may have to honeycomb the ball and have part of the work the machine does operate a big hot air pump; but we can work it out.'

All that day, I worked with lathe, milling machine and hacksaw. After clamping the new big ball securely to a workbench, Farnsworth pitched in to help me. But we weren't able to finish by nightfall and Farnsworth turned his spare bedroom over to me for the night. I was too tired to go home.

And too tired to sleep soundly, too. Farnsworth lived on the edge of San Francisco, by a big truck by-pass, and almost all night I wrestled with the pillow and sheets, listening half-consciously to those heavy trucks rumbling by, and in my mind, always, that little grey ball, bouncing and bouncing and bouncing …

At daybreak, I came abruptly fully awake with the sound of crashing echoing in my ears, a battering sound that seemed to come from the basement. I grabbed my coat and pants, rushed out of the room, almost knocked over Farnsworth, who was struggling to get his shoes on out in the hall, and we scrambled down the two flights of stairs together.

The place was a chaos, battered and bashed equipment everywhere, and on the floor, overturned against the far wall, the table that the ball had been clamped to. The ball itself was gone.

I had not been fully asleep all night, and the sight of that mess, and what it meant, jolted me immediately awake. Something, probably a heavy truck, had started a tiny oscillation in that ball. And the ball had been heavy enough to start the table bouncing with it until, by dancing that table around the room, it had literally torn the clamp off and shaken itself free. What had happened afterwards was obvious, with the ball building up velocity with every successive bounce.

But where was the ball now?

Suddenly Farnsworth cried out hoarsely, 'Look!' and I followed his outstretched, pudgy finger to where, at one side of the basement, a window had been broken open—a small window, but plenty big enough for something the size of a basketball to crash through it.

There was a little weak light coming from outdoors. And then I saw the ball. It was in Farnsworth's back yard, bouncing a little sluggishly on the grass. The grass would damp it, hold it back, until we could get to it. Unless ...

I took off up the basement steps like a streak. Just beyond the back yard, I had caught a glimpse of something that frightened me. A few yards from where I had seen the ball was the edge of the big six-lane highway, a broad ribbon of smooth, hard concrete.

I got through the house to the back porch, rushed out and was in the back yard just in time to see the ball take its first bounce on to the concrete. I watched it, fascinated, when it hit—after the soft, energy absorbing turf, the concrete was like a springboard. Immediately the ball flew high in the air. I was running across the yard towards it, praying under my breath, *Fall on that grass next time.*

It hit before I got to it, and right on the concrete again, and this time I saw it go straight up at least fifty feet.

My mind was suddenly full of thoughts of dragging mattresses from the house, or making a net or something to stop that hurtling thirty-five pounds; but I stood where I was, unable to move, and saw it come down again on the highway. It went up a hundred feet. And down again on the concrete, about fifteen feet further down the road. In the direction of the city.

That time it was two hundred feet, and when it hit again, it made a thud that you could have heard for a quarter of a mile. I could practically see it flatten out on the road before it took off upward again, at twice the speed it had hit at.

Suddenly generating an idea, I whirled and ran back to Farnsworth's house. He was standing in the yard now, shivering from the morning air, looking at me like a little lost and badly scared child.

'Where are your car keys?' I almost shouted at him.

'In my pocket.'

'Come on!'

I took him by the arm and half dragged him to the carport. I got the keys from him, started the car, and by mangling about seven traffic laws and three prize rosebushes, managed to get on the highway, facing in the direction that the ball was heading.

'Look,' I said, trying to drive down the road and search for the ball at the same time. 'It's risky, but if I can get the car under it and we can hop out in time, it should crash through the roof. That ought to slow it down enough for us to nab it.'

'But—what about my car?' Farnsworth bleated.

'What about that first building—or first person—it hits in San Francisco?'

'Oh,' he said. 'Hadn't thought of that.'

I slowed the car and stuck my head out the window. It was lighter now, but no sign of the ball. 'If it happens to get to town—any town, for that matter—it'll be falling from about ten or twenty miles. Or forty.'

'Maybe it'll go high enough first so that it'll burn. Like a meteor.'

'No chance,' I said. 'Built-in cooling system, remember?'

Farnsworth formed his mouth into an 'Oh' and exactly at that moment there was a resounding thump and I saw the ball hit in a field, maybe twenty yards from the edge of the road, and take off again. This time it didn't seem to double its velocity, and I figured the ground was soft enough to hold it back—but it wasn't slowing down either, not with a bounce factor of better than two to one.

Without watching for it to go up, I drove as quickly as I could off the road and over—carrying part of a wire fence with me—to where it had hit. There was no mistaking it; there was a depression about three feet deep, like a small crater.

I jumped out of the car and stared up. It took me a few seconds to spot it, over my head. One side caught by the pale and slanting morning sunlight, it was only a bright diminishing speck.

The car motor was running and I waited until the ball disappeared for a moment and then reappeared. I watched for another couple of seconds until I felt I could make a decent guess on its direction, hollered at Farnsworth to get out of the car—it had just occurred to me that there was no use risking his life, too—dived in and drove a hundred yards or so to the spot I had anticipated.

I stuck my head out the window and up. The ball was the size of an egg now. I adjusted the car's position, jumped out and ran for my life.

It hit instantly after—about sixty feet from the car. And at the same time, it occurred to me that what I was trying to do was completely impossible. Better to hope that the ball hit a pond, or bounced out to sea, or landed in a sand dune. All we could do would be to follow, and if it ever was damped down enough, grab it.

It had hit soft ground and didn't double its height that time, but it had still gone higher. It was out of sight for almost a lifelong minute.

And then—incredibly rotten luck—it came down, with an ear-shattering thwack, on the concrete highway again. I had seen it hit, and instantly afterwards I saw a crack as wide as a finger open along the entire width of the road. And the ball had flown back up like a rocket.

My God, I was thinking, *now it means business. And on the next bounce ...*

It seemed like an incredibly long time that we craned our necks, Farnsworth and I, watching for it to reappear in the sky. And when it finally did, we could hardly follow it. It whistled like a bomb and we saw the grey streak come plummeting to earth almost a quarter of a mile away from where we were standing.

But we didn't see it go back up again.

For a moment, we stared at each other silently. Then Farnsworth almost whispered, 'Perhaps it's landed in a pond.'

'Or in the world's biggest cowpile,' I said. 'Come on!'

We could have met our deaths by rock salt and buckshot that day, if the farmer who owned that field had been home. We tore up everything we came to getting across it—including cabbages and rhubarb. But we had to search for ten minutes, and even then we didn't find the ball.

What we found was a hole in the ground that could have been a small-scale meteor crater. It was a good twenty feet deep. But at the bottom, no ball.

I stared wildly at it for a full minute before I focused my eyes enough to see, at the bottom, a thousand little grey fragments.

And immediately it came to both of us at the same time. A poor conductor, the ball had used up all its available heat on that final impact. Like a golfball that has been dipped in liquid air and dropped, it had smashed into thin splinters.

The hole had sloping sides and I scrambled down in it and picked up one of the pieces, using my handkerchief, folded—

there was no telling just how cold it would be.

It was the stuff, all right. And colder than an icicle.

I climbed out. 'Let's go home,' I said.

Farnsworth looked at me thoughtfully. Then he sort of cocked his head to one side and asked, 'What do you suppose will happen when those pieces thaw?'

I stared at him. I began to think of a thousand tiny slivers whizzing around erratically, ricocheting off buildings, in downtown San Francisco and in twenty counties, and no matter what they hit, moving and accelerating as long as there was any heat in the air to give them energy.

And then I saw a tool shed, on the other side of the pasture from us.

But Farnsworth was ahead of me, waddling along, puffing. He got the shovels out and handed one to me.

We didn't say a word, neither of us, for hours. It takes a long time to fill a hole twenty feet deep—especially when you're shovelling very, very carefully and packing down the dirt very, very hard.

THE BIG BOUNCE

Among the basic rules that seem to govern the workings of the universe are the first and second laws of thermodynamics. (There is also a third law of thermodynamics but it doesn't involve everyday life.)

Thermodynamics is the science involving the interchange of work and energy. The first law of thermodynamics can be stated as: 'Energy can neither be created nor destroyed, but can be changed from one form to another.' Another way of putting it is: 'The total amount of energy in the universe is constant.' Sometimes the first law of thermodynamics is called 'The law of conservation of energy' and it is probably *the* most basic and important scientific generalization.

The second law of thermodynamics is a lot harder to define clearly, but the simplest way of putting it is that: 'In every spontaneous change, the total amount of *usable* energy decreases.' Thus, there is a steady vast loss of usable energy in the universe even though the total quantity doesn't change, so that the universe is steadily running down.

Another way of phrasing the second law is to say that: 'The amount of disorder in the universe is constantly increasing.' Since the most disorderly form of energy is heat, there is a constant increase of heat at the expense of other forms of energy. To make it worse there is a constant levelling-out of the intensity of heat; that is the temperature of the universe generally is steadily becoming 'medium' at the expense of the very hot and very cold.

In *The Big Bounce*, we have a ball that moves higher with every bounce. It gains kinetic energy steadily, and kinetic energy is usable. Since usable energy is increasing with each bounce, the ball is defying the second law of thermodynamics.

This is impossible, of course. No ball, of whatever composition can gain energy and velocity and height with every bounce. We can be quite sure that Tevis knew it, too, but deliberately introduced this impossibility to start off his story and to demonstrate what an odd world we would live in if the second law could be violated.

Interestingly enough, he escapes from catastrophe by making use of the first law of thermodynamics, which he does *not* violate. If the ball gains energy with each bounce, where does that energy come from? If it came from nowhere, that would be a violation of the first law, so Tevis has it come from the heat content of the ball. The more energy of motion the ball gains, the colder it gets.

That, too, is a violation of the second law for the only way to convert heat into motion is to have two volumes of matter, one much hotter than the other, and allow them to come to intermediate temperature. In this way, some of the heat energy can be put to useful work at the expense of much more of the heat energy becoming more disorderly by evening out in temperature.

Questions and Suggestions

1. What is the stand of the U.S. Patent Office on 'perpetual motion' machines. All of these, incidentally, break either the first or the second laws of thermodynamics. Why?

2. The ocean has vast quantities of heat in it. Even a polar ocean does. Why do ocean vessels have to burn fuel? Why can't they just use the heat of the ocean water over which they pass?

3. In view of the first law of thermodynamics, where does the tremendous energy radiated by the Sun and all the other stars come from?

4. Look up the history of some perpetual motion machines designed in the past. What was the 'catch' in each case? Why wouldn't they work? Were some of them outright hoaxes?

5. The laws of thermodynamics are based on the general experience of scientists. They have never observed the laws to be broken. Scientists, however, merely observe their own section of the universe and their own general type of environment. What about outer space ten billion light-years away? What about the centre of the Sun? How sure can we be that scientific laws are the same everywhere under all conditions?

6. Suppose a scientist discovered some easily produced phenomenon which seemed to defy either the first or second law of thermodynamics? Should he assume at once there was some mistake and forget the whole thing? Should he instantly proclaim the phenomenon and declare the laws broken? What would *you* do?

17. Neutron Star

Larry Niven

I

The Skydiver dropped out of hyperspace an even million miles above the neutron star. I needed a minute to place myself against the stellar background and another to find the distortion Sonya Laskin had mentioned before she died. It was to my left, an area the apparent size of the Earth's moon. I swung the ship around to face it.

Curdled stars, muddled stars, stars that had been stirred with a spoon.

The neutron star was in the centre, of course, though I couldn't see it and hadn't expected to. It was only eleven miles across, and cool. A billion years had passed since BVS-1 burned by fusion fire. Millions of years, at least, since the cataclysmic two weeks during which BVS-1 was an X-ray star, burning at a temperature of five billion degrees Kelvin. Now it showed only by its mass.

The ship began to turn by itself. I felt the pressure of the fusion drive. Without help from me, my faithful metal watch-dog was putting me in hyperbolic orbit that would take me within one mile of the neutron star's surface. Twenty-four hours to fall, twenty-four hours to rise ... and during that time, something would try to kill me. As something had killed the Laskins.

The same type of autopilot, with the same programme, had chosen the Laskins's orbit. It had not caused their ship to collide with the star. I could trust the autopilot. I could even change its programme.

I really ought to.

How did I get myself into this hole?

The drive went off after ten minutes of manoeuvring. My orbit was established, in more ways than one. I knew what would happen if I tried to back out now.

All I'd done was walk into a drugstore to get a new battery for my lighter!

Right in the middle of the store, surrounded by three floors of sales counters, was the new 2603 Sinclair intrasystem yacht. I'd come for a battery, but I stayed to admire. It was a beautiful job, small and sleek and streamlined and blatantly different from anything that's ever been built. I wouldn't have flown it for anything, but I had to admit it was pretty. I ducked my head through the door to look at the control panel. You never saw so many dials. When I pulled my head out, all the customers were looking in the same direction. The place had gone startlingly quiet.

I can't blame them for staring. A number of aliens were in the store, mainly shopping for souvenirs, but they were staring too. A puppeteer is unique. Imagine a headless, three-legged centaur wearing two Cecil the Seasick Sea Serpent puppets on his arms, and you'll have something like the right picture. But the arms are weaving necks, and the puppets are real heads, flat and brainless, with wide flexible lips. The brain is under a bony hump set between the bases of the necks. This puppeteer wore only its own coat of brown hair, with a mane that extended all the way up its spine to form a thick mat over the brain. I'm told that the way they wear the mane indicates their status in society, but to me it could have been anything from a dock worker to a jeweller to the president of General Products.

I watched with the rest as it came across the floor, not because I'd never seen a puppeteer, but because there is something beautiful about the dainty way they move on those slender legs and tiny hooves. I watched it come straight towards me, closer and closer. It stopped a foot away, looked me over and said, 'You are Beowulf Shaeffer, former chief pilot for Nakamura Lines.'

Its voice was a beautiful contralto with not a trace of accent. A puppeteer's mouths are not only the most flexible speech organs around, but also the most sensitive hands. The tongues are forked and pointed, the wide, thick lips have little fingerlike knobs along the rims. Imagine a watchmaker with a sense of taste in his fingertips . . .

I cleared my throat. 'That's right.'

It considered me from two directions. 'You would be interested in a high-paying job?'

'I'd be fascinated in a high-paying job.'

'I am our equivalent of the regional president of General Products. Please come with me, and we will discuss this elsewhere.'

I followed it into a displacement booth. Eyes followed me all the way. It was embarrassing, being accosted in a public drugstore by a two-headed monster. Maybe the puppeteer knew it. Maybe it was testing me to see how badly I needed money.

My need was great. Eight months had passed since Nakamura Lines folded. For some time before that, I had been living very high on the hog, knowing that my back pay would cover my debts. I never saw that back pay. It was quite a crash, Nakamura Lines. Respectable middle-aged businessmen took to leaving their hotel windows without their life belts. Me, I kept spending. If I'd started living frugally, my creditors would have done some checking . . . and I'd have ended in debtor's prison.

The puppeteer dialled thirteen fast digits with its tongue. A moment later we were elsewhere. Air puffed out when I opened the booth door, and I swallowed to pop my ears.

'We are on the roof of the General Products building.' The rich contralto voice thrilled along my nerves, and I had to remind myself that it was an alien speaking, not a lovely woman. 'You must examine this spacecraft while we discuss your assignment.'

I stepped outside a little cautiously, but it wasn't the windy season. The roof was at ground level. That's the way we build on We Made It. Maybe it has something to do with the fifteen-hundred-mile-an-hour winds we get in summer and winter, when the planet's axis of rotation runs through its primary, Procyon. The winds are our planet's only tourist attraction, and it would be a shame to slow them down by planting skyscrapers in their path. The bare, square concrete roof was surrounded by endless square miles of desert, not like the deserts of other inhabited worlds, but an utterly lifeless expanse of fine sand just crying to be planted with ornamental cactus. We've tried that. The wind blows the plants away.

The ship lay on the sand beyond the roof. It was a #2 General Products hull: a cylinder three hundred feet long and twenty feet through, pointed at both ends and with a slight wasp-waist constriction near the tail. For some reason it was lying on its side, with the landing shocks still folded in at the tail.

Ever notice how all ships have begun to look the same? A good ninety-five per cent of today's spacecrafts are built around one of the four General Products hulls. It's easier and safer to build that way, but somehow all ships end as they began: mass-produced look-alikes.

The hulls are delivered fully transparent, and you use paint where you feel like it. Most of this particular hull had been left transparent. Only the nose had been painted, around the lifesystem. There was no major reaction drive. A series of retractable attitude jets had been mounted in the sides, and the hull was pierced with smaller holes, square and round—for observational instruments. I could see them gleaming through the hull.

The puppeteer was moving towards the nose, but something made me turn towards the stern for a closer look at the landing shocks.

They were bent. Behind the curved, transparent hull panels, some tremendous pressure had forced the metal to flow like warm wax, back and into the pointed stern.

'What did this?' I asked.

'We do not know. We wish strenuously to find out.'

'What do you mean?'

'Have you heard of the neutron star BVS-1?'

I had to think a moment. 'First neutron star ever found, and so far the only. Someone located it two years ago by stellar displacement.'

'BVS-1 was found by the Institute of Knowledge on Jinx. We learned through a go-between that the Institute wished to explore the star. They needed a ship to do it. They had not yet sufficient money. We offered to supply them with a ship's hull, with the usual guarantees, if they would turn over to us all data they acquired through using our ship.'

'Sounds fair enough.' I didn't ask why they hadn't done their own exploring. Like most sentient vegetarians, puppeteers find discretion to be the *only* part of valour.

'Two humans named Peter Laskin and Sonya Laskin wished to use the ship. They intended to come within one mile of the surface in a hyperbolic orbit. At some point during their trip, an unknown force apparently reached through the hull to do this to the landing shocks. The unknown force also seems to have killed the pilots.'

'But that's impossible. Isn't it?'

'You see the point. Come with me.' The puppeteer trotted towards the bow.

I saw the point, all right. Nothing, but nothing can get through a General Products hull. No kind of electromagnetic energy except visible light. No kind of matter, from the smallest subatomic particle to the fastest meteor. That's what the company's advertisements claim, and the guarantee backs them up. I've never doubted it, and I've never heard of a General Products hull damaged by a weapon or by anything else.

On the other hand, a General Products hull is as ugly as it is functional. The puppeteer-owned company could be badly hurt if it got around that something *could* get through a company hull. But I didn't see where I came in.

We rode an escalladder into the nose.

The lifesystem was in two compartments. Here the Laskins had used heat-reflective paint. In the conical control cabin the hull had been divided into windows. The relaxation room behind it was a windowless reflective silver. From the back wall of the relaxation room an access tube ran aft, opening on various instruments and the hyperdrive motors.

There were two acceleration couches in the control cabin. Both had been torn loose from their mountings and wadded into the nose like so much tissue paper, crushing the instrument panel. The backs of the crumpled couches were splashed with rust brown. Flecks of the same colour were all over everything, the walls, the windows, the viewscreens. It was as if something had hit the couches from behind: something like a dozen paint-filled toy balloons, striking with tremendous force.

'That's blood,' I said.

'That is correct. Human circulatory fluid.'

II

Twenty-four hours to fall.

I spent most of the first twelve hours in the relaxation room, trying to read. Nothing significant was happening, except that a few times I saw the phenomenon Sonya Laskin had mentioned in her last report. When a star went directly behind the invisible BVS-1, a halo formed. BVS-1 was heavy enough to bend light around it, displacing most stars to the sides; but when a star went directly behind the neutron star, its light was displaced to all sides at once. Result: a tiny circle which flashed once and was gone almost before the eye could catch it.

I'd known next to nothing about neutron stars the day the puppeteer picked me up. Now I was an expert. But I still had no idea what was waiting for me when I got down there.

All the matter you're ever likely to meet will be normal matter, composed of a nucleus of protons and neutrons surrounded by electrons in quantum energy states. In the heart of any star there is a second kind of matter: for there, the tremendous pressure is enough to smash the electron shells. The result is degenerate matter: nuclei forced together by pressure and gravity, but held apart by the mutual repulsion of the more or less continuous electron 'gas' around them. The right circumstances may create a third type of matter.

Given: a burnt-out white dwarf with a mass greater than 1.44 times the mass of the Sun—Chandrasekhar's Limit, named for an Indian-American astronomer of the nineteen hundreds. In such a mass the electron pressure alone would not be able to hold the electrons back from the nuclei. Electrons would be forced against protons—to make neutrons. In one blazing explosion most of the star would change from a compressed mass of degenerate matter to a closely packed lump of neutrons: neutronium, theoretically the densest matter possible in this universe. Most of the remaining normal and degenerate matter would be blown away by the liberated heat.

For two weeks the star would give off X-rays, as its core temperature dropped from five billion degrees Kelvin to five hundred million. After that it would be a light-emitting body perhaps ten to twelve miles across: the next best thing to invisible. It was not strange that BVS-1 was the first neutron star ever found.

Neither is it strange that the Institute of Knowledge on Jinx would have spent a good deal of time and trouble looking. Until BVS-1 was found, neutronium and neutron stars were only theories. The examination of an actual neutron star could be of tremendous importance. Neutron stars could give us the key to true gravity control.

Mass of BVS-1: 1·3 times the mass of Sol, approximately.

Diameter of BVS-1 (estimated): eleven miles of neutronium, covered by half a mile of degenerate matter, covered by maybe twelve feet of ordinary matter.

Escape velocity: 130,000 mps, approximately.

Nothing else was known of the tiny black star until the Laskins went in to look. Now the Institute knew one thing more. The star's spin.

* * *

'A mass that large can distort space by its rotation,' said the puppeteer. 'The Institute ship's projected hyperbola was twisted across itself in such a way that we can deduce the star's period of rotation to be two minutes, twenty-seven seconds.'

The bar was somewhere in the General Products building. I don't know just where, and with the transfer booths it doesn't matter. I kept staring at the puppeteer bartender. Naturally only a puppeteer would be served by a puppeteer bartender, since any biped would resent knowing that somebody made his drink with his mouth. I had already decided to get dinner somewhere else.

'I see your problem,' I said. 'Your sales will suffer if it gets out that something can reach through one of your hulls and smash a crew to bloody smears. But where do I fit in?'

'We wish to repeat the experiment of Sonya Laskin and Peter Laskin. We must find—'

'With me?'

'Yes. We must find out what it is that our hulls cannot stop. Naturally you may—'

'But I won't.'

'We are prepared to offer one million stars.'

I was tempted, but only for a moment. 'Forget it.'

'Naturally you will be allowed to build your own ship, starting with a #2 General Products hull.'

'Thanks, but I'd like to go on living.'

'You would dislike being confined. I find that We Made It has re-established the debtor's prison. If General Products made public your accounts . . .'

'Now, *just* a—'

'You owe money in the close order of five hundred thousand stars. We will pay your creditors before you leave. If you return'—I had to admire the creature's honesty in not saying *when*—'we will pay you the remainder. You may be asked to speak to news commentators concerning the voyage, in which case there will be more stars.'

'You say I can build my own ship?'

'Naturally. This is not a voyage of exploration. We want you to return safely.'

'It's a deal,' I said.

After all, the puppeteer had tried to blackmail me. What happened next would be its own fault.

They built my ship in two weeks flat. They started with a #2 General Products hull, just like the one around the Institute of Knowledge ship, and the lifesystem was practically a duplicate of the Laskins', but there the resemblance ended. There were no instruments to observe neutron stars. Instead, there was a fusion motor big enough for a Jinx warliner. In my ship, which I now called Skydiver, the drive would produce thirty gees at the safety limit. There was a laser cannon big enough to punch a hole through We Made It's moon. The puppeteer wanted me to feel safe and now I did, for I could fight and I could run. Especially I could run.

I heard the Laskins' last broadcast through half a dozen times. Their unnamed ship had dropped out of hyperspace a million miles above BVS-1. Gravity warp would have prevented their getting closer in hyperspace. While her husband was crawling through the access tube for an instrument check, Sonya Laskin had called the Institute of Knowledge. '... we can't see it yet, not with the naked eye. But we can see where it is. Every time some star or other goes behind it, there's a little ring of light. Just a minute. Peter's ready to use the telescope ...'

Then the star's mass had cut the hyperspacial link. It was expected and nobody had worried—then. Later, the same effect must have stopped them from escaping whatever attacked them, into hyperspace.

When would-be rescuers found the ship, only the radar and the cameras were still running. They didn't tell us much. There had been no camera in the cabin. But the forward camera gave us, for one instant, a speed-blurred view of the neutron star. It was a featureless disc the orange colour of perfect barbecue coals, if you know someone who can afford to burn wood. This object has been a neutron star a long time.

'There'll be no need to paint the ship,' I told the president. 'You should not make such a trip with the walls transparent. You would go insane.'

'I'm no flatlander. The mind-wrenching sight of naked space fills me with mild, but waning interest. I want to know nothing's sneaking up behind me.'

The day before I left, I sat alone in the General Products bar letting the puppeteer bartender make me drinks with his mouth. He did it well. Puppeteers were scattered around the bar in twos and threes, with a couple of men for variety; but the drinking hour had not yet arrived. The place felt empty.

I was pleased with myself. My debts were all paid, not that that would matter where I was going. I would leave with not a mini-credit to my name; with nothing but the ship . . .

All told, I was well out of a sticky situation. I hoped I'd like being a rich exile.

I jumped when the newcomer sat down across from me. He was a foreigner, a middle-aged man wearing an expensive night-black business suit and a snow-white asymmetric beard. I let my face freeze and started to get up.

'Sit down, Mr. Shaeffer.'

'Why?'

He told me by showing me a blue disc. An Earth-government ident. I looked it over to show I was alert, not because I'd know an ersatz from the real thing.

'My name is Sigmund Ausfaller,' said the government man. 'I wish to say a few words concerning your assignment on behalf of General Products.'

I nodded, not saying anything.

'A record of your verbal contract was sent to us as a matter of course. I noticed some peculiar things about it. Mr. Shaeffer, will you really take such a risk for only five hundred thousand stars?'

'I'm getting twice that.'

'But you only keep half of it. The rest goes to pay debts. Then there are taxes. But never mind. What occurred to me was that a spaceship is a spaceship, and yours is very well armed and has powerful legs. An admirable fighting ship, if you were moved to sell it.'

'But it isn't mine.'

'There are those who would not ask. On Canyon, for example, or the Isolationist party of Wonderland.'

I said nothing.

'Or, you might be planning a career of piracy. A risky business, piracy, and I don't take the notion seriously.'

I hadn't even thought about piracy. But I'd have to give up on Wonderland ...

'What I would like to say is this, Mr. Shaeffer. A single entrepreneur, if he were sufficiently dishonest, could do terrible damage to the reputation of all human beings everywhere. Most species find it necessary to police the ethics of their own members, and we are no exception. It occurred to me that you might not take your ship to the neutron star at all; that you would take it elsewhere and sell it. The puppeteers do not make invulnerable war vessels. They are pacifists. Your Skydiver is unique.

'Hence I have asked General Products to allow me to install a remote control bomb in the Skydiver. Since it is inside the hull, the hull cannot protect you. I had it installed this afternoon.

'Now, notice! If you have not reported within a week I will set off the bomb. There are several worlds within a week's hyperspace flight of here, but all recognize the dominion of Earth. If you flee, you must leave your ship within a week, so I hardly think you will land on a non-habitable world. Clear?'

'Clear.'

'If I am wrong, you may take a lie-detector test and prove it. Then you may punch me in the nose, and I will apologize handsomely.'

I shook my head. He stood up, bowed and left me sitting there cold sober.

Four films had been taken from the Laskins' cameras. In

the time left to me, I ran through them several times, without seeing anything out of the way. If the ship had run through a gas cloud, the impact could have killed the Laskins. At perihelion they were moving at better than half the speed of light. But there would have been friction, and I saw no sign of heating in the films. If something alive had attacked them, the beast was invisible to radar and to an enormous range of light frequencies. If the attitude jets had fired accidentally—I was clutching at straws—the light showed on none of the films.

There would be savage magnetic forces near BVS-1, but that couldn't have done any damage. No such force could penetrate a General Products hull. Neither could heat, except in special bands of radiated light, bands visible to at least one of the puppeteers' alien customers. I hold adverse opinions on the General Products hull, but they all concern the dull anonymity of the design. Or maybe I resent the fact that General Products holds a near-monopoly on spacecraft hulls and isn't owned by human beings. But if I'd had to trust my life to, say, the Sinclair yacht I'd seen in the drugstore, I'd have chosen jail.

Jail was one of my three choices. But I'd be there for life. Ausfaller would see to that.

Or I could run for it in the Skydiver. But no world within reach would have me, that is. Of course if I could find an undiscovered Earthlike world within a week of We Made It . . .

Fat chance. I preferred BVS-1 to that any day.

III

I thought that flashing circle of light was getting bigger, but it flashed so seldom I couldn't be sure. BVS-1 wouldn't show even in my telescope. I gave that up and settled for just waiting.

Waiting, I remembered a long-ago summer I spent on Jinx. There were days when, unable to go outside because a dearth of clouds had spread the land with raw blue-white sunlight, we amused ourselves by filling party balloons with tap water and dropping them on the sidewalk from three stories up. They made lovely splash patterns—which dried out too fast. So we put a little ink in each balloon before filling it. Then the patterns stayed.

Sonya Laskin had been in her chair when the chairs collapsed. Blood samples showed that it was Peter, who had struck them from behind, like a water balloon from a great height.

What could get through a General Products hull?

Ten hours to fall.

I unfastened the safety net and went for an inspection tour. The access tunnel was three feet wide, just right to push through in free fall. Below me was the length of the fusion tube; to the left, the laser cannon; to the right, a set of curved side tubes leading to inspection points for the gyros, the batteries and generator, the air plant, the hyperspace shunt motors. All was in order—except me. I was clumsy. My jumps were always too short or too long. There was no room to turn at the stern end, so I had to back fifty feet to a side tube.

Six hours to go, and still I couldn't find the neutron star. Probably I would see it only for an instant, passing at better than half the speed of light. Already my speed must be enormous.

Were the stars turning blue?

Two hours to go, I was sure they were turning blue. Was my speed that high? Then the stars behind should be red. Machinery blocked the view behind me, so I used the gyros. The ship turned with peculiar sluggishness. And the stars behind were blue, not red. All around me were blue-white stars.

Imagine light falling into a savagely steep gravitational well. It won't accelerate. Light can't move faster than light. But it can gain in energy, in frequency. The light was falling on me, harder and harder as I dropped.

I told the dictaphone about it. That dictaphone was probably the best protected item on the ship. I had already decided to earn my money by using it, just as if I expected to collect. Privately I wondered just how intense the light would get.

Skydiver had drifted back to vertical, with its axis through the neutron star, but now it faced outward. I'd thought I had the ship stopped horizontally. More clumsiness. I used the gyros. Again the ship moved mushily, until it was halfway through the swing. Then it seemed to fall automatically into place. It was as if the Skydiver preferred to have its axis through the neutron star.

I didn't like that in the least.

I tried the manoeuvre again, and again the Skydiver fought back. But this time there was something else. Something was pulling at me.

So I unfastened my safety net and fell headfirst into the nose.

The pull was light, about a tenth of a gee. It felt more like sinking through honey than falling. I climbed back into my chair, tied myself in with the net, now hanging face down, turned on the dictaphone. I told my story in such nit-picking detail that my hypothetical listeners could not but doubt my hypothetical sanity. 'I think this is what happened to the Laskins,' I finished. 'If the pull increases, I'll call back.'

Think? I never doubted it. This strange, gentle pull was inexplicable. Something inexplicable had killed Peter and Sonya Laskin. *Q.E.D.*

Around the point where the neutron star must be, the stars were like smeared dots of oilpaint, smeared radially. They glared with an angry, painful light. I hung face down in the net and tried to think.

It was an hour before I was sure. The pull was increasing. And I still had an hour to fall.

Something was pulling on me, but not on the ship.

No, that was nonsense. What could reach out to me through a General Products hull? It must be the other way around. Something was pushing on the ship, pushing it off course.

If it got worse I could use the drive to compensate. Meanwhile, the ship was being pushed *away* from BVS-1, which was fine by me.

But if I was wrong, if the ship were not somehow being

pushed away from BVS-1, the rocket motor would send the Skydiver crashing into eleven miles of neutronium.

And why wasn't the rocket already firing? If the ship was being pushed off course, the autopilot should be fighting back. The accelerometer was in good order. It had looked fine when I made my inspection tour down the access tube.

Could something be pushing on the ship *and* on the accelerometer but not on me?

It came down to the same impossibility. Something that could reach through a General Products hull.

To hell with theory, said I to myself, said I. I'm getting out of here. To the dictaphone I said, 'The push has increased dangerously. I'm going to try to alter my orbit.'

Of course, once I turned the ship outward and used the rocket, I'd be adding my own acceleration to the X force. It would be a strain, but I could stand it for awhile. If I came within a mile of BVS-1, I'd end like Sonya Laskin.

She must have waited face down in a net like mine, waited without a drive unit, waited while the pressure rose and the net cut into her flesh, waited until the net snapped and dropped her into the nose, to lie crushed and broken until the X force tore the very chairs loose and dropped them on her.

I hit the gyros.

The gyros weren't strong enough to turn me. I tried it three times. Each time the ship rotated about fifty degrees and hung there, motionless, while the whine of the gyros went up and up. Released, the ship immediately swung back to position. I was nose down to the neutron star, and I was going to stay that way.

Half an hour to fall, and the X force was over a gee. My sinuses were in agony. My eyes were ripe and ready to fall out. I don't know if I could have stood a cigarette, but I didn't get the chance. My pack of Fortunados had fallen out of my pocket, when I dropped into the nose. There it was, four feet beyond my fingers, proof that the X force acted on other objects besides me. Fascinating.

I couldn't take any more. If it dropped me shrieking into the neutron star, I had to use the drive. And I did. I ran the thrust up until I was approximately in free fall. The blood which had pooled in my extremities went back where it belonged. The gee dial registered one point two gee. I cursed it for a lying robot.

The soft-pack was bobbing around in the nose, and it occurred to me that a little extra nudge on the throttle would bring it to me. I tried it. The pack drifted towards me, and I reached, and like a sentient thing it speeded up to avoid my clutching hand. I snatched at it again as it went past my ear, but again it was moving too fast. That pack was going at a hell of a clip, considering that here I was, practically in free fall. It dropped through the door to the relaxation room, still picking up speed, blurred and vanished as it entered the access tube. Seconds later I heard a solid Thump.

But that was *crazy*. Already the X force was pulling blood into my face. I pulled my lighter out, held it at arm's length and let go. It fell gently into the nose. But the pack of Fortunados had hit like I'd dropped it from a *building*.

Well.

I nudged the throttle again. The mutter of fusing hydrogen reminded me that if I tried to keep this up all the way, I might well put the General Products hull to its toughest test yet: smashing it into a neutron star at half lightspeed. I could see it now: a transparent hull containing only a few cubic inches of dwarf star matter wedged into the tip of the nose.

At one point four gee, according to that lying gee dial, the lighter came loose and drifted towards me. I let it go. It was clearly falling when it reached the doorway. I pulled the throttle back. The loss of power jerked me violently forward, but I kept my face turned. The lighter slowed and hesitated at the entrance to the access tube. Decided to go through. I cocked my ears for the sound, then jumped as the whole ship rang like a gong.

And the accelerometer was right at the ship's centre of mass. Otherwise the ship's mass would have thrown the needle off. The puppeteers were fiends for ten-decimal-point accuracy.

I favoured the dictaphone with a few fast comments, then got to work reprogramming the autopilot. Luckily what I wanted was simple. The X force was but an X force to me, but now I knew how it behaved. I might actually live through this.

The stars were fiercely blue, warped to streaked lines near that special point. I thought I could see it now, very small and dim and red; but it might have been imagination. In twenty minutes, I'd be rounding the neutron star. The drive grumbled behind me. In effective free fall, I unfastened the safety net and pushed myself out of the chair.

A gentle push aft—and ghostly hands grasped my legs. Ten pounds of weight hung by my fingers from the back of the chair. The pressure should drop fast. I'd programmed the autopilot to reduce the thrust from two gees to zero during the next two minutes. All I had to do was be at the centre of mass, in the access tube, when the thrust went to zero.

Something gripped the ship through a General Products hull. A psychokinetic life form stranded on a sun twelve miles in diameter? But how could anything alive stand such gravity?

Something might be stranded in orbit. There is life in space: outsiders and sailseeds and maybe others we haven't found yet. For all I knew or cared, BVS-1 itself might be alive. It didn't matter. I knew what the X force was trying to do. It was trying to pull the ship apart.

There was no pull on my fingers. I pushed aft and landed on the back wall, on bent legs. I knelt over the door, looking aft/down. When free fall came, I pulled myself through and was in the relaxation room looking down/forward into the nose.

Gravity was changing faster than I liked. The X force was growing as zero hour approached, while the compensating rocket thrust dropped. The X force tended to pull the ship apart; it was two gee forward at the nose, two gee backward at the tail and diminished to zero at the centre of mass. Or so I hoped. The pack and lighter had behaved as if the force pulling them had increased for every inch they moved sternward.

The dictaphone was fifty feet below, utterly unreachable.

If I had anything more to say to General Products, I'd have to say it in person. Maybe I'd get the chance. Because I knew what force was trying to tear the ship apart.

It was the tide.

The motor was off, and I was at the ship's midpoint. My spread-eagled position was getting uncomfortable. It was four minutes to perihelion.

Something creaked in the cabin below me. I couldn't see what it was, but I could clearly see a red point glaring among blue radial lines, like a lantern at the bottom of a well. To the sides, between the fusion tube and the tanks and other equipment, the blue stars glared at me with a light that was almost violet. I was afraid to look too long. I actually thought they might blind me.

There must have been hundreds of gravities in the cabin. I could even feel the pressure change. The air was thin at this height, one hundred and fifty feet above the control room.

And now, almost suddenly, the red dot was more than a dot. My time was up. A red disc leapt up at me; the ship swung around me; and I gasped and shut my eyes tight. Giants' hands gripped my arms and legs and head, gently but with great firmness, and tried to pull me in two. In that moment it came to me that Peter Laskin had died like this. He'd made the same guesses I had, and he'd tried to hide in the access tube. But he'd slipped. As I was slipping ...

When I got my eyes open the red dot was shrinking into nothing.

IV

The puppeteer president insisted I be put in a hospital for observation. I didn't fight the idea. My face and hands were flaming red, with blisters rising, and I ached like I'd been beaten. Rest and tender loving care, that's what I wanted.

I was floating between a pair of sleeping plates, hideously uncomfortable, when the nurse came to announce a visitor. I knew who it was from her peculiar expression.

'What can get through a General Products hull?' I asked it.

'I hoped you would tell me.' The president rested on its single back leg, holding a stick that gave off green, incense-smelling smoke.

'And so I will. Gravity.'

'Do not play with me, Beowulf Shaeffer. This matter is vital.'

'I'm not playing. Does your world have a moon?'

'That information is classified.' The puppeteers are cowards. Nobody knows where they come from, and nobody is likely to find out.

'Do you know what happens when a moon gets too close to its primary?'

'It falls apart.'

'Why?'

'I do not know.'

'Tides.'

'What is a tide?'

Oho, said I to myself, said I. 'I'm going to try to tell you. The Earth's moon is almost two thousand miles in diameter and does not rotate with respect to Earth. I want you to pick two rocks on the Moon, one at the point nearest the Earth, one at the point furthest away.'

'Very well.'

'Now, isn't it obvious that if those rocks were left to themselves they'd fall away from each other? They're in two different orbits, mind you, concentric orbits, one almost two thousand miles outside the other. Yet these rocks are forced to move at the same orbital speed.'

'The one outside is moving faster.'

'Good point. So there *is* a force trying to pull the Moon apart. Gravity holds it together. Bring the Moon close enough to Earth, and those two rocks would simply float away.'

'I see. Then this *tide* tried to pull your ship apart. It was powerful enough in the lifesystem of the Institute ship to pull the acceleration chairs out of their mounts.'

'And to crush a human being. Picture it. The ship's nose was just seven miles from the centre of BVS-1. The tail was three hundred feet further out. Left to themselves they'd have gone in completely different orbits. My head and feet tried to do the same thing, when I got close enough.'

'I see. Are you moulting?'

'What?'

'I noticed you are losing your outer integument in spots.'

'Oh, *that*. I got a bad sunburn from exposure to starlight.'

Two heads stared at each other for an eyeblink. A shrug? The puppeteer said, 'We have deposited the remainder of your pay with the Bank of We Made It. One Sigmund Ausfaller, human, has frozen the account until your taxes are computed.'

'Figures.'

'If you will talk to reporters now, explaining what happened to the Institute ship, we will pay you ten thousand stars. We will pay cash so that you may use it immediately. It is urgent. There have been rumours.'

'Bring 'em in.' As an afterthought I added, 'I can also tell them that your world is moonless. That should be good for a footnote somewhere.'

'I do not understand.' But two long necks had drawn back, and the puppeteer was watching me like a pair of pythons.

'You'd know what a tide was if you had a moon. You couldn't avoid it.'

'Would you be interested in . . .'

'. . . a million stars? I'd be fascinated. I'll even sign a contract if it includes what we're hiding. How do *you* like being blackmailed?'

NEUTRON STAR

In 1962, astronomers discovered that there were X-rays coming from certain points in the sky. (These were absorbed by our atmosphere and it was only when rockets with appropriate instruments could be sent beyond the atmosphere that these X-rays could be detected.)

The problem was to work out what could possibly serve as a source for those X-rays. To send out so many X-rays that they were still detectable after spreading out over many, many light-years, the source would have to be the size of a star at least and very, very hot. Ordinary stars could not be that hot, and astronomers began to suspect the existence of very tiny stars with unusual properties.

The Sun has very dense matter at its centre, where atomic nuclei are pushed unusually close together; much closer than in normal matter. Some stars, like the tiny companion of Sirius, are made up mostly of this crushed matter. What if, in some stars, the atomic nuclei are crushed together till they touch, so that they become solid 'neutronium'. Such a 'neutron star' would contain all the mass of the Sun compressed into a sphere just under ten miles across. These might produce vast quantities of X-rays.

Scientists didn't expect to be able to see such tiny stars, but they studied the X-rays carefully, hoping to deduce from them whether neutron stars definitely existed or not. For a variety of reasons, hope waned and by 1966, when *Neutron Star* was published, a good deal of the earlier enthusiasm had vanished. Nevertheless, Niven was still justified in basing a story upon the existence of such an object—it had not been ruled out altogether.

Then in 1968, two years after the story was published, astronomers discovered a new phenomenon—radio-wave pulses in the sky that came and went very regularly, in some cases as quickly as thirty times a second, in other cases as slowly as once in three seconds. This new phenomenon was referred to as 'pulsars'.

Something in space had to be pulsing, revolving, or rotating fast enough to account for this and the best suggestion seemed to be that of a rotating neutron star. A neutron star would be small enough to rotate in seconds or fractions of a second and the results of such a rotation seemed to fit the observed facts. At the moment neutron stars are big again and Niven seems to have been right to have held on to his notion.

Questions and Suggestions

1. What observations in connection with 'X-ray stars' made it seem less likely that they represented neutron stars. How were pulsars discovered? What other suggestions were made, in addition to neutron stars, concerning their nature?

2. Suppose the Sun's mass were condensed into a ball of matter ten miles across. How much would a cubic inch of its matter weigh?

3. If the Sun suddenly became a neutron star without loss of mass, would that affect its gravitational pull on us? What changes would take place on Earth?

4. What would be the gravitational pull on the surface of a neutron star as compared with that on the surface of the Earth?

5. What causes tides? The Moon's tidal effect on Earth is greater than the Sun's, even though the Sun's gravitational pull on Earth is greater than the Moon's. Explain that. Calculate the tidal effect of the neutron star on the man in the spaceship in the story as compared with the tidal effect of the Moon on the Earth.

Appendix

Further Reading

1. A MARTIAN ODYSSEY by Stanley G. Weinbaum
   Is There Life on Other Worlds? by Paul Anderson (Macmillan, 1963)
   We Are Not Alone by Walter Sullivan (Hodder, 1965)

2. NIGHT by Don A. Stuart
   Frontiers of Astronomy by Fred Hoyle (Heinemann, 1955)
   Great Ideas and Theories of Modern Cosmology by Jagjit Singh (Constable, 1963)

3. THE DAY IS DONE by Lester del Rey
   Mankind in the Making by William Howells (Secker and Warburg, 1961)
   Man, Time, & Fossils by Ruth Moore (Jonathan Cape, 1962)

4. HEAVY PLANET by Lee Gregor
   Weather on the Planets by George Ohring (Doubleday, 1966)
   Earth, Moon, and Planets by Fred L. Whipple (Oxford University Press, 1968)

5. '—AND HE BUILT A CROOKED HOUSE—' by Robert A. Heinlein
   A New Look at Geometry by Irving Adler (Dobson, 1967)
   Introduction to Geometry by H. S. M. Coxeter (2nd ed., Wiley, 1969)

6. PROOF by Hal Clement
   The Sun by Giorgio Abetti (Faber and Faber, 1957)
   The Stars by W. Kruse and W. Dieckvoss (Mayflower, 1960)

7. A SUBWAY NAMED MOBIUS by A. J. Deutsch
   Intuitive Concepts in Elementary Topology by B. H. Arnold (Prentice-Hall, 1962)
   Experiments in Topology by Stephen Barr (John Murray, 1965)

8. SURFACE TENSION by James Blish
   Cells and Cell Structure by E. H. Mercer (Hutchinson Educational, 1961)
   The Procession of Life by Alfred S. Romer (Weidenfeld and Nicolson, 1968)

9. COUNTRY DOCTOR by William Morrison
   Life on the Planets by Robert Tocquet (Grove, 1962)
   Life in the Universe by Michael W. Ovenden (Heinemann, 1964)

10. THE HOLES AROUND MARS by Jerome Bixby
    Celestial Mechanics by Y. Riabov (Dover, 1961)
    Astronautics for Science Teachers by John G. Meitner (Wiley, 1965)

11. THE DEEP RANGE by Arthur C. Clarke
    The Sea by Leonard Engel (Time, Inc., 1961)
    Whales by E. J. Slijper (Hutchinson, 1962)

12. THE CAVE OF NIGHT by James E. Gunn
    Appointment on the Moon by Richard S. Lewis (Viking, 1968) (revised edition, Ballantine, 1969)
    We Reach the Moon by John Noble Wilford (Bantam, 1969)

13. DUST RAG by Hal Clement
    Pictorial Guide to the Moon by Dinsmore Alter (Thomas Y. Crowell, 1967)

The Case for Going to the Moon by Neil P. Ruzic (Putnam, 1965)

14. PÂTÉ DE FOIE GRAS by Isaac Asimov
Isotopic Tracers in Biology by Martin David Kamen (3rd ed., Academic Press, 1957)
Isotopes by J. L. Putnam (Pelican, 1960)

15. OMNILINGUAL by H. Beam Piper
Lost Worlds by Leonard Cottrell (Elek Books, 1964)
To the Rock of Darius: The Story of Henry Rawlinson by Robert Silverberg (Holt, Rinehart and Winston, 1966)

16. THE BIG BOUNCE by Walter S. Tevis
The Laws of Physics by Milton A. Rothman (Basic Books, 1963)
Understanding Physics by Isaac Asimov (Volume I, Allen and Unwin, 1967)

17. NEUTRON STAR by Larry Niven
The Tides by Edward P. Clancy (McCorquodale, 1968)
The Astounding Pulsars, Science Year, 1969, page 37 (Field Enterprises, 1969)